paul Bourget

# COSMOPOLIS

BY

## PAUL BOURGET

*Crowned by the French Academy*

With a Preface by JULES LEMAÎTRE
of the French Academy  ::  ::  ::  ::

NEW YORK
Wm. H. Wise & Co.

# PAUL BOURGET

ORN in Amiens, September 2, 1852, Paul Bourget was a pupil at the Lycée Louis le Grand, and then followed a course at the Ecole des Hautes Etudes, intending to devote himself to Greek philology. He, however, soon gave up linguistics for poetry, literary criticism, and fiction. When yet a very young man, he became a contributor to various journals and reviews, among others to the *Revue des deux Mondes, La Renaissance, Le Parlement, La Nouvelle Revue,* etc. He has since given himself up almost exclusively to novels and fiction, but it is necessary to mention here that he also wrote poetry. His poetical works comprise: *Poësies* (1872–1876), *La Vie Inquiète* (1875), *Edel* (1878), and *Les Aveux* (1882).

With riper mind and to far better advantage, he appeared a few years later in literary essays on the writers who had most influenced his own development—the philosophers Renan, Taine, and Amiel, the poets Baudelaire and Leconte de Lisle; the dramatist Dumas fils, and the novelists Turgenieff, the Goncourts, and Stendhal. Brunetière says of Bourget that "no one knows more, has read more, read better, or meditated more

profoundly upon what he has read, or assimilated it
more completely." So much "reading" and so much
"meditation," even when accompanied by strong as-
similative powers, are not, perhaps, the most desirable
and necessary tendencies in a writer of verse or of
fiction. To the philosophic critic, however, they must
evidently be invaluable; and thus it is that in a certain
self-allotted domain of literary appreciation allied to
semi-scientific thought, Bourget stands to-day without a
rival. His *Essais de Psychologie Contemporaine* (1883),
*Nouveaux Essais* (1885), and *Etudes et Portraits* (1888)
are certainly not the work of a week, but rather the out-
come of years of self-culture and of protracted determined endeavor upon the sternest lines. In fact, for a
long time, Bourget rose at 3 A.M. and elaborated anxiously study after study, and sketch after sketch, well
satisfied when he sometimes noticed his articles in the
theatrical *feuilleton* of the *Globe* and the *Parlement*,
until he finally contributed to the great *Débats* itself.
A period of long, hard, and painful probation must always be laid down, so to speak, as the foundation of
subsequent literary fame. But France, fortunately for
Bourget, is not one of those places where the foundation
is likely to be laid in vain, or the period of probation to
endure for ever and ever.

In fiction, Bourget carries realistic observation beyond the externals (which fixed the attention of Zola
and Maupassant) to states of the mind: he unites the
method of Stendhal to that of Balzac. He is always
interesting and amusing. He takes himself seriously
and persists in regarding the art of writing fiction as a

# PREFACE

science. He has wit, humor, charm, and lightness of touch, and ardently strives after philosophy and intellectuality—qualities that are rarely found in fiction. It may well be said of M. Bourget that he is innocent of the creation of a single stupid character. The men and women we read of in Bourget's novels are so intellectual that their wills never interfere with their hearts.

The list of his novels and romances is a long one, considering the fact that his first novel, *L'Irreparable*, appeared as late as 1884. It was followed by *Cruelle Enigme* (1885); *Un Crime d'Amour* (1886); *André Cornelis* and *Mensonges* (1887); *Le Disciple* (1889); *La Terre promise; Cosmopolis* (1892), crowned by the Academy; *Drames de Famille* (1899); *Monique* (1902); his romances are *Une Idylle tragique* (1896); *La Duchesse Bleue* (1898); *Le Fantôme* (1901); and *L'Etape* (1902).

*Le Disciple* and *Cosmopolis* are certainly notable books. The latter marks the cardinal point in Bourget's fiction. Up to that time he had seen environment more than characters; here the dominant interest is psychic, and, from this point on, his characters become more and more like Stendhal's, "different from normal clay." *Cosmopolis* is perfectly charming. Bourget is, indeed, the past-master of "psychological" fiction.

To sum up: Bourget is in the realm of fiction what Frédéric Amiel is in the realm of thinkers and philosophers—a subtle, ingenious, highly gifted student of his time. With a wonderful dexterity of pen, a very acute, almost womanly intuition, and a rare diffusion

# PREFACE

of grace about all his writings, it is probable that Bourget will remain less known as a critic than as a romancer. Though he neither feels like Loti nor sees like Maupassant—he reflects.

_Jules Lemaître_

de l'Académie Française.

# CONTENTS

[ ix ]

# CONTENTS

## CHAPTER X

## AUTHOR'S INTRODUCTION

 SEND you, my dear Primoli, from beyond the Alps, the romance of international life, begun in Italy almost under your eyes, to which I have given for a frame that ancient and noble Rome of which you are so ardent an admirer.

To be sure, the drama of passion which this book depicts has no particularly Roman features, and nothing was farther from my thoughts than to trace a picture of the society so local, so traditional, which exists between the Quirinal and the Vatican. The drama is not even Italian, for the scene might have been laid, with as much truth, at Venice, Florence, Nice, St. Moritz, even Paris or London, the various cities which are like quarters scattered over Europe of the fluctuating *Cosmopolis*, christened by Beyle: *Vengo adesso da Cosmopoli*. It is the contrast between the rather incoherent ways of the rovers of high life and the character of perennity impressed everywhere in the great city of the Cæsars and of the Popes which has caused me to choose the spot where even the corners speak of a secular past, there to evoke some representatives of the most modern, as well as the most arbitrary and the most momentary, life. You,

I

# INTRODUCTION

who know better than any one the motley world of cosmopolites, understand why I have confined myself to painting here only a fragment of it. That world, indeed, does not exist, it can have neither defined customs nor a general character. It is composed of exceptions and of singularities. We are so naturally creatures of custom, our continual mobility has such a need of gravitating around one fixed axis, that motives of a personal order alone can determine us upon an habitual and voluntary exile from our native land. It is so, now in the case of an artist, a person seeking for instruction and change; now in the case of a business man who desires to escape the consequences of some scandalous error; now in the case of a man of pleasure in search of new adventures; in the case of another, who cherishes prejudices from birth, it is the longing to find the "happy mean;" in the case of another, flight from distasteful memories. The life of the cosmopolite can conceal all beneath the vulgarity of its whims, from snobbery in quest of higher connections to swindling in quest of easier prey, submitting to the brilliant frivolities of the sport, the sombre intrigues of policy, or the sadness of a life which has been a failure.

Such a variety of causes renders at once very attractive and almost impracticable the task of the author who takes as a model that ever-changing society so like unto itself in the exterior rites and fashions, so really, so intimately complex and composite in its fundamental elements. The writer is compelled to take from it a series of leading facts, as I have done, essaying to deduce a law which governs them. That law, in the present

[2]

instance, is the permanence of race. Contradictory as may appear this result, the more one studies the cosmopolites, the more one ascertains that the most irreducible idea within them is that special strength of heredity which slumbers beneath the monotonous uniform of superficial relations, ready to reawaken as soon as love stirs the depths of the temperament. But there again a difficulty, almost insurmountable, is met with.   Obliged to concentrate his action to a limited number of personages, the novelist can not pretend to incarnate in them the confused *whole* of characters which the vague word *race* sums up.   Again, taking this book as an example, you and I, my dear Primoli, know a number of Venetians and of English women, of Poles and of Romans, of Americans and of French who have nothing in common with Madame Steno, Maud and Boleslas Gorka, Prince d'Ardea, Marquis Cibo, Lincoln Maitland, his brother-in-law, and the Marquis de Montfanon, while Justus Hafner only represents one phase out of twenty of the European adventurer, of whom one knows neither his religion, his family, his education, his point of setting out, nor his point of arriving, for he has been through various ways and means.   My ambition would be satisfied were I to succeed in creating here a group of individuals not representative of the entire race to which they belong, but only as possibly existing in that race—or those races.   For several of them, Justus Hafner and his daughter Fanny, Alba Steno, Florent Chapron, Lydia Maitland, have mixed blood in their veins.   May these personages interest you, my dear friend, and become

# INTRODUCTION

to you as real as they have been to me for some time, and may you receive them in your palace of Tor di Nona as faithful messengers of the grateful affection felt for you by your companion of last winter.

PAUL BOURGET.

PARIS, November 16, 1892.

# COSMOPOLIS

## CHAPTER I

### A DILETTANTE AND A BELIEVER

LTHOUGH the narrow stall, flooded with heaped-up books and papers, left the visitor just room enough to stir, and although that visitor was one of his regular customers, the old bookseller did not deign to move from the stool upon which he was seated, while writing on an unsteady desk. His odd head, with its long, white hair, peeping from beneath a once black felt hat with a broad brim, was hardly raised at the sound of the opening and shutting of the door. The newcomer saw an emaciated, shriveled face, in which, from behind spectacles, two brown eyes twinkled slyly. Then the hat again shaded the paper, which the knotty fingers, with their dirty nails, covered with uneven lines traced in a handwriting belonging to another age, and from the thin, tall form, enveloped in a greenish, worn-out coat, came a faint voice, the voice of a man afflicted with chronic laryngitis, uttering as an apology, with a strong Italian accent, this phrase in French:

# PAUL BOURGET

·"One moment, Marquis, the muse will not wait."

"Very well, I will; I am no muse. Listen to your inspiration comfortably, Ribalta," replied, with a laugh, he whom the vendor of old books received with such original unconstraint. He was evidently accustomed to the eccentricities of the strange merchant. In Rome —for this scene took place in a shop at the end of one of the most ancient streets of the Eternal City, a few paces from the Place d'Espagne, so well known to tourists—in the city which serves as a confluent for so many from all points of the world, has not that sense of the odd been obliterated by the multiplicity of singular and anomalous types stranded and sheltering there?  You will find there revolutionists like boorish Ribalta, who is ending in a curiosity-shop a life more eventful than the most eventful of the sixteenth century.

Descended from a Corsican family, this personage came to Rome when very young, about 1835, and at first became a seminarist.  On the point of being ordained a priest, he disappeared only to return, in 1849, so rabid a republican that he was outlawed at the time of the reëstablishment of the pontifical government. He then served as secretary to Mazzini, with whom he disagreed for reasons which clashed with Ribalta's honor.  Would passion for a woman have involved him in such extravagance?  In 1870 Ribalta returned to Rome, where he opened, if one may apply such a term to such a hole, a book-shop.  But he is an amateur bookseller, and will refuse you admission if you displease him.  Having inherited a small income, he

[6]

sells or he does not, following his fancy or the requirements of his own purchases, to-day asking you twenty
francs for a wretched engraving for which he paid ten
sous, to-morrow giving you at a low price a costly book,
the value of which he knows. Rabid Gallophobe, he
never pardoned his old general the campaign of Dijon
any more than he forgave Victor Emmanuel for having
left the Vatican to Pius IX. "The house of Savoy
and the papacy," said he, when he was confidential,
"are two eggs which we must not eat on the same
dish." And he would tell of a certain pillar of St.
Peter's hollowed into a staircase by Bernin, where a
cartouch of dynamite was placed. If you were to ask
him why he became a book collector, he would bid
you step over a pile of papers, of boarding and of folios.
Then he would show you an immense chamber, or
rather a shed, where thousands of pamphlets were piled
up along the walls: "These are the rules of all the convents suppressed by Italy. I shall write their history."
Then he would stare at you, for he would fear that
you might be a spy sent by the king with the sole object of learning the plans of his most dangerous enemy
—one of those spies of whom he has been so much in
awe that for twenty years no one has known where he
slept, where he ate, where he hid when the shutters of
his shop in the Rue Borgognona were closed. He expected, on account of his past, and his secret manner,
to be arrested at the time of the outrage of Passanante
as one of the members of those *Circoli Barsanti*, to
whom a refractory corporal gave his name.

But, on examining the dusty cartoons of the old

[ 7 ]

book-stall, the police discovered nothing except a prodigious quantity of grotesque verses directed against
the Piedmontese and the French, against the Germans
and the Triple Alliance, against the Italian republicans
and the ministers, against Cavour and Signor Crispi,
against the University of Rome and the Inquisition,
against the monks and the capitalists! It was, no
doubt, one of those pasquinades which his customers
watched him at work upon, thinking, as he did so,
how Rome abounded in paradoxical meetings.

For, in 1867, that same old Garibaldian exchanged
shots at Mentana with the Pope's Zouaves, among
whom was Marquis de Montfanon, for so was called
the visitor awaiting Ribalta's pleasure. Twenty-three
years had sufficed to make of the two impassioned
soldiers of former days two inoffensive men, one of
whom sold old volumes to the other! And there is a
figure such as you will not find anywhere else—the
French nobleman who has come to die near St.
Peter's.

Would you believe, to see him with his coarse boots,
dressed in a simple coat somewhat threadbare, a round
hat covering his gray head, that you have before you
one of the famous Parisian dandies of 1864? Listen to
this other history. Scruples of devoutness coming in
the wake of a serious illness cast at one blow the frequenter of the *Café Anglais* and gay suppers into the
ranks of the pontifical zouaves. A first sojourn in
Rome during the last four years of the government of
Pius IX, in that incomparable city to which the presentiment of the approaching termination of a secular rule,

the advent of the Council, and the French occupation gave a still more peculiar character, was enchantment. All the germs of piety instilled in the nobleman by the education of the Jesuits of Brughetti ended by reviving a harvest of noble virtues, in the days of trial which came only too quickly. Montfanon made the campaign of France with the other zouaves, and the empty sleeve which was turned up in place of his left arm attested with what courage he fought at Patay, at the time of that sublime charge when the heroic General de Sonis unfurled the banner of the Sacred Heart. He had been a duelist, sportsman, gambler, lover, but to those of his old companions of pleasure whom chance brought to Rome he was only a devotee who lived economically, notwithstanding the fact that he had saved the remnants of a large fortune for alms, for reading and for collecting.

Every one has that vice, more or less, in Rome, which is in itself the most surprising museum of history and of art. Montfanon is collecting documents in order to write the history of the French nobility and of the Church. His mistresses of the time when he was the rival of the Gramont-Caderousses and the Demidoffs would surely not recognize him any more than he would them. But are they as happy as he seems to have remained through his life of sacrifice? There is laughter in his blue eyes, which attest his pure Germanic origin, and which light up his face, one of those feudal faces such as one sees in the portraits hung upon the walls of the priories of Malta, where plainness has race. A thick, white moustache, in which glim-

mers a vague reflection of gold, partly hides a scar
which would give to that red face a terrible look were
it not for the expression of those eyes, in which there
is fervor mingled with merriment. For Montfanon
is as fanatical on certain subjects as he is genial and
jovial on others. If he had the power he would undoubtedly have Ribalta arrested, tried, and condemned
within twenty-four hours for the crime of free-thinking.
Not having it, he amused himself with him, so much
the more so as the vanquished Catholic and the discontented Socialists have several common hatreds.
Even on this particular morning we have seen with
what indulgence he bore the brusqueness of the old
bookseller, at whom he gazed for ten minutes without
disconcerting him in the least. At length the revolu-
tionist seemed to have finished his epigram, for with a
quiet smile he carefully folded the sheet of paper, put
it in a wooden box which he locked. Then he turned
around.

"What do you desire, Marquis?" he asked, without
any further preliminary.

"First of all, you will have to read me your poem,
old red-shirt," said Montfanon, "which will only be
my recompense for having awaited your good pleasure
more patiently than an ambassador. Let us see whom
are you abusing in those verses? Is it Don Ciccio or
His Majesty? You will not reply? Are you afraid
that I shall denounce you at the Quirinal?"

"No flies enter a closed mouth," replied the old con-
spirator, justifying the proverb by the manner in which
he shut his toothless mouth, into which, indeed, at

that moment, neither a fly nor the tiniest grain of dust could enter.

"An excellent saying," returned the Marquis, with a laugh, "and one I should like to see engraved on the façade of all the modern parliaments. But between your poetry and your adages have you taken the time to write for me to that bookseller at Vienna, who owns the last copy of the pamphlet on the trial of the bandit Hafner?"

"Patience," said the merchant. "I will write."

"And my document on the siege of Rome, by Bourbon, those three notarial deeds which you promised me, have you dislodged them?"

"Patience, patience," repeated the merchant, adding, as he pointed with a comical mixture of irony and of despair to the disorder in his shop, "How can you expect me to know where I am in the midst of all this?"

"Patience, patience," repeated Montfanon. "For a month you have been singing that old refrain. If, instead of composing wretched verses, you would attend to your correspondence, and, if, instead of buying continually, you would classify this confused mass. . . . But," said he, more seriously, with a brusque gesture, "I am wrong to reproach you for your purchases, since I have come to speak to you of one of the last. Cardinal Guerillot told me that you showed him, the other day, an interesting prayer-book, although in very bad condition, which you found in Tuscany. Where is it?"

"Here it is," said Ribalta, who, leaping over several

piles of volumes and thrusting aside with his foot an enormous heap of cartoons, opened the drawer of a tottering press. In that drawer he rummaged among an accumulation of odd, incongruous objects: old medals and old nails, bookbindings and discolored engravings, a large leather box gnawed by insects, on the outside of which could be distinguished a partly effaced coat-of-arms. He opened that box and extended toward Montfanon a volume covered with leather and studded. One of the clasps was broken, and when the Marquis began to turn over the pages, he could see that the interior had not been better taken care of than the exterior. Colored prints had originally ornamented the precious work; they were almost effaced. The yellow parchment had been torn in places. Indeed, it was a shapeless ruin which the curious nobleman examined, however, with the greatest care, while Ribalta made up his mind to speak.

"A widow of Montalcino, in Tuscany, sold it to me. She asked me an enormous price, and it is worth it, although it is slightly damaged. For those are miniatures by Matteo da Siena, who made them for Pope Pius II Piccolomini. Look at the one which represents Saint Blaise, who is blessing the lions and panthers. It is the best preserved. Is it not fine?"

"Why try to deceive me, Ribalta?" interrupted Montfanon, with a gesture of impatience. "You know as well as I that these miniatures are very mediocre, and that they do not in the least resemble Matteo's compact work; and another proof is that the prayer-book is dated 1554. See!" and, with his remaining hand, very adroitly he showed the merchant the figures; "and as I have quite a memory for dates, and as I am interested in Siena, I have not forgotten that Matteo died before 1500. I did not go to college with Macchiavelli," continued he, with some brusqueness, "but I will tell you that which the Cardinal would have told you if you had not deceived him by your finesse, as you tried to deceive me just now. Look at this partly effaced signature, which you have not been able to read. I will decipher it for you. *Blaise de Mo*, and then a *c*, with several letters missing, just three, and that makes *Montluc* in the orthography of the time, and the *b* is in a handwriting which you might have examined in the archives of that same Siena, since you come from there. Now, with regard to this coat-of-arms," and he closed the book to detail to his stupefied companion the arms hardly visible on the cover, "do you see a wolf, which was originally of gold, and turtles of gules? Those are the arms which Montluc has borne since the year 1554, when he was made a citizen of Siena for having defended it so bravely against the terrible Marquis de Marignan. As for the box," he took it in its turn to study it, "these are really the half-moons of the Piccolominis. But what does that prove? That after the siege, and just as it was necessary to retire to Montalcino, Montluc gave his prayer-book, as a souvenir, to some of that family. The volume was either lost or stolen, and finally reduced to the state in which it now is. This book, too, is proof that a little French blood was shed in the service of Italy. But those who have sold it have forgotten that, like Magenta and

Solferino, you have only memory for hatred. Now that you know why I want your prayer-book, will you sell it to me for five hundred francs?"

The bookseller listened to that discourse with twenty contradictory expressions upon his face. From force of habit he felt for Montfanon a sort of respect mingled with animosity, which evidently rendered it very painful for him to have been surprised in the act of telling an untruth. It is necessary, to be just, to add that in speaking of the great painter Matteo and of Pope Pius II in connection with that unfortunate volume, he had not thought that the Marquis, ordinarily very economical and who limited his purchases to the strict domain of ecclesiastical history, would have the least desire for that prayer-book. He had magnified the subject with a view to forming a legend and to taking advantage of some rich, unversed amateur.

On the other hand, if the name of Montluc meant absolutely nothing to him, it was not the same with the direct and brutal allusion which his interlocutor had made to the war of 1859. It is always a thorn in the flesh of those of our neighbors from beyond the Alps who do not love us. The pride of the Garibaldian was not far behind the generosity of the former zouave. With an abruptness equal to that of Montfanon, he took up the volume and grumbled as he turned it over and over in his inky fingers:

"I would not sell it for six hundred francs. No, I would not sell it for six hundred francs."

"It is a very large sum," said Montfanon.

"No," continued the good man, "I would not sell

[ 14 ]

it." Then extending it to the Marquis, in evident excitement, he cried: "But to you I will sell it for four hundred francs."

"But I have offered you five hundred francs for it," said the nonplussed purchaser. "You know that is a small sum for such a curiosity."

"Take it for four," insisted Ribalta, growing more and more eager, "not a sou less, not a sou more." It is what it cost me. And you shall have your documents in two days and the Hafner papers this week. But was that Bourbon who sacked Rome a Frenchman?" he continued. "And Charles d'Anjou, who fell upon us to make himself King of the two Sicilies? And Charles VIII, who entered by the Porte du Peuple? Were they Frenchmen? Why did they come to meddle in our affairs? Ah, if we were to calculate closely, how much you owe us! Was it not we who gave you Mazarin, Massena, Bonaparte and many others who have gone to die in your army in Russia, in Spain and elsewhere? And at Dijon? Did not Garibaldi stupidly fight for you, who would have taken from him his country? We are quits on the score of service. . . . But take your prayer-book — good-evening, good-evening. You can pay me later."

And he literally pushed the Marquis out of the stall, gesticulating and throwing down books on all sides. Montfanon found himself in the street before having been able to draw from his pocket the money he had got ready.

"What a madman! My God, what a madman!" said he to himself, with a laugh. He left the shop at a brisk pace, with the precious book under his arm. He understood, from having frequently come in contact with them, those southern natures, in which swindling and chivalry elbow without harming one another —Don Quixotes who set their own windmills in motion. He asked himself:

"How much would he still make after playing the magnamimous with me?" His question was never to be answered, nor was he to know that Ribalta had bought the rare volume among a heap of papers, engravings, and old books, paying twenty-five francs for all. Moreover, two encounters which followed one upon the other on leaving the shop, prevented him from meditating on that problem of commercial psychology. He paused for a moment at the end of the street to cast a glance at the Place d'Espagne, which he loved as one of those corners unchanged for the last thirty years. On that morning in the early days of May, the square, with its sinuous edge, was indeed charming with bustle and light, with the houses which gave it a proper contour, with the double staircase of La Trinité-des-Monts lined with idlers, with the water which gushed from a large fountain in the form of a bark placed in the centre—one of the innumerable caprices in which the fancy of Bernin, that illusive decorator, delighted to indulge. Indeed, at that hour and in that light, the fountain was as natural in effect as were the nimble hawkers who held in their extended arms baskets filled with roses, narcissus, red anemones, fragile cyclamens and dark pansies. Barefooted, with sparkling eyes, entreaties upon their lips, they glided among the carriages which passed along rapidly, fewer than in the height of the season, still quite numerous, for spring was very late this year, and it came with delightful freshness. The flower-sellers besieged the hurried passers-by, as well as those who paused at the shop-windows, and, devout Catholic as Montfanon was, he tasted, in the face of the picturesque scene of a beautiful morning in his favorite city, the pleasure of crowning that impression of a bright moment by a dream of eternity. He had only to turn his eyes to the right, toward the Collége de la Propagande, a seminary from which all the missions of the world set out.

But it was decreed that the impassioned nobleman should not enjoy undisturbed the bibliographical trifle obtained so cheaply and which he carried under his arm, nor that feeling so thoroughly Roman; a sudden apparition surprised him at the corner of a street, at an angle of the sidewalk. His bright eyes lost their serenity when a carriage passed by him, a carriage, perfectly appointed, drawn by two black horses, and in which, notwithstanding the early hour, sat two ladies. The one was evidently an inferior, a companion who acted as chaperon to the other, a young girl of almost sublime beauty, with large black eyes, which contrasted strongly with a pale complexion, but a pallor in which there was warmth and life. Her profile, of an Oriental purity, was so much on the order of the Jewish type that it left scarcely a doubt as to the Hebrew origin of the creature, a veritable vision of loveliness, who seemed created, as the poets say, "To draw all hearts in her wake." But no! The jovial, kindly face of the Marquis suddenly darkened as he watched the girl about to turn the corner of the street, and who bowed to a very fashionable young man, who undoubtedly knew the late pontifical zouave, for he approached him familiarly, saying, in a mocking tone and in a French which came direct from France:

"Well! Now I have caught you, Marquis Claude-François de Montfanon! . . . She has come, you have seen her, you have been conquered. Have your eyes feasted upon divine Fanny Hafner? Tremble! I shall denounce you to his Eminence, Cardinal Gueril-lot; and if you malign his charming catechist I will be there to testify that I saw you hypnotized as she passed, as were the people of Troy by Helen. And I know very positively that Helen had not so modern a grace, so beautiful a mind, so ideal a profile, so deep a glance, so dreamy a mouth and such a smile. Ah, how lovely she is! When shall you call?"

"If Monsieur Julien Dorsenne," replied Montfanon, in the same mocking tone, "does not pay more attention to his new novel than he is doing at this moment, I pity his publisher. Come here," he added, brusquely, dragging the young man to the angle of Rue Borgo-gnona. "Did you see the victoria stop at No. 13, and the divine Fanny, as you call her, alight? . . . She has entered the shop of that old rascal, Ribalta. She will not remain there long. She will come out, and she will drive away in her carriage. It is a pity she will not pass by us again. We should have had the pleasure of seeing her disappointed air. This is what she is in search of," added he, with a gay laugh, ex-

hibiting his purchase, "but which she could not have
were she to offer all the millions which her honest
father has stolen in Vienna. Ha, ha!" he concluded,
laughing still more heartily, "Monsieur de Montfanon
rose first; this morning has not been lost, and you,
Monsieur, can see what I obtained at the curiosity-shop
of that old fellow who will not make a plaything of this
object, at least," he added, extending the book to his
interlocutor, at whom he glanced with a comical expression of triumph.

"I do not wish to look at it," responded Dorsenne.
"But, yes," he continued, as Montfanon shrugged his
shoulders, "in my capacity of novelist and observer,
since you cast it at my head, I know already what it is.
What do you bet? . . . It is a prayer-book which bears
the signature of Marshal de Montluc, and which Cardinal Guerillot discovered. Is that true? He spoke
to Mademoiselle Hafner about it, and he thought he
would mitigate your animosity toward her by telling
you she was an enthusiast and wished to buy it. Is
that true as well? And you, wretched man, had only
one thought, to deprive that poor little thing of the
trifle. Is that true? We spent the evening before
last together at Countess Steno's; she talked to me of
nothing but her desire to have the book on which the
illustrious soldier, the great believer, had prayed. She
told me of all her heroic resolutions. Later she went
to buy it. But the shop was closed; I noticed it on
passing, and you certainly went there, too. . . . Is
that true? . . . And, now that I have detailed to you
the story, explain to me, you who are so just, why you

cherish an antipathy so bitter and so childish—excuse the word!—for an innocent, young girl, who has never speculated on 'Change, who is as charitable as a whole convent, and who is fast becoming as devout as yourself. Were it not for her father, who will not listen to the thought of conversion before marriage, she would already be a Catholic, and—Protestants as they are for the moment—she would never go anywhere but to church. . . . When she is altogether a Catholic, and under the protection of a Sainte-Claudine and a Sainte-Françoise, as you are under the protection of Saint-Claude and Saint-François, you will have to lay down your arms, old leaguer, and acknowledge the sincerity of the religious sentiments of that child who has never harmed you."

"What! She has done nothing to me?" . . . interrupted Montfanon. "But it is quite natural that a sceptic should not comprehend what she has done to me, what she does to me daily, not to me personally, but to my opinions. When one has, like you, learned intellectual athletics in the circus of the Sainte-Beuves and Renans, one must think it fine that Catholicism, that grand thing, should serve as a plaything for the daughter of a pirate who aims at an aristocratic marriage. It may, too, amuse you that my holy friend, Cardinal Guerillot, should be the dupe of that intriguer. But I, Monsieur, who have received the sacrament by the side of a Sonis, I can not admit that one should make use of what was the faith of that hero to thrust one's self into the world. I do not admit that one should play the *rôle* of dupe and accomplice to an old

man whom I venerate and whom I shall enlighten, I give
you my word."

"And as for this ancient relic," he continued, again
showing the volume, "you may think it childish that
I do not wish it mixed up in the shameful comedy. But
no, it shall not be. They shall not exhibit with words
of emotion, with tearful eyes, this breviary on which
once prayed that grand soldier; yes, Monsieur, that
great believer. She has done nothing to me," he repeated, growing more and more excited, his red face
becoming purple with rage, "but they are the quin-
tessence of what I detest the most, people like her and
her father. They are the incarnation of the modern
world, in which there is nothing more despicable than
these cosmopolitan adventurers, who play at *grand
seigneur* with the millions filibustered in some stroke
on the Bourse. First, they have no country. What
is this Baron Justus Hafner—German, Austrian,
Italian? Do you know? They have no religion.
The name, the father's face, that of the daughter, pro-
claim them Jews, and they are Protestants—*for the
moment*, as you have too truthfully said, while they
prepare themselves to become Mussulmen or what not.
*For the moment*, when it is a question of God! . . . They
have no family. Where was this man reared? What
did his father, his mother, his brothers, his sisters do?
Where did he grow up? Where are his traditions?
Where is his past, all that constitutes, all that estab-
lishes the moral man? . . . Just look. All is mystery
in this personage, excepting this, which is very clear:
if he had received his due in Vienna, at the time of the

suit of the *Crédit Austro-Dalmate*, in 1880, he would be in the galleys, instead of in Rome. The facts were these: there were innumerable failures. I know something about it. My poor cousin De Saint-Rémy, who was with the Comte de Chambord, lost the bread of his old age and his daughter's dowry. There were suicides and deeds of violence, notably that of a certain Schroeder, who went mad on account of that crash, and who killed himself, after murdering his wife and his two children. And the Baron came out of it unsullied. It is not ten years since the occurrence, and it is forgotten. When he settled in Rome he found open doors, extended hands, as he would have found them in Madrid, London, Paris, or elsewhere. People go to his house; they receive him! And you wish me to believe in the devoutness of that man's daughter! . . . No, a thousand times no; and you yourself, Dorsenne, with your mania for paradoxes and sophisms, you have the right spirit in you, and these people horrify you in reality, as they do me."

"Not the least in the world," replied the writer, who had listened to the Marquis's tirade; with an unconvinced smile, he repeated: "Not the least in the world. . . . You have spoken of me as an acrobat or an athlete. I am not offended, because it is you, and because I know that you love me dearly. Let me at least have the suppleness of one. First, before passing judgment on a financial affair I shall wait until I understand it. Hafner was acquitted. That is enough, for one thing. Were he even the greatest rogue in the universe, that would not prevent his daughter from be-

ing an angel, for another. As for that cosmopolitanism for which you censure him, we do not agree there;
it is just that which interests me in him. Thirdly, . . .
I should not consider that I had lost the six months
spent in Rome, if I had met only him. Do not look at
me as if I were one of the patrons of the circus, Uncle
Beuve, or poor Monsieur Renan himself," he continued,
tapping the Marquis's shoulder. "I swear to you that I
am very serious. Nothing interests me more than these
exceptions to the general rule—than those who have
passed through two, three, four phases of existence.
Those individuals are my museum, and you wish me
to sacrifice to your scruples one of my finest subjects. . . .
Moreover,"—and the malice of the remark he was
about to make caused the young man's eyes to sparkle
—"revile Baron Hafner as much as you like," he continued; "call him a thief and a snob, an intriguer and
a knave, if it pleases you. But as for being a person
who does not know where his ancestors lived, I reply,
as did Bonhomet when he reached heaven and the Lord
said to him: 'Still a chimney-doctor, Bonhomet?'
'And you, Lord?' . . . For you were born in Bour-
gogne, Monsieur de Montfanon, of an ancient family,
related to all the nobility—upon which I congratulate you—and you have lived here in Rome for almost twenty-four years, in the *Cosmopolis* which you
revile."

"First of all," replied the Pope's former soldier,
holding up his mutilated arm, "I might say that I no
longer count, I do not live. And then," his face became inspired, and the depths of that narrow mind,

often blinded but very exalted, suddenly appeared, "and then, my Rome to me, Monsieur, has nothing in common with that of Monsieur Hafner nor with yours, since you are come, it seems, to pursue studies of moral teratology. Rome to me is not *Cosmopolis*, as you say, it is *Metropolis*, it is the mother of cities. You forget that I am a Catholic in every fibre, and that I am at home here. I am here because I am a monarchist, because I believe in old France as you believe in the modern world; and I serve her in my fashion, which is not very efficacious, but which is one way, nevertheless. . . . The post of trustee of Saint Louis, which I accepted from Corcelle, is to me my duty, and I will sustain it in the best way in my power. . . . Ah! that ancient France, how one feels her grandeur here, and what a part she is known to have had in Christianity! It is that chord which I should like to have heard vibrate in a fluent writer like you, and not eternally those paradoxes, those sophisms. But what matters it to you who date from yesterday and who boast of it," he added, almost sadly, "that in the most insignificant corners of this city centuries of history abound? Does your heart blush at the sight of the façade of the church of Saint-Louis, the salamander of François I and the lilies? Do you know why the Rue Bargognona is called thus, and that near by is Saint-Claude-des-Bourguignons, our church? Have you visited, you who are from the Vosges, that of your province, Saint-Nicolas-des-Lorrains? Do you know Saint-Yves-des-Bretons?

"But," and here his voice assumed a gay accent, "I have thoroughly charged into that rascal of a Haf-

ner. I have laid him before you without any hesitation. I have spoken to you as I feel, with all the fervor of my heart, although it may seem sport to you.
You will be punished, for I shall not allow you to escape. I will take you to the France of other days.
You shall dine with me at noon, and between this and
then we will make the tour of those churches I have
just named. During that time we will go back one
hundred and fifty years in the past, into that world in
which there were neither cosmopolites nor dilettantes.
It is the old world, but it is hardy, and the proof is
that it has endured; while your society—look where
it is after one hundred years in France, in Italy, in
England—thanks to that detestable Gladstone, of
whom pride has made a second Nebuchadnezzar. It
is like Russia, your society; according to the only de-
cent words of the obscene Diderot, 'rotten before mature!' Come, will you go?"

"You are mistaken," replied the writer, "in thinking that. I do not love your old France, but that does
not prevent me from enjoying the new. One can like
wine and champagne at the same time. But I am
not at liberty. I must visit the exposition at Palais
Castagna this morning."

"You will not do that," exclaimed impetuous Montfanon, whose severe face again expressed one of those
contrarieties which caused it to brighten when he was
with one of whom he was fond as he was of Dorsenne.
"You would not have gone to see the King assassinated
in '93? The selling at auction of the old dwelling of
Pope Urban VII is almost as tragical! It is the be-

ginning of the agony of what was Roman nobility. I
know. They deserve it all, since they were not killed
to the last man on the steps of the Vatican when the
Italians took the city. We should have done it, we who
had no popes among our grand-uncles, if we had not
been busy fighting elsewhere. But it is none the less
pitiful to see the hammer of the appraisers raised above
a palace with which is connected centuries of history.
Upon my life, if I were Prince d'Ardea—if I had inherited the blood, the house, the titles of the Castagnas,
and if I thought I should leave nothing behind me of
that which my fathers had amassed—I swear to you,
Dorsenne, I should die of grief. And if you recall the
fact that the unhappy youth is a spoiled child of eight-
and-twenty, surrounded by flatterers, without parents,
without friends, without counsellors, that he risked his
patrimony on the Bourse among thieves of the integrity of Monsieur Hafner, that all the wealth collected
by that succession of popes, of cardinals, of warriors,
of diplomatists, has served to enrich ignoble men, you
would think the occurrence too lamentable to have
any share in it, even as a spectator. Come, I will take
you to Saint-Claude."

"I assure you I am expected," replied Dorsenne,
disengaging his arm, which his despotic friend had
already seized. "It is very strange that I should
meet you on the way, having the rendezvous I have.
I, who dote on contrasts, shall not have lost my morning. Have you the patience to listen to the enumera-
tion of the persons whom I shall join immediately?
It will not be very long, but do not interrupt me. You

will be angry if you will survive the blow I am about
to give you. Ah, you do not wish to call your Rome
a *Cosmopolis;* then what do you say to the party with
which, in twenty minutes, I shall visit the ancient palace of Urban VII? First of all, we have your beautiful enemy, Fanny Hafner, and her father, the Baron,
representing a little of Germany, a little of Austria, a
little of Italy and a little of Holland. For it seems the
Baron's mother was from Rotterdam. Do not interrupt. We shall have Countess Steno to represent
Venice, and her charming daughter, Alba, to represent
a small corner of Russia, for the Chronicle claims that
she was the child, not of the defunct Steno, but of
Werekiew—André, you know, the one who killed himself in Paris five or six years ago, by casting himself
into the Seine, not at all aristocratically, from the
Pont de la Concorde. We shall have the painter, the
celebrated Lincoln Maitland, to represent America.
He is the lover of Steno, whom he stole from Gorka
during the latter's trip to Poland. We shall have the
painter's wife, Lydia Maitland, and her brother, Florent Chapron, to represent a little of France, a little
of America, and a little of Africa; for their grandfather was the famous Colonel Chapron mentioned in
the *Memorial*, who, after 1815, became a planter in
Alabama. That old soldier, without any prejudices,
had, by a mulattress, a son whom he recognized and
to whom he left—I do not know how many dollars.
*Inde* Lydia and Florent. Do not interrupt, it is almost finished. We shall have, to represent England, a
Catholic wedded to a Pole, Madame Gorka, the wife

of Boleslas, and, lastly, Paris, in the form of your servant. It is now I who will essay to drag you away, for were you to join our party, you, the feudal, it would be complete. . . . Will you come?"

"Has the blow satisfied you?" asked Montfanon. "And the unhappy man has talent," he exclaimed, talking of Dorsenne as if the latter were not present, "and he has written ten pages on Rhodes which are worthy of Chateaubriand, and he has received from God the noblest gifts—poetry, wit, the sense of history; and in what society does he delight! But, come, once for all, explain to me the pleasure which a man of your genius can find in frequenting that international Bohemia, more or less gilded, in which there is not one being who has standing or a history. I no longer allude to that scoundrel Hafner and his daughter, since you have for her, novelist that you are, the eyes of Monsieur Guerillot. But that Countess Steno, who must be at least forty, who has a grown daughter, should she not remain quietly in her palace at Venice, respectably, bravely, instead of holding here that species of salon for transients, through which pass all the libertines of Europe, instead of having lover after lover, a Pole after a Russian, an American after a Pole? And that Maitland, why did he not obey the only good sentiment with which his compatriots are inspired, the aversion to negro blood, an aversion which would prevent them from doing what he has done—from marrying an octoroon? If the young woman knows of it, it is terrible, and if she does not it is still more terrible. And Madame Gorka, that honest creature, for I believe she is, and truly pious as well, who has not observed for the past two years that her husband was the Countess's lover, and who does not see, moreover, that it is now Maitland's turn. And that poor Alba Steno, that child of twenty, whom they drag through these improper intrigues! Why does not Florent Chapron put an end to the adultery of her sister's husband? I know him. He once came to see me with regard to a monument he was raising in Saint-Louis in memory of his cousin. He respects the dead, that pleased me. But he is a dupe in this sinister comedy at which you are assisting, you, who know all, while your heart does not revolt."

"Pardon, pardon!" interrupted Dorsenne, "it is not a question of that. You wander on and you forget what you have just asked me. . . . What pleasure do I find in the human mosaic which I have detailed to you? I will tell you, and we will not talk of the morals, if you please, when we are simply dealing with the intellect. I do not pride myself on being a judge of human nature, sir leaguer; I like to watch and to study it, and among all the scenes it can present I know of none more suggestive, more peculiar, and more modern than this: You are in a salon, at a dining-table, at a party like that to which I am going this morning. You are with ten persons who all speak the same language, are dressed by the same tailor, have read the same morning paper, think the same thoughts and feel the same sentiments. . . . But these persons are like those I have just enumerated to you, creatures from very different points of the world and of history. You study them with all that you know of their origin and their heredity, and little by little beneath the varnish of cosmopolitanism you discover their race, irresistible, indestructible race! In the mistress of the house, very elegant, very cultured, for example, a Madame Steno, you discover the descendant of the Doges, the patrician of the fifteenth century, with the form of a queen, strength in her passion and frankness in her incomparable immorality; while in a Florent Chapron or a Lydia you discover the primitive slave, the black hypnotized by the white, the unfreed being produced by centuries of servitude; while in a Madame Gorka you recognize beneath her smiling amiability the fanaticism of truth of the Puritans; beneath the artistic refinement of a Lincoln Maitland you find the squatter, invincibly coarse and robust; in Boleslas Gorka all the nervous irritability of the Slav, which has ruined Poland. These lineaments of race are hardly visible in the civilized person, who speaks three or four languages fluently, who has lived in Paris, Nice, Florence, here, that same fashionable, monotonous life. But when passion strikes its blow, when the man is stirred to his inmost depths, then occurs the conflict of characteristics, more surprising when the people thus brought together have come from afar. And that is why," he concluded with a laugh, "I have spent six months in Rome without hardly having seen a Roman, busy, observing the little clan which is so revolting to you. It is probably the twentieth I have studied, and I shall no doubt study twenty more, for not one resembles another. Are you indulgently inclined to-

ward me, now that you have got even with me in
making me hold forth at this corner, like the hero of
a Russian novel? Well, now adieu."

Montfanon had listened to the discourse with an in-
penetrable air. In the religious solitude in which he
was awaiting the end, as he said, nothing afforded
him greater pleasure than the discussion of ideas. But
he was inspired by the enthusiasm of a man who
feels with extreme ardor, and when he was met by the
partly ironical dilettanteism of Dorsenne he was almost
pained by it, so much the more so as the author and he
had some common theories, notably an extreme fancy
for heredity and race. A sort of discontented grimace
distorted his expressive face. He clicked his tongue
in ill-humor, and said:

"One more question! . . . And the result of all
that, the object? To what end does all this observation lead you?"

"To what should it lead me? To comprehend, as
I have told you," replied Dorsenne.

"And then?"

"There is no *then*," answered the young man, "one
debauchery is like another."

"But among the people whom you see living thus,"
said Montfanon, after a pause, "there are some surely
whom you like and whom you dislike, for whom you
entertain esteem and for whom you feel contempt?
Have you not thought that you have some duties toward them, that you can aid them in leading better
lives?"

"That," said Dorsenne, "is another subject which

[ 31 ]

we will treat of some other day, for I am afraid now of being late. . . . Adieu."

"Adieu," said the Marquis, with evident regret at parting. Then, brusquely: "I do not know why I like you so much, for in the main you incarnate one of those vices of mind which inspire me with the most horror, that dilettanteism set in vogue by the disciples of Monsieur Renan, and which is the very foundation of the decline. You will recover from it, I hope. You are so young!" Then becoming again jovial and mocking: "May you enjoy yourself in your descent of Courtille; I almost forgot that I had a message to give to you for one of the supernumeraries of your troop. Will you tell Gorka that I have dislodged the book for which he asked me before his departure?"

"Gorka," replied Julien, "has been in Poland three months on family business. I just told you how that trip cost him his mistress."

"What," said Montfanon, "in Poland? I saw him this morning as plainly as I see you. He passed the Fountain du Triton in a cab. If I had not been in such haste to reach Ribalta's in time to save the Montluc, I could have stopped him, but we were both in too great a hurry."

"You are sure that Gorka is in Rome—Boleslas Gorka?" insisted Dorsenne.

"What is there surprising in that?" said Montfanon. "It is quite natural that he should not wish to remain away long from a city where he has left a wife and a mistress. I suppose your Slav and your Anglo-Saxon have no prejudices, and that they share their Venetian with a dilettanteism quite modern. It is cosmopolitan, indeed. . . . Well, once more, adieu. . . . Deliver my message to him if you see him, and," his face again expressed a childish malice, "do not fail to tell Mademoiselle Hafner that her father's daughter will never, never have this volume. It is not for intriguers!" And, laughing like a mischievous schoolboy, he pressed the book more tightly under his arm, repeating: "She shall not have it. Listen. . . . And tell her plainly. She shall not have it!"

# CHAPTER II

## THE BEGINNING OF A DRAMA

"THERE is an intelligent man, who never questions his ideas," said Dorsenne to himself, when the Marquis had left him. "He is like the Socialists. What vigor of mind in that old worn-out machine!" And for a brief moment he watched, with a glance in which there was at least as much admiration as pity, the Marquis, who was disappearing down the Rue de la Propagande, and who walked at the rapid pace characteristic of monomaniacs. They follow their thoughts instead of heeding objects. However, the care he exercised in avoiding the sun's line for the shade attested the instincts of an old Roman, who knew the danger of the first rays of spring beneath that blue sky. For a moment Montfanon paused to give alms to one of the numerous mendicants who abound in the neighborhood of the Place d'Espagne, meritorious in him, for with his one arm and burdened with the prayer-book it required a veritable effort to search in his pocket. Dorsenne was well enough acquainted with that original personage to know that he had never been able to say "no" to any one who asked charity, great or small, of him. Thanks to that sys-

tem, the enemy of beautiful Fanny Hafner was always short of cash with forty thousand francs' income and leading a simple existence. The costly purchase of the relic of Montluc proved that the antipathy conceived for Baron Justus's charming daughter had become a species of passion. Under any other circumstances, the novelist, who delighted in such cases, would not have failed to meditate ironically on that feeling, easy enough of explanation. There was much more irrational instinct in it than Montfanon himself suspected. The old leaguer would not have been logical if he had not had in point of race an inquisition partiality, and the mere suspicion of Jewish origin should have prejudiced him against Fanny. But he was just, as Dorsenne had told him, and if the young girl had been an avowed Jewess, living up zealously to her religion, he would have respected but have avoided her, and he never would have spoken of her with such bitterness.

The true motive of his antipathy was that he loved Cardinal Guerillot, as was his habit in all things, with passion and with jealousy, and he could not forgive Mademoiselle Hafner for having formed an intimacy with the holy prelate in spite of him, Montfanon, who had vainly warned the old Bishop de Clermont against her whom he considered the most wily of intriguers. For months vainly did she furnish proofs of her sincerity of heart, the Cardinal reporting them in due season to the Marquis, who persisted in discrediting them, and each fresh good deed of his enemy augmented his hatred by aggravating the uneasiness which was caused him, notwithstanding all, by a vague sense of his in-iquity.

But Dorsenne no sooner turned toward the direc-tion of the Palais Castagna than he quickly forgot both Mademoiselle Hafner's and Montfanon's prejudices, in thinking only of one sentence uttered by the latter— that which related to the return of Boleslas Gorka. The news was unexpected, and it awakened in the writer such grave fears that he did not even glance at the shop-window of the French bookseller at the cor-ner of the Corso to see if the label of the "Fortieth thousand" flamed upon the yellow cover of his last book, the *Eclogue Mondaine*, brought out in the autumn, with a success which his absence of six months from Paris, had, however, detracted from. He did not even think of ascertaining if the regimen he practised, in imi-tation of Lord Byron, against *embonpoint*, would pre-serve his elegant form, of which he was so proud, and yet mirrors were numerous on the way from the Place d'Espagne to the Palais Castagna, which rears its som-bre mass on the margin of the Tiber, at the extremity of the Via Giulia, like a pendant of the Palais Sacchetti, the masterwork of Sangallo. Dorsenne did not indulge in his usual pastime of examining the souvenirs along the streets which met his eye, and yet he passed in the twenty minutes which it took him to reach his rendez-vous a number of buildings teeming with centuries of historical reminiscences. There was first of all the vast Palais Borghese—the piano of the Borghese, as it has been called, from the form of a clavecin adopted by the architect—a monument of splendor, which was, less than two years later, to serve as the scene of a situation more melancholy than that of the Palais Castagna.

Dorsenne had not an absent glance for the sumptuous building—he passed unheeding the façade of St.-Louis, the object of Montfanon's admiration. If the writer did not profess for that relic of ancient France the piety of the Marquis, he never failed to enter there to pay his literary respects to the tomb of Madame de Beaumont, to that *quia non sunt* of an epitaph which Chateaubriand inscribed upon her tombstone, with more vanity, alas, than tenderness. For the first time Dorsenne forgot it; he forgot also to gaze with delight upon the rococo fountain on the Place Navonne, that square upon which Domitian had his circus, and which recalls the cruel pageantries of imperial Rome. He forgot, too, the mutilated statue which forms the angle of the Palais Braschi, two paces farther—two paces still farther, the grand artery of the Corso Victor-Emmanuel demonstrated the effort at regeneration of present Rome; two paces farther yet, the Palais Farnese recalls the grandeur of modern art, and the tragedy of contemporary monarchies. Does not the thought of Michelangelo seem to be still imprinted on the sombre cross-beam of that immense sarcophagus, which was the refuge of the last King of Naples? But it requires a mind entirely free to give one's self up to the charm of historical dilettanteism which cities built upon the past conjure up, and although Julien prided himself, not without reason, on being above emotion, he was not possessed of his usual independence of mind

[ 37 ]

during the walk which took him to his "human mosaic," as he picturesquely expressed it, and he pondered and repondered the following questions:

"Boleslas Gorka returned? And two days ago I saw his wife, who did not expect him until next month. Montfanon is not, however, imaginative. Boleslas Gorka returned? At the moment when Madame Steno is mad over Maitland—for she is mad! The night before last, at her house at dinner, she looked at him—it was scandalous. Gorka had a presentiment of it this winter. When the American attempted to take Alba's portrait the first time, the Pole put a stop to it. It was fine for Montfanon to talk of division between these two men. When Boleslas left here, Maitland and the Countess were barely acquainted and now—— If he has returned it is because he has discovered that he has a rival. Some one has warned him—an enemy of the Countess, a *confrère* of Maitland. Such pieces of infamy occur among good friends. If Gorka, who is a shot like Casal, kills Maitland in a duel, it will make one deceiver less. If he avenges himself upon his mistress for that treason, it would be a matter of indifference to me, for Catherine Steno is a great rogue. . . . But my little friend, my poor, charming Alba, what would become of her if there should be a scandal, bloodshed, perhaps, on account of her mother's folly? Gorka returned? And he did not write it to me, to me who have received several letters from him since he went away; to me, whom he selected last autumn as the confidant of his jealousies, under the pretext that I knew women, and, with the vain hope of inspiring me. . . . His silence and return no longer seem like a romance; they savor rather of a drama, and with a Slav, as much a Slav as he is, one may expect anything. I know not what to think of it, for he will be at the Palais Castagna. Poor, charming Alba!"

The monologue did not differ much from a monologue uttered under similar circumstances by any young man interested in a young girl whose mother does not conduct herself becomingly. It was a touch-ing situation, but a very common one, and there was no necessity for the author to come to Rome to study it, one entire winter and spring. If that interest went beyond a study, Dorsenne possessed a very simple means of preventing his little friend, as he said, from being rendered unhappy by the conduct of that mother whom age did not conquer. Why not propose for her hand? He had inherited a fortune, and his suc-cess as an author had augmented it. For, since the first book which had established his reputation, the *Etudes de Femmes*, published in 1879, not a single one of the fifteen novels or selections from novels had remained unnoticed. His personal celebrity could, strictly speaking, combine with it family celebrity, for he boasted that his grandfather was a cousin of that brave General Dorsenne whom Napoleon could only replace at the head of his guard by Friant. All can be told in a word. Although the heirs of the hero of the Empire had never recognized the relationship, Julien believed in it, and when he said, in reply to compliments on his books, "At my age my grand-uncle, the Colonel of the Guard, did greater things," he was sincere in his belief. But it was unnecessary to mention it, for, situated as he was, Countess Steno would gladly have accepted him as a son-in-law. As for gaining the love of the young girl, with his handsome face, intelligent and refined, and his elegant form, which he had retained intact in spite of his thirty-seven years, he might have done so. Nothing, however, was farther from his thoughts than such a project, for, as he ascended the steps of the staircase of the palace formerly occupied by Urban VII, he continued, in very different terms, his monologue, a species of involuntary "copy" which is written instinctively in the brain of the man of letters when he is particularly fond of literature.

At times it assumes a written form, and it is the most marked of professional distortions, the most unintelligible to the illiterate, who think waveringly and who do not, happily for them, suffer the continual servitude to precision of word and to too conscientious thought.

"Yes; poor, charming Alba!" he repeated to himself. "How unfortunate that the marriage with Countess Gorka's brother could not have been arranged four months ago. Connection with the family of her mother's lover would be tolerably immoral! But she would at least have had less chance of ever knowing it; and the convenient combination by which the mother has caused her to form a friendship with that wife in order the better to blind the two, would have bordered a little more on propriety. To-day Alba would be Lady Ardrahan, leading a prosaic English life, instead of being united to some imbecile whom they will find for her here or elsewhere. She will then deceive him as her mother deceived the late Steno—with me, perhaps, in remembrance of our pure intimacy of to-day. That would be too sad! Do not let us think of it! It is the future, of the existence of which we are ignorant, while we do know that the present exists and that it has all rights. I owe to the Contessina my best impressions of Rome, to the vision of her loveliness in this scene of so grand a past. And this is a sensation which is enjoyable; to visit the Palais Castagna with the adorable creature upon whom rests the menace of a drama. To enjoy the Countess Steno's kindness, otherwise the house would not have that tone and I would never have obtained the little one's friendship. To rejoice that Ardea is a fool, that he has lost his fortune on the Bourse, and that the syndicate of his creditors, presided over by Monsieur Ancona, has laid hands upon his palace. For, otherwise, I should not have ascended the steps of this papal staircase, nor have seen this *débris* of Grecian sarcophagi fitted into the walls, and this garden of so intense a green. As for Gorka, he may have returned for thirty-six other reasons than jealousy, and Montfanon is right: Caterina is cunning enough to inveigle both the painter and him. She will make Maitland believe that she received Gorka for the sake of Madame Gorka, and to prevent him from ruining that excellent woman at gaming. She will tell Boleslas that there was nothing more between her and Maitland than Platonic discussions on the merits of Raphael and Perugino. . . .

[41]

And I should be more of a dupe than the other two for missing the visit. It is not every day that one has a chance to see auctioned, like a simple Bohemian, the grand-nephew of a pope."

The second suite of reflections resembled more than the first the real Dorsenne, who was often incomprehensible even to his best friends. The young man with the large, black eyes, the face with delicate features, the olive complexion of a Spanish monk, had never had but one passion, too exceptional not to baffle the ordinary observer, and developed in a sense so singular that to the most charitable it assumed either an attitude almost outrageous or else that of an abominable egotism and profound corruption.

Dorsenne had spoken truly, he loved to comprehend —to comprehend as the gamester loves to game, the miser to accumulate money, the ambitious to obtain position—there was within him that appetite, that taste, that mania for ideas which makes the scholar and the philosopher. But a philosopher united by a caprice of nature to an artist, and by that of fortune and of education to a worldly man and a traveller. The abstract speculations of the metaphysician would not have sufficed for him, nor would the continuous and simple creation of the narrator who narrates to amuse himself, nor would the ardor of the semi-animal of the man-of-pleasure who abandons himself to the frenzy of vice. He invented for himself, partly from instinct, partly from method, a compromise between his contradictory tendencies, which he formulated in a fashion slightly pedantic, when he said that his sole aim was to "intellectualize the forcible sensations;" in clearer terms, he dreamed of meeting with, in human life, the greatest number of impressions it could give and to think of them after having met them.

He thought, with or without reason, to discover in his two favorite writers, Goethe and Stendhal, a constant application of a similar principle. His studies had, for the past fourteen years when he had begun to live and to write, passed through the most varied spheres possible to him. But he had passed through them, lending his presence without giving himself to them, with this idea always present in his mind: that he existed to become familiar with other customs, to watch other characters, to clothe other personages and the sensations which vibrated within them. The period of his revival was marked by the achievement of each one of his books which he composed then, persuaded that, once written and construed, a sentimental or social experience was not worth the trouble of being dwelt upon. Thus is explained the incoherence of custom and the atmospheric contact, if one may so express it, which are the characteristics of his work. Take, for example, his first collection of novels, the *Etudes de Femmes*, which made him famous. They are about a sentimental woman who loved unwisely, and who spent hours from excess of the romantic studying the avowed or disguised *demi-monde*. By the side of that, *Sans Dieu*, the story of a drama of scientific consciousness, attests a continuous frequenting of the Museum, the Sorbonne and the College of France, while *Monsieur le Premier* presents one of the most striking pictures

of the contemporary political world, which could only
have been traced by a familiar of the Palais Bourbon.

On the other hand, the three books of travel pre-
tentiously named *Tourisime*, *Les Profils d'Etrangères*
and the *Eclogue Mondaine*, which fluctuated between
Florence and London, St.-Moritz and Bayreuth, revealed long sojourns out of France; a clever analysis
of the Italian, English, and German worlds; a superficial but true knowledge of the languages, the history
and literature, which in no way accords with *l'odor di
femina*, exhale from every page. These contrasts are
brought out by a mind endowed with strangely complex qualities, dominated by a firm will and, it must
be said, a very mediocre sensibility. The last point
will appear irreconcilable with the extreme and almost
morbid delicacy of certain of Dorsenne's works. It is
thus however. He had very little heart. But, on the
other hand, he had an abundance of nerves and nerves,
and their irritability suffice for him who desires to
paint human passions, above all, love, with its joys and
its sorrows, of which one does not speak to a certain
extent when one experiences them. Success had come
to Julien too early not to have afforded him occasion
for several adventures. In each of the centres traversed
in the course of his sentimental vagabondage he tried
to find a woman in whom was embodied all the
scattered charms of the district. He had formed innumerable intimacies. Some had been frankly affectionate. The majority were Platonic. Others had consisted of the simple coquetry of friendship, as was the
case with Mademoiselle Steno. The young man had

never employed more vanity than enthusiasm. Every woman, mistress or friend, had been to him, nine times out of ten, a curiosity, then a model. But as he held that the model could not be recognized by any exterior sign, he did not think that he was wrong in making use of his prestige as a writer, for what he called his "culture." He was capable of justice, the defense which he made of Fanny Hafner to Montfanon proved it; of admiration, his respect for the noble qualities of that same Montfanon testify to it; of compassion, for without it he would not have apprehended at once with so much sympathy the result which the return of Count Gorka would have on the destiny of innocent Alba Steno.

On reaching the staircase of the Palais Castagna, instead of hastening, as was natural, to find out at least what meant the return to Rome of the lover whom Madame Steno deceived, he collected his startled sensibilities before meeting Alba, and, pausing, he scribbled in a note-book which he drew from his pocket, with a pencil always within reach of his fingers, in a firm hand, precise and clear, this note savoring somewhat of sentimentalism:

"25 April, '90. Palais Castagna.—Marvellous staircase constructed by Balthazar Peruzzi, so broad and long, with double rows of stairs, like those of Santa Colomba, near Siena. Enjoyed above all the sight of an interior garden so arranged, so designed that the red flowers, the regularity of the green shrubs, the neat lines of the graveled walks resemble the features of a face. The idea of the Latin garden, opposed to the

[ 45 ]

Germanic or Anglo-Saxon, the latter respecting the irregularity of nature, the other all in order, humanizing and administering even to the flower-garden.

"Subject the complexity of life to a thought harmonious and clear, a constant mark of the Latin genus, for a group of trees as well as an entire nation, an entire religion—Catholicism. It is the contrary in the races of the North. Significance of the word: the forests have taught man liberty."

He had hardly finished writing that oddly interpreted memorandum, and was closing his note-book, when the sound of a familiar voice caused him to turn suddenly. He had not heard ascend the stairs a personage who waited until he finished writing, and who was no other than one of the actors in his "troupe"— to use his expression, one of the persons of the party of that morning organized the day before at Madame Steno's, and just the one whom the intolerable marquis had defamed with so much ardor, the father of beautiful Fanny Hafner, Baron Justus himself. The renowned founder of the *Crédit Austro-Dalmate* was a small, thin man, with blue eyes of an acuteness almost insupportable, in a face of neutral color. His ever-courteous manner, his attire, simple and neat, his speech serious and discreet, gave to him that species of distinction so common to old diplomatists. But the dangerous adventurer was betrayed by the glance which Hafner could not succeed in veiling with indifferent amiability. The man-of-the-world, which he prided himself upon having become, was visible through all by certain indefinable trifles, and above all by those eyes, of

COSMOPOLIS

a restlessness so singular in so wealthy a man, indicating
an enigmatical and obscure past of dark and contrasting
struggles, of covetous sharpness, of cold calculation
and indomitable energy. Fanatical Montfanon, who
abused the daughter with such unjustness, judged the
father justly. The son of a Jew of Berlin and of a
Dutch Protestant, Justus Hafner was inscribed on the
civil state registers as belonging to his mother's faith.
But the latter died when Justus was very young, and he
was not reared in any other liturgy than that of *money*.
From his father, a persevering and skilful jeweller, but
too prudent to risk or gain much, he learned the business of precious stones, to which he added that of laces,
paintings, old materials, tapestries, rare furniture.

An infallible eye, the patience of a German united
with his Israelitish and Dutch extraction, soon amassed
for him a small capital, which his father's bequest
augmented. At twenty-seven Justus had not less than
five hundred thousand marks. Two imprudent operations on the Bourse, enterprises to force fortune and
to obtain the first million, ruined the too-audacious
courtier, who began again the building up of his fortune by becoming a diamond broker.

He went to Paris, and there, in a wretched little
room on the Rue Montmartre, in three years, he made
his second capital. He then managed it so well that
in 1870, at the time of the war, he had made good his
losses. The armistice found him in England, where
he had married the daughter of a Viennese agent, in
London, for the purpose of starting a vast enterprise
of revictualing the belligerent armies. The enormous

profits made by the father-in-law and the son-in-law during that year determined them to found a banking-house which should have its principal seat in Vienna and a branch in Berlin. Justus Hafner, a passionate admirer of Herr von Bismarck, controlled, besides, a newspaper. He tried to gain the favor of the great statesman, who refused to aid the former diamond merchant in gratifying political ambitions cherished from an early age.

It was a bitter disappointment to the persevering man, who, having tried his luck in Prussia, emigrated definitively to Vienna. The establishment of the *Crédit Austro-Dalmate*, launched with extraordinary claims, permitted him at length to realize at least one of his chimeras. His wealth, while not equaling that of the mighty financiers of the epoch, increased with a rapidity almost magical to a cipher high enough to permit him, from 1879, to indulge in the luxurious life which can not be led by any one with an income short of five hundred thousand francs. Contrary to the custom of speculators of his genus, Hafner in time invested his earnings safely. He provided against the coming demolition of the structure so laboriously built up. The *Crédit Austro-Dalmate* had suffered in great measure owing to innumerable public and private disasters and scandals, such as the suicide and murder in the Schroeder family.

Suits were begun against a number of the founders, among them Justus Hafner. He was acquitted, but with such damage to his financial integrity and in the face of such public indignation that he abandoned

Austria for Italy and Vienna for Rome. There, heedless of first rebuffs, he undertook to realize the third great object of his life, the gaining of social position. To the period of avidity had succeeded, as it frequently does with those formidable handlers of money, the period of vanity. Being now a widower, he aimed at his daughter's marriage with a strength of will and a complication of combinations equal to his former efforts, and that struggle for connection with high life was disguised beneath the cloak of the most systematically adopted politeness of deportment. How had he found the means, in the midst of struggles and hardships, to refine himself so that the primitive broker and speculator were almost unrecognizable in the baron of fifty-four, decorated with several orders, installed in a magnificent palace, the father of a charming daughter, and himself an agreeable conversationalist, a courteous gentleman, an ardent sportsman? It is the secret of those natures created for social conquest, like a Napoleon for war and a Talleyrand for diplomacy. Dorsenne asked himself the question frequently, and he could not solve it. Although he boasted of watching the Baron with an intellectual curiosity, he could not restrain a shudder of antipathy each time he met the eyes of the man.

And on this particular morning it was especially disagreeable to him that those eyes had seen him making his unoffending notes, although there was scarcely a shade of gentle condescension—that of a great lord who patronizes a great artist—in the manner in which Hafner addressed him.

4      [ 49 ]

"Do not inconvenience yourself for me, dear sir,"
said he to Dorsenne. "You work from nature, and
you are right. I see that your next novel will touch
upon the ruin of our poor Prince d'Ardea. Do not be
too hard on him, nor on us."

The artist could not help coloring at that benign
pleasantry. It was all the more painful to him because
it was at once true and untrue. How should he explain
the sort of literary alchemy, thanks to which he was enabled to affirm that he never drew portraits, although
not a line of his fifteen volumes was traced without a
living model? He replied, therefore, with a touch of
ill-humor:

"You are mistaken, my dear Baron. I do not make
notes on persons."

"All authors say that," answered the Baron, shrugging his shoulders with the assumed good-nature which
so rarely forsook him, "and they are right. . . . At
any rate, it is fortunate that you had something to
write, for we shall both be late in arriving at a rendezvous where there are ladies. . . . It is almost a quarter past eleven, and we should have been there at eleven
precisely. . . . But I have one excuse, I waited for
my daughter."

"And she has not come?" asked Dorsenne.

"No," replied Hafner, "at the last moment she
could not make up her mind. She had a slight annoyance this morning—I do not know what old book she
had set her heart on. Some rascal found out that she
wanted it, and he obtained it first. . . . But that is
not the true cause of her absence. The true cause is

that she is too sensitive, and she finds it so sad that
there should be a sale of the possessions of this ancient
family. . . I did not insist. What would she have
experienced had she known the late Princess Nicoletta,
Pepino's mother? When I came to Rome on a visit
for the first time, in '75, what a salon that was and
what a Princess! . . . She was a Condolmieri, of the
family of Eugene IV."

"How absurd vanity renders the most refined man,"
thought Julien, suiting his pace to the Baron's. "He
would have me believe that he was received at the
house of that woman who was politically the *blackest of
the black*, the most difficult to please in the recruiting of
her salon. . . . Life is more complex than the Montfanons even know of! This girl feels by instinct that
which the *chouan* of a marquis feels by doctrine, the
absurdity of this striving after nobility, with a father
who forgets the broker and who talks of the popes of
the Middle Ages as of a trinket! . . . While we are
alone, I must ask this old fox what he knows of Boleslas
Gorka's return. He is the confidant of Madame Steno.
He should be informed of the doings and whereabouts
of the Pole."

The friendship of Baron Hafner for the Countess,
whose financial adviser he was, should have been for
Dorsenne a reason for avoiding such a subject, the more
so as he was convinced of the man's dislike for him.
The Baron could, by a single word perfidiously repeated,
injure him very much with Alba's mother. But the
novelist, similar on that point to the majority of professional observers, had only the power of analysis of a ret-

rospective order. Never had his keen intelligence served him to avoid one of those slight errors of conversation which are important mistakes on the pitiful checker-board of life. Happily for him, he cherished no ambition except for his pleasure and his art, without which he would have found the means of making for himself, gratuitously, enough enemies to clear all the academies.

He, therefore, chose the moment when the Baron arrived at the landing on the first floor, pausing somewhat out of breath, and after the agent had verified their passes, to say to his companion:

"Have you seen Gorka since his arrival?"

"What? Is Boleslas here?" asked Justus Hafner, who manifested his astonishment in no other manner than by adding: "I thought he was still in Poland."

"I have not seen him myself," said Dorsenne. He already regretted having spoken too hastily. It is always more prudent not to spread the first report. But the ignorance of that return of Countess Steno's best friend, who saw her daily, struck the young man with such surprise that he could not resist adding: "Some one, whose veracity I can not doubt, met him this morning." Then, brusquely: "Does not this sudden return make you fearful?"

"Fearful?" repeated the Baron. "Why so?" As he uttered those words he glanced at the writer with his usual impassive expression, which, however, a very slight sign, significant to those who knew him, belied. In exchanging those few words the two men had passed into the first room of "objects of art," having belonged

to the apartment of "His Eminence Prince d'Ardea,"
as the catalogue said, and the Baron did not raise the
gold glass which he held at the end of his nose when
near the smallest display of bric-à-brac, as was his
custom. As he walked slowly through the collection
of busts and statues of that first room, called "Mar-
bles" on the catalogue, without glancing with the eye
of a practised judge at the Gobelin tapestry upon the
walls, it must have been that he considered as very
grave the novelist's revelation. The latter had said too
much not to continue:

"Well, I who have not been connected with Madame
Steno for years, like you, trembled for her when that
return was announced to me. She does not know
what Gorka is when he is jealous, or of what he is
capable."

"Jealous? Of whom?" interrupted Hafner. "It is
not the first time I have heard the name of Boleslas
uttered in connection with the Countess. I confess I
have never taken those words seriously, and I should
not have thought that you, a frequenter of her salon,
one of her friends, would hesitate on that subject.
Rest assured, Gorka is in love with his charming wife,
and he could not make a better choice. Countess
Caterina is an excellent person, very Italian. She is
interested in him, as in you, as in Maitland, as in me;
in you because you write such admirable books, in
Maitland because he paints like our best masters, in
Boleslas on account of the sorrow he had in the death
of his first child, in me because I have so delicate a
charge. She is more than an excellent person, she is

[ 53 ]

a truly superior woman, very superior." He uttered his hypocritical speech with such perfect ease that Dorsenne was surprised and irritated. That Hafner did not believe one treacherous word of what he said the novelist was sure, he who, from the indiscreet confidences of Gorka, knew what to think of the Venetian's manner, and he, too, understood the Baron's glance! At any other time he would have admired the policy of the old stager. At that moment the novelist was vexed by it, for it caused him to play a *rôle*, very common but not very elevating, that of a calumniator, who has spoken ill of a woman with whom he dined the day before. He, therefore, quickened his pace as much as politeness would permit, in order not to remain *tête-à-tête* with the Baron, and also to rejoin the persons of their party already arrived.

They emerged from the first room to enter a second, marked "Porcelain;" then a third, "Frescoes of Perino del Vaga," on account of the ceiling upon which the master painted a companion to his vigorous piece at Genoa—"Jupiter crushing the Giants"—and, lastly, into a fourth, called "The Arazzi," from the wonderful panels with which it was decorated.

A few visitors were lounging there, for the season was somewhat advanced, and the date which M. Ancona had chosen for the execution proved either the calculation of profound hatred or else the adroit ruse of a syndicate of retailers. All the magnificent objects in the palace were adjudged at half the value they would have brought a few months sooner or later. The small group of curios stood out in contrast to the pro-

COSMOPOLIS

fusion of furniture, materials, objects of art of all kinds, which filled the vast rooms. It was the residence of five hundred years of power and of luxury, where masterpieces, worthy of the great Medicis, and executed in their time, alternated with the gewgaws of the eighteenth century and bronzes of the First Empire, with silver trinkets ordered but yesterday in London. Baron Justus could not resist these. He raised his glass and called Dorsenne to show him a curious armchair, the carving of a cartel, the embroidery on some material. One glance sufficed for him to judge. . . . If the novelist had been capable of observing, he would have perceived in the detailed knowledge the banker had of the catalogue the trace of a study too deep not to accord with some mysterious project.

"There are treasures here," said he. "See these two Chinese vases with convex lids, with the orange ground decorated with gilding. Those are pieces no longer made in China. It is a lost art. And this *tête-à-tête* decorated with flowers; and this pluvial cope in this case. What a marvel! It is as good as the one of Pius Second, which was at Pienza and which has been stolen. I could have bought it at one time for fifteen hundred francs. It is worth fifteen thousand, twenty thousand, all of that. Here is some *faïence*. It was brought from Spain when Cardinal Castagna came from Madrid, when he took the place of Pius Fifth as sponsor of Infanta Isabella. Ah, what treasures! But you go like the wind," he added, "and perhaps it is better, for I would stop, and Cavalier Fossati, the auctioneer, to whom those terrible creditors of Peppino have given charge of the sale, has spies everywhere. You notice an object, you are marked as a *solid man*, as they say in Germany. You are noted. I shall be down on his list. I have been caught by him enough. Ha! He is a very shrewd man! But come, I see the ladies. We should have remembered that they were here," and smiling—but at whom?—at Fossati, at himself or his companion?—he made the latter read the notice hung on the door of a transversal room, which bore this inscription: "Salon of marriage-chests."

There were, indeed, ranged along the walls about fifteen of those wooden cases painted and carved, of those *cassoni* in which it was the fashion, in grand Italian families, to keep the trousseaux destined for the brides. Those of the Castagnas proved, by their escutcheons, what alliances the last of the grand-nephews of Urban VII, the actual Prince d'Ardea, entered into. Three very elegant ladies were examining the chests; in them Dorsenne recognized at once fair and delicate Alba Steno, Madame Gorka, with her tall form, her fair hair, too, and her strong English profile, and pretty Madame Maitland, with her olive complexion, who did not seem to have inherited any more negro blood than just enough to tint her delicate face. Florent Chapron, the painter's brother-in-law, was the only man with those three ladies. Countess Steno and Lincoln Maitland were not there, and one could hear the musical voice of Alba spelling the heraldry carved on the coffers, formerly opened with tender curiosity by young girls, laughing and dreaming by turns like her.

"Look, Maud," said she to Madame Gorka, "there is the oak of the Della Rovere, and there the stars of the Altieri."

"And I have found the column of the Colonna," replied Maud Gorka.

"And you, Lydia?" said Mademoiselle Steno to Madame Maitland.

"And I, the bees of the Barberini."

"And I, the lilies of the Farnese," said in his turn Florent Chapron, who, having raised his head first, perceived the newcomers. He greeted them with a pleasant smile, which was reflected in his eyes and which showed his white teeth. "We no longer expected you, sirs. Every one has disappointed us. Lincoln did not wish to leave his atelier. It seems that Mademoiselle Hafner excused herself yesterday to these ladies. Countess Steno has a headache. We did not even count on the Baron, who is usually promptness personified."

"I was sure Dorsenne would not fail us," said Alba, gazing at the young man with her large eyes, of a blue as clear as those of Madame Gorka were dark. "Only that I expected we should meet him on the staircase as we were leaving, and that he would say to us, in surprise: 'What, I am not on time?' Ah," she continued, "do not excuse yourself, but reply to the examination in Roman history we are about to put you through. We have to follow here a veritable course studying all these old chests. What are the arms of this family?" she asked, leaning with Dorsenne over one of the *cassoni*. "You do not know? The Carafa,

famous man! And what Pope did they have? You
do not know that either? Paul Fourth, sir novelist. If
ever you visit us in Venice, you will be surprised at the
Doges."

She employed so affectionate a grace in that speech,
and she was so apparently in one of her moods—so
rare, alas!—of childish joyousness, that Dorsenne,
preoccupied as he was, felt his heart contract on her
account. The simultaneous absence of Madame Steno
and Lincoln Maitland could only be fortuitous. But
persuaded that the Countess loved Maitland, and not
doubting that she was his mistress, the absence of both
appeared singularly suspicious to him. Such a thought
sufficed to render the young girl's innocent gayety
painful to him. That gayety would become tragical if
it were true that the Countess's other lover had returned
unexpectedly, warned by some one. Dorsenne experienced genuine agitation on asking Madame Gorka:

"How is Boleslas?"

"Very well, I suppose," said his wife. "I have not
had a letter to-day. Does not one of your proverbs
say, 'No news is good news?'"

Baron Hafner was beside Maud Gorka when she
uttered that sentence. Involuntarily Dorsenne looked
at him, and involuntarily, master as he was of himself,
he looked at Dorsenne. It was no longer a question
of a simple hypothesis. That Boleslas Gorka had
returned to Rome unknown to his wife constituted,
for any one who knew of his relations with Madame
Steno, and of the infidelity of the latter, an event full
of formidable consequences. Both men were possessed

by the same thought. Was there still time to prevent a catastrophe? But each of them in this circumstance, as is so often the case in important matters of life, was to show the deepness of his character. Not a muscle of Hafner's face quivered. It was a question, perhaps, of rendering a service to a woman in danger, whom he loved with all the feeling of which he was capable. That woman was the mainspring of his social position in Rome. She was still more. A plan for Fanny's marriage, as yet secret, but on the point of being consummated, depended upon Madame Steno. But he felt it impossible to attempt to render her any service before having spent half an hour in the rooms of the Palais Castagna, and he began to employ that half hour in a manner which would be most profitable to his possible purchases, for he turned to Madame Gorka and said to her, with the rather exaggerated politeness habitual to him:

"Countess, if you will permit me to advise you, do not pause so long before these coffers, interesting as they may be. First, as I have just told Dorsenne, Cavalier Fossati, the agent, has his spies everywhere here. Your position has already been remarked, you may be sure, so that if you take a fancy for one, he will know it in advance, and he will manage to make you pay double, triple, and more for it. And then we have to see so much, notably a cartoon of twelve designs by old masters, which Ardea did not even suspect he had, and which Fossati discovered— would you believe?—worm-eaten, in a cupboard in one of the granaries."

"There is some one whom your collection would interest," said Florent, "my brother-in-law."

"Well," replied Madame Gorka to Hafner with her habitual good-nature, "there are at least two of these coffers that I like and wish to have. I said it in so loud a tone that it is not worth the trouble of hoping that your Cavalier Fossati does not know it, if he really has that mode of espionage in practice. But forty or fifty pounds more make no difference—nor forty thousand even."

"Baron Hafner will warn you that your tone is not low enough," laughed Alba Steno, "and he will add his great phrase: 'You will never be diplomatic.' But," added the girl, turning toward Dorsenne, having drawn back from silent Lydia Maitland, and arranging to fall behind with the young man, "I am about to employ a little diplomacy in order to find out whether you have any trouble." And here her mobile face changed its expression, looking into Julien's with genuine anxiety. "Yes," said she, "I have never seen you so preoccupied as you seem to be this morning. Do you not feel well? Have you received ill news from Paris? What ails you?"

"I preoccupied?" replied Dorsenne. "You are mistaken. There is absolutely nothing, I assure you." It was impossible to lie with more apparent awkwardness, and if any one merited the scorn of Baron Hafner, it was he. Hardly had Madame Gorka spoken, when he had, with the rapidity of men of vivid imagination, seen Countess Steno and Maitland surprised by Gorka, at that very moment, in some place of rendezvous, and that surprise followed by a challenge, perhaps an immediate murder. And, as Alba continued to laugh merrily, his presentiment of her sad fate became so vivid that his face actually clouded over. He felt impelled to ascertain, when she questioned him, how great a friendship she bore him. But his effort to hide his emotion rendered his voice so harsh that the young girl resumed:

"I have vexed you by my questioning?"

"Not the least in the world," he replied, without being able to find a word of friendship. He felt at that moment incapable of talking, as they usually did, in that tone of familiarity, partly mocking, partly sentimental, and he added: "I simply think this exposition somewhat melancholy, that is all." And, with a smile, "But we shall lose the opportunity of having it shown us by our incomparable *cicerone*," and he obliged her, by quickening her pace, to rejoin the group piloted by Hafner through the magnificence of the almost deserted apartment.

"See," said the former broker of Berlin and of Paris, now an enlightened amateur—"see, how that charlatan of a Fossati has taken care not to increase the number of trinkets now that we are in the reception-rooms. These armchairs seem to await invited guests. They are known. They have been illustrated in a magazine of decorative art in Paris. And that dining-room through that door, with all the silver on the table, would you not think a *fête* had been prepared?"

"Baron," said Madame Gorka, "look at this material; it is of the eighteenth century, is it not?"

"Baron," asked Madame Maitland, "is this cup with the lid old Vienna or Capadimonte?"

"Baron," said Florent Chapron, "is this armor of Florentine or Milanese workmanship?"

The eyeglass was raised to the Baron's thin nose, his small eyes glittered, his lips were pursed up, and he replied, in words as exact as if he had studied all the details of the catalogue verbatim. Their thanks were soon followed by many other questions, in which two voices alone did not join, that of Alba Steno and that of Dorsenne. Under any other circumstances, the latter would have tried to dissipate the increasing sadness of the young girl, who said no more to him after he repulsed her amicable anxiety. In reality, he attached no great importance to it. Those transitions from excessive gayety to sudden depression were so habitual with the Contessina, above all when with him. Although they were the sign of a vivid sentiment, the young man saw in them only nervous unrest, for his mind was absorbed with other thoughts.

He asked himself if, at any hazard, after the manner in which Madame Gorka had spoken, it would not be more prudent to acquaint Lincoln Maitland with the secret return of his rival. Perhaps the drama had not yet taken place, and if only the two persons threatened were warned, no doubt Hafner would put Countess Steno upon her guard. But when would he see her? What if he, Dorsenne, should at once tell Maitland's brother-in-law of Gorka's return, to that Florent Chapron whom he saw at the moment glancing at all the objects of the princely exposition? The step was

an enormous undertaking, and would have appeared
so to any one but Julien, who knew that the relations
between Florent Chapron and Lincoln Maitland were
of a very exceptional nature.  Julien knew that Florent—sent when very young to the Jesuits of Beaumont, in England, by a father anxious to spare him
the humiliation which his blood would call down upon
him in America—had formed a friendship with Lincoln, a pupil in the same school.  He knew that the
friendship for the schoolmate had turned to enthusiasm
for the artist, when the talent of his old comrade had
begun to reveal itself.  He knew that the marriage,
which had placed the fortune of Lydia at the service
of the development of the painter, had been the work
of that enthusiasm at an epoch when Maitland, spoiled
by the unwise government of his mother, and unap-
preciated by the public, was wrung by despair.  The
exceptional character of the marriage would have surprised a man less heeding of moral peculiarities than
was Dorsenne, who had observed, all too frequently,
the silence and reserve of that sister not to look upon
her as a sacrifice.  He fancied that admiration for his
brother-in-law's genius had blinded Florent to such a
degree that he was the first cause of the sacrifice.

"Drama for drama," said he to himself, as the visit
drew near its close, and after a long debate with himself.  "I should prefer to have it one rather than the
other in that family.  I should reproach myself all
my life for not having tried every means."  They
were in the last room, and Baron Hafner was just
fastening the strings of an album of drawings, when

[63]

the conviction took possession of the young man in a definite manner. Alba Steno, who still maintained silence, looked at him again with eyes which revealed the struggle of her interest for him and of her wounded pride. She longed, without doubt, at the moment they were about to separate, to ask him, according to their intimate and charming custom, when they should meet again. He did not heed her—any more than he did the other pair of eyes which told him to be more prudent, and which were those of the Baron; any more than he did the observation of Madame Gorka, who, having remarked the ill-humor of Alba, was seeking the cause, which she had long since divined was the heart of the young girl; any more than the attitude of Madame Maitland, whose eyes at times shot fire equal to her brother's gentleness. He took the latter by the arm, and said to him aloud:

"I should like to have your opinion on a small portrait I have noticed in the other room, my dear Chapron." Then, when they were before the canvas which had served as a pretext for the aside, he continued, in a low voice: "I heard very strange news this morning. Do you know Boleslas Gorka is in Rome unknown to his wife?"

"That is indeed strange," replied Maitland's brother-in-law, adding simply, after a silence: "Are you certain of it?"

"As certain as that we are here," said Dorsenne. "One of my friends, Marquis de Montfanon, met him this morning."

A fresh silence ensued between the two, during

which Julien felt that the arm upon which he rested trembled. Then they joined the party, while Florent said aloud: "It is an excellent piece of painting, which has, unfortunately, been revarnished too much."

"May I have done right!" thought Julien. "He understood me."

## CHAPTER III

### BOLESLAS GORKA

ARDLY ten minutes had passed since Dorsenne had spoken as he had to Florent Chapron, and already the imprudent novelist began to wonder whether it would not have been wiser not to interfere in any way in an adventure in which his intervention was of the least importance.

The apprehension of an immediate drama which had possessed him, for the first time, after the conversation with Montfanon, for the second time, in a stronger manner, by proving the ignorance of Madame Gorka on the subject of the husband's return—that frightful and irresistible evocation in a clandestine chamber, suddenly deluged with blood, was banished by the simplest event. The six visitors exchanged their last impressions on the melancholy and magnificence of the Castagna apartments, and they ended by descending the grand staircase with the pillars, through the windows of which staircase smiled beneath the scorching sun the small garden which Dorsenne had compared to a face. The young man walked a little in advance, beside Alba Steno, whom he now tried, but in vain, to cheer. Suddenly, at the last turn of the broad steps which tempered the decline gradually, her face brightened with surprise and pleasure. She uttered a slight cry and said: "There is my mother!" And Julien saw the Madame Steno, whom he had seen, in an access of almost delirious anxiety, surprised, assassinated by a betrayed lover. She was standing upon the gray and black mosaic of the peristyle, dressed in the most charming morning toilette. Her golden hair was gathered up under a large hat of flowers, over which was a white veil; her hand toyed with the silver handle of a white parasol, and in the reflection of that whiteness, with her clear, fair complexion, with her lovely blue eyes in which sparkled passion and intelligence, with her faultless teeth which gleamed when she smiled, with her form still slender notwithstanding the fulness of her bust, she seemed to be a creature so youthful, so vigorous, so little touched by age that a stranger would never have taken her to be the mother of the tall young girl who was already beside her and who said to her:

"What imprudence! Ill as you were this morning, to go out in this sun. Why did you do so?"

"To fetch you and to take you home!" replied the Countess gayly. "I was ashamed of having indulged myself! I rose, and here I am. Good-day, Dorsenne. I hope you kept your eyes open up there. A story might be written on the Ardea affair. I will tell it to you. Good-day, Maud. How kind of you to make lazy Alba exercise a little! She would have quite a different color if she walked every morning. Good-day, Florent. Good-day, Lydia. The *master* is not here? And you, old friend, what have you done with Fanny?"

She distributed these simple "good-days" with a grace so delicate, a smile so rare for each one—tender for her daughter, *spirituelle* for the author, grateful for Madame Gorka, amicably surprised for Chapron and Madame Maitland, familiar and confiding for her *old friend*, as she called the Baron. She was evidently the soul of the small party, for her mere presence seemed to have caused animation to sparkle in every eye.

All talked at once, and she replied, as they walked toward the carriages, which waited in a court of honor capable of holding seventy gala chariots. One after the other these carriages advanced. The horses pawed the ground; the harnesses shone; the footmen and coachmen were dressed in perfect liveries; the porter of the Palais Castagna, with his long redingote, on the buttons of which were the symbolical chestnuts of the family, had beneath his laced hat such a dignified bearing that Julien suddenly found it absurd to have imagined an impassioned drama in connection with such people. The last one left, while watching the others depart, he once more experienced the sensation so common to those who are familiar with the worst side of the splendor of society and who perceive in them the moral misery and ironical gayety.

"You are becoming a great simpleton, my friend, Dorsenne," said he, seating himself more democratically in one of those open cabs called in Rome a *botte*. "To fear a tragical adventure for the woman who is mistress of herself to such a degree is something like casting one's self into the water to prevent a shark from drowning. If she had not upon her lips Maitland's kisses, and in her eyes the memory of happiness, I am very much mistaken. She came from a rendezvous. It was written for me, in her toilette, in the color upon her cheeks, in her tiny shoes, easy to remove, which had not taken thirty steps. And with what mastery she uttered her string of falsehoods! Her daughter, Madame Gorka, Madame Maitland, how quickly she included them all! That is why I do not like the theatre, where one finds the actress who employs that tone to utter her: 'Is the master not here?'"

He laughed aloud, then his thoughts, relieved of all anxiety, took a new course, and, using the word of German origin familiar to Cosmopolitans, to express an absurd action, he said: "I have made a pretty *schlemylade*, as Hafner would say, in relating to Florent Gorka's unexpected arrival. It was just the same as telling him that Maitland was the Countess's lover. That is a conversation at which I should like to assist, that which will take place between the two brothers-in-law. Should I be very much surprised to learn that this unattached negro is the confidant of his great friend? It is a subject to paint, which has never been well treated; the passionate friendships of a Tattet for a Musset, of an Eckermann for a Goethe, of an Asselineau for a Beaudelaire, the total absorption of the admirer in the admired. Florent found that the genius of the great painter had need of a fortune, and he gave him his sister. Were he to find that that genius re-

[ 69 ]

PAUL BOURGET

quired a passion in order to develop still more, he would not object. My word of honor! He glanced at the Countess just now with gratitude! Why not, after all? Lincoln is a colorist of the highest order, although his desire to be with the tide has led him into too many imitations. But it is his race. Young Madame Maitland has as much sense as the handle of a basket; and Madame Steno is one of those extraordinary women truly created to exalt the ideals of an artist. Never has he painted anything as he painted the portrait of Alba. I can hear this dialogue:

"'You know the Pole has returned? What Pole? The Countess's. What? You believe those calumnies?' Ah, what comedies here below! 'Gad! The cabman has also committed his *schlemylade*. I told him Rue Sistina, near La Trinité-des-Monts, and here he is going through Place Barberini instead of cutting across Capo le Case. It is my fault as well. I should not have heeded it had there been an earthquake. Let us at least admire the Triton of Bernin. What a sculptor that man was! yet he never thought of nature except to falsify it."

These incoherent remarks were made with a good-nature decidedly optimistic, as could be seen, when the *fiacre* finally drew up at the given address. It was that of a very modest restaurant decorated with this signboard: *Trattoria al Marzocco*. And the Marzocco, the lion symbolical of Florence, was represented above the door, resting his paw on the escutcheon ornamented with the national *lys*. The appearance of that front did not justify the choice which the elegant Dorsenne had made of the place at which to dine when he did not dine in society. But his dilettantism liked nothing better than those sudden leaps from society, and M. Egiste Brancadori, who kept the Marzocco, was one of those unconscious buffoons of whom he was continually in search in real life, one of those whom he called his "Thebans", in reference to King Lear. "I'll talk a word with this same learned Theban," cried the mad king, one knows not why, when he meets "poor Tom" on the heath.

That Dorsenne's Parisian friends, the Casals, the Machaults, the De Vardes, those habitués of the club, might not judge him too severely, he explained that the Theban born in Florence was a cook of the first order and that the modest restaurant had its story. It amused so paradoxical an observer as Julien was. He often said, "Who will ever dare to write the truth of the history?" This, for example: Pope Pius IX, having asked the Emperor to send him some troops to protect his dominions, the latter agreed to do so—an occupation which bore two results: a Corsican hatred of the half of Italy against France and the founding of the Marzocco by Egiste Brancadori, says the Theban or the doctor. It was one of the pleasantries of the novelist to pretend to have cured his dyspepsia in Italy, thanks to the wise and wholesome cooking of the said Egiste. In reality, and more simply, Brancadori was the old cook of a Russian lord, one of the Werekiews, the cousin of pretty Alba Steno's real father. That Werekiew, renowned in Rome for the daintiness of his dinners, died suddenly in 1866. Several of the frequenters of his house, advised by a French officer of the army of occupation, and tired of clubs, hotels, and ordinary restaurants, determined to form a syndicate and to employ his former cook. They, with his coöperation, established a sort of superior café, to which with some pride they gave the name of the Culinary Club. By assuring to each one a minimum of sixteen meals for seven francs, they kept for four years an excellent table, at which were to be found all the distinguished tourists in Rome. The year 1870 had disbanded that little society of connoisseurs and of conversationalists, and the club was metamorphosed into a restaurant, almost unknown, except to a few artists or diplomats who were attracted by the ancient splendors of the place, and, above all, by the knowledge of the "doctor's" talents.

It was not unusual at eight o'clock for the three small rooms which composed the establishment to be full of men in white cravats, white waistcoats and evening coats. To cosmopolitan Dorsenñe this was a singularly interesting sight; a member of the English embassy here, of the Russian embassy farther on, two German attachés elsewhere, two French secretaries near at hand from St. Siège, another from the Quirinal. What interested the novelist still more was the conversation of the doctor himself, genial Brancadori, who could neither read nor write. But he had preserved a faithful remembrance of all his old customers, and when he felt confidential, standing erect upon the threshold of his kitchen, of the possession of which he was so insolently proud, he repeated curious

stories of Rome in the days of his youth. His gestures, so conformable to the appearance of things, his
mobile face and his Tuscan tongue, which softened into
*h* all the harsh *e*'s between two vowels, gave a savor to
his stories which delighted a seeker after local truths.
It was in the morning especially, when there was no
one in the restaurant, that he voluntarily left his ovens
to chat, and if Dorsenne gave the address of the Marzocco to his cabman, it was in the hope that the old
cook would in his manner sketch for him the story of
the ruin of Ardea. Brancadori was standing by the
bar where was enthroned his niece, Signorina Sabatina, with a charming Florentine face, chin a trifle
long, forehead somewhat broad, nose somewhat short,
a sinuous mouth, large, black eyes, an olive complexion
and waving hair, which recalled in a forcible manner
the favorite type of the first of the Ghirlandajos.

"Uncle," said the young girl, as soon as she perceived Dorsenne, "where have you put the letter
brought for the Prince?"

In Italy every foreigner is a prince or a count, and
the profound good-nature which reigns in the habit
gives to those titles, in the mouths of those who employ
them, an amiability often free from calculation. There
is no country in the world where there is a truer, a
more charming familiarity of class for class, and Brancadori immediately gave a proof of it in addressing as
"carolei"—that is to say, "my dear"—him whom his
daughter had blazoned with a coronet, and he cried,
fumbling in the pockets of the alpaca waistcoat which
he wore over his apron of office:

[ 73 ]

"The brain is often lacking in a gray head. I put it in the pocket of my coat in order to be more sure of not forgetting it. I changed my coat, because it was warm, and left it with the letter in my apartments."

"You can look for it after lunch," said Dorsenne.

"No," replied the young girl, rising, "it is not two steps from here; I will go. The *concierge* of the palace where your Excellency lives brought it himself, and said it must be delivered immediately."

"Very well, go and fetch it," replied Julien, who could not suppress a smile at the honor paid his dwelling, "and I will remain here and talk with my doctor, while he gives me the prescription for this morning— that is to say, his bill of fare. Guess whence I come, Brancadori," he added, assured of first stirring the cook's curiosity, then his power of speech. "From the Palais Castagna, where they are selling everything."

"Ah! *Per Bacco!*" exclaimed the Tuscan, with evident sorrow upon his old parchment-like face, scorched from forty years of cooking. "If the deceased Prince Urban can see it in the other world, his heart will break, I assure you. The last time he came to dine here, about ten years ago, on Saint Joseph's Day, he said to me: 'Make me some fritters, Egiste, like those we used to have at Monsieur d'Epinag's, Monsieur Clairin's, Fortuny's, and poor Henri Regnault's.' And he was happy! 'Egiste,' said he to me, 'I can die contented! I have only one son, but I shall leave him six millions and the palace. If it was Gigi I should be less easy, but Peppino!' Gigi was the other one, the elder, who died, the gay one, who used to come here every day—a fine fellow, but bad ! You should have heard him tell of his visit to Pius Ninth on the day upon which he converted an Englishman. Yes, Excellency, he converted him by lending him by mistake a pious book instead of a novel. The Englishman took the book, read it, read another, a third, and became a Catholic. Gigi, who was not in favor at the Vatican, hastened to tell the Holy Father of his good deed. 'You see, my son,' said Pius Ninth, 'what means our Lord God employs!' Ah, he would have used those millions for his amusement, while Peppino ! They were all squandered in signatures. Just think, the name of Prince d'Ardea meant money! He speculated, he lost, he won, he lost again, he drew up bills of exchange after bills of exchange. And every time he made a move such as I am making with my pencil—only I can not sign my name—it meant one hundred, two hundred thousand francs to go into the world. And now he must leave his house and Rome. What will he do, Excellency, I ask you?" With a shake of his head he added: "He should reconstruct his fortune abroad. We have this saying: 'He who squanders gold with his hands will search for it with his feet.' But Sabatino is coming! She has been as nimble as a cat."

The good man's invaluable mimetic art, his proverbs, the story of the *fête* of St. Joseph, the original evocation of the heir of the Castagnas continually signing and signing, the coarse explanation of his ruin

[ 75 ]

—very true, however—everything in the recital had amused Dorsenne. He knew enough Italian to appreciate the untranslatable passages of the language of the man of the people. He was again on the verge of laughter, when the *fresco madonna*, as he sometimes designated the young girl, handed him an envelope the address upon which soon converted his smile into an undisguised expression of annoyance. He pushed aside the day's bill of fare which the old cook presented to him and said, brusquely: "I fear I can not remain to breakfast." Then, opening the letter: "No, I can not; adieu." And he went out, in a manner so precipitate and troubled that the uncle and niece exchanged smiling glances. Those typical Southerners could not think of any other trouble in connection with so handsome a man as Dorsenne than that of the heart.

"*Chi ha l'amor nel petto*," said Signorina Sabatina.

"*Ha lo spron nei fianchi*," replied the uncle.

That naïve adage which compares the sharp sting which passion drives into our breasts to the spurring given the flanks of a horse, was not true of Dorsenne. The application of the proverb to the circumstance was not, however, entirely erroneous, and the novelist commented upon it in his passion, although in another form, by repeating to himself, as he went along the Rue Sistina: "No, no, I can not interfere in that affair, and I shall tell him so firmly."

He examined again the note, the perusal of which had rendered him more uneasy than he had been twice before that morning. He had not been mistaken in recognizing on the envelope the handwriting of Boleslas Gorka, and these were the terms, teeming with mystery under the circumstances, in which the brief message was worded:

"I know you to be such a friend to me, dear Julien, and I have for your character, so chivalrous and so French, such esteem that I have determined to turn to you in an era of my life thoroughly tragical. I wish to see you *immediately*. I shall await you at your lodging. I have sent a similar note to the Cercle de la Chasse, another to the bookshop on the Corso, another to your antiquary's. Wheresoever my appeal finds you, leave all and come at once. You will save more for me than life. For a reason which I will tell you, my return is a profound secret. *No one*, you understand, knows of it but you. I need not write more to a friend as sincere as you are, and whom I embrace with all my heart.

"B. G."

"It is unequalled!" said Dorsenne, crumpling the letter with rising anger. "He embraces me with all his heart. I am his most sincere friend! I am chivalrous, French, the only person he esteems! What disagreeable commission does he wish me to undertake for him? Into what scrape is he about to ask me to enter, if he has not already got me into it? I know that school of protestation. We are allied for life and death, are we not? Do me a favor! And they upset your habits, encroach upon your time, embark you in tragedies, and when you say 'No' to them—then they squarely accuse you of selfishness and of treason! It is my fault, too. Why did I listen to his confidences? Have I not known for years that a man who relates his love-affairs on so short an ac-

[ 77 ]

quaintance as ours is a scoundrel and a fool? And with such people there can be no possible connection. He amused me at the beginning, when he told me his sly intrigue, *without naming the person*, as they all do at first. He amused me still more by the way he managed to name her without violating that which people in society call honor. And to think that the women believe in that honor and that discretion! And yet it was the surest means of entering Steno's, and approaching Alba. . . . I believe I am about to pay for my Roman flirtation. If Gorka is a Pole, I am from Lorraine, and the heir of the Castellans will only make me do what I agree to, nothing more."

In such an ill-humor and with such a resolution, Julien reached the door of his house. If that dwelling was not the palace alluded to by Signorina Sabatina, it was neither the usually common house as common to-day in new Rome as in contemporary Paris, modern Berlin, and in certain streets of London opened of late in the neighborhood of Hyde Park. It was an old building on the Place de la Trinité-des-Monts, at an angle of the two streets Sistina and Gregoriana. Although reduced to the state of a simple *pension*, more or less *bourgeoise*, that house had its name marked in certain guide-books, and like all the corners of ancient Rome it preserved the traces of a glorious, artistic history. The small columns of the porch gave it the name of the *tempietto*, or little temple, while several personages dear to *littérateurs* had lived there, from the landscape painter Claude Lorrain to the poet François Coppée. A few paces distant, almost opposite, lived Poussin, and one of the greatest among modern English poets, Keats, died quite near by, the John Keats whose tomb is to be seen in Rome, with that melencholy epitaph upon it, written by himself:

*Here lies one whose name was writ in water.*

It was seldom that Dorsenne returned home without repeating to himself the translation he had attempted of that beautiful *Ci-gît un dont le nom fut ecrit sur de l'eau.*

Sometimes he repeated, at evening, this delicious fragment:

*The sky was tinged with tender green and pink.*

This time he entered in a more prosaic manner; for he addressed the *concierge* in the tone of a jealous husband or a debtor hunted by creditors:

"Have you given the key to any one, Tonino?" he asked.

"Count Gorka said that your Excellency asked him to await you here," replied the man, with a timidity rendered all the more comical by the formidable cut of his gray moustache and his imperial, which made him a caricature of the late King Victor Emmanuel.

He had served in '59 under the *Galantuomo*, and he paid the homage of a veteran of Solferino to that glorious memory. His large eyes rolled with fear at the least confusion, and he repeated:

"Yes, he said that your Excellency asked him to wait," while Dorsenne ascended the staircase, saying aloud: "More and more perfect. But this time the

[ 79 ]

familiarity passes all bounds; and it is better so. I have been so surprised and annoyed from the first that I shall be easily able to refuse the imprudent fellow what he will ask of me." In his anger the novelist sought to arm himself against his weakness, of which he was aware—not the weakness of insufficient will, but of a too vivid perception of the motives which the person with whom he was in conflict obeyed. He, however, was to learn that there is no greater dissolvent of rancor than intelligent curiosity. His was, indeed, aroused by a simple detail, which consisted in ascertaining under what conditions the Pole had travelled; his dressing-case, his overcoat and his hat, still white with the dust of travel, were lying upon the table in the antechamber.

Evidently he had come direct from Warsaw to the Place de la Trinité-des-Monts. A prey to what delirium of passion? Dorsenne had not time to ask the question any more than he had presence of mind to compose his manner to such severity that it would cut short all familiarity on the part of his strange visitor. At the noise made by the opening of the antechamber door, Boleslas started up. He seized both hands of the man into whose apartments he had obtruded himself. He pressed them. He gazed at him with feverish eyes, with eyes which had not closed for hours, and he murmured, drawing the novelist into the tiny salon:

"You have come, Julien, you are here! Ah, I thank you for having answered my call at once! Let me look at you, for I am sure I have a friend beside me, one in whom I can trust, with whom I can speak frankly, upon whom I can depend. If this solitude had lasted much longer I should have become mad."

Although Madame Steno's lover belonged to the class of excitable, nervous people who exaggerate their feelings by an unconscious wildness of tone and of manner, his face bore the traces of a trouble too deep not to be startling.

Julien, who had seen him set out, three months before, so radiantly handsome, was struck by the change which had taken place during such a brief absence. He was the same Boleslas Gorka, that handsome man, that admirable human animal, so refined and so strong, in which was embodied centuries of aristocracy — the Counts de Gorka belong to the ancient house of Lodzia, with which are connected so many illustrious Polish families, the Opalenice-Opalenskis, the Bnin-Bninskis, the Ponin-Poniniskis and many others—but his cheeks were sunken beneath his long, brown beard, in which were glints of gold; his eyes were heavy as if from wakeful nights, his nostrils were pinched and his face was pale. The travel-stains upon his face accentuated the alteration.

Yet the native elegance of that face and form gave grace to his lassitude. Boleslas, in the vigorous and supple maturity of his thirty-four years, realized one of those types of manly beauty so perfect that they resist the strongest tests. The excesses of emotion, as those of libertinism, seem only to invest the man with a new prestige; the fact is that the novelist's room, with its collection of books, photographs, en-

6              [ 81 ]

gravings, paintings and moldings, invested that form, tortured by the bitter sufferings of passion, with a poesy to which Dorsenne could not remain altogether insensible. The atmosphere, impregnated with Russian tobacco and the bluish vapor which filled the room, revealed in what manner the betrayed lover had diverted his impatience, and in the centre of the writing-table a cup with a bacchanal painted in red on a black ground, of which Julien was very proud, contained the remains of about thirty cigarettes, thrown aside almost as soon as lighted. Their paper ends had been gnawed with a nervousness which betrayed the young man's condition, while he repeated, in a tone so sad that it almost called forth a shudder:

"Yes, I should have gone mad."

"Calm yourself, my dear Boleslas, I implore you," replied Dorsenne. What had become of his ill-humor? How could he preserve it in the presence of a person so evidently beside himself? Julien continued, speaking to his companion as one speaks to a sick child: "Come, be seated. Be a little more tranquil, since I am here, and you have reason to count on my friendship. Speak to me. Explain to me what has happened. If there is any advice to give you, I am ready. I am prepared to render you a service. My God! In what a state you are!"

"Is it not so?" said the other, with a sort of ironical pride. It was sufficient that he had a witness of his grief for him to display it with secret vanity. "Is it not so?" he continued. "Could you only know how I have suffered. This is nothing," said he, alluding to his haggard appearance. "It is here that you should read," he struck his breast, then passing his hands over his brow and his eyes, as if to exorcise a nightmare. "You are right. I must be calm, or I am lost."

After a prolonged silence, during which he seemed to have gathered together his thoughts and to collect his will, for his voice had become decided and sharp, he began: "You know that I am here unknown to any one, even to my wife."

"I know it," replied Dorsenne. "I have just left the Countess. This morning I visited the Palais Castagna with her, Hafner, Madame Maitland, Florent Chapron." He paused and added, thinking it better not to lie on minor points, "Madame Steno and Alba were there, too."

"Any one else?" asked Boleslas, with so keen a glance that the author had to employ all his strength to reply:

"No one else."

There was a silence between the two men.

Dorsenne anticipated from his question toward what subject the conversation was drifting. Gorka, now lying rather than sitting upon the divan in the small room, appeared like a beast that, at any moment, might bound. Evidently he had come to Julien's a prey to the mad desire *to find out something*, which is to jealousy what thirst is to certain punishments. When one has tasted the bitter draught of certainty, one does not suffer less. Yet one walks toward it, barefooted, on the heated pavement, heedless of the heat. The motives which led Boleslas to choose the French novelist as the one from whom to obtain his information, demonstrated that the feline character of his physiognomy was not deceptive. He understood Dorsenne much better than Dorsenne understood him. He knew him to be nervous, on the one hand, and perspicacious on the other. If there was an intrigue between Maitland and Madame Steno, Julien had surely observed it, and, approached in a certain manner, he would surely betray it. Moreover—for that violent and crafty nature abounded in perplexities—Boleslas, who passionately admired the author's talent, experienced a sort of indefinable attraction in exhibiting himself before him in the *rôle* of a frantic lover. He was one of the persons who would have his photograph taken on his deathbed, so much importance did he attach to his person. He would, no doubt, have been insulted, if the author of *Une Eglogue Mondaine* had portrayed in a book himself and his love for Countess Steno, and yet he had only approached the author, had only chosen him as a confidant with the vague hope of impressing him. He had even thought of suggesting to him some creation resembling himself. Yes, Gorka was very complex, for he was not contented with deceiving his wife, he allowed the confiding creature to form a friendship with the daughter of her husband's mistress. Still, he deceived her with remorse, and had never ceased bearing her an affection as sorrowful as it was respectful. But it required Dorsenne to admit the like anomalies, and the rare sensation of being observed in his passionate frenzy

[ 84 ]

attracted the young man to some one who was at once a sure confidant, a possible portrayer, a moral accomplice. It was necessary now, but it would not be an easy matter, to make of him his involuntary detective.

"You see," resumed he suddenly, "to what miserable, detailed inquiries I have descended, I who always had a horror of espionage, as of some terrible degradation. I shall question you frankly, for you are my friend. And what a friend! I intended to use artifice with you at first, but I was ashamed. Passion takes possession of me and distorts me. No matter what infamy presents itself, I rush into it, and then I am afraid. Yes, I am afraid of myself! But I have suffered so much! You do not understand? Well! Listen," continued he, covering Dorsenne with one of those glances so scrutinizing that not a gesture, not a quiver of his eyelids, escaped him, "and tell me if you have ever imagined for one of your romances a situation similar to mine. You remember the mortal fear in which I lived last winter, with the presence of my brother-in-law, and the danger of his denouncing me to my poor Maud, from stupidity, from a British sense of virtue, from hatred. You remember, also, what that voyage to Poland cost me, after those long months of anxiety? The press of affairs and the illness of my aunt coming just at the moment when I was freed from Ardrahan, inspired me with miserable forebodings. I have always believed in presentiments. I had one. I was not mistaken. From the first letter I received—from whom you can guess—I saw that there was taking place in Rome something which threatened me in what I held dearest on earth, in that love for which I sacrificed all, toward which I walked by trampling on the noblest of hearts. Was Catherine ceasing to love me? When one has spent two years of one's life in a passion—and what years!—one clings to it with every fibre! I will spare you the recital of those first weeks spent in going here and there, in paying visits to relatives, in consulting lawyers, in caring for my sick aunt, in fulfilling my duty toward my son, since the greater part of the fortune will go to him. And always with this firm conviction: She no longer writes to me as formerly, she no longer loves me. Ah! if I could show you the letter she wrote when I was absent once before. You have a great deal of talent, Julien, but you have never composed anything more beautiful."

He paused, as if the part of the confession he was approaching cost him a great effort, while Dorsenne interpolated:

"A change of tone in correspondence is not, however, sufficient to explain the fever in which I see you."

"No," resumed Gorka, "but it was not merely a change of tone. I complained. For the first time my complaint found no echo. I threatened to cease writing. No reply. I wrote to ask forgiveness. I received a letter so cold that in my turn I wrote an angry one. Another silence! Ah! You can imagine the terrible effect produced upon me by an unsigned letter which I received fifteen days since. It arrived one morning. It bore the Roman postmark. I did not recognize the handwriting. I opened it. I saw two sheets of paper on which were pasted cuttings from a French journal. I repeat it was unsigned; it was an anonymous letter."

"And you read it?" interrupted Dorsenne. "What folly!"

"I read it," replied the Count. "It began with words of startling truth relative to my own situation. That our affairs are known to others we may be sure, since we know theirs. We should, consequently, remember that we are at the mercy of their indiscretion, as they are at ours. The beginning of the note served as a guarantee of the truth of the end, which was a detailed, minute recital of an intrigue which Madame Steno had been carrying on during my absence, and with whom? With the man whom I always mistrusted, that dauber who wanted to paint Alba's portrait—but whose desires I nipped in the bud— with the fellow who degraded himself by a shameful marriage for money, and who calls himself an artist —with that American—with Lincoln Maitland!"

Although the childish and unjust hatred of the jealous —the hatred which degrades us in lowering the one we love—had poisoned his discourse with its bitterness, he did not cease watching Dorsenne. He partly raised himself on the couch and thrust his head forward as he uttered the name of his rival, glancing keenly at the novelist meanwhile. The latter fortunately had been rendered indignant at the news of the anonymous letter, and he repeated, with an astonishment which in no way aided his interlocutor:

"What infamy, what infamy!"

"Wait," resumed Boleslas; "that was merely a beginning. The next day I received another letter, written and sent under the same conditions; the day after, a third. I have twelve of them—do you hear? twelve—in my portfolio, and all composed with the same atrocious knowledge of the circle in which we move, as was the first. At the same time I was receiving letters from my poor wife, and all coincided, in the terrible series, in a frightful concordance. The anonymous letter told me: 'To-day they were together two hours and a quarter,' while Maud wrote: 'I could not go out to-day, as agreed upon, with Madame Steno, for she had a headache.' Then the portrait of Alba, of which they told me incidentally. The anonymous letters detailed to me the events, the prolongation of sitting, while my wife wrote: 'We again went to see Alba's portrait yesterday. The painter erased what he had done.' Finally it became impossible for me to endure it. With their abominable minuteness of detail, the anonymous letters gave me even the address of their rendezvous! I set out. I said to myself, 'If I announce my arrival to my wife they will find it out, they will escape me.' I intended to surprise them. I wanted—Do I know what I wanted? I wanted to suffer no longer the agony of uncertainty. I took the train. I stopped neither day nor night. I left my valet yesterday in Florence, and this morning I was in Rome.

"My plan was made on the way. I would hire apartments near theirs, in the same street, perhaps in the same house. I would watch them, one, two days, a week. And then—would you believe it? It was in the cab which was bearing me directly toward that street that I saw suddenly, clearly within me, and that I was startled. I had my hand upon this revolver." He drew the weapon from his pocket and laid it upon the divan, as if he wished to repulse any new temptation. "I saw myself as plainly as I see you, killing those two beings like two animals, should I surprise them. At the same time I saw my son and my wife. Between murder and me there was, perhaps, just the distance which separated me from the street, and I felt that it was necessary to fly at once—to fly that street, to fly from the guilty ones, if they were really guilty; to fly from myself! I thought of you, and I have come to say to you, 'My friend, this is how things are; I am drowning, I am lost; save me.'"

"You have yourself found the salvation," replied Dorsenne. "It is in your son and your wife. See them first, and if I can not promise you that you will not suffer any more, you will no longer be tempted by that horrible idea." And he pointed to the pistol, which gleamed in the sunlight that entered through the casement. Then he added: "And you will have the idea still less when you will have been able to prove *de visu* what those anonymous letters were worth. Twelve letters in fifteen days, and cuttings from how many papers? And they claim that we invent heinousness in our books ! If you like, we will search together for the person who can have elaborated that little piece of villany. It must be a Judas, a Rodin, an Iago—or Iaga. But this is not the moment to waste in hypotheses.

Are you sure of your valet? You must send him a despatch, and in that despatch the copy of another addressed to Madame Gorka, which your man will send this very evening. You will announce your arrival for to-morrow, making allusion to a letter written, so to speak, from Poland, and which was lost. This evening from here you will take the train for Florence, from which place you will set out again this very night. You will be in Rome again to-morrow morning. You will have avoided, not only the misfortune of having become a murderer, though you would not have surprised any one, I am sure, but the much more grave misfortune of awakening Madame Gorka's suspicions. Is it a promise?"

Dorsenne rose to prepare a pen and paper: "Come, write the despatch immediately, and render thanks to your good genius which led you to a friend whose business consists in imagining the means of solving insoluble situations."

"You are quite right," Boleslas replied, after taking in his hand the pen which he offered to the other, "it is fortunate." Then, casting aside the pen as he had the revolver, "I can not. No, I can not, as long as I have this doubt within me. Ah, it is too horrible! I can see them plainly. You speak to me of my wife; but you forget that she loves me, and at the first glance she would read me, as you did. You can not imagine what an effort it has cost me for two years never to arouse suspicion. I was happy, and it is easy to deceive when one has nothing to hide but happiness. To-day we should not be together five minutes before she would seek, and she would find. No, no; I can not. I need something more."

"Unfortunately," replied Julien, "I can not give it to you. There is no opium to lull asleep doubts such as those horrible anonymous letters have awakened. What I know is this, that if you do not follow my advice Madame Gorka will not have a suspicion, but certainty. It is now perhaps too late. Do you wish me to tell you what I concealed from you on seeing you so troubled? You did not lose much time in coming from the station hither, and probably you did not look out of your cab twice. But you were seen. By whom? By Montfanon. He told me so this morning almost on the threshold of the Palais Castagna. If I had not gathered from some words uttered by your wife that she was ignorant of your presence in Rome, I—do you hear?—I should have told her of it. Judge now of your situation!"

He spoke with an agitation which was not assumed, so much was he troubled by the evidence of danger which Gorka's obstinacy presented. The latter, who had begun to collect himself, had a strange light in his eyes. Without doubt his companion's nervousness marked the moment he was awaiting to strike a decisive blow. He rose with so sudden a start that Dorsenne drew back. He seized both of his hands, but with such force that not a quiver of the muscles escaped him:

"Yes, Julien, you have the means of consoling me, you have it," said he in a voice again hoarse with emotion.

[ 91 ]

"What is it?" asked the novelist.

"What is it? You are an honest man, Dorsenne; you are a great artist; you are my friend, and a friend allied to me by a sacred bond, almost a brother-in-arms; you, the grand-nephew of a hero who shed his blood by the side of my grandfather at Somo-Sierra. Give me your word of honor that you are absolutely certain Madame Steno is not Maitland's mistress, that you never thought it, have never heard it said, and I will believe you, I will obey you! Come," continued he, pressing the writer's hand with more fervor, "I see you hesitate!"

"No," said Julien, disengaging himself from the wild grasp, "I do not hesitate. I am sorry for you. Were I to give you that word, would it have any weight with you for five minutes? Would you not be persuaded immediately that I was perjuring myself to avoid a misfortune?"

"You hesitate," interrupted Boleslas. Then, with a burst of wild laughter, he said, "It is then true! I like that better! It is frightful to know it, but one suffers less— To know it! As if I did not know she had lovers before me, as if it were not written on Alba's every feature that she is Werekiew's child, as if I had not heard it said seventy times before knowing her that she had loved Branciforte, San Giobbe, Strabane, ten others. Before, during, or after, what difference does it make? Ah, I was sure on knocking at your door—at this door of honor—I should hear the truth, that I would touch it as I touch this object," and he laid his hand upon a marble bust on the table.

# COSMOPOLIS

"You see I hear it like a man. You can speak to me now. Who knows? Disgust is a great cure for passion. I will listen to you. Do not spare me!"

"You are mistaken, Gorka," replied Dorsenne. "What I have to say to you, I can say very simply. I was, and I am, convinced that in a quarter of an hour, in an hour, to-morrow, the day after, you will consider me a liar or an imbecile. But, since you misinterpreted my silence, it is my duty to speak, and I do so. I give you my word of honor I have never had the least suspicion of a connection between Madame Steno and Maitland, nor have their relations seemed changed to me for a second since your absence. I give you my word of honor that no one, do you hear, no one has spoken of it to me. And, now, act as you please, think as you please. I have said all I can say."

The novelist uttered those words with a feverish energy which was caused by the terrible strain he was making upon his conscience. But Gorka's laugh had terrified him so much the more as at the same instant the jealous lover's disengaged hand was voluntarily or involuntarily extended toward the weapon which gleamed upon the couch. The vision of an immediate catastrophe, this time inevitable, rose before Julien. His lips had spoken, as his arm would have been outstretched, by an irresistible instinct, to save several lives, and he had made the false statement, the first and no doubt the last in his life, without reflecting. He had no sooner uttered it than he experienced such an excess of anger that he would at that moment almost

[ 93 ]

have preferred not to be believed. It would indeed have been a comfort to him if his visitor had replied by one of those insulting negations which permit one man to strike another, so great was his irritation. On the contrary, he saw the face of Madame Steno's lover turned toward him with an expression of gratitude upon it. Boleslas's lips quivered, his hands were clasped, two large tears gushed from his burning eyes and rolled down his cheeks. When he was able to speak, he moaned:

"Ah, my friend, how much good you have done me ! From what a nightmare you have relieved me. Ah! Now I am saved! I believe you, I believe you. You are intimate with them. You see them every day. If there had been anything between them you would know it. You would have heard it talked of. Ah! Thanks! Give me your hand that I may press it. Forget all I said to you just now, the slander I uttered in a moment of delirium. I know very well it was untrue. And now, let me embrace you as I would if you had really saved me from drowning. Ah, my friend, my only friend!"

And he rushed up to clasp to his bosom the novelist, who replied with the words uttered at the beginning of this conversation: "Calm yourself, I beseech you, calm yourself!" and repeating to himself, brave and loyal man that he was: "I could not act differently, but it is hard!"

# CHAPTER IV

"O, I could not act differently," re-
peated Dorsenne on the evening of
that eventful day. He had given his
entire afternoon to caring for Gorka.
He made him lunch. He made him
lie down. He watched him. He
took him in a closed carriage to Por-
tonaccio, the first stopping-place on
the Florence line. Indeed, he made every effort not
to leave alone for a moment the man whose frenzy he
had rather suspended than appeased, at the price,
alas, of his own peace of mind! For, once left alone, in
solitude and in the apartments on the Place de la Trin-
ité, where twenty details testified to the visit of Gorka,
the weight of the perjured word of honor became a
heavy load to the novelist, so much the more heavy
when he discovered the calculating plan followed by
Boleslas. His tardy penetration permitted him to re-
view the general outline of their conversation. He
perceived that not one of his interlocutor's sentences,
not even the most agitated, had been uttered at ran-
dom. From reply to reply, from confidence to confidence, he, Dorsenne, had become involved in the
dilemma without being able to foresee or to avoid it;

he would either have had to accuse a woman or to lie
with one of those lies which a manly conscience does
not easily pardon. He did not forgive himself for it.

"It is so much worse," said he to himself, "as it
will prevent nothing. A person vile enough to pen
anonymous letters will not stop there. She will find
the means of again unchaining the madman. . . . But
who wrote those letters? Gorka may have forged
them in order to have an opportunity to ask me the
question he did. . . . And yet, no. . . . There are two
indisputable facts—his state of jealousy and his extraordinary return. Both would lead one to suppose
a third, a warning. But given by whom? . . . He told
me of twelve anonymous letters. . . . Let us assume
that he received one or two. . . . But who is the author
of those?"

The immediate development of the drama in which
Julien found himself involved was embodied in the
answer to the question. It was not easy to formulate.
The Italians have a proverb of singular depth which
the novelist recalled at that moment. He had laughed
a great deal when he heard sententious Egiste Brancadori repeat it. He repeated it to himself, and he
understood its meaning. *Chi non sa fingersi amico,
non sa essere nemico.* "He who does not know how to
disguise himself as a friend, does not know how to be
an enemy." In the little corner of society in which
Countess Steno, the Gorkas and Lincoln Maitland
moved, who was hypocritical and spiteful enough to
practise that counsel?

"It is not Madame Steno," thought Julien; "she has

related all herself to her lover. I knew a similar case. But it involved degraded Parisians, not a *Dogesse* of the sixteenth century found intact in the Venice of to-day, like a flower of that period preserved. Let us strike her off. Let us strike off, too, Madame Gorka, the truthful creature who could not even condescend to the smallest lie for a trinket which she desires. It is that which renders her so easily deceived. What irony! . . . Let us strike off Florent. He would allow himself to be killed, if necessary, like a Mameluke at the door of the room where his genial brother-in-law was dallying with the Countess. . . . Let us strike off the American himself. I have met such a case, a lover weary of a mistress, denouncing himself to her in order to be freed from his love-affair. But he was a *roué*, and had nothing in common with this booby, who has a talent for painting as an elephant has a trunk—what irony! He married this octoroon to have money. But it was a base act which freed him from commerce, and permitted him to paint all he wanted, as he wanted. He allows Steno to love him because she is diabolically pretty, notwithstanding her forty years, and then she is, in spite of all, a real noblewoman, which flattered him. He has not one dollar's worth of moral delicacy in his heart. But he has an abundance of knavery. . . Let us, too, strike out his wife. She is such a veritable slave whom the mere presence of a white person annihilates to such a degree that she dares not look her husband in the face. . . . It is not Hafner. The sly fox is capable of doing anything by cunning, but is he capable of under-

taking a useless and dangerous piece of rascality?
Never. . . . Fanny is a saint escaped from the Golden
Legend, no matter what Montfanon thinks! I have
now reviewed the entire coterie. . . . I was about to
forget Alba. . . . It is too absurd even to think of
her. . . . Too absurd? Why?"

Dorsenne was, on formulating that fantastic thought,
upon the point of retiring. He took up, as was his
habit, one of the books on his table, in order to read a
few pages, when once in bed. He had thus within
his reach the works by which he strengthened his doctrine of intransitive intellectuality; they were Goethe's
*Mémoirs;* a volume of George Sand's correspondence,
in which were the letters to Flaubert; the *Discours de
la Méthode* by Descartes, and the essay by Burckhart
on the Renaissance.

But, after turning over the leaves of one of those
volumes, he closed it without having read twenty lines.
He extinguished his lamp, but he could not sleep. The
strange suspicion which crossed his mind had something monstrous about it, applied thus to a young girl.
What a suspicion and what a young girl! The preferred friend of his entire winter, she on whose account
he had prolonged his stay in Rome, for she was the
most graceful vision of delicacy and of melancholy in
the framework of a tragical and solemn past. Any
other than Dorsenne would not have admitted such
an idea without being inspired with horror. But Dorsenne, on the contrary, suddenly began to dive into
that sinister hypothesis, to help it forward, to justify
it. No one more than he suffered from a moral de-

formity which the abuse of a certain literary work inflicts on some writers. They are so much accustomed to combining artificial characters with creations of their imaginations that they constantly fulfil an analogous need with regard to the individuals they know best. They have some friend who is dear to them, whom they see almost daily, who hides nothing from them and from whom they hide nothing. But if they speak to you of him you are surprised to find that, while continuing to love that friend, they trace to you in him two contradictory portraits with the same sincerity and the same probability.

They have a mistress, and that woman, even in the space sometimes of one day, sees them, with fear, change toward her, who has remained the same. It is that they have developed in them to a very intense degree the imagination of the human soul, and that to observe is to them only a pretext to construe. That infirmity had governed Julien from early maturity. It was rarely manifested in a manner more unexpected than in the case of charming Alba Steno, who was possibly dreaming of him at the very moment when, in the silence of the night, he was forcing himself to prove that she was capable of that species of epistolary parricide.

"After all," he said to himself, for there is iconoclasm in the excessively intellectual, and they delight in destroying their dearest moral or sentimental idols, the better to prove their strength, "after all, have I really understood her relations toward her mother? When I came to Rome in November, when I was to be presented to the Countess, what did not only one, but nine or ten persons tell me? That Madame Steno had a *liaison* with the husband of her daughter's best friend, and that the little one was grieving about it. I went to the house. I saw the child. She was sad that evening. I had the curiosity to wish to read her heart. . . . It is six months since then. We have met almost daily, often twice a day. She is so hermetically sealed that I am no farther advanced than I was on the first day. I have seen her glance at her mother as she did this morning, with loving, admiring eyes. I have seen her turn pale at a word, a gesture, on her part. I have seen her embrace Maud Gorka, and play tennis with that same friend so gayly, so innocently. I have seen that she could not bear the presence of Maitland in a room, and yet she asked the American to take her portrait. . . Is she guileless? . . Is she a hypocrite? Or is she tormented by doubt—divining, not divining—believing, not believing in—her mother? Is she underhand in any case, with her eyes the color of the sea? Has she the ambiguous mind at once of a Russian and an Italian? . . . This would be a solution of the problem, that she was a girl of extraordinary inward energy, who, both aware of her mother's intrigues and detesting them with an equal hatred, had planned to precipitate the two men upon each other. For a young girl the undertaking is great. I will go to the Countess's to-morrow night, and I will amuse myself by watching Alba, to see. . . If she is innocent, my deed will be inoffensive. If perchance she is not? . . ."

# COSMOPOLIS

It is vain to profess to one's own heart a complaisant dandyism of misanthropy. Such reflections leave behind them a tinge of a remorse, above all when they are, as these, absolutely whimsical and founded on a simple paradox of dilettantism. Dorsenne experienced a feeling of shame when he awoke the following morning, and, thinking of the mystery of the letters received by Gorka, he recalled the criminal romance he had constructed around the charming and tender form of his little friend; happily for his nerves, which were strained by the consideration of the formidable problem. If it is not some one in the Countess's circle, who has written those letters? He received, on rising, a voluminous package of proofs with the inscription: "Urgent." He was preparing to give to the public a collection of his first articles, under the title of *Poussière d'Idées*.

Dorsenne was a faithful literary worker. Usually, involved titles serve to hide in a book-stall shop-made goods, and romance writers or dramatic authors who pride themselves on living to write, and who seek inspiration elsewhere than in regularity of habits and the work-table, have their efforts marked from the first by sterility. Obscure or famous, rich or poor, an artist must be an artisan and practise these fruitful virtues —patient application, conscientious technicality, absorption in work. When he seated himself at his table Dorsenne was heart and soul in his business. He closed his door, he opened no letters nor telegrams, and he spent ten hours without taking anything but two eggs and some black coffee, as he did on this particular day, when looking over the essays of his twenty-fifth year with the talent of his thirty-fifth, retouching here a word, rewriting an entire page, dissatisfied here, smiling there at his thought. The pen flew, carrying with it all the sensibility of the intellectual man who had completely forgotten Madame Steno, Gorka, Maitland, and the calumniated Contessina, until he should awake from his lucid intoxication at nightfall. As he counted, in arranging the slips, the number of articles prepared, he found there were twelve.

"Like Gorka's letters," said he aloud, with a laugh. He now felt coursing through his veins the lightness which all writers of his kind feel when they have labored on a work they believe good. "I have earned my evening," he added, still in a loud voice. "I must now dress and go to Madame Steno's. A good dinner at the doctor's. A half-hour's walk. The night promises to be divine. I shall find out if they have news of the *Palatine*,"—the name he gave Gorka in his moments of gayety. "I shall talk in a loud voice of anonymous letters. If the author of those received by Boleslas is there, I shall be in the best position to discover him; provided that it is not Alba. . . Decidedly—that would be sad!" . . .

It was ten o'clock in the evening, when the young man, faithful to his programme, arrived at the door of the large house on the Rue du Vingt Septembre occupied by Madame Steno. It was an immense modern structure, divided into two distinct parts; to the left a revenue building and to the right a house on the order

of those which are to be seen on the borders of Park
Monceau. The Villa Steno, as the inscription in gold
upon the black marble door indicated, told the entire
story of the Countess's fortune—that fortune appraised
by rumor, with its habitual exaggeration, now at twenty,
now at thirty, millions. She had in reality two hundred and fifty thousand francs' income. But as, in
1873, Count Michel Steno, her husband, died, leaving
only debts, a partly ruined palace at Venice and much
property heavily mortgaged, the amount of that income
proved the truth of the title, "superior woman," applied by her friends to Alba's mother. Her friends
likewise added: "She has been the mistress of Hafner, who has aided her with his financial advice," an
atrocious slander which was so much the more false
as it was before ever knowing the Baron that she had begun to amass her wealth. This is how she managed it:

At the close of 1873, when, as a young widow, living
in retirement in the sumptuous and ruined dwelling
on the Grand Canal, she was struggling with her creditors, one of the largest bankers in Rome came to
propose to her a very advantageous scheme. It dealt
with a large piece of land which belonged to the Steno
estate, a piece of land in Rome, in one of the suburbs,
between the Porta Salara and the Porta Pia, a sort
of village which the deceased Cardinal Steno, Count
Michel's uncle, had begun to lay out. After his demise,
the land had been rented in lots to kitchen-gardeners,
and it was estimated that it was worth about forty
centimes a square metre. The financier offered four
francs for it, under the pretext of establishing a factory

on the site. It was a large sum of money. The Countess required twenty-four hours in which to consider, and, at the end of that time, she refused the offer, which won for her the admiration of the men of business who knew of the refusal. In 1882, less than ten years later, she sold the same land for ninety francs a metre. She saw, on glancing at a plan of Rome, and in recalling the history of modern Italy, first, that the new masters of the Eternal City would centre all their ambition in rebuilding it, then that the portion comprised between the Quirinal and the two gates of Salara and Pia would be one of the principal points of development; finally, that if she waited she would obtain a much greater sum than the first offer. And she had waited, applying herself to watching the administration of her possessions like the severest of intendants, depriving herself, stopping up gaps with unhoped-for profits. In 1875, she sold to the National Gallery a suite of four panels by Carpaccio, found in one of her country houses, for one hundred and twenty thousand francs. She had been as active and practical in her material life as she had been light and audacious in her sentimental experiences. The story circulated of her infidelity to Steno with Werekiew at St. Petersburg, where the diplomatist was stationed, after one year of marriage, was confirmed by the wantonness of her conduct, of which she gave evidence as soon as free.

At Rome, where she lived a portion of the year after the sale of her land, out of which she retained enough to build the double house, she continued to increase her fortune with the same intelligence. A very advantageous investment in Acqua Marcia enabled her to double in five years the enormous profits of her first operation. And what proved still more the exceptional good sense with which the woman was endowed, when love was not in the balance, she stopped on those two gains, just at the time when the Roman aristocracy, possessed by the delirium of speculation, had begun to buy stocks which had reached their highest value.

To spend the evening at the Villa Steno, after spending all the morning of the day before at the Palais Castagna, was to realize one of those paradoxes of contradictory sensations such as Dorsenne loved, for poor Ardea had been ruined in having attempted to do a few years later that which Countess Catherine had done at the proper moment. He, too, had hoped for an increase in the value of property. Only he had bought the land at seventy francs a metre, and in '90 it was not worth more than twenty-five. He, too, had calculated that Rome would improve, and on the high-priced land he had begun to build entire streets, imagining he could become like the Dukes of Bedford and of Westminster in London, the owner of whole districts. His houses finished, they did not rent, however. To complete the rest he had to borrow. He speculated in order to pay his debts, lost, and contracted more debts in order to pay the difference. His signature, as the proprietor of the Marzocco had said, was put to innumerable bills of exchange. The result was that on all the walls of Rome, including that of the

Rue Vingt Septembre on which was the Villa Steno, were posted multi-colored placards announcing the sale, under the management of Cavalier Fossati, of the collection of art and of furniture of the Palais Castagna.

"To foresee is to possess power," said Dorsenne to himself, ringing at Madame Steno's door and summing up thus the invincible association of ideas which recalled to him the palace of the ruined Roman Prince at the door of the villa of the triumphant Venetian: "It is the real Alpha and Omega."

The comparison between the lot of Madame Steno and that of the heir of the Castagnas had almost caused the writer to forget his plan of inquiry as to the author of the anonymous letters. It was to be impressed upon him, however, when he entered the hall where the Countess received every evening. Ardea himself was there, the centre of a group composed of Alba Steno, Madame Maitland, Fanny Hafner and the wealthy Baron, who, standing aloof and erect, leaning against a console, seemed like a beneficent and venerable man in the act of blessing youth. Julien was not surprised on finding so few persons in the vast salon, any more than he was surprised at the aspect of the room filled with old tapestry, bric-à-brac, furniture, flowers, and divans with innumerable cushions.

He had had the entire winter in which to observe the interior of that house, similar to hundreds of others in Vienna, Madrid, Florence, Berlin, anywhere, indeed, where the mistress of the house applies herself to realizing an ideal of Parisian luxury. He had amused himself many an evening in separating from the almost

international framework local features, those which
distinguished the room from others of the same kind.
No human being succeeds in being absolutely factitious
in his home or in his writings. The author had thus
noted that the salon bore a date, that of the Countess's
last journey to Paris in 1880. It was to be seen in the
plush and silk of the curtains. The general coloring,
in which green predominated, a liberty egotistical in
so brilliant a blonde, had too warm a tone and betrayed the Italian. Italy was also to be found in the
painted ceiling and in the frieze which ran all around,
as well as in several paintings scattered about. There
were two panels by Moretti de Brescia in the second
style of the master, called his silvery manner, on account of the delicate and transparent fluidity of the
coloring; a *Souper chez le Pharisien* and a *Jésus res-
suscité sur le rivage*, which could only have come from
one of the very old palaces of a very ancient family.
Dorsenne knew all that, and he knew, too, for what
reasons he found almost empty at that time of the
year the hall so animated during the entire winter, the
hall through which he had seen pass a veritable car-
nival of visitors: great lords, artists, political men,
Russians and Austrians, English and French—pell-
mell. The Countess was far from occupying in Rome
the social position which her intelligence, her fortune
and her name should have assured her. For, having
been born a Navagero, she combined on her escutcheon
the cross of gold of the Sebastien Navagero who was
the first to mount the walls of Lepante, with the star
of the grand Doge Michel.

But one particular trait of character had always prevented her from succeeding on that point. She could not bear *ennui* nor constraint, nor had she any vanity. She was positive and impassioned, in the manner of the men of wealth to whom their meditated-upon combinations serve to assure the conditions of their pleasures. Never had Madame Steno displayed diplomacy in the changes of her passions, and they had been numerous before the arrival of Gorka, to whom she had remained faithful two years, an almost incomprehensible thing ! Never had she, save in her own home, observed the slightest bounds when there was a question of reaching the object of her desire. Moreover, she had not in Rome to support her any member of the family to which she belonged, and she had not joined either of the two sets into which, since 1870, the society of the city was divided. Of too modern a mind and of a manner too bold, she had not been received by the admirable woman who reigns at the Quirinal, and who had managed to gather around her an atmosphere of such noble elevation.

These causes would have brought about a sort of semi-ostracism, had the Countess not applied herself to forming a salon of her own, the recruits for which were almost altogether foreigners. The sight of new faces, the variety of conversation, the freedom of manner, all in that moving world, pleased the thirst for diversion which, in that puissant, spontaneous, and almost manly immoral nature, was joined with very just clear-sightedness. If Julien paused for a moment surprised at the door of the hall, it was not, therefore, on finding it empty at the end of the season; it was on beholding there, among the inmates, Peppino Ardea, whom he had not met all winter. Truly, it was a strange time to appear in new scenes when the hammer of the appraiser was already raised above all which had been the pride and the splendor of his name. But the grand-nephew of Urban VII, seated between sublime Fanny Hafner, in pale blue, and pretty Alba Steno, in bright red, opposite Madame Maitland, so graceful in her mauve toilette, had in no manner the air of a man crushed by adversity.

The subdued light revealed his proud manly face, which had lost none of its gay *hauteur*. His eyes, very black, very brilliant, and very unsteady, seemed almost in the same glance to scorn and to smile, while his mouth, beneath its brown moustache, wore an expression of disdain, disgust, and sensuality. The shaven chin displayed a bluish shade, which gave to the whole face a look of strength, belied by the slender and nervous form. The heir of the Castagnas was dressed with an affectation of the English style, peculiar to certain Italians. He wore too many rings on his fingers, too large a bouquet in his buttonhole, and above all he made too many gestures to allow for a moment, with his dark complexion, of any doubt as to his nationality. It was he who, of all the group, first perceived Julien, and he said to him, or rather called out familiarly:

"Ah, Dorsenne! I thought you had gone away. We have not seen you at the club for fifteen days."

"He has been working," replied Hafner, "at some

new masterpiece, at a romance which is laid in Roman society, I am sure. Mistrust him, Prince, and you, ladies, disarm the portrayer.''

"I," resumed Ardea, laughing pleasantly, "will give him notes upon myself, if he wants them, as long as this, and I will illustrate his romance into the bargain with photographs which I once had a rage for taking. . . See, Mademoiselle,'' he added, turning to Fanny, "that is how one ruins one's self. I had a mania for the instantaneous ones. It was very innocent, was it not? It cost me thirty thousand francs a year, for four years."

Dorsenne had heard that it was a watchword between Peppino Ardea and his friends to take lightly the disaster which came upon the Castagna family in its last and only scion. He was not expecting such a greeting. He was so disconcerted by it that he neglected to reply to the Baron's remark, as he would have done at any other time. Never did the founder of the *Crédit Austro-Dalmate* fail to manifest in some such way his profound aversion for the novelist. Men of his species, profoundly cynical and calculating, fear and scorn at the same time a certain literature. Moreover, he had too much tact not to be aware of the instinctive repulsion with which he inspired Julien. But to Hafner, all social strength was tariffed, and literary success as much as any other. As he was afraid, as on the staircase of the Palais Castagna, that he had gone too far, he added, laying his hand with its long, supple fingers familiarly upon the author's shoulder:

"This is what I admire in him: It is that he allows

profane persons, such as we are, to plague him, without ever growing angry. He is the only celebrated author who is so simple. . . But he is better than an author; he is a veritable man-of-the-world."

"Is not the Countess here?" .asked Dorsenne, addressing Alba Steno, and without replying any more to the action, so involuntarily insulting, of the Baron than he had to his sly malice or to the Prince's facetious offer. Madame Steno's absence had again inspired him with an apprehension which the young girl dissipated by replying:

"My mother is on the terrace. . . We were afraid it was too cool for Fanny." . . It was a very simple phrase, which the Contessina uttered very simply, as she fanned herself with a large fan of white feathers. Each wave of it stirred the meshes of her fair hair, which she wore curled upon her rather high forehead. Julien understood her too well not to perceive that her voice, her gestures, her eyes, her entire being, betrayed a nervousness at that moment almost upon the verge of sadness.

Was she still reserved from the day before, or was she a prey to one of those inexplicable transactions, which had led Dorsenne in his meditations of the night to such strange suspicions? Those suspicions returned to him with the feeling that, of all the persons present, Alba was the only one who seemed to be aware of the drama which undoubtedly was brewing. He resolved to seek once more for the solution of the living enigma which that singular girl was. How lovely she appeared to him that evening with those two expressions which gave her an almost tragical look! The corners of her mouth drooped somewhat; her upper lip, almost too short, disclosed her teeth, and in the lower part of her pale face was a bitterness so prematurely sad! Why? It was not the time to ask the question. First of all, it was necessary for the young man to go in search of Madame Steno on the terrace, which terminated in a paradise of Italian voluptuousness, the salon furnished in imitation of Paris. Shrubs blossomed in large terra-cotta vases. Statuettes were to be seen on the balustrade, and, beyond, the pines of the Villa Bonaparte outlined their black umbrellas against a sky of blue velvet, strewn with large stars. A vague aroma of acacias, from a garden near by, floated in the air, which was light, caressing, and warm. The soft atmosphere sufficed to convict of falsehood the Contessina, who had evidently wished to justify the *tête-à-tête* of her mother and of Maitland. The two lovers were indeed together in the perfume, the mystery and the solitude of the obscure and quiet terrace.

It took Dorsenne, who came from the bright glare of the salon, a moment to distinguish in the darkness the features of the Countess who, dressed all in white, was lying upon a willow couch with soft cushions of silk. She was smoking a cigarette, the lighted end of which, at each breath she drew, gave sufficient light to show that, notwithstanding the coolness of the night, her lovely neck, so long and flexible, about which was clasped a collar of pearls, was bare, as well as her fair shoulders and her perfect arms, laden with bracelets, which were visible through her wide, flowing sleeves. On advancing, Julien recognized, through the vegetable odors of that spring night, the strong scent of the Virginian tobacco which Madame Steno had used since she had fallen in love with Maitland, instead of the Russian "papyrus" to which Gorka had accustomed her. It is by such insignificant traits that amorous women recognize a love profoundly, insatiably sensual, the only one of which the Venetian was capable. Their passionate desire to give themselves up still more leads them to espouse, so to speak, the slightest habits of the men whom they love in that way. Thus are explained those metamorphoses of tastes, of thoughts, even of appearance, so complete, that in six months, in three months of separation they become like different people. By the side of that graceful and supple vision, Lincoln Maitland was seated on a low chair. But his broad shoulders, which his evening coat set off in their amplitude, attested that before having studied "Art"—and even while studying it—he had not ceased to practise the athletic sports of his English education. As soon as he was mentioned, the term "large" was evoked. Indeed, above the large frame was a large face, somewhat red, with a large, red moustache, which disclosed, in broad smiles, his large, strong teeth.

Large rings glistened on his large fingers. He presented a type exactly opposite to that of Boleslas Gorka. If the grandson of the Polish Castellan recalled the dangerous finesse of a feline, of a slender and beautiful panther, Maitland could be compared to one of those mastiffs in the legends, with a jaw and muscles strong enough to strangle lions. The painter in him was only in the eye and in the hand, in consequence of a gift as physical as the voice to a tenor. But that instinct, almost abnormal, had been developed, cultivated to excess, by the energy of will in refinement, a trait so marked in the Anglo-Saxons of the New World when they like Europe, instead of detesting it. For the time being, the longing for refinement seemed reduced to the passionate inhalations of that divine, fair rose of love which was Madame Steno, a rose almost too full-blown, and which the autumn of forty years had begun to fade. But she was still charming. And how little Maitland heeded the fact that his wife was in the room near by, the windows of which cast forth a light which caused to stand out more prominently the shadow of the voluptuous terrace! He held his mistress's hand within his own, but abandoned it when he perceived Dorsenne, who took particular pains to move a chair noisily on approaching the couple, and to say, in a loud voice, with a merry laugh:

"I should have made a poor gallant abbé of the last century, for at night I can really see nothing. If your cigarette had not served me as a beacon-light I should have run against the balustrade."

"Ah, it is you, Dorsenne," replied Madame Steno, with a sharpness contrary to her habitual amiability, which proved to the novelist that first of all he was the "inconvenient third" of the classical comedies, then that Hafner had reported his imprudent remarks of the day before.

"So much the better," thought he, "I shall have forewarned her. On reflection she will be pleased. It is true that at this moment there is no question of reflection." As he said those words to himself, he talked aloud of the temperature of the day, of the probabilities of the weather for the morrow, of Ardea's good-humor. He made, indeed, twenty trifling remarks, in order to manage to leave the terrace and to leave the lovers to their *tête-à-tête*, without causing his withdrawal to become noticeable by indiscreet haste, as disagreeable as suggestive.

"When may we come to your atelier to see the portrait finished, Maitland?" he asked, still standing, in order the better to manage his retreat.

"Finished?" exclaimed the Countess, who added, employing a diminutive which she had used for several weeks: "Do you then not know that Linco has again effaced the head?" "Not the entire head," said the painter, "but the face is to be done over. You remember, Dorsenne, those two canvases by Pier della Francesca, which are at Florence, Duc Federigo d'Urbino and his wife Battista Sforza. Did you not see them in the same room with *La Calomnie* by Botticelli, with a landscape in the background? It is drawn like this," and he made a gesture with his thumb, "and that is what I am trying to obtain, the necessary curve on which all faces depend. There is no better painter in Italy."

"And Titian and Raphael?" interrupted Madame Steno.

"And the Sienese and the Lorenzetti, of whom

[115]

you once raved? You wrote to me of them, with regard to my article on your exposition of 'eighty-six;
do you remember?" inquired the writer.

"Raphael?" replied Maitland. . . "Do you wish
me to tell you what Raphael really was? A sublime
builder. And Titian? A sublime upholsterer. It is
true, I admired the Sienese very much," he added,
turning toward Dorsenne. "I spent three months in
copying the Simone Martini of the municipality, the
Guido Riccio, who rides between two strongholds on
a gray heath, where there is not a sign of a tree or a
house, but only lances and towers. Do I remember
Lorenzetti? Above all, the fresco at San Francesco,
in which Saint François presents his order to the Pope,
that was his best work. . . Then, there is a cardinal,
with his fingers on his lips, thus!"—another gesture.
"Well, I remember it, you see, because there is an
anecdote. It is portrayed on a wall—oh, a grand
portrayal, but without the subject, flutt!" . . and he
made a hissing sound with his lips, "while Pier della
Francesca, Carnevale, Melozzo," . . he paused to find
a word which would express the very complicated
thought in his head, and he concluded: "That is
painting!"

"But the *Assumption* by Titian, and the *Transfig-
uration* by Raphael," resumed the Countess, who added in Italian, with an accent of enthusiasm: "*Ah, che
bellezza!*"

"Do not worry, Countess," said Dorsenne, laughing
heartily, "those are an artist's opinions. Ten years
ago, I said that Victor Hugo was an amateur and

Alfred de Musset a *bourgeois*. But," he added, "as
I am not descended from the Doges nor the Pilgrim
Fathers, I, a poor, degenerate Gallo-Roman, fear the
dampness on account of my rheumatism, and ask
your permission to reënter the house." Then, as he
passed through the door of the salon: "Raphael, a
builder! Titian, an upholsterer! Lorenzetti, a re-
producer!" he repeated to himself. "And the descendant of the Doges, who listened seriously to those
speeches, her ideal should be a madonna *en chromo!*
Of the first order! As for Gorka, if he had not made
me lose my entire day yesterday, I should think I had
been dreaming, so little is there any question of him.
. . . And Ardea, who continues to laugh at his ruin.
He is not bad for an Italian. But he talks too much
about his affairs, and it is in bad taste!" . . . Indeed,
as he turned toward the group assembled in a corner of
the salon, he heard the Prince relating a story about
Cavalier Fossati, to whom was entrusted the charge
of the sale:

"How much do you think will be realized on all?"
I asked him, finally. "Oh," he replied, "very little. . .
But a little and a little more end by making a great
deal. With what an air he added: '*E già il moschino
è conte* — Already the gnat is a count.' The gnat
was himself. 'A few more sales like yours, my Prince,
and my son, the Count of Fossati, will have half a
million. He will enter the club and address you with the
familiar 'thou' when playing *goffo* against you. That is
what there is in this *già* (already). . . On my honor, I
have not been happier than since I have not a sou."

[ 117 ]

PAUL BOURGET

"You are an optimist, Prince," said Hafner, "and whatsoever our friend Dorsenne here present may claim, it is necessary to be optimistic."

"You are attacking him again, father," interrupted Fanny, in a tone of respectful reproach.

"Not the man," returned the Baron, "but his ideas —yes, and above all those of his school. . . . Yes, yes," he continued, either wishing to change the conversation, which Ardea persisted in turning upon his ruin, or finding very well organized a world in which strokes like that of the *Crédit Austro-Dalmate* are possible, he really felt a deep aversion to the melancholy and pessimism with which Julien's works were tinged. And he continued: "On listening to you, Ardea, just now, and on seeing this great writer enter, I am reminded by contrast of the fashion now in vogue of seeing life in a gloomy light."

"Do you find it very gay?" asked Alba, brusquely.

"Good," said Hafner; "I was sure that, in talking against pessimism, I should make the Contessina talk. . . . Very gay?" he continued. "No. But when I think of the misfortunes which might have come to all of us here, for instance, I find it very tolerable. Better than living in another epoch, for example. One hundred and fifty years ago, Contessina, in Venice, you would have been liable to arrest any day under a warrant of the Council of Ten. . . . And you, Dorsenne, would have been exposed to the cudgel like Monsieur de Voltaire, by some jealous lord. . . And Prince d'Ardea would have run the risk of being assassinated or beheaded at each change of Pope. And

# COSMOPOLIS

I, in my quality of Protestant, should have been driven from France, persecuted in Austria, molested in Italy, burned in Spain."

As can be seen, he took care to choose between his two inheritances. He had done so with an enigmatical good-nature which was almost ironical. He paused, in order not to mention what might have come to Madame Maitland before the suppression of slavery. He knew that the very pretty and elegant young lady shared the prejudices of her American compatriots against negro blood, and that she made every effort to hide the blemish upon her birth to the point of never removing her gloves. It may, however, in justice be added, that the slightly olive tinge in her complexion, her wavy hair, and a vague bluish reflection in the whites of her eyes would scarcely have betrayed the mixture of race. She did not seem to have heeded the Baron's pause, but she arranged, with an absent air, the folds of her mauve gown, while Dorsenne replied: "It is a fine and specious argument. . . . Its only fault is that it has no foundation. For I defy you to imagine yourself what you would have been in the epoch of which you speak. We say frequently, 'If I had lived a hundred years ago.' We forget that a hundred years ago we should not have been the same; that we should not have had the same ideas, the same tastes, nor the same requirements. It is almost the same as imagining that you could think like a bird or a serpent."

"One could very well imagine what it would be never to have been born," interrupted Alba Steno.

She uttered the sentence in so peculiar a manmer that the discussion begun by Hafner was nipped in the bud.

The words produced their effect upon the chatter of the idlers who only partly believed in the ideas they put forth. Although there is always a paradox in condemning life amid a scene of luxury when one is not more than twenty, the Contessina was evidently sincere. Whence came that sincerity? From what corner of her youthful heart, wounded almost to death? Dorsenne was the only person who asked himself the question, for the conversation turned at once, Lydia Maitland having touched with her fan the sleeve of Alba, who was two seats from her, to ask her this question with an irony as charming, after the young girl's words, as it was involuntary:

"It is silk muslin, is it not?"

"Yes," replied the Contessina, who rose and leaned over, to offer to the curious gaze of her pretty neighbor her arm, which gleamed frail, nervous, and softly fair through the transparent red material, with a bow of ribbon of the same color tied at her slender shoulder and her graceful wrist, while Ardea, by the side of Fanny, could be heard saying to the daughter of Baron Justus, more beautiful than ever that evening, in her pallor slightly tinged with pink by some secret agitation:

"You visited my palace yesterday, Mademoiselle?"

"No," she replied.

"Ask her why not, Prince," said Hafner.

"Father!" cried Fanny, with a supplication in her

black eyes which Ardea had the delicacy to obey, as he resumed:

"It is a pity. Everything there is very ordinary. But you would have been interested in the chapel. Indeed, I regret that the most, those objects before which my ancestors have prayed so long and which end by being listed in a catalogue. . . . They even took the reliquary from me, because it was by Ugolina da Siena. I will buy it back as soon as I can. Your father applauds my courage. I could not part from those objects without real sorrow."

"But it is the feeling she has for the entire palace," said the Baron.

"Father!" again implored Fanny.

"Come, compose yourself, I will not betray you," said Hafner, while Alba, taking advantage of having risen, left the group. She walked toward a table at the other extremity of the room, set in the style of an English table, with tea and iced drinks, saying to Julien, who followed her:

"Shall I prepare your brandy and soda, Dorsenne?"

"What ails you, Contessina?" asked the young man, in a whisper, when they were alone near the plateau of crystal and the collection of silver, which gleamed so brightly in the dimly lighted part of the room.

"Yes," he persisted, "what ails you? Are you still vexed with me?"

"With you?" said she. "I have never been. Why should I be?" she repeated. "You have done nothing to me."

"Some one has wounded you?" asked Julien.

He saw that she was sincere, and that she scarcely remembered the ill-humor of the preceding day. "You can not deceive a friend such as I am," he continued. "On seeing you fan yourself, I knew that you had some annoyance. I know you so well."

"I have no annoyance," she replied, with an impatient frown. "I can not bear to hear lies of a certain kind. That is all !"

"And who has lied?" resumed Dorsenne.

"Did you not hear Ardea speak of his chapel just now, he who believes in God as little as Hafner, of whom no one knows whether he is a Jew or a Gentile! . . . Did you not see poor Fanny look at him the while? And did you not remark with what tact the Baron made the allusion to the delicacy which had prevented his daughter from visiting the Palais Castagna with us? And did that comedy enacted between the two men give you no food for thought?"

"Is that why Peppino is here?" asked Julien. "Is there a plan on foot for the marriage of the heiress of Papa Hafner's millions and the grand-nephew of Pope Urban VII? That will furnish me with a fine subject of conversation with some one of my acquaintance!" . . . And the mere thought of Montfanon learning such news caused him to laugh heartily, while he continued: "Do not look at me so indignantly, dear Contessina. . . . But I see nothing so sad in the story. Fanny to marry Peppino? Why not? You yourself have told me that she is partly Catholic, and that her father is only awaiting her marriage to have her baptized. She will be happy then. Ardea will keep the magnificent palace we saw yesterday, and the Baron will crown his career in giving to a man ruined on the Bourse, in the form of a dowry, that which he has taken from others."

"Be silent," said the young girl, in a very grave voice, "you inspire me with horror. That Ardea should have lost all scruples, and that he should wish to sell his title of a Roman prince at as high a price as possible, to no matter what bidder, is so much the more a matter of indifference, for we Venetians do not allow ourselves to be imposed upon by the Roman nobility. We all had Doges in our families when the fathers of these people were bandits in the country, waiting for some poor monk of their name to become Pope. That Baron Hafner sells his daughter as he once sold her jewels is also a matter of indifference to me. But you do not know her. You do not know what a creature, charming and enthusiastic, simple and sincere, she is, and who will never, never mistrust that, first of all, her father is a thief, and, then, that he is selling her like a trinket in order to have grand-children who shall be at the same time grand-nephews of the Pope, and, finally, that Peppino does not love her, that he wants her dowry, and that he will have for her as little feeling as they have for her." She glanced at Madame Maitland. "It is worse than I can tell you," she said, enigmatically, as if vexed by her own words, and almost frightened by them.

"Yes," said Julien, "it would be very sad; but are you sure that you do not exaggerate the situation?

There is not so much calculation in life. It is more mediocre and more facile. Perhaps the Prince and the Baron have a vague project."

"A vague project?" interrupted Alba, shrugging her shoulders. "There is never anything vague with a Hafner, you may depend. What if I were to tell you that I am positive—do you hear—positive that it is he who holds between his fingers the largest part of the Prince's debts, and that he caused the sale by Ancona to obtain the bargain?"

"It is impossible!" exclaimed Dorsenne. "You saw him yourself yesterday thinking of buying this and that object."

"Do not make me say any more," said Alba, passing over her brow and her eyes two or three times her hand, upon which no ring sparkled—that hand, very supple and white, whose movements betrayed extreme nervousness. "I have already said too much. It is not my business, and poor Fanny is only to me a recent friend, although I think her very attractive and affectionate. . . When I think that she is on the point of pledging herself for life, and that there is no one, that there can be no one, to cry: They lie to you! I am filled with compassion. That is all. It is childish!"

It is always painful to observe in a young person the exact perception of the sinister dealings of life, which, once entered into the mind, never allows of the care-lessness so natural at the age of twenty.

The impression of premature disenchantment Alba Steno had many times given to Dorsenne, and it had indeed been the principal attraction to the curious observer of the feminine character, who still was struck by the terrible absence of illusion which such a view of the projects of Fanny's father revealed. Whence did she know them? Evidently from Madame Steno herself. Either the Baron and the Countess had talked of them before the young girl too openly to leave her in any doubt, or she had divined what they did not tell her, through their conversation. On seeing her thus, with her bitter mouth, her bright eyes, so visibly a prey to the fever of suppressed loathing, Dorsenne again was impressed by the thought of her perfect perspicacity. It was probable that she had applied the same force of thought to her mother's conduct. It seemed to him that on raising, as she was doing, the wick of the silver lamp beneath the large tea-kettle, that she was glancing sidewise at the terrace, where the end of the Countess's white robe could be seen through the shadow. Suddenly the mad thoughts which had so greatly agitated him on the previous day possessed him again, and the plan he had formed of imitating his model, Hamlet, in playing in Madame Steno's salon the *rôle* of the Danish prince before his uncle occurred to him. Absently, with his customary air of indifference, he continued:

"Rest assured, Ardea does not lack enemies. Hafner, too, has plenty of them. Some one will be found to denounce their plot, if there is a plot, to lovely Fanny. An anonymous letter is so quickly written."

He had no sooner uttered those words than he interrupted himself with the start of a man who handles a

**weapon** which he thinks unloaded and which suddenly discharges.

It was, really, to discharge a duty in the face of his own scepticism that he had spoken thus, and he did not expect to see another shade of sadness flit across Alba's mobile and proud face.

There was in the corners of her mouth more disgust, her eyes expressed more scorn, while her hands, busy preparing the tea, trembled as she said, with an accent so agitated that her friend regretted his cruel plan:

"Ah! Do not speak of it! It would be still worse than her present ignorance. At least, now she knows nothing, and if some miserable person were to do as you say she would know in part without being sure. . . . How could you smile at such a supposition? . . . No! Poor, gentle Fanny! I hope she will receive no anonymous letters. They are so cowardly and make so much trouble!"

"I ask your pardon if I have wounded you," replied Dorsenne. He had touched, he felt it, a tender spot in that heart, and perceived with grief that not only had Alba Steno not written the anonymous letters addressed to Gorka, but that, on the contrary, she had received some herself. From whom? Who was the mysterious denunciator who had warned in that abominable manner the daughter of Madame Steno after the lover? Julien shuddered as he continued: "If I smiled, it was because I believe Mademoiselle Hafner, in case the misfortune should come to her, sensible enough to treat such advice as it merits. An anonymous letter does not deserve to be read. Any one

COSMOPOLIS

infamous enough to make use of weapons of that sort
does not deserve that one should do him the honor
even to glance at what he has written."

"Is it not so?" said the girl. There was in her
eyes, the pupils of which suddenly dilated, a gleam of
genuine gratitude which convinced her companion
that he had seen correctly. He had uttered just the
words of which she had need. In the face of that
proof, he was suddenly overwhelmed by an access of
shame and of pity—of shame, because in his thoughts
he had insulted the unhappy girl—of pity, because she
had to suffer a blow so cruel, if, indeed, her mother
had been exposed to her. It must have been on the
preceding afternoon or that very morning that she
had received the horrible letter, for, during the visit to
the Palais Castagna, she had been, by turns, gay and
quiet, but so childish, while on that particular evening
it was no longer the child who suffered, but the woman.
Dorsenne resumed:

"You see, we writers are exposed to those abomi-
nations. A book which succeeds, a piece which pleases,
an article which is extolled, calls forth from the envious unsigned letters which wound us or those whom
we love. In such cases, I repeat, I burn them un-
read, and if ever in your life such come to you, listen
to me, little Countess, and follow the advice of your
friend, Dorsenne, for he is your friend; you know it,
do you not, your true friend?"

"Why should I receive anonymous letters?" asked
the girl, quickly. "I have neither fame, beauty, nor
wealth, and am not to be envied."

As Dorsenne looked at her, regretting that he had
said so much, she forced her sad lips to smile, and
added: "If you are really my friend, instead of making me lose time by your advice, of which I shall probably never have need, for I shall never become a great
authoress, help me to serve the tea, will you? It
should be ready." And with her slender fingers
she raised the lid of the kettle, saying: "Go and ask
Madame Maitland if she will take some tea this evening, and Fanny, too. . . . Ardea takes whiskey and
the Baron mineral water. . . . You can ring for his
glass of vichy. . . . There. . . . You have delayed me.
. . . There are more callers and nothing is ready.
. . . Ah," she cried, "it is Maud!"—then, with surprise, "and her husband!"

Indeed, the folding doors of the hall opened to
admit Maud Gorka, a robust British beauty, radiant
with happiness, attired in a gown of black *crêpe de
Chine* with orange ribbons, which set off to advantage
her fresh color. Behind her came Boleslas. But he
was no longer the traveller who, thirty-six hours before,
had arrived at the Place de la Trinité-des-Monts, mad
with anxiety, wild with jealousy, soiled by the dust
of travel, his hair disordered, his hands and face dirty.
It was, though somewhat thinner, the elegant Gorka
whom Dorsenne had known—tall, slender, and per-
fumed, in full dress, a bouquet in his buttonhole, his
lips smiling. To the novelist, knowing what he knew,
the smile and the composure had something in them
more terrible than the frenzy of the day before. He
comprehended it by the manner in which the Pole gave

him his hand. One night and a day of reflection had undermined his work, and if Boleslas had enacted the comedy to the point of lulling his wife's suspicions and of deciding on the visit of that evening, it was because he had resolved not to consult any one and to lead his own inquiry. He was succeeding in the beginning; he had certainly perceived Madame Steno's white gown upon the terrace, while radiant Maud explained his unexpected return with her usual ingenuousness.

"This is what comes of sending to a doting father accounts of our boy's health. . . . I wrote him the other day that Luc had a little fever. He wrote to ask about its progress. I did not receive his letter. He became uneasy, and here he is."

"I will tell mamma," said Alba, passing out upon the terrace, but her haste seemed too slow to Dorsenne. He had such a presentiment of danger that he did not think of smiling, as he would have done on any other occasion, at the absolute success of the deception which he and Boleslas had planned on the preceding day, and of which the Count had said, with a fatuity now proven: "Maud will be so happy to see me that she will believe all."

It was a scene both simple and tragical—of that order in which in society the most horrible incidents occur without a sound, without a gesture, amid phrases of conventionality and in a festal framework! Two of the spectators, at least, besides Julien, understood its importance—Ardea and Hafner. For neither the one nor the other had failed to notice the relations

9 [ 129 ]

between Madame Steno and Maitland, much less her position with regard to Gorka. The writer, the *grand seigneur*, and the business man had, notwithstanding the differences of age and of position, a large experience of analogous circumstances.

They knew of what presence of mind a courageous woman was capable, when surprised, as was the Venetian. All these have declared since that they had never imagined more admirable self-possession, a composure more superbly audacious, than that displayed by Madame Steno, at that decisive moment. She appeared on the threshold of the French window, surprised and delighted, just in the measure she conformably should be. Her fair complexion, which the slightest emotion tinged with carmine, was bewitchingly pink. Not a quiver of her long lashes veiled her deep blue eyes, which gleamed brightly. With her smile, which exhibited her lovely teeth, the color of the large pearls which were twined about her neck, with the emeralds in her fair hair, with her fine shoulders displayed by the slope of her white corsage, with her delicate waist, with the splendor of her arms from which she had removed the gloves to yield them to the caresses of Maitland, and which gleamed with more emeralds, with her carriage marked by a certain haughtiness, she was truly a woman of another age, the sister of those radiant princesses whom the painters of Venice evoke beneath the marble porticoes, among apostles and martyrs. She advanced to Maud Gorka, whom she embraced affectionately, then, pressing Boleslas's hand, she said in a voice so warm, in which at times there were deep tones, softened by the habitual use of the caressing dialect of the lagoon:

"What a surprise! And you could not come to dine with us? Well, sit down, both of you, and relate to me the Odyssey of the traveller," and, turning toward Maitland, who had followed her into the salon with the insolent composure of a giant and of a lover:

"Be kind, my little Linco, and fetch me my fan and my gloves, which I left on the couch."

At that moment Dorsenne, who had only one fear, that of meeting Gorka's eyes—he could not have borne their glance—was again by the side of Alba Steno. The young girl's face, just now so troubled, was radiant. It seemed as if a great weight had been lifted from the pretty Contessina's mind.

"Poor child," thought the writer, "she would not think her mother could be so calm were she guilty. The Countess's manner is the reply to the anonymous letter. Have they written all to her? My God! Who can it be?"

And he fell into a deep revery, interrupted only by the hum of the conversation, in which he did not participate. It would have satisfied him had he observed, instead of meditated, that the truth with regard to the author of the anonymous letters might have become clear to him, as clear as the courage of Madame Steno in meeting danger—as the blind confidence of Madame Gorka—as the disdainful imperturbability of Maitland before his rival and the suppressed rage of that rival—as the finesse of Hafner in sustaining the general conversation—as the assiduous attentions of Ardea to Fanny—as the emotion of the latter—as clear as Alba's sense of relief. All those faces, on Boleslas's entrance, had expressed different feelings. Only one had, for several minutes, expressed the joy of crime and the avidity of ultimately satisfied hatred. But as it was that of little Madame Maitland, the silent creature, considered so constantly by him as stupid and insignificant, Dorsenne had not paid more attention to it than had the other witnesses the surprising reappearance of the betrayed lover.

Every country has a metaphor to express the idea that there is no worse water than that which is stagnant. *Still waters run deep,* say the English, and the Italians, *Still waters ruin bridges.*

These adages would not be accurate if one did not forget them in practise, and the professional analyst of the feminine heart had entirely forgotten them on that evening.

# CHAPTER V

O a woman less courageous than the Countess, less capable of looking a situation in the face and of advancing to it, such an evening would have marked the prelude to one of those nights of insomnia when the mind exhausts in advance all the agonies of probable danger. Countess Steno did not know what weakness and fear were.

A creature of energy and of action, who felt herself to be above all danger, she attached no meaning to the word uneasiness. So she slept, on the night which followed that *soirée*, a sleep as profound, as refreshing, as if Gorka had never returned with vengeance in his heart, with threats in his eyes. Toward ten o'clock the following morning, she was in the tiny salon, or rather, the office adjoining her bedroom, examining several accounts brought by one of her men of business. Rising at seven o'clock, according to her custom, she had taken the cold bath in which, in summer as well as winter, she daily quickened her blood. She had breakfasted, *à l'anglaise*, following the rule to which she claimed to owe the preservation of her digestion, upon eggs cold meat, and tea. She had made her complicated toilette, had visited her daughter to ascertain how she had slept, had written five letters, for her cosmopolitan salon compelled her to carry on an immense correspondence, which radiated between Cairo and New York, St. Petersburg and Bombay, taking in Munich, London, and Madeira, and she was as faithful in friendship as she was inconstant in love. Her large handwriting, so elegant in its composition, had covered pages and pages before she said: "I have a rendezvous at eleven o'clock with Maitland. Ardea will be here at ten to talk of his marriage. I have accounts from Finoli to examine. I hope that Gorka will not come, too, this morning." . . . Persons in whom the feeling of love is very complete, but very physical, are thus. They give themselves and take themselves back altogether. The Countess experienced no more pity than fear in thinking of her betrayed lover. She had determined to say to him, "I no longer love you," frankly, openly, and to offer him his choice between a final rupture or a firm friendship.

The only annoyance depended upon the word of explanation, which she desired to see postponed until afternoon, when she would be free, an annoyance which, however, did not prevent her from examining with her usual accuracy the additions and multiplications of her intendant, who stood near her with a face such as Bonifagio gave to his Pharisees. He managed the seven hundred *hectares* of Piove, near Padua, Madame Steno's favorite estate. She had increased the revenue from it tenfold, by the draining of a sterile and often malignant lagoon, which, situated a metre below the water-level, had proved of surprising fertility; and she calculated the probable operations for weeks in advance with the detailed and precise knowledge of rural cultivation which is the characteristic of the Italian aristocracy and the permanent cause of its vitality.

"Then you estimate the gain from the silkworms at about fifty kilos of cocoons to an ounce?"

"Yes, Excellency," replied the intendant.

"One hundred ounces of yellow; one hundred times fifty makes five thousand," resumed the Countess. "At four francs fifty?"

"Perhaps five, Excellency," said the intendant.

"Let us say twenty-two thousand five hundred," said the Countess, "and as much for the Japanese. . . . That will bring us in our outlay for building."

"Yes, Excellency. And about the wine?"

"I am of the opinion, after what you have told me of the vineyard, that you should sell as quickly as possible to Kauffmann's agent all that remains of the last crop, but not at less than six francs. You know it is necessary that our casks be emptied and cleaned after the month of August. . . . If we were to fail this time, for the first year that we manufacture our wine with the new machine, it would be too bad."

"Yes, Excellency. And the horses?"

"I think that is an opportunity we should not let escape. My advice is that you take the express to Florence to-day at two o'clock. You will reach Verona to-morrow morning. You will conclude the bargain. The horses will be sent to Piove the same evening. . .

We have finished just in time," she continued, arranging the intendant's papers. She put them herself in their envelope, which she gave him. She had an extremely delicate sense of hearing, and she knew that the door of the antechamber opened. It seemed that the administrator took away in his portfolio all the preoccupation of this extraordinary woman. For, after concluding that dry conversation, or rather that monologue, she had her clearest and brightest smile with which to receive the new arrival, who was, fortunately, Prince d'Ardea. She said to the servant:

"I wish to speak with the Prince. If any one asks for me, do not admit him and do not send any one hither. Bring me the card." Then, turning toward the young man, "Well, *Simpaticone*," it was the nickname she gave him, "how did you finish your evening?"

"You would not believe me," replied Peppino Ardea, laughing; "I, who no longer have anything, not even my bed. I went to the club and I played. . . . For the first time in my life I won."

He was so gay in relating his childish prank, he jested so merrily about his ruin, that the Countess looked at him in surprise, as he had looked at her on entering. . . . We understand ourselves so little, and we know so little about our own singularities of character, that each one was surprised at finding the other so calm. Ardea could not comprehend that Madame Steno should not be at least uneasy about Gorka's return and the consequences which might result therefrom. She, on the other hand, admired the strange youth who, in his misfortune, could find such joviality at his command. He had evidently expended as much care upon his toilette as if he had not to take some immediate steps to assure his future, and his waistcoat, the color of his shirt, his cravat, his yellow shoes, the flower in his buttonhole, all united to make of him an amiable and incorrigibly frivolous dandy. She felt the need which strong characters have in the presence of weak ones; that of acting for the youth, of aiding him in spite of himself, and she attacked at once the question of marriage with Fanny Hafner. With her usual common-sense, and with her instinct of arranging everything, Madame Steno perceived in the union so many advantages for every one that she was in haste to conclude it as quickly as if it involved a personal affair.

The marriage was earnestly desired by the Baron, who had spoken of it to her for months. It suited Fanny, who would be converted to Catholicism with the consent of her father. It suited the Prince, who at one stroke would be freed from his embarrassment. Finally, it suited the name of Castagna. Although Peppino was its only representative at that time, and as, by an old family tradition, he bore a title different from the patronymic title of Pope Urban VII, the sale of the celebrated palace had called forth a scandal to which it was essential to put an end. The Countess had forgotten that she had assisted, without a protestation, in that sale. Had she not known through Hafner that he had bought at a low price an enormous heap of the Prince's bills of exchange? Did she not know the Baron well enough to be sure that M. Noé Ancona, the implacable creditor who sold the palace, was only the catspaw of this terrible friend? In a fit of ill-humor at the Baron, had she not herself accused him in Alba's presence of this very simple plan, to bring Ardea to a final catastrophe in order to offer him salvation in the form of the union with Fanny, and to execute at the same time an excellent operation? For, once freed from the mortgages which burdened them, the Prince's lands and buildings would regain their true value, and the imprudent speculator would find himself again as rich, perhaps richer.

"Come," said Madame Steno to the Prince, after a moment's silence and without any preamble, "it is now time to talk business. You dined by the side of my little friend yesterday; you had the entire evening in which to study her. Answer me frankly, would she not make the prettiest little Roman princess who could kneel in her wedding-gown at the tomb of the apostles? Can you not see her in her white gown, under her veil, alighting at the staircase of Saint Peter's from the carriage with the superb horses which her father has given her? Close your eyes and see her in your thoughts. Would she not be pretty? Would she not?"

"Very pretty," replied Ardea, smiling at the tempting vision Madame Steno had conjured up, "but she is not fair. And you know, to me, a woman who is not fair—ah, Countess! What a pity that in Venice, five years ago, on a certain evening—do you remember?"

COSMOPOLIS

"How much like you that is!" interrupted she, laughing her deep, clear laugh. "You came to see me this morning to talk to me of a marriage, unhoped for with your reputation of gamester, of supper-giver, of *mauvais sujet;* of a marriage which fulfils conditions almost improbable, so perfect are they—beauty, youth, intelligence, fortune, and even, if I have read my little friend aright, the beginning of an interest, of a very deep interest. And, for a little, you would make a declaration to me. Come, come!" and she extended to him for a kiss her beautiful hand, on which gleamed large emeralds. "You are forgiven. But answer— yes or no. Shall I make the proposal? If it is yes, I will go to the Palace Savorelli at two o'clock. I will speak to my friend Hafner. He will speak to his daughter, and it will not depend upon me if you have not their reply this evening or to-morrow morning. Is it yes? Is it no?"

"This evening? To-morrow?" exclaimed the Prince, shaking his head with a most comical gesture. "I can not decide like that. It is an ambush! I come to talk, to consult you."

"And on what?" asked Madame Steno, with a vivacity almost impatient. "Can I tell you anything you do not already know? In twenty-four hours, in forty-eight, in six months, what difference will there be, I pray you? We must look at things as they are, however. To-morrow, the day after, the following days, will you be less embarrassed?"

"No," said the Prince, "but——"

"There is no but," she resumed, allowing him to say

[ 139 ]

no more than she had allowed her intendant. The despotism natural to puissant personalities scorned to be disguised in her, when there were practical decisions in which she was to take part. "The only serious objection you made to me when I spoke to you of this marriage six months ago was that Fanny was not a Catholic. I know to-day that she has only to be asked to be converted. So do not let us speak of that."

"No," said the Prince, "but——"

"As for Hafner," continued the Countess, "you will say he is my friend and that I am partial, but that partiality even is an opinion. He is precisely the father-in-law you need. Do not shake your head. He will repair all that needs repairing in your fortune. You have been robbed, my poor Peppino. You told me so yourself. . . Become the Baron's son-in-law, and you will have news of your robbers. I know. . . . There is the Baron's origin and the suit of ten years ago with all the *pettogolezzi* to which it gave rise. All that has not the common meaning. The Baron began life in a small way. He was from a family of Jewish origin—you see, I do not deceive you—but converted two generations back, so that the story of his change of religion since his stay in Italy is a calumny, like the rest. He had a suit in which he was acquitted. You would not require more than the law, would you?"

"No, but——"

"For what are you waiting, then?" concluded Madame Steno. "That it may be too late? How about your lands?"

"Ah! let me breathe, let me fan myself," said Ardea, who, indeed, took one of the Countess's fans from the desk. "I, who have never known in the morning what I would do in the evening, I, who have always lived according to my pleasure, you ask me to take in five minutes the resolution to bind myself forever!"

"I ask you to decide what you wish to do," returned the Countess. "It is very amusing to travel at one's pleasure. But when it is a question of arranging one's life, this childishness is too absurd. I know of only one way: to see one's aim and to march directly to it. Yours is very clear—to get out of this dilemma. The way is not less clear; it is marriage with a girl who has five millions dowry. Yes or no, will you have her? . . . Ah," said she, suddenly interrupting herself, "I shall not have a moment to myself this morning, and I have an appointment at eleven o'clock!" . . . She looked at the timepiece on her table, which indicated twenty-five minutes past ten. She had heard the door open. The footman was already before her and presented to her a card upon a salver. She took the card, looked at it, frowned, glanced again at the clock, seemed to hesitate, then: "Let him wait in the small salon, and say that I will be there immediately," said she, and turning again toward Ardea: "You think you have escaped. You have not. I do not give you permission to go before I return. I shall return in fifteen minutes. Would you like some newspapers? There are some. Books? There are some. Tobacco? This box is filled with cigars. . . . In a quarter of an hour I shall be here and I will have your reply. I wish it, do you hear? ɪ wish it." . . . And, on the threshold, with another smile, using that time a term of *patois* common in Northern Italy and which is only a corruption of *schiavo* or servant: *Ciao Simpaticone.*

"What a woman!" said Peppino Ardea, when the door was closed upon the Countess. "Yes, what a pity that five years ago in Venice I was not free! Who knows? If I had dared, when she took me to my hotel in her gondola. She was about to leave San Giobbe. She had not yet accepted Boleslas. She would have advised—have directed me. I should have speculated on the Bourse, as she did, with Hafner's counsel. But not in the quality of son-in-law. I should not have been obliged to marry. And she would not now have such bad tobacco." . . . He was on the point of lighting one of the Virginian cigarettes, a present from Maitland. He threw it away, making a grimace with his air of a spoiled child, at the risk of scorching the rug which lay upon the marble floor; and he passed into the antechamber in order to fetch his own case in the pocket of the light overcoat he had prudently taken on coming out after eight o'clock.

As he lighted one of the cigarettes in that case, filled with so-called Egyptian tobacco, mixed with opium and saltpetre, which he preferred to the tobacco of the American, he mechanically glanced at the card which the servant had left on going from the room—the card of the unknown visitor for whom Madame Steno had left him.

Ardea read upon it, with astonishment, these words: *Count Boleslas Gorka.*

"She is better than I thought her," said he, on re-entering the deserted office. "She had no need to bid me not to go. I think I should wait to see her return from that conversation."

It was indeed Boleslas whom the Countess found in the salon, which she had chosen as the room the most convenient for the stormy explanation she anticipated. It was isolated at the end of the hall, and was like a pendant to the terrace. It formed, with the dining-room, the entire ground-floor, or, rather, the *entresol* of the house. Madame Steno's apartments, as well as the other small salon in which Peppino was, were on the first floor, together with the rooms set apart for the Contessina and her German governess, Fraulein Weber, for the time being on a journey.

The Countess had not been mistaken. At the first glance exchanged on the preceding day with Gorka, she had divined that he knew all. She would have suspected it, nevertheless, since Hafner had told her the few words indiscreetly uttered by Dorsenne on the clandestine return of the Pole to Rome. She had not at that time been mistaken in Boleslas's intentions, and she had no sooner looked in his face than she felt herself to be in peril. When a man has been the lover of a woman as that man had been hers, with the vibrating communion of a voluptuousness unbroken for two years, that woman maintains a sort of physiological, quasi-animal instinct. A gesture, the accent of a word, a sigh, a blush, a pallor, are signs for her that her intuition interprets with infallible certainty. How and why is that instinct accompanied by absolute oblivion of former caresses? It is a particular case of that insoluble and melancholy problem of the birth and death of love. Madame Steno had no taste for reflection of that order. Like all vigorous and simple creatures, she acknowledged and accepted it. As on the previous day, she became aware that the presence of her former lover no longer touched in her being the chord which had rendered her so weak to him during twenty-five months, so indulgent to his slightest caprices. It left her as cold as the marble of the bas-relief by Mino da Fiesole fitted into the wall just above the high chair upon which he leaned.

Boleslas, notwithstanding the paroxysm of lucid fury which he suffered at that moment, and which rendered him capable of the worst violence, had on his part a knowledge of the complete insensibility in which his presence left her. He had seen her so often, in the course of their long *liaison*, arrive at their morning rendezvous at that hour, in similar toilettes, so fresh, so supple, so youthful in her maturity, so eager for kisses, tender and ardent. She had now in her blue eyes, in her smile, in her entire person, something at once so gracious and so inaccessible, which gives to an abandoned lover the mad longing to strike, to murder, a woman who smiles at him with such a smile. At the same time she was so beautiful in the morning light, subdued by the lowered blinds, that she inspired him with an equal desire to clasp her in his arms whether she would or no. He had recognized, when she entered the room, the aroma of a preparation which she had used in her bath, and that trifle

alone had aroused his passion far more than when the
servant told him Madame Steno was engaged, and
he wondered whether she was not alone with Maitland.
Those impassioned, but suppressed, feelings trembled
in the accent of the very simple phrase with which he
greeted her.  At certain moments, words are nothing;
it is the tone in which they are uttered.  And to the
Countess that of the young man was terrible.

"I am disturbing you?" he asked, bowing and barely
touching with the tips of his fingers the hand she had
extended to him on entering.  "Excuse me, I thought
you alone.  Will you be pleased to name another time
for the conversation which I take the liberty of de-
manding?"

"No, no," she replied, not permitting him to finish
his sentence.  "I was with Peppino Ardea, who will
await me," said she, gently.  "Moreover, you know
I am in all things for the immediate.  When one has
something to say, it should be said, one, two, three!
. . . First, there is not much to say, and then it is
better said. . . . There is nothing that will sooner
render difficult easy explanations and embroil the best
of friends than delay and maintaining silence."

"I am very happy to find you in such a mind,"
replied Boleslas, with a sarcasm which distorted his
handsome face into a smile of atrocious hatred.  The
good-nature displayed by her cut him to the heart,
and he continued, already less self-possessed: "It is
indeed an explanation which I think I have the right
to ask of you, and which I have come to claim."

"To claim, my dear?" said the Countess, looking

10                    [ 145 ]

him fixedly in the face without lowering her proud eyes, in which those imperative words had kindled a flame.

If she had been admirable the preceding evening in facing as she had done the return of her discarded lover, on coming direct from the *tête-à-tête* with her new one, perhaps, at that moment, she was doubly so, when she did not have her group of intimate friends to support her. She was not sure that the madman who confronted her was not armed, and she believed him perfectly capable of killing her, while she could not defend herself. But a part had to be played sooner or later, and she played it without flinching. She had not spoken an untruth in saying to Peppino Ardea: "I know only one way: to see one's aim and to march directly to it." She wanted a definitive rupture with Boleslas. Why should she hesitate as to the means?

She was silent, seeking for words. He continued:

"Will you permit me to go back three months, although that is, it seems, a long space of time for a woman's memory? I do not know whether you recall our last meeting? Pardon, I meant to say the last but one, since we met last night. Do you concede that the manner in which we parted then did not presage the manner in which we met?"

"I concede it," said the Countess, with a gleam of angry pride in her eyes, "although I do not very much like your style of expression. It is the second time you have addressed me as an accuser, and if you assume that attitude it will be useless to continue."

"Catherine!" . . . That cry of the young man, whose anger was increasing, decided her whom he thus addressed to precipitate the issue of a conversation in which each reply was to be a fresh burst of rancor.

"Well?" she inquired, crossing her arms in a manner so imperious that he paused in his menace, and she continued: "Listen, Boleslas, we have talked ten minutes without saying anything, because neither of us has the courage to put the question such as we know and feel it to be. Instead of writing to me, as you did, letters which rendered replies impossible to me; instead of returning to Rome and hiding yourself like a malefactor; instead of coming to my home last night with that threatening face; instead of approaching me this morning with the solemnity of a judge, why did you not question me simply, frankly, as one who knows that I have loved him very, very much? . . . Having been lovers, is that a reason for detesting each other when we cease those relations?"

"'When we cease those relations!'" replied Gorka. "So you no longer love me? Ah, I knew it; I guessed it after the first week of that fatal absence! But to think that you should tell it to me some day like that, in that calm voice which is a horrible blasphemy for our entire past. No, I do not believe it. I do not yet believe it. Ah, it is too infamous."

"Why?" interrupted the Countess, raising her head with still more haughtiness. "There is only one thing infamous in love, and that is a falsehood. Ah, I know it. You men are not accustomed to meeting true women, who have the respect, the religion of their

sentiment. I have that respect; I practise that religion. I repeat that I loved you a great deal, Boleslas.
I did not hide it from you formerly. I was as loyal
to you as truth itself. I have the consciousness of being so still, in offering you, as I do, a firm friendship,
the friendship of man for man, who only asks to prove
to you the sincerity of his devotion."

"I, a friendship with you, I—I—I?" exclaimed
Boleslas. "Have I had enough patience in listening
to you as I have listened? I heard you lie to me
and scented the lie in the same breath. Why do you
not ask me as well to form a friendship for him with
whom you have replaced me? Ah, so you think I
am blind, and you fancy I did not see that Maitland
near you, and that I did not know at the first glance
what part he was playing in your life? You did not
think I might have good reasons for returning as I
did? You did not know that one does not dally with
one whom one loves as I love you? . . . It is not true.
. . . You have not been loyal to me, since you took
this man for a lover while you were still my mistress.
You had not the right, no, no, no, you had not the
right! . . . And what a man! . . . If it had been
Ardea, Dorsenne, no matter whom, that I might not
blush for you. . . . But that brute, that idiot, who
has nothing in his favor, neither good looks, birth,
elegance, mind nor talent, for he has none—he has
nothing but his neck and shoulders of a bull. . . . It
is as if you had deceived me with a lackey. . . .No.
. . . . it is too terrible. . . . Ah, Catherine, swear to
me that it is not true. Tell me that you no longer

love me, I will submit, I will go away, I will accept all, provided that you swear to me you do not love that man—swear, swear!" . . . he added, grasping her hands with such violence that she uttered a slight exclamation, and, disengaging herself, said to him:

"Cease; you pain me. You are mad, Gorka; that can be your sole excuse. . . . I have nothing to swear to you. What I feel, what I think, what I do no longer concerns you after what I have told you. . . . Believe what it pleases you to believe. . . . But," and the irritation of an enamored woman, wounded in the man she adores, possessed her, "you shall not speak twice of one of my friends as you have just spoken. You have deeply offended me, and I will not pardon you. In place of the friendship I offered you so honestly, we will have no further connections excepting those of society. That is what you desired. . . . Try not to render them impossible to yourself. Be correct at least in form. Remember you have a wife, I have a daughter, and that we owe it to them to spare them the knowledge of this unhappy rupture. . . . God is my witness, I wished to have it otherwise."

"My wife! Your daughter!" cried Boleslas with bitterness. "This is indeed the hour to remember them and to put them between you and my just vengeance! They never troubled you formerly, the two poor creatures, when you began to win my love? . . . It was convenient for you that they should be friends! And I lent myself to it! . . . I accepted such baseness—that to-day you might take shelter behind the two innocents! . . . No, it shall not be. . . . No, you shall not escape me thus. Since it is the only point on which I can strike you, I will strike you there. I hold you by that means, do you hear, and I will keep you. Either you dismiss that man, or I will no longer respect anything. My wife shall know all! Her! So much the better! For some time I have been stifled by my lies. . . . Your daughter, too, shall know all. She shall judge you now as she would judge you one day."

As he spoke he advanced to her with a manner so cruel that she recoiled. A few more moments and the man would have carried out his threat. He was about to strike her, to break objects around him, to call forth a terrible scandal. She had the presence of mind of an audacity more courageous still. An electric bell was near at hand. She pressed it, while Gorka said to her, with a scornful laugh, "That was the only affront left you to offer me—to summon your servants to defend you."

"You are mistaken," she replied. "I am not afraid. I repeat you are mad, and I simply wish to prove it to you by recalling you to the reality of your situation. . . . Bid Mademoiselle Alba come down," said she to the footman whom her ring had summoned. That phrase was the drop of cold water which suddenly broke the furious jet of vapor. She had found the only means of putting an end to the terrible scene. For, notwithstanding his menace, she knew that Maud's husband always recoiled before the young girl, the friend of his wife, of whose delicacy and sensibility he was aware.

Gorka was capable of the most dangerous and most

cruel deeds, in an excess of passion augmented by vanity.

He had in him a chivalrous element which would paralyze his frenzy before Alba. As for the immorality of that combination of defence which involved her daughter in her rupture with a vindictive lover, the Countess did not think of that. She often said: "She is my comrade, she is my friend." . . . And she thought so. To lean upon her in that critical moment was only natural to her. In the tempest of indignation which shook Gorka, the sudden appeal to innocent Alba appeared to him the last degree of cynicism. During the short space of time which elapsed between the departure of the footman and the arrival of the young girl, he only uttered these words, repeating them as he paced the floor, while his former mistress defied him with her bold gaze:

"I scorn you, I scorn you; ah, how I scorn you!" Then, when he heard the door open: "We will resume our conversation, Madame."

"When you wish," replied Countess Steno, and to her daughter, who entered, she said: "You know the carriage is to come at ten minutes to eleven, and it is now the quarter. Are you ready?"

"You can see," replied the young girl, displaying her pearl-gray gloves, which she was just buttoning, while on her head a large hat of black tulle made a dark and transparent aureole around her fair head. Her delicate bust was displayed to advantage in the corsage Maitland had chosen for her portrait, a sort of cuirass of a dark-blue material, finished at the neck

and wrists with bands of velvet of a darker shade.
The fine lines of cuffs and a collar gave to that pure
face a grace of youth younger than her age.

She had evidently come at her mother's call, with
the haste and the smile of that age. Then, to see
Gorka's expression and the feverish brilliance of the
Countess's eyes had given her what she called, in an
odd but very appropriate way, the sensation of "a
needle in the heart," of a sharp, fine point, which entered her breast to the left. She had slept a sleep so
profound, after the *soirée* of the day before, on which
she had thought she perceived in her mother's attitude
between the Polish count and the American painter a
proof of certain innocence.

She admired her mother so much, she thought her
so intelligent, so beautiful, so good, that to doubt her
was a thought not to be borne! There were times
when she doubted her. A terrible conversation about
the Countess, overheard in a ballroom, a conversation between two men, who did not know Alba to be
behind them, had formed the principal part of the
doubt, which, by turns, had increased and diminished,
which had abandoned and tortured her, according to
the signs, as little decisive as Madame Steno's tranquillity of the preceding day or her confusion that
morning. It was only an impression, very rapid, instantaneous, the prick of a needle, which merely leaves
after it a drop of blood, and yet she had a smile with
which to say to Boleslas:

"How did Maud rest? How is she this morning?
And my little friend Luc?"

"They are very well," replied Gorka. The last stage of his fury, suddenly arrested by the presence of the young girl, was manifested, but only to the Countess, by the simple phrase to which his eyes and his voice lent an extreme bitterness: "I found them as I left them. . . . Ah! They love me dearly. . . . I leave you to Peppino, Countess," added he, walking toward the door. "Mademoiselle, I will bear your love to Maud." . . . He had regained all the courtesy which a long line of savage *grands seigneurs*, but *grands seigneurs* nevertheless, had instilled in him. If his bow to Madame Steno was very ceremonious, he put a special grace in the low bow with which he took leave of the Contessina. It was merely a trifle, but the Countess was keen enough to perceive it. She was touched by it, she whom despair, fury, and threats had found so impassive. For an instant she was vaguely humiliated by the success which she had gained over the man whom she would, voluntarily, five minutes before, have had cast out of doors by her servants. She was silent, oblivious even of her daughter's presence, until the latter recalled her to herself by saying:

"Shall I put on my veil and fetch my parasol?"

"You can join me in the office, whither I am going to talk with Ardea," replied her mother; adding, "I shall perhaps have some news to tell you in the carriage which will give you pleasure!" . . . She had again her bright smile, and she did not mistrust while she resumed her conversation with Peppino that poor Alba, on reëntering her chamber, wiped from her pale cheeks two large tears, and that she opened, to re-read it, the infamous anonymous letter received the day before. She knew by heart all the perfidious phrases. Must it not have been that the mind which had composed them was blinded by vengeance to such a degree that it had no scruples about laying before the innocent child a denunciation which ran thus:

*"A true friend of Mademoiselle Steno warns her that she is compromised, more than a marriageable young girl should be, in playing, with regard to M. Maitland the rôle she has already played with regard to M. Gorka. There are conditions of blindness so voluntary that they become complicity."*

Those words, enigmatical to any one else, but to the Contessina horribly clear, had been, like the letters of which Boleslas had told Dorsenne, cut from a journal and pasted on a sheet of paper. How had Alba trembled on reading that note for the first time, with an emotion increased by the horror of feeling hovering over her and her mother a hatred so relentless! Later in the day how much had the words exchanged with Dorsenne comforted her, and how reassured had she been by the Countess's imperturbability on the entrance of Boleslas Gorka! Fragile peace, which had vanished when she saw her mother and the husband of her best friend face to face, with traces in their eyes, in their gestures, upon their countenances, of an angry scene! The thought "Why were they thus! What had they said?" again occurred to her to sadden her. Suddenly she crushed in her hand with violence the anonymous letter, which gave a concrete form to her sorrow and her suspicion, and, lighting a taper, she held it to the paper, which the flames soon reduced to ashes. She ran her fingers through the *débris* until there was very little left, and then, opening the window, she cast it to the winds.

She looked at her glove after doing this—her glove, a few moments before, of so delicate a gray, now stained by the smoky dust. It was symbolical of the stain which the letter, even when destroyed, had left upon her mind. The gloves, too, inspired her with horror. She hastily drew them off, and, when she descended to rejoin Madame Steno, it was not any more possible to perceive on those hands, freshly gloved, the traces of that tragical childishness, than it was possible to discern, beneath the large veil which she had tied over her hat, the traces of tears. She found the mother for whom she was suffering so much, wearing, too, a large sun-hat, but a white one with a white veil, beneath which could be seen her fair hair, her sparkling blue eyes and pink-and-white complexion; her form was enveloped in a gown of a material and cut more youthful than her daughter's, while, radiant with delight, she said to Peppino Ardea:

"Well, I congratulate you on having made up your mind. The step shall be taken to-day, and you will be grateful to me all your life!"

"Yet," replied the young man, "I understand myself. I shall regret my decision all the afternoon. It is true," he added, philosophically, "that I should regret it—just as much if I had not made it."

"You have guessed that we were talking of Fanny's marriage," said Madame Steno to her daughter several minutes later, when they were seated side by side, like two sisters, in the victoria which was bearing them toward Maitland's studio.

"Then," asked the Contessina, "you think it will be arranged?"

"It *is* arranged," gayly replied Madame Steno. "I am commissioned to make the proposition. . . . How happy all three will be! . . . Hafner has aimed at it this long time! I remember how, in 1880, after his suit, he came to see me in Venice—you and Fanny played on the balcony of the palace—he questioned me about the Quirinal, the Vatican and society. . . . Then he concluded, pointing to his daughter, 'I shall make a Roman princess of the little one!'"

The *dogaresse* was so delighted at the thought of the success of her negotiations, so delighted, too, to go, as she was going, to Maitland's studio, behind her two English cobs, which trotted so briskly, that she did not see on the sidewalk Boleslas Gorka, who watched her pass.

Alba was so troubled by that fresh proof of her mother's lack of conscience that she did not notice Maud's husband either. Baron Hafner's and Prince d'Ardea's manner toward Fanny had inspired her the day before with a dolorous analogy between the atmosphere of falsehood in which that poor girl lived and the atmosphere in which she at times thought she herself lived. That analogy again possessed her, and she again felt the "needle in the heart" as she recalled what she had heard before from the Countess of the intrigue by which Baron Justus Hafner had, indeed, ensnared his future son-in-law. She was overcome by infinite sadness, and she lapsed into one of her usual silent moods, while the Countess related to her Peppino's indecision. What cared she for Boleslas's anger at that moment? What could he do to her? Gorka was fully aware of her utter carelessness of the scene which had taken place between them, as soon as he saw the victoria pass. For some time he remained standing, watching the large white and black hats disappear down the Rue du Vingt Septembre.

This thought took possession of him at once. Madame Steno and her daughter were going to Maitland's atelier. . . . He had no sooner conceived that bitter suspicion than he felt the necessity of proving it at once. He entered a passing cab, just as Ardea, having left the Villa Steno after him, sauntered up, saying:

"Where are you going? May I go with you that we may have a few moments' conversation?"

"Impossible," replied Gorka. "I have a very urgent appointment, but in an hour I shall perhaps have occasion to ask a service of you. . . . Where shall I find you?"

"At home," said Peppino, "lunching."

"Very well," replied Boleslas, and, raising himself, he whispered in the cabman's ear, in a voice too low for his friend to hear what he said: "Ten francs for you if in five minutes you drive me to the corner of the Rue Napoleon III and the Place de la Victor-Emmanuel."

# PAUL BOURGET

The man gathered up his reins, and, by some sleight-of-hand, the jaded horse which drew the *botte* was suddenly transformed into a fine Roman steed, the *botte* itself into a light carriage as swift as the Tuscan *carrozzelle*, and the whole disappeared in a cross street, while Peppino said to himself:

"There is a fine fellow who would do so much better to remain with his friend Ardea than to go whither he is going. This affair will end in a duel. If I had not to liquidate that folly," and he pointed out with the end of his cane a placard relative to the sale of his own palace, "I would amuse myself by taking Caterina from both of them. But those little amusements must wait until after my marriage."

As we have seen, the cunning Prince had not been mistaken as to the course taken by the cab Gorka had hailed. It was indeed into the neighborhood of the atelier occupied by Maitland that the discarded lover hastened, but not to the atelier. The madman wished to prove to himself that the exhibition of his despair had availed him nothing, and that, scarcely rid of him, Madame Steno had repaired to the other. What would it avail him to know it and what would the evidence prove? Had the Countess concealed those sittings—those convenient sittings—as the jealous lover had told Dorsenne? The very thought of them caused the blood to flow in his veins much more feverishly than did the thoughts of the other meetings. For those he could still doubt, notwithstanding the anonymous letters, notwithstanding the *tête-à-tête* on the terrace, notwithstanding the insolent "Linco," whom she had addressed thus before him, while of the long intimacies of the studio he was certain. They maddened him, and, at the same time, by that strange contradiction which is characteristic of all jealousy, he hungered and thirsted to prove them.

He alighted from his cab at the corner he had named to his cabman, and from which point he could watch the Rue Leopardi, in which was his rival's house. It was a large structure in the Moorish style, built by the celebrated Spanish artist, Juan Santigosa, who had been obliged to sell all five years before—house, studio, horses, completed paintings, sketches begun— in order to pay immense losses at gaming. Florent Chapron had at the time bought the sort of counterfeit Alhambra, a portion of which he rented to his brother-in-law. During the few moments that he stood at the corner, Boleslas Gorka recalled having visited that house the previous year, while taking, in the company of Madame Steno, Alba, Maud,' and Hafner, one of those walks of which fashionable women are so fond in Rome as well as in Paris. An irrational instinct had rendered the painter and his paintings antipathetic to him at their first meeting. Had he had sufficient cause? Suddenly, on leaning forward in such a manner as to see without being seen, he perceived a victoria which entered the Rue Leopardi, and in that victoria the black hat of Mademoiselle Steno and the light one of her mother. In two minutes more the elegant carriage drew up at the Moorish structure, which gleamed among the other buildings in that street, for the most part unfinished, with a sort of insolent sumptuousness.

# PAUL BOURGET

The two ladies alighted and disappeared through the door, which closed upon them, while the coachman started up his horses at the pace of animals which are returning to their stable. He checked them that they might not become overheated, and the fine cobs trembled impatiently in their harnesses. Evidently the Countess and Alba were in the studio for a long sitting. What had Boleslas learned that he did not already know? Was he not ridiculous, standing upon the sidewalk of the square in the centre of which rose the ruin of an antique reservoir, called, for a reason more than doubtful, the trophy of Marius. With one glance the young man took in this scene—the empty victoria turning in the opposite direction, the large square, the ruin, the row of high houses, his cab. He appeared to himself so absurd for being there to spy out that of which he was only too sure, that he burst into a nervous laugh and reëntered his cab, giving his own address to the cabman: *Palazzetto Doria, Place de Venise.* The cab that time started off leisurely, for the man comprehended that the mad desire to arrive hastily no longer possessed his fare. By a sudden metamorphosis, the swift Roman steed became a common nag, and the vehicle a heavy machine which rumbled along the streets. Boleslas yielded to depression, the inevitable reaction of an excess of violence such as he had just experienced. His composure could not last. The studio, in which was Madame Steno, began to take a clear form in the jealous lover's mind in proportion as he drove farther from it. In his thoughts he saw his former mistress walking about in the framework of tapestry, armor, studies begun, as he had frequently seen her walking in his smoking-room, with the smile upon her lips of an amorous woman, touching the objects among which her lover lives. He saw impassive Alba, who served as chaperon in the new intrigue of her mother's with the same *naïveté* she had formerly employed in shielding their *liaison*. He saw Maitland with his indifferent glance of the day before, the glance of a preferred lover, so sure of his triumph that he did not even feel jealous of the former lover.

The absolute tranquillity of one who replaces us in an unfaithful mistress's affections augments our fury still more if we have the misfortune to be placed in a position similar to Gorka's. In a moment his rival's evocation became to him impossible to bear. He was very near his own home, for he was just at that admirable square encumbered with the débris of basilica, the Forum of Trajan, which the statue of St. Peter at the summit of the column overlooks. Around the base of the sculptured marble, legends attest the triumph of the humble Galilean fisherman who landed at the port of the Tiber 1800 years ago, unknown, persecuted, a beggar. What a symbol and what counsel to say with the apostle: "Whither shall we go, Lord? Thou alone hast the words of eternal life!"

But Gorka was neither a Montfanon nor a Dorsenne to hear within his heart or his mind the echo of such precepts. He was a man of passion and of action, who only saw his passion and his actions in the position in which fortune threw him. A fresh access of

fury recalled to him Maitland's attitude of the preceding day. This time he would no longer control himself. He violently pulled the surprised coachman's
sleeve, and called out to him the address of the Rue
Leopardi in so imperative a tone that the horse began
again to trot as he had done before, and the cab to
go quickly through the labyrinth of streets. A wave
of tragical desire rolled into the young man's heart.
No, he would not bear that affront. He was too bitterly wounded in the most sensitive chords of his being,
in his love as well as his pride. Both struggled within
him, and another instinct as well, urging him to the
mad step he was about to take. The ancient blood
of the Palatines, with regard to which Dorsenne always
jested, boiled in his veins. If the Poles have furnished
many heroes for dramas and modern romances, they
have remained, through their faults, so dearly atoned
for, the race the most chivalrously, the most madly
brave in Europe. When men of so intemperate and
so complex an excitability are touched to a certain
depth, they think of a duel as naturally as the descendants of a line of suicides think of killing themselves.

Joyous Ardea, with his Italian keenness, had seen at
a glance the end to which Gorka's nature would lead
him. The betrayed lover required a duel to enable
him to bear the treason. He might wound, he might,
perhaps, kill his rival, and his passion would be satisfied, or else he would risk being killed himself, and the
courage he would display braving death would suffice
to raise him in his own estimation. A mad thought

possessed him and caused him to hasten toward the Rue Leopardi, to provoke his rival suddenly and before Madame Steno! Ah, what pleasure it would give him to see her tremble, for she surely would tremble when she saw him enter the studio! But he would be *correct*, as she had so insolently asked him to be. He would go, so to speak, to see Alba's portrait. He would dissemble, then he would be better able to find a pretext for an argument. It is so easy to find one in the simplest conversation, and from an argument a quarrel is soon born. He would speak in such a manner that Maitland would have to answer him. The rest would follow. But would Alba Steno be present? Ha, so much the better! He would be so much more at ease, if the altercation arose before her, to deceive his own wife as to the veritable reason of the duel. Ah, he would have his dispute at any price, and from the moment that the seconds had exchanged visits the American's fate would be decided. He knew how to render it impossible for the fellow to remain longer in Rome. The young man was greatly wrought up by the romance of the provocation and the duel.

"How it refreshes the blood to be avenged upon two fools," said he to himself, descending from his cab and inquiring at the door of the Moorish house.

"Monsieur Maitland?" he asked the footman, who at one blow dissipated his excitement by replying with this simple phrase, the only one of which he had not thought in his frenzy:

"Monsieur is not at home."

"He will be at home to me," replied Boleslas. "I have an appointment with Madame and Mademoiselle Steno, who are awaiting me."

"Monsieur's orders are strict," replied the servant.

Accustomed, as are all servants entrusted with the defence of an artist's work, to a certain rigor of orders, he yet hesitated, in the face of the untruth which Gorka had invented on the spur of the moment, and he was about to yield to his importunity when some one appeared on the staircase of the hall. That some one was none other than Florent Chapron. Chance decreed that the latter should send for a carriage in which to go to lunch, and that the carriage should be late. At the sound of wheels stopping at the door, he looked out of one of the windows of his apartment, which faced the street. He saw Gorka alight. Such a visit, at such an hour, with the persons who were in the atelier, seemed to him so dangerous that he ran downstairs immediately. He took up his hat and his cane, to justify his presence in the hall by the very natural excuse that he was going out. He reached the middle of the staircase just in time to stop the servant, who had decided to "go and see," and, bowing to Boleslas with more formality than usual:

"My brother-in-law is not there, Monsieur," said he; and he added, turning to the footman, in order to dispose of him in case an altercation should arise between the importunate visitor and himself, "Nero, fetch me a handkerchief from my room. I have forgotten mine."

"That order could not be meant for me, Monsieur," insisted Boleslas. "Monsieur Maitland has made an

appointment with me, with Madame Steno, in order
to show us Alba's portrait."

"It is no order," replied Florent. "I repeat to you
that my brother-in-law has gone out. The studio is
closed, and it is impossible for me to undertake to
open it to show you the picture, since I have not the
key. As for Madame and Mademoiselle Steno, they
have not been here for several days; the sittings have
been interrupted."

"What is still more extraordinary, Monsieur," replied
the other, "is that I saw them with my own eyes, five
minutes ago, enter this house and I, too, saw their
carriage drive away." . . . He felt his anger increase
and direct itself altogether against the watch-dog so
suddenly raised upon the threshold of his rival's house.

Florent, on his part, had begun to lose patience.
He had within him the violent irritability of the negro
blood, which he did not acknowledge, but which
slightly tinted his complexion. The manner of Madame
Steno's former lover seemed to him so outrageous that
he replied very dryly, as he opened the door, in order
to oblige the caller to leave:

"You are mistaken, Monsieur, that is all."

"You are aware, Monsieur," replied Boleslas, "of the
fact that you just addressed me in a tone which is not
the one which I have a right to expect from you. . . .
When one charges one's self with a certain business, it
is at least necessary to introduce a little form."

"And I, Monsieur," replied Chapron, "would be
very much obliged to you if, when you address me, you
would not do so in enigmas. I do not know what you

mean by 'a certain business,' but I know that it is unbefitting a gentleman to act as you have acted at the door of a house which is not yours and for reasons that I can not comprehend."

"You will comprehend them very soon, Monsieur," said Boleslas, beside himself, "and you have not constituted yourself your brother's slave without motives."

He had no sooner uttered that sentence than Florent, incapable any longer of controlling himself, raised his cane with a menacing gesture, which the Polish Count arrested just in time, by seizing it in his right hand. It was the work of a second, and the two men were again face to face, both pale with anger, ready to collar one another rudely, when the sound of a door closing above their heads recalled to them their dignity. The servant descended the stairs. It was Chapron who first regained his self-possession, and he said to Boleslas, in a voice too low to be heard by any one but him:

"No scandal, Monsieur, eh? I shall have the honor of sending two of my friends to you."

"It is I, Monsieur," replied Gorka, "who will send you two. You shall answer to me for your manner, I assure you."

"Ha! Whatsoever you like," said the other. "I accept all your conditions in advance. . . . But one thing I ask of you," he added, "that no names be mentioned. There would be too many persons involved. Let it appear that we had an argument on the street, that we disagreed, and that I threatened you."

"So be it," said Boleslas, after a pause. "You have my word. There is a man," said he to himself five minutes later, when again rolling through the streets in his cab, after giving the cabman the address of the Palais Castagna. "Yes, there is a man. . . . He was very insolent just now, and I lacked composure. I am too nervous. I should be sorry to injure the boy. But, patience, the other will lose nothing by waiting."

# CHAPTER VI

## THE INCONSISTENCY OF AN OLD CHOUAN

HILE the madman, Boleslas, hastened to Ardea to ask his coöperation in the most unreasonable of encounters, with a species of savage delight, Florent Chapron was possessed by only one thought: at any price to prevent his brother-in-law from suspecting his quarrel with Madame Steno's former lover and the duel which was to be the result. His passionate friendship for Lincoln was so strong that it prevented the nervousness which usually precedes a first duel, above all when he who appears upon the ground has all his life neglected practising with the sword or pistol. To a fencer, and to one accustomed to the use of firearms, a duel means a number of details which remove the thought of danger. The man conceives the possibilities of the struggle, of a deed to be bravely accomplished. That is sufficient to inspire him with a composure which absolute ignorance can not inspire, unless it is supported by one of those deep attachments often so strong within us. Such was the case with Florent.

Dorsenne's instinct, which could so easily read the heart, was not mistaken there; the painter had in his wife's brother a friend of self-sacrificing dévotion. He could exact anything of the Mameluke, or, rather, of that slave, for it was the blood of the slaves, of his ancestors, which manifested itself in Chapron by so total an absorption of his personality. The atavism of servitude has these two effects which are apparently contradictory: it produces fathomless capacities of sacrifice or of perfidy. Both of these qualities were embodied in the brother and in the sister. As happens, sometimes, the two characteristics of their race were divided between them; one had inherited all the virtue of self-sacrifice, the other all the puissance of hypocrisy.

But the drama called forth by Madame Steno's infidelity, and finally by Gorka's rashness, would only expose to light the moral conditions which Dorsenne had foreseen without comprehending. He was completely ignorant of the circumstances under which Florent had developed, of those under which Maitland and he had met, of how Maitland had decided to marry Lydia; finally an exceptional and lengthy history which it is necessary to sketch here at least, in order to render clear the singular relations of those three beings.

As we have seen, the allusion coarsely made by Boleslas to negro blood marked the moment when Florent lost all self-control, to the point even of raising his cane to his insolent interlocutor. That blemish, hidden with the most jealous care, represented to the young man what it had represented to his father, the vital point of self-love, secret and constant humiliation. It was very faint, the trace of negro blood which flowed in their veins, so faint that it was necessary to be told of it, but it was sufficient to render a stay in America so much the more intolerable to both, as they had inherited all the pride of their name, a name which the Emperor mentioned at St. Helena as that of one of his bravest officers. Florent's grandfather was no other, indeed, than the Colonel Chapron who, as Napoleon desired information, swam the Dniéper on horseback, followed a Cossack on the opposite shore, hunted him like a stag, laid him across his saddle and took him back to the French camp. When the Empire fell, that hero, who had compromised himself in an irreparable manner in the army of the Loire, left his country and, accompanied by a handful of his old comrades, went to found in the southern part of the United States, in Alabama, a sort of agricultural colony, to which they gave the name—which it still preserves—of Arcola, a naïve and melancholy tribute to the fabulous epoch which, however, had been dear to them.

Who would have recognized the brilliant colonel, who penetrated by the side of Montbrun the heart of the Grande Redoute, in the planter of forty-five, busy with his cotton and his sugar-cane, who made a fortune in a short time by dint of energy and good sense? His success, told of in France, was the indirect cause of another emigration to Texas, led by General Lallemand, and which terminated so disastrously. Colonel Chapron had not, as can be believed, acquired in roaming through Europe very scrupulous notions on the relations of the two sexes. Having made the mother of his child a pretty and sweet-tempered mulattress whom he met on a short trip to New Orleans, and whom he brought back to Arcola, he became deeply attached to the charming creature and to his son, so much the more so as, with a simple difference of complexion and of hair, the child was the image of him. Indeed, the old warrior, who had no relatives in his native land, on dying, left his entire fortune to that son, whom he had christened Napoleon. While he lived, not one of his neighbors dared to treat the young man differently from the way in which his father treated him.

But it was not the same when the prestige of the Emperor's soldier was not there to protect the boy against that aversion to race which is morally a prejudice, but socially interprets an instinct of preservation of infallible surety. The United States has grown only on that condition. The mixture of blood would there have dissolved the admirable Anglo-Saxon energy which the struggle against a nature at once very rich and very mutinous has exalted to such surprising splendor. It is not necessary to ask those who are the victims of such an instinct to comprehend the legal injustice. They only feel its ferocity. Napoleon Chapron, rejected in several offers of marriage, thwarted in his plans, humiliated under twenty trifling circumstances by the Colonel's former companions, became a species of misanthrope. He lived, sustained by a twofold desire, on the one hand to increase his fortune, and on the other to wed a white woman. It was not until 1857, at the age of thirty-five, that he realized the second of his two projects. In the course of a trip to

Europe, he became interested on the steamer in a young English governess, who was returning from Canada, summoned home by family troubles. He met her again in London. He helped her with such delicacy in her distress, that he won her heart, and she consented to become his wife. From that union were born, one year apart, Florent and Lydia.

Lydia had cost her mother her life, at the moment when the War of Secession jeoparded the fortune of Chapron, who, fortunately for him, had, in his desire to enrich himself quickly, invested his money a little on all sides. He was only partly ruined, but that semiruin prevented him from returning to Europe, as he had intended. He was compelled to remain in Alabama to repair that disaster, and he succeeded, for at his death, in 1880, his children inherited more than four hundred thousand dollars each. The incomparable father's devotion had not limited itself to the building up of a large fortune. He had the courage to deprive himself of the presence of the two beings whom he adored, to spare them the humiliation of an American school, and he sent them after their twelfth year to England, the boy to the Jesuits of Beaumont, the girl to the convent of the Sacred Heart, at Roehampton. After four years there, he sent them to Paris, Florent to Vaugirard, Lydia to the Rue de Varenne, and just at the time that he had realized the amount he considered requisite, when he was preparing to return to live near them in a country without prejudices, a stroke of apoplexy took him off suddenly. The double wear of toil and care had told upon one of those organisms which the mixture of the black and white races often produces, athletic in appearance, but of a very keen sensibility, in which the vital resistance is not in proportion to the muscular vigor.

Whatever care the man, so deeply grieved by the blemish upon his birth, had taken to preserve his children from a similar experience, he had not been able to do so, and soon after his son entered Beaumont his trials began. The few boys with whom Florent was thrown in contact, in the hotels or in his walks, during his sojourn in America, had already made him feel that humiliation from which his father had suffered so much. The youth of twelve, silent and absurdly sensitive, who made his appearance on the lawn of the peaceful English college on an autumn morning, brought with him a self-love already bleeding, to whom it was a delightful surprise to find himself among comrades of his age who did not even seem to suspect that any difference separated them from him. It required the perception of a Yankee to discern, beneath the nails of the handsome boy with the dark complexion, the tiny drops of negro blood, so far removed. Between an octoroon and a creole a European can never tell the difference. Florent had been represented as what he really was, the grandson of one of the Emperor's best officers. His father had taken particular pains to designate him as French, and his companions only saw in him a pupil like themselves, coming from Alabama—that is to say, from a country almost as chimerical as Japan or China.

All who in early youth have known the torture

of apprehension will be able to judge of the poor
child's agony when, after four months of a life amid
the warmth of sympathy, one of the Jesuit fathers
who directed the college announced to him, thinking
it would afford him pleasure, the expected arrival of
an American, of young Lincoln Maitland. This was to
Florent so violent a shock that he had a fever for forty-
eight hours. In after years he could remember what
thoughts possessed him on the day when he descended
from his room to the common refectory, sure that as
soon as he was brought face to face with the new
pupil he would have to sustain the disdainful glance
suffered so frequently in the United States. There
was no doubt in his mind that, his origin once discovered, the atmosphere of kindness in which he
moved with so much surprise would soon be changed
to hostility. He could again see himself crossing the
yard; could hear himself called by Father Roberts—
the master who had told him of the expected new
arrival—and his surprise when Lincoln Maitland had
given him the hearty handshake of one demi-com-
patriot who meets another. He was to learn later that
that reception was quite natural, coming from the son
of an Englishman, educated altogether by his mother,
and taken from New York to Europe before his fifth
year, there to live in a circle as little American as possible. Chapron did not reason in that manner. He
had an infinitely tender heart. Gratitude entered it
—gratitude as impassioned as had been his fear. One
week later Lincoln Maitland and he were friends, and
friends so intimate that they never parted.

# COSMOPOLIS

The affection, which was merely to the indifferent nature of Maitland a simple college episode, became to Florent the most serious, most complete sentiment of his life. Those fraternities of election, the loveliest and most delicate of the heart of man, usually dawn thus in youth. It is the ideal age of passionate friendship, that period between ten and sixteen, when the spirit is so pure, so fresh, still so virtuous, so fertile in generous projects for the future. One dreams of a companionship almost mystical with the friend from whom one has no secret, whose character one sees in such a noble light, on whose esteem one depends as upon the surest recompense, whom one innocently desires to resemble. Indeed, they are, between the innocent lads who work side by side on a problem of geometry or a lesson in history, veritable poems of tenderness at which the man will smile later, finding so far different from him in all his tastes, him whom he desired to have for a brother. It happens, however, in certain natures of a sensibility particularly precocious and faithful at the same time, that the awakening of effective life is so strong, so encroaching, that the impassioned friendship persists, first through the other awakening, that of sensuality, so fatal to all the senses of delicacy, then through the first tumult of social experience, not less fatal to our ideal of youth. That was the case with Florent Chapron, whether his character, at once somewhat wild and yet submissive, rendered him more qualified for that renunciation of his personality than friendship demands, whether, far from his father and his sister and not

[ 175 ]

having any mother, his loving heart had need of attaching itself to some one who could fill the place of his relatives, or whether Maitland exercised over him a special prestige by his opposite qualities. Fragile and somewhat delicate, was he seduced by the strength and dexterity which his friend exhibited in all his exercises? Timid and naturally taciturn, was he governed by the assurance of that athlete with the loud laugh, with the invincible energy? Did the surprising tendency toward art which the other one showed conquer him, as well as sympathy for the misfortunes which were confided to him and which touched him more than they touched him who experienced them?

Gordon Maitland, Lincoln's father, of an excellent family of New York, had been killed at the battle of Chancellorsville, during the same war which had ruined Florent's father in part. Mrs. Maitland, the poor daughter of a small rector of a Presbyterian church at Newport, and who had only married her husband for his money, had but one idea, when once a widow—to go abroad. Whither? To Europe, vague and fascinating spot, where she fancied she would be distinguished by her intelligence and her beauty. She was pretty, vain and silly, and that voyage in pursuit of a part to play in the Old World caused her to pass two years first in one hotel and then in another, after which she married the second son of a poor Irish peer, with the new chimera of entering that Olympus of British aristocracy of which she had dreamed so much. She became a Catholic, and her son with her, to obtain

# COSMOPOLIS

the result which cost her dear, for not only was the
lord who had given her his name brutal, a drunkard
and cruel, but he added to all those faults that of
being one of the greatest gamblers in the entire United
Kingdom. He kept his stepson away from home,
beat his wife, and died toward 1880, after dissipating
the poor creature's fortune and almost all of Lincoln's.
At that time the latter, whom his stepfather had naturally left to develop in his own way, and who, since
leaving Beaumont, had studied painting at Venice,
Rome and Paris, was in the latter city and one of the
first pupils in Bonnat's studio. Seeing his mother
ruined, without resources at forty-four years of age, persuaded himself of his glorious future, he had one of
those magnificent impulses such as one has in youth and
which prove much less the generosity than the pride
of life. Of the fifteen thousand francs of income remaining to him, he gave up to his mother twelve thousand five hundred. It is expedient to add that in less
than a year afterward he married the sister of his
college friend and four hundred thousand dollars.
He had seen poverty and he was afraid of it. His
action with regard to his mother seemed to justify in
his own eyes the purely interested character of the
combination which freed his brush forever. There
are, moreover, such artistic consciences. Maitland
would not have pardoned himself a concession of art.
He considered rascals the painters who begged success
by compromise in their style, and he thought it quite
natural to take the money of Mademoiselle Chapron,
whom he did not love, and for whom, now that he

12          [ 177 ]

had grown to manhood and knew several of her compatriots, he likewise felt the prejudice of race. "The glory of the colonel of the Empire and friendship for that good Florent," as he said, "covered all."

Poor and good Florent! That marriage was to him the romance of his youth realized. He had desired it since the first week that Maitland had given him the cordial handshake which had bound them. To live in the shadow of his friend, become at once his brother-in-law and his ideal—he did not dream of any other solution of his own destiny. The faults of Maitland, developed by age, fortune, and success—we recall the triumph of his *Femme en violet et en jaune* in the Salon of 1884—found Florent as blind as at the epoch when they played cricket together in the fields at Beaumont. Dorsenne very justly diagnosed there one of those hypnotisms of admiration such as artists, great or small, often inspire around them. But the author, who always generalized too quickly, had not comprehended that the admirer with Florent was grafted on a friend worthy to be painted by La Fontaine or by Balzac, the two poets of friendship, the one in his sublime and tragic *Cousin Pons*, the other in that short but fine fable, in which is this verse, one of the most tender in the French language:

*Vous mètes, en dormant, un peu triste apparu.*

Florent did not love Lincoln because he admired him; he admired him because he loved him. He was not wrong in considering the painter as one of the most gifted who had appeared for thirty years. But

[ 178 ]

Lincoln would have had neither the bold elegance of his drawing, nor the vivid strength of coloring, nor the ingenious finesse of imagination if the other had lent himself with less ardor to the service of the work and to the glory of the artist. When Lincoln wanted to travel he found his brother-in-law the most diligent of couriers. When he had need of a model he had only to say a word for Florent to set about finding one. Did Lincoln exhibit at Paris or London, Florent took charge of the entire proceeding—seeing the journalists and picture dealers, composing letters of thanks for the articles, in a handwriting so like that of the painter that the latter had only to sign it. Lincoln desired to return to Rome. Florent had discovered the house on the Rue Leopardi, and he settled it even before Maitland, then in Egypt, had finished a large study begun at the moment of the departure of the other.

Florent had, by virtue of the affection felt for his brother-in-law, come to comprehend the paintings as well as the painter himself. These words will be clear to those who have been around artists and who know what a distance separates them from the most enlightened amateur. The amateur can judge and feel. The artist only, who has wielded the implements, knows, before a painting, how it is done, what stroke of the brush has been given, and why; in short, the trituration of the matter by the workman. Florent had watched Maitland work so much, he had rendered him so many effective little services in the studio, that each of his brother-in-law's canvases became animated to him, even to the slightest details. When he saw them on the wall of the gallery they told him of an intimacy which was at once his greatest joy and his greatest pride. In short, the absorption of his personality in that of his former comrade was so complete that it had led to this anomaly, that Dorsenne himself, notwithstanding his indulgence for psychological singularities, had not been able to prevent himself from finding almost monstrous: Florent was Lincoln's brother-in-law, and he seemed to find it perfectly natural that the latter should have adventures outside, if the emotion of those adventures could be useful to his talent!

Perhaps this long and yet incomplete analysis will permit us the better to comprehend what emotions agitated the young man as he reascended the staircase of his house—of their house, Lincoln's and his—after his unexpected dispute with Boleslas Gorka. It will attenuate, at least with respect to him, the severity of simple minds. All passion, when developed in the heart, has the effect of etiolating around it the vigor of other instincts. Chapron was too fanatical a friend to be a very equitable brother. It seemed to him very simple and very legitimate that his sister should be at the service of the genius of Lincoln, as he himself was. Moreover, if, since the marriage with her brother's friend, his sister had been stirred by the tempest of a moral tragedy, Florent did not suspect it. When had he studied Lydia, the silent, reserved Lydia, of whom he had once for all formed an opinion, as is the almost invariable custom of relative with relative? Those who have seen us when young are like those who see us daily. The images which they trace of us always reproduce what we were at a certain moment—scarcely ever what we are. Florent considered his sister very good, because he had formerly found her so; very gentle, because she had never resisted him; not intelligent, because she did not seem sufficiently interested in the painter's work; as for the suffering and secret rebellion of the oppressed creature, crushed between his blind partiality and the selfishness of a scornful husband, he did not even suspect them, much less the terrible resolution of which that apparent resignation was capable.

If he had trembled when Madame Steno began to interest herself in Lincoln, it was solely for the work of the latter, so much the more as for a year he had perceived not a decline but a disturbance in the painting of that artist, too voluntary not to be unequal. Then Florent had seen, on the other hand, the nerve of Maitland reawakened in the warmth of that little intrigue.

The portrait of Alba promised to be a magnificent study, worthy of being placed beside the famous *Femme en violet et en jaune*, which those envious of Lincoln always remembered. Moreover, the painter had finished with unparalleled ardor two large compositions partly abandoned. In the face of that proof of a fever of production more and more active, how would not Florent have blessed Madame Steno, instead of cursing her, so much the more that it sufficed him to close his eyes and to know that his conscience was in repose when opposite his sister? He knew all, however. The proof of it was in his shudder when Dorsenne announced to him the clandestine arrival in Rome of Madame Steno's other lover, and one proof still more certain, the impulse which had precipitated him upon Boleslas, who was parleying with the servant, and now it was he who had accepted the duel which an exasperated rival had certainly come to propose to his dear Lincoln, and he thought only of the latter.

"He must know nothing until afterward. He would take the affair upon himself, and I have a chance to kill him, that Gorka—to wound him, at least. In any case, I will arrange it so that a second duel will be rendered difficult to that lunatic. . . . But, first of all, let us make sure that we have not spoken too loudly and that they have not heard upstairs the ill-bred fellow's loud voice."

It was in such terms that he qualified his adversary of the morrow. For very little more he would have judged Gorka unpardonable not to thank Lincoln, who had done him the honor to supplant him in the Countess's favor!

In the meantime, let us cast a glance at the atelier! When the friend, devoted to complicity, but also to heroism, entered the vast room, he could see at the first glance that he had been mistaken and that no sound of voices had reached that peaceful retreat.

The atelier of the American painter was furnished with a harmonious sumptuousness which real artists know how to gather around them. The large strip of sky seen through the windows looked down upon a corner veritably Roman—of the Rome of to-day, which attests an uninterrupted effort toward forming a new city by the side of the old one. One could see an angle of the old garden and the fragment of an antique building, with a church steeple beyond. It was on a background of azure, of verdure and of ruins, in a horizon larger and more distant, but composed of the same elements, that was to arise the face of the young girl, designed after the manner, so sharp and so modelled, of the Pier della Francesca, with whom Maitland had been preoccupied for six months.

All great composers, of an originality more composite than genitive, have these infatuations.

Maitland was at his easel, dressed with that correct elegance which is the almost certain mark of Anglo-Saxon artists. With his little varnished shoes, his fine black socks, spotted with red, his coat of quilted silk, his light cravat and the purity of his linen, he had the air of a gentleman who applied himself to an amateur effort, and not of the patient and laborious worker he really was. But his canvases and his studies, hung on all sides, among tapestries, arms and trinkets, bespoke patient labor. It was the history of an energy bent upon the acquisition of a personality constantly fleeting. Maitland manifested in a supreme degree the trait common to almost all his compatriots, even those who came in early youth to Europe, that intense desire not to lack civilization, which is explained by the fact that the American is a being entirely new, endowed with an activity incomparable, and deprived of traditional saturation. He is not born cultivated, matured, already fashioned virtually, if one may say so, like a child of the Old World. He can create himself at his will. With superior gifts, but gifts entirely physical, Maitland was a self-made man of art, as his grandfather had been a self-made man of money, as his father had been a self-made man of war. He had in his eye and in his hand two marvellous implements for painting, and in his perseverence in developing a still more marvellous one. He lacked constantly the something necessary and local which gives to certain very inferior painters the inexpressible superiority of a savor of soil. It could not be said that he was not inventive and new, yet one experienced on seeing no matter which one of his paintings that he was a creature of culture and of acquisition. The scattered studies in the atelier first of all displayed the influence of his first master, of solid and simple Bonnat. Then he had been tempted by the English pre-Raphaelites, and a fine copy of the famous *Song of Love*, by Burne-Jones, attested that reaction on the side of an art more subtle, more impressed by that poetry which professional painters treat scornfully as literary. But Lincoln was too vigorous for the languors of such an ideal, and he quickly turned to other teachings. Spain conquered him, and Velasquez, the colorist of so peculiar a fancy that, after a visit to the Museum of the Prado, one carries away the idea that one has just seen the only painting worthy of the name.

The spirit of the great Spaniard, that despotic stroke of the brush which seems to draw the color in the groundwork of the picture, to make it stand out in almost solid lights, his absolute absence of abstract intentions and his newness which affects entirely to ignore the past, all in that formula of art, suited Maitland's temperament. To him, too, he owed his masterpiece, the *Femme en violet et en jaune*, but the restless seeker did not adhere to that style. Italy and the Florentines next influenced him, just those the most opposed to Velasquez; the Pollajuoli, Andrea del Castagna, Paolo Uccello and Pier della Francesca. Never would one have believed that the same hand which had wielded with so free a brush the color of the *Femme en violet* could be that which sketched the contour of the portrait of Alba with so severe, so rigid a drawing.

At the moment Florent entered the studio that work so completely absorbed the attention of the painter that he did not hear the door open any more than did Madame Steno, who was smoking cigarettes, reclining indolently and blissfully upon the divan, her half-closed eyes fixed upon the man she loved. Lincoln only divined another presence by a change in Alba's face. God! How pale she was, seated in the immobility of her pose in a large, heraldic armchair, with a back of carved wood, her hands grasping the arms, her mouth so bitter, her eyes so deep in their fixed glance! . . . Did she divine that which she could not, however, know, that her fate was approaching with the visitor who entered, and who, having left the studio fifteen minutes before, had to justify his return by an excuse.

"It is I," said he. "I forgot to ask you, Lincoln, if you wish to buy Ardea's three drawings at the price they offer."

"Why did you not tell me of it yesterday, my little Linco?" interrupted the Countess. "I saw Peppino again this morning. . . . I would have from him his lowest figure."

"That would only be lacking," replied Maitland, laughing his large laugh. "He does not acknowledge those drawings, dear *dogaresse*. . . . They are a part of the series of trinkets he carefully subtracted from his creditor's inventory and put in different places. There are some at seven or eight antiquaries', and we may expect that for the next ten years all the cockneys of my country will be allured by this phrase, 'This is from the Palais Castagna. I have it by a little arrangement.'"

His eyes sparkled as he imitated one of the most celebrated bric-à-brac dealers in Rome, with the incomparable art of imitation which distinguishes all the old *habitués* of Parisian studios.

"At present these three drawings are at an antiquary's of Babuino, and very authentic."

"Except when they are represented as Vincis," said Florent, "when Leonardo was left-handed, and their hatchings are made from left to right."

"And you think Ardea would not agree with me in it?" resumed the Countess.

"Not even with you," said the painter. "He had the assurance last night, when I mentioned them before him, to ask me the address in order to go to see them."

"How did you learn their production?" questioned Madame Steno.

"Ask him," said Maitland, pointing to Chapron
with the end of his brush. "When there is a question
of enriching his old Maitland's collection, he becomes
more of a merchant than the merchants themselves.
They tell him all. . . . Vinci or no Vinci, it is the
pure Lombard style. Buy them. I want them."

"I will go, then," replied Florent. "Countess. . . .
Contessina."

He bowed to Madame Steno and her daughter.
The mother bestowed upon him her pleasantest smile.
She was not one of those mistresses to whom their
lovers' intimate friends are always enemies. On the
contrary, she enveloped them in the abundant and
blissful sympathy which love awoke in her. Besides,
she was too cunning not to feel that Florent approved
of her love. But, on the other hand, the intense
aversion which Alba at that moment felt toward her
mother's suspected intrigues was expressed by the formality with which she inclined her head in response
to the farewell of the young man, who was too happy
to have found that the dispute had not been heard.

"From now until to-morrow," thought he, on re-
descending the staircase, "there will be no one to warn
Lincoln. . . . The purchase of the drawings was an
invention to demonstrate my tranquillity. . . . Now I
must find two discreet seconds."

Florent was a very deliberate man, and a man who
had at his command perfect evenness of temperament
whenever it was not a question of his enthusiastic
attachment to his brother-in-law. He had the power
of observation habitual to persons whose sensitive

*amour propre* has frequently been wounded. He therefore deferred until later his difficult choice and went to luncheon, as if nothing had happened, at the restaurant where he was expected. Certainly the proprietor did not mistrust, in replying to the questions of his guest relative to the most recent portraits of Lenbach, that the young man, so calm, so smiling, had on hand a duel which might cost him his life. It was only on leaving the restaurant that Florent, after mentally reviewing ten of his older acquaintances, resolved to make a first attempt upon Dorsenne. He recalled the mysterious intelligence given him by the novelist, whose sympathy for Maitland had been publicly manifested by an eloquent article. Moreover, he believed him to be madly in love with Alba Steno. That was one probability more in favor of his discretion.

Dorsenne would surely maintain silence with regard to a meeting in connection with which, if it were known, the cause of the contest would surely be mentioned. It was only too clear that Gorka and Chapron had no real reason to quarrel and fight a duel. But at ten-thirty, that is to say, three hours after the unreasonable altercation in the vestibule, Florent rang at the door of Julien's apartments. The latter was at home, busy upon the last correction of the proofs of *Poussière d'Idées*. His visitor's confidence upset him to such a degree that his hands trembled as he arranged his scattered papers. He remembered the presence of Boleslas on that same couch, at the same time of the day, forty-eight hours before. How the

[ 188 ]

drama would progress if that madman went away in that mood! He knew only too well that Maitland's brother-in-law had not told him all.

"It is absurd," he cried, "it is madness, it is folly! . . . You are not going to fight about an argument such as you have related to me? You talked at the corner of the street, you exchanged a few angry words, and then, suddenly, seconds, a duel. . . . Ah, it is absurd."

"You forget that I offered him a violent insult in raising my cane to him," interrupted Florent, "and since he demands satisfaction I must give it to him."

"Do you believe," said the writer, "that the public will be contented with those reasons? Do you think they will not look for the secret motives of the duel? Do I know the story of a woman? . . . You see, I ask no questions. I rely upon what you confide in me. But the world is the world, and you will not escape its remarks."

"It is precisely for that reason that I ask absolute discretion of you," replied Florent, "and for that reason that I have come to ask you to serve me as a second. . . . There is no one in whom I trust as implicitly as I do in you. . . . It is the only excuse for my step."

"I thank you," said Dorsenne. He hesitated a moment. Then the image of Alba, which had haunted him since the previous day, suddenly presented itself to his mind. He recalled the sombre anguish he had surprised in the young girl's eyes, then her comforted glance when her mother smiled at once upon Gorka and Maitland. He recalled the anonymous letter and the mysterious hatred which impended over Madame Steno. If the quarrel between Boleslas and Florent became known, there was no doubt that it would be said generally that Florent was fighting for his brother-in-law on account of the Countess. No doubt, too, that the report would reach the poor Contessina. It was sufficient to cause the writer to reply: "Very well! I accept. I will serve you. Do not thank me. We are losing valuable time. You will require another second. Of whom have you thought?"

"Of no one," returned Florent. "I confess I have counted on you to aid me."

"Let us make a list," said Julien. "It is the best way, and then cross off the names."

Dorsenne wrote down a number of their acquaintances, and they indeed crossed them off, according to his expression, so effectually that after a minute examination they had rejected all of them. They were then as much perplexed as ever, when suddenly Dorsenne's eyes brightened, he uttered a slight exclamation, and said brusquely:

"What an idea! But it *is* an idea! . . . Do you know the Marquis de Montfanon?" he asked Florent.

"He with one arm?" replied the latter. "I saw him once with reference to a monument I put up at Saint Louis des Français."

"He told me of it," said Dorsenne. "For one of your relatives, was it not?"

"Oh, a distant cousin," replied Florent; "one

Captain Chapron, killed in 'forty-nine in the trenches before Rome."

"Now, to our business," cried Dorsenne, rubbing his hands. "It is Montfanon who must be your second. First of all, he is an experienced duellist, while I have never been on the ground. That is very important. You know the celebrated saying: 'It is neither swords nor pistols which kill; it is the seconds.' . . . And then if the matter has to be arranged, he will have more prestige than your servant."

"It is impossible," said Florent; "Marquis de Montfanon. . . . He will never consent. I do not exist for him."

"That is my affair," cried Dorsenne. "Let me take the necessary steps in my own name, and then if he agrees you can make it in yours. . . . Only we have no time to lose. Do not leave your house until six o'clock. By that time I shall know upon what to depend."

If, at first, the novelist had felt great confidence in the issue of his strange attempt with reference to his old friend, that confidence changed to absolute apprehension when he found himself, half an hour later, at the house which Marquis Claude François occupied in one of the oldest parts of Rome, from which location he could obtain an admirable view of the Forum. How many times had Julien come, in the past six months, to that Marquis who dived constantly in the sentiment of the past, to gaze upon the tragical and grand panorama of the historical scene! At the voice of the recluse, the broken columns rose, the ruined temples were rebuilt, the triumphal view was cleared from its mist.  He talked, and the formidable *épopée* of the Roman legend was evoked, interpreted by the fervent Christian in that mystical and providential sense, which all, indeed, proclaims in that spot, where the Mamertine prison relates the trial of St. Peter, where the portico of the temple of Faustine serves as a pediment to the Church of St. Laurent, where Ste.-Marie-Liberatrice rises upon the site of the Temple of Vesta — *Sancta Maria, libera nos a pœnis inferni*—Montfanon always added when he spoke of it, and he pointed out the Arch of Titus, which tells of the fulfilment of the prophecies of Our Lord against Jerusalem, while, opposite, the groves reveal the outlines of a nunnery upon the ruins of the dwellings of the Cæsars.  And, at the extreme end, the Coliseum recalls to mind the ninety thousand spectators come to see the martyrs suffer.

Such were the sights where lived the former pontifical zouave, and, on ringing the bell of the third *étage*, Julien said to himself: "I am a simpleton to come to propose to such a man what I have to propose.  Yet it is not to be a second in an ordinary duel, but simply to prevent an adventure which might cost the lives of two men in the first place, then the honor of Madame Steno, and, lastly, the peace of mind of three innocent persons, Madame Gorka, Madame Maitland and my little friend Alba. . . . He alone has sufficient authority to arrange all.  It will be an act of charity, like any other. . . . I hope he is at home," he concluded, hearing the footstep of the servant, who recognized the visitor and who anticipated all questions.

"The Marquis went out this morning before eight o'clock. He will not return until dinner-time."

"Do you know where he has gone?"

"To hear mass in a catacomb, and to be present at a procession," replied the footman, who took Dorsenne's card, adding: "The Trappists of Saint Calixtus certainly know where the Marquis is. . . . He lunched with them."

"We shall see," said the young man to himself, somewhat disappointed. His carriage rolled in the direction of Porte St. Sebastien, near which was the catacomb and the humble dwelling contiguous to it —the last morsel of the Papal domains kept by the poor monks. "Montfanon will have taken communion this morning," thought he, "and at the very word *duel* he will listen to nothing more. However, the matter must be arranged; it must be. . . . What would I not give to know the truth of the scene between Gorka and Florent? By what strange and diabolical *ricochet* did the Palatine hit upon the latter when his business was with the brother-in-law? . . . Will he be angry that I am his adversary's second? . . . Bah! . . . After our conversation of the other day our friendship is ended. . . . Good, I am already at the little church of *Domine, quo vadis.** I might say to myself: '*Juliane, quo vadis?*' 'To perform an act a little better than the majority of my actions,' I might reply."

*"Lord, whither art thou going?"

# PAUL BOURGET

That impressionable soul which vibrated at the slightest contact was touched by the souvenir of one of the innumerable pious legends which nineteen centuries of Catholicism have suspended at all the corners of Rome and its surrounding districts. He recalled the touching story of St. Peter flying from persecution and meeting our Lord: "Lord, whither art thou going?" asked the apostle. "To be crucified a second time," replied the Saviour, and Peter was ashamed of his weakness and returned to martyrdom. Montfanon himself had related that episode to the novelist, who again began to reflect upon the Marquis's character and the best means of approaching him. He forgot to glance at the vast solitude of the Roman suburbs before him, and so deep was his reverie that he almost passed unheeded the object of his search. Another disappointment awaited him at the first point in his voyage of exploration.

The monk who came at his ring to open the door of the inclosure contiguous to St. Calixtus, informed him that he of whom he was in search had left half an hour before.

"You will find him at the Basilica of Saint Nerée and Saint Achilles," added the Trappist; "it is the *fête* of those two saints, and at five o'clock there will be a procession in their catacombs. . . . It is a fifteen minutes' ride from here, near the tower Marancia, on the Via Ardeatina."

"Shall I miss him a third time?" thought Dorsenne, alighting from the carriage finally, and proceeding on foot to the opening which leads to the subterranean

# COSMOPOLIS

Necropolis dedicated to the two saints who were the eunuchs of Domitilla, the niece of Emperor Vespasian. A few ruins and a dilapidated house alone mark the spot where once stood the pious Princess's magnificent villa. The gate was open, and, meeting no one who could direct him, the young man took several steps in the subterranean passage. He perceived that the long gallery was lighted. He entered there, saying to himself that the row of tapers, lighted every ten paces, assuredly marked the line which the procession would follow, and which led to the central basilica. Although his anxiety as to the issue of his undertaking was extreme, he could not help being impressed by the grandeur of the sight presented by the catacomb thus illuminated. The uneven niches reserved for the dead, asleep in the peace of the Lord for so many centuries, made recesses in the corridors and gave them a solemn and tragical aspect. Inscriptions were to be seen there, traced on the stone, and all spoke of the great hope which those first Christians had cherished, the same which believers of our day cherish.

Julien knew enough of symbols to understand the significance of the images between which the persecuted of the primitive church had laid their fathers. They are so touching and so simple! The anchor represents safety in the storm; the gentle dove and the ewe, symbols of the soul, which flies away and seeks its shepherd; the phœnix, whose wings announce the resurrection. Then there were the bread and the wine, the branches of the olive and the palm. The silent cemetery was filled with a faint aroma of incense,

noticed by Dorsenne on entering. High mass, celebrated in the morning, left the sacred perfume diffused
among those bones, once the forms of human beings
who kneeled there amid the same holy aroma. The
contrast was strong between that spot, where everything spoke of things eternal, and the drama of passion, worldly and culpable, the progress of which
agitated even Dorsenne. At that moment he appeared
to himself in the light of a profaner, although he was
obeying generous and humane instincts. He experienced a sense of relief when, at a bend in one of the
corridors which he had selected from among many
others, he found himself face to face with a priest,
who held in his hand a basket filled with the petals
of flowers, destined, no doubt, for the procession.
Dorsenne inquired of him the way to the Basilica in
Italian, while the reply was given in perfect French.

"Perhaps you know the Marquis de Montfanon,
father?" asked the novelist.

"I am one of the chaplains of Saint Louis," said
the priest, with a smile, adding: "You will find him
in the Basilica."

"Now, the moment has come," thought Dorsenne,.
"I must be subtle. . . . After all, it is charity I am
about to ask him to do. . . . Here I am. I recognize the staircase and the opening above."

A corner of the sky, indeed, was to be seen, and a
ray of light entered which permitted the writer to
distinguish him whom he was seeking among the few
persons assembled in the ruined chapel, the most venerable of all those which encircle Rome with a hidden

girdle of sanctuaries. Montfanon, too recognizable, alas! by the empty sleeve of his black redingote, was seated on a chair, not very far from the altar, on which burned enormous tapers. Priests and monks were arranging baskets filled with petals, like those of the chaplain, whom Dorsenne had just met. A group of three curious visitors commented in whispers upon the paintings, scarcely visible on the discolored stucco of the ceiling. Montfanon was entirely absorbed in the book which he held in his one hand. The large features of his face, ennobled and almost transfigured by the ardor of devotion, gave him the admirable expression of an old Christian soldier. *Bonus miles Christi*—a good soldier of Christ—had been inscribed upon the tomb of the chief under whom he had been wounded at Patay. One would have taken him for a guardian layman of the tombs of the martyrs, capable of confessing his faith like them, even to the death. And when Julien determined to approach and to touch him lightly on the shoulder, he saw that, in the nobleman's clear, blue eyes, ordinarily so gay, and sometimes so choleric, sparkled unshed tears. His voice, too, naturally sharp, was softened by the emotion of the thought which his reading, the place, the time, the occupation of his day had awakened within him.

"Ah, you here?" said he to his young friend, without any astonishment. "You have come for the procession. That is well. You will hear sung the lovely lines: *Hi sunt quos fatuè mundus abhorruit.*" He pronounced *ou* as *u*, *à l' Italienne*, for his liturgic

[ 197 ]

training had been received in Rome. "The season is favorable for the ceremonies. The tourists have gone. There will only be people here who pray and who feel, like you. . . . And to feel is half of prayer. The other half is to believe. You will become one of us. I have always predicted it. There is no peace but here."

"I would gladly have come only for the procession," replied Dorsenne, "but my visit has another motive, dear friend," said he, in a still lower tone. "I have been seeking for you for more than an hour, that you might aid me in rendering a great service to several people, in preventing a very great misfortune, perhaps."

"I can help you to prevent a very great misfortune?" repeated Montfanon.

"Yes," replied Dorsenne, "but this is not the place in which to explain to you the details of the long and terrible adventure. . . . At what hour is the ceremony? I will wait for you, and tell it to you on leaving here."

"It does not begin until five o'clock—five-thirty," said Montfanon, looking at his watch, "and it is now fifteen minutes past four. Let us leave the catacomb, if you wish, and you can repeat your story to me up above. A very great misfortune? Well," he added, pressing the hand of the young man whom, personally, he liked as much as he detested his views, "rest assured, my dear child, we will prevent it!"

There was in the manner in which he uttered those words the tranquillity of a mind which knows not uneasiness, that of a believer who feels sure of always accomplishing all that he wishes to do. It would not have been Montfanon, that is to say, a species of visionary, who loved to argue with Dorsenne, because he knew that in spite of all he was understood, if he had not continued, as they walked along the lighted corridor, while remounting toward daylight:

"If it is all the same to you, sir apologist of the modern world, I should like to pause here and ask you frankly: Do you not feel yourself more contemporary with all the dead who slumber within these walls than with a radical elector or a free-mason deputy? Do you not feel that if these martyrs had not come to pray beneath these vaults eighteen hundred years ago, the best part of your soul would not exist? Where will you find a poetry more touching than that of these symbols and of these epitaphs? That admirable De Rossi showed me one at Saint Calixtus last year. My tears flow as I recall it. *'Pete pro Phœbe et pro virginio ejus.* Pray for Phœbus and for—How do you translate the word *virginius*, the husband who has known only one wife, the virgin husband of a virgin spouse? Your youth will pass, Dorsenne. You will one day feel what I feel, the happiness which is wanting on account of bygone errors, and you will comprehend that it is only to be found in Christian marriage, whose entire sublimity is summed up in this prayer: *Pro virginio ejus.* . . . You will be like me then, and you will find in this book," he held up *l'Eucologe*, which he clasped in his hand, "something through which to offer up to God your remorse and your regrets. Do you know the hymn of the Holy

# PAUL BOURGET

Sacrament, *Adoro te, devotè?* No. Yet you are capable of feeling what is contained in these lines. Listen. It is this idea: That on the cross one sees only the man, not the God; that in the host one does not even see the man, and that yet one believes in the real presence.

*In cruce latebat sola Deitas.*
*At hic latet simul et humanitas.*
*Ambo tamen credens atque confitens . . .*

"And now this last verse:

*Peto quod petivit latro pœnitens !* *

"What a cry! Ah, but it is beautiful! It is beautiful! What words to say in dying! And what did the poor thief ask, that Dixmas of whom the church has made a saint for that one appeal: '*Remember me, Lord, in Thy kingdom !*' But we have arrived. Stoop, that you may not spoil your hat. Now, what do you want with me? You know the motto of the Montfanons: *Excelsior et firmior—Always higher and always firmer. . . .* One can never do too many good deeds. If it be possible, *present*, as we said to the roll-call."

A singular mixture of fervor and of good-nature, of enthusiastic eloquence and of political or religious fanaticism, was Montfanon. But the good-nature rapidly vanished from his face, at once so haughty and so simple, in proportion as Dorsenne's story proceeded. The writer, indeed, did not make the error

* I ask that which the penitent thief asked.

[ 200 ]

of at once formulating his proposition. He felt that he could not argue with the pontifical zouave of by-gone days. Either the latter would look upon it as monstrous and absurd, or he would see in it a char-itable duty to be accomplished, and then, whatever annoyance the matter might occasion him, he would accept it, as he would bestow alms. It was that chord of generosity which Julien, diplomatic for once in his life, essayed to touch by his confidence. Gaining authority by their conversation of a few days before, he related all he could of Gorka's visit, concealing the fact of that word of honor so falsely given, which still oppressed him with a mortal weight. He told how he had soothed the madman, how he conducted him to the station, then he described the meeting of the two rivals twenty-four hours later. He dwelt upon Alba's manner that evening and the infamy of the anonymous letters written to Madame Steno's dis-carded lover and to her daughter. And after he had reported the mysterious quarrel which had suddenly arisen between Gorka and Chapron:

"I, therefore, promised to be his second," he con-cluded, "because I believe it my absolute duty to do all I can to prevent the duel from taking place. Only think of it. If it should take place, and if one of them is killed or wounded, how can the affair be kept secret in this gossiping city of Rome? And what remarks it will call forth! It is evident that these two boys have quarrelled only on account of the rela-tions between Madame Steno and Maitland. By what strange coincidence? Of that I know nothing.

But there will not be a doubt in public opinion. And can you not see additional anonymous letters written to Alba, Madame Gorka, Madame Maitland? . . . The men I do not care for. . . . Two out of three merit all that comes to them. But those innocent creatures—is it not frightful?"

"Frightful, indeed," replied Montfanon; "it is that which renders those adulterous adventures so hideous. There are many people who are affected by it besides the guilty ones. . . . You see that, you who thought that society so pleasant, so refined, so interesting, the day before yesterday? But it does no good to recriminate. I understand. You have come to ask me to advise you in your *rôle* of second. My follies of youth will enable me to direct you. . . . Correctness in the slightest detail and no nerves, when one has to arrange a duel. Oh! You will have trouble. Gorka is mad. I know the Poles. They have great faults, but they are brave. Lord, but they are brave! And little Chapron, I know him, too; he has one of those stubborn natures, which would allow their breasts to be pierced without saying 'Ouf!' And *amour propre*. He has good soldier's blood in his veins, that child, notwithstanding the mixture. And with that mixture, do you not see what a hero the first of the three Dumas, the mulatto general, has been? . . . Yes. You have there a hard job, my good Dorsenne. . . . You will need another second to assist you, who will have the same views as you and—pardon me—more experience, perhaps."

"Marquis," replied Julien, whose voice trembled

with anxiety, "there is only one person in Rome who would be respected enough, venerated by all, so that his intervention in that delicate and dangerous matter be decisive, one person who could suggest excuses to Chapron, or obtain them from the other. . . . In short, there is only one person who has the authority of a hero before whom they will remain silent when he speaks of honor, and that person is you."

"I," exclaimed Montfanon, "I, you wish me to be"—

"One of Chapron's seconds," interrupted Dorsenne. "Yes. It is true. I come on his part and for that. Do not tell me what I already know, that your position will not allow of such a step. It is because it is what it is, that I thought of coming to you. Do not tell me that your religious principles are opposed to duels. It is that there may be no duel that I conjure you to accept. . . . It is essential that it does not take place. I swear to you, that the peace of too many innocent persons is concerned."

And he continued, calling into service at that moment all the intelligence and all the eloquence of which he was capable. He could follow on the face of the former duellist, who had become the most ardent of Catholics and the most monomaniacal of old bachelors, twenty diverse expressions. At length Montfanon laid his hand with veritable solemnity on his interlocutor's arm and said to him:

"Listen, Dorsenne, do not tell me any more. . . . I consent to what you ask of me, but on two conditions. They are these: The first is that Monsieur

Chapron will trust absolutely to my judgment, whatsoever it may be; the second is that you will retire with me if these gentlemen persist in their childishness. . . . I promise to aid you in fulfilling a mission of charity, and not anything else; I repeat, not anything else. Before bringing Monsieur Chapron to me you will repeat to him what I have said, word for word."

"Word for word," replied the other, adding: "He is at home awaiting the result of my undertaking."

"Then," said the Marquis, "I will return to Rome with you at once. He has probably already received Gorka's seconds, and if they really wish to arrange a duel the rule is not to put it off. . . . I shall not see my procession, but to prevent misfortune is to do a good deed, and it is one way of praying to God."

"Let me press your hand, my noble friend," said Dorsenne; "never have I better understood what a truly brave man is."

When the writer alighted, three-quarters of an hour later, at the house on the Rue Leopardi, after having seen Montfanon home, he felt sustained by such moral support that was almost joyous. He found Florent in his species of salon-smoking-room, arranging his papers with methodical composure.

"He accepts," were the first words the young men uttered, almost simultaneously, while Dorsenne repeated Montfanon's words.

"I depend absolutely on you two," replied the other. "I have no thirst for Monsieur de Gorka's blood. . . . But that gentleman must not accuse the

grandson of Colonel Chapron of cowardice. . . .
For that I rely upon the relative of General Dorsenne
and on the old soldier of Charette."

As he spoke, Florent handed a letter to Julien, who
asked: "From whom is this?"

"This," said Florent, "is a letter addressed to you,
on this very table half an hour ago by Baron Hafner.
. . . There is some news. I have received my adversary's seconds. The Baron is one, Ardea the
other."

"Baron Hafner!" exclaimed Dorsenne. "What a
singular choice!" He paused, and he and Florent
exchanged glances. They understood one another
without speaking. Boleslas could not have found a
surer means of informing Madame Steno as to the
plan he intended to employ in his vengeance. On the
other hand, the known devotion of the Baron for the
Countess gave one chance more for a pacific solution,
at the same time that the fanaticism of Montfanon
would be confronted with Fanny's father, an episode
of comedy suddenly cast across Gorka's drama of
jealousy.

Julien resumed with a smile: "You must watch
Montfanon's face when we inform him of those two
witnesses. He is a man of the fifteenth century,
you know, a Montluc, a Duc d'Alba, a Philippe II.
I do not know which he detests the most, the Free-
masons, the Free-thinkers, the Protestants, the Jews, or
the Germans. And as this obscure and tortuous Hafner is a little of everything, he has vowed hatred against
him! . . . Leaving that out of the question, he sus-

pects him of being a secret agent in the service of the Triple Alliance! But let us see the letter."

He opened and glanced through it. "This craftiness serves for something, it is equivalent almost to kindness. He, too, has felt that it is necessary to end our affair, were it only to avoid scandal. He appoints a meeting at his house between six and seven o'clock with me and your second. Come, time is flying. You must come to the Marquis to make your request officially. Begin this way. Obtain his promise before mentioning Hafner's name. I know him. He will not retract his word. But it is just."

The two friends found Montfanon awaiting them in his office, a large room filled with books, from which could be obtained a fine view of the panorama of the Forum, more majestic still on that afternoon when the shadows of the columns and arches grew longer on the sidewalk. The room with its brick floor had no other comfort than a carpet under the large desk littered with papers—no doubt fragments of the famous work on the relations of the French nobility and the Church. A crucifix stood upon the desk. On the wall were two engravings, that of Monseigneur Pie, the holy Bishop of Poitiers, and that of General de Sonis, on foot, with his wooden leg, and a painting representing St. François, the patron of the house. Those were the only artistic decorations of the modest habitation. The nobleman often said: "I have freed myself from the tyranny of objects." But with that marvellous background of grandiose ruins and that sky, the simple spot was an incomparable retreat in which to end in meditation and renouncement a life already shaken by the tempests of the senses and of the world.

The hermit of that Thébaïde rose to greet his two visitors, and pointing out to Chapron an open volume on his table, he said to him:

"I was thinking of you. It is Chateauvillars's book on duelling. It contains a code which is not very complete. I recommend it to you, however, if ever you have to fulfil a mission like ours," and he pointed to Dorsenne and himself, with a gesture which constituted the most amicable of acceptations. "It seems you had too hasty a hand. . . . Ha! ha! Do not defend yourself. Such as you see me, at twenty-one I threw a plate in the face of a gentleman who bantered Comte de Chambord before a number of Jacobins at a *table d'hôte* in the provinces. See," continued he, raising his white moustache and disclosing a scar, "this is the souvenir. The fellow was once a dragoon; he proposed the sabre. I accepted, and this is what I got, while he lost two fingers. . . . That will not happen to us this time at least. . . . Dorsenne has told you our conditions."

"And I replied that I was sure I could not intrust my honor to better hands," replied Florent.

"Cease!" replied Montfanon, with a gesture of satisfaction. "No more phrases. It is well. Moreover, I judged you, sir, from the day on which you spoke to me at Saint Louis. You honor your dead. That is why I shall be happy, very happy, to be useful to you."

# PAUL BOURGET

"Now tell me very clearly the recital you made to Dorsenne."

Then Florent related concisely that which had taken place between him and Gorka—that is to say, their argument and his passion, carefully omitting the details in which the name of his brother-in-law would be mixed.

"The deuce!" said Montfanon, familiarly, "the affair looks bad, very bad. . . . You see, a second is a confessor. You have had a discussion in the street with Monsieur Gorka, but about what? You can not reply? What did he say to you to provoke you to the point of wishing to strike him? That is the first key to the position."

"I can not reply," said Florent.

"Then," resumed the Marquis, after a silence, "there only remains to assert that the gesture on your part was—how shall I say? Unmeditated and unfinished. That is the second key to the position. . . . You have no special grudge against Monsieur Gorka?"

"None."

"Nor he against you?"

"None."

"The affair looks better," said Montfanon, who was silent for a time, to resume, in the voice of a man who is talking to himself, "Count Gorka considers himself offended? But is there any offence? It is that which we should discuss. . . . An assault or the threat of an assault would afford occasion for an arrangement. . . . But a gesture restrained, since it was not carried into effect. . . . Do not interrupt me," he continued.

COSMOPOLIS

"I am trying to understand it clearly. . . . We must arrive at a solution. We shall have to express our regret, leaving the field open to another reparation, if Gorka requires it. . . . And he will not require it. The entire problem now rests on the choice of his seconds. . . . Whom will he select?"

"I have already received visits from them," said Florent. "Half an hour ago. One is Prince d'Ardea."

"He is a gentleman," replied Montfanon. "I shall not be sorry to see him to tell him my feelings with regard to the public sale of his palace, to which he should never have allowed himself to be driven. . . . And the other?"

"The other?" interrupted Dorsenne. "Prepare yourself for a blow. . . . I swear to you I did not know his name when I went in search of you at the catacomb. It is—in short—it is Baron Hafner."

"Baron Hafner!" exclaimed Montfanon. "Boleslas Gorka, the descendant of the Gorkas, of that grand Luc Gorka who was Palatine of Posen and Bishop of Cujavie, has chosen for his second Monsieur Justus Hafner, the thief, the scoundrel, who had the disgraceful suit! . . . No, Dorsenne, do not tell me that; it is not possible." Then, with the air of a combatant: "We will challenge him, that is all, for his lack of honor. I take it upon myself, as well as to tell of his deeds to Boleslas. We will spend an enjoyable quarter of an hour there, I promise you."

"You will not do that," said Dorsenne, quickly. "First, with regard to official honor, there is only one law, is there not? Hafner was acquitted and his

14          [ 209 ]

adversaries condemned. You told me so the other day. . . . And then, you forget the conversation we just had."

"Pardon," interrupted Florent, in his turn. "Monsieur de Montfanon, in promising to assist me, has done me a great honor, which I shall never forget. If there should result from it any annoyance to him I should be deeply grieved, and I am ready to release him from his promise."

"No," said the Marquis, after another silence. "I will not take it back." . . . He was so magnanimous when his two or three hobbies were not involved that the slightest delicacy awoke an echo in him. He again extended his hand to Chapron and continued, but with an accent which betrayed suppressed irritation: "After all, it does not concern us if Monsieur Gorka has chosen to be represented in an affair of honor by one whom he should not even salute. . . . You will, then, give our two names to those two gentlemen . . . and Dorsenne and I will await them, as is the rule. . . . It is their place to come, since they are the proxies of the person insulted."

"They have already arranged a meeting for this evening," replied Chapron.

"What's arranged? With whom? For whom?" exclaimed Montfanon, a prey to a fresh access of choler. "With you? . . . For us? . . . Ah, I do not like such conduct where such grave matters are concerned. . . . The code is absolute on that subject. . . . Their challenge once made, to which you, Monsieur Chapron, have to reply by *yes* or *no*, these gentlemen should withdraw immediately. . . . It is not your fault, it is Ardea's, who has allowed that dabbler in spurious dividends to perform his part of intriguer. . . . But we will rectify all in the right way, which is the French. . . . And where is the rendezvous?"

"I will read to you the letter which the Baron left for me with Florent," said Dorsenne, who indeed read the very courteous note Hafner had written to him, in which he excused himself for choosing his own house as a rendezvous for the four witnesses. "One can not ignore so polite a note?"

"There are too many *dear sirs*, and too many *compliments*," said Montfanon, brusquely. "Sit here," he continued, relinquishing his armchair to Florent, "and inform the two men of our names and address, adding that we are at their service and ignoring the first inaccuracy on their part. Let them return! . . . And you, Dorsenne, since you are afraid of wounding that gentleman, I will not prevent you from going to his house—personally, do you hear—to warn him that Monsieur Chapron, here present, has chosen for his first second a disagreeable person, an old duellist, anything you like, but who desires strict form, and, first of all, a correct call made upon us by them, in order to settle officially upon a rendezvous."

"What did I tell you?" asked Dorsenne, when he with Florent descended Montfanon's staircase. "He is a different man since you mentioned the Baron to him. The discussion between them will be a hot one. I hope he will not spoil all by his folly. On my honor, if I had guessed whom Gorka would choose I should

not have suggested to you the old leaguer, as I call
him."

"And I, if Monsieur de Montfanon should make me
fight at five paces," replied Chapron, with a laugh,
"would be grateful to you for having brought me into
relations with him. He is a whole-souled man, as was
my poor father, as is Maitland. I adore such people."

"Is there no means of having at once heart and
head?" said Julien to himself, on reaching the Palais
Savorelli, where Hafner lived, and recalling the Marquis's choler on the one hand, and on the other the
egotism of Maitland, of which Florent's last words
reminded him. His apprehension of the afternoon
returned in a greater degree, for he knew Montfanon
to be very sensitive on certain points, and it was one
of those points which would be wounded to the quick
by the forced relations with Gorka's witnesses. "I
do not trust Hafner," thought he; "if the cunning
fellow has accepted the mission utterly contrary to his
tastes, his habits, almost to his age, it must be to con-
nive with his future son-in-law and to conciliate all.
Perhaps even the marriage had been already settled?
I hope not. The Marquis would be so furious he
would require the duel to a letter."

The young man had guessed aright. Chance, which
often brings one event upon another, decreed that
Ardea, at the very moment that he was deliberating
with Gorka as to the choice of another second, received
a note from Madame Steno containing simply these
words: *"Your proposal has been made, and the answer
is yes. May I be the first to embrace you, Simpaticone?"*

An ingenious idea occurred to him; to have arranged by his future father-in-law the quarrel which he considered at once absurd, useless, and dangerous. The eagerness with which Gorka had accepted Hafner's name, proved, as Dorsenne and Florent had divined, his desire that his perfidious mistress should be informed of his doings. As for the Baron, he consented —oh, irony of coincidences!—by saying to Peppino Ardea words almost identical with those which Montfanon had uttered to Dorsenne:

"We will draw up, in advance, an official plan of conciliation, and, if the matter can not be arranged, we will withdraw."

It was in such terms that the memorable conversation was concluded, a conversation truly worthy of the *combinazione* which poor Fanny's marriage represented. There had been less question of the marriage itself than that of the services to be rendered to the infidelity of the woman who presided over the sorry traffic! Is it necessary to add that neither Ardea nor his future father-in-law had made the shadow of an allusion to the true side of the affair? Perhaps at any other time the excessive prudence innate to the Baron and his care never to compromise himself would have deterred him from the possible annoyances which might arise from an interference in the adventure of an exasperated and discarded lover. But his joy at the thought that his daughter was to become a Roman princess—and with what a name!—had really turned his brain.

He had, however, the good sense to say to the

stunned Ardea: "Madame Steno must know nothing of it, at least beforehand. She would not fail to inform Madame Gorka, and God knows of what the latter would be capable."

In reality, the two men were convinced that it was essential, directly or indirectly, to beware of warning Maitland. They employed the remainder of the afternoon in paying their visit to Florent, then in sending telegram after telegram to announce the betrothal, with which charming Fanny seemed more satisfied since Cardinal Guerillot had consented, at simply a word from her, to preside at her baptism. The Baron, in the face of that consent, could not restrain his joy. He loved his daughter, strange man, somewhat in the manner in which a breeder loves a favorite horse which has won the *Grand Prix* for him. When Dorsenne arrived, bearing Chapron's note and Montfanon's message, he was received with a cordiality and a complaisance which at once enlightened him upon the result of the matrimonial intrigue of which Alba had spoken to him.

"Anything that your friend wishes, my dear sir. . . . Is it not so, Peppino?" said the Baron, seating himself at his table. "Will you dictate the letter yourself, Dorsenne? . . . See, is this all right? You will understand with what sentiments we have accepted this mission when you learn that Fanny is betrothed to Prince Ardea, here present. The news dates from three o'clock. So you are the first to know it, is he not, Peppino?" He had drawn up not less than two hundred despatches. "Return whenever you like with the Marquis. . . . I simply ask, under the circumstances, that the interview take place, if it be possible, between six and seven, or between nine and ten, in order not to interfere with our little family dinner."

"Let us say nine o'clock," said Dorsenne. "Monsieur de Montfanon is somewhat formal. He would like to have your reply by letter."

"Prince Ardea to marry Mademoiselle Hafner!" That cry which the news brought by Julien wrested from Montfanon was so dolorous that the young man did not think of laughing. He had thought it wiser to prepare his irascible friend, lest the Baron might make some allusion to the grand event during the course of the conversation, and that the other might. not make some impulsive remark.

"Did I not tell you that the girl's Catholicism was a farce? Did I not tell Monseigneur Guerillot? This was what she aimed at all those years, with such perfect hypocrisy? It was the Palais Castagna. And she will enter there as mistress! . . . She will bring there the dishonor of that pirated gold on which there are stains of blood! Warn them, that they do not speak to me of it, or I will not answer for myself. . . . The second of a Gorka, the father-in-law of an Ardea, he triumphs, the thief who should by rights be a convict! . . . But we shall see. Will not all the other Roman princes who have no blots upon their escutcheons, the Orsinis, the Colonnas, the Odeschalchis, the Borgheses, the Rospigliosis, not combine to prevent this monstrosity? Nobility is like love, those who buy those sacred things degrade them in paying for them, and those to whom they are given are no better than mire. . . . Princess d'Ardea! That creature! Ah, what a disgrace! . . . But we must remember our engagement relative to that brave young Chapron. The boy pleases me; first, because very probably he is going to fight for some one else and out of a devotion which I can not very well understand! It is devotion all the same, and it is chivalry! . . . He desires to prevent that miserable Gorka from calling forth a scandal which would have warned his sister. . . . And then, as I told him, he respects the dead. . . . Let us. . . . I have my wits no longer about me, that intelligence has so greatly disturbed me. . . . Princess d'Ardea! . . . Well, write that we will be at Monsieur Hafner's at nine o'clock. . . . I do not want any of those people at my house. . . . At yours it would not be proper; you are too young. And I prefer going to the father-in-law's rather than to the son-in-law's. The rascal has made a good bargain in buying what he has bought with his stolen millions. But the other. . . . And his great-great-uncle might have been Jules Second, Pie Fifth, Hildebrand; he would have sold all just the same! . . . He can not deceive himself! He has heard the suit against that man spoken of! He knows whence come those millions! He has heard their family, their lives spoken of! And he has not been inspired with too great a horror to accept the gold of that adventurer. Does he not know what a name is? Our name! It is ourselves, our honor, in the mouths, in the thoughts, of others! How happy I am, Dorsenne, to have been fifty-two

years of age last month. I shall be gone before having seen what you will see, the agony of all the aris-
tocrats and royalties. It was only in blood that they
fell! But they do not fall. Alas! They fix themselves upon the ground, which is the saddest of all.
Still, what matters it? The monarchy, the nobility,
and the Church are everlasting. The people who disregard them will die, that is all. Come, write your
letter, which I will sign. Send it away, and you will
dine with me. We must go into the den provided
with an argument which will prevent this duel, and
sustaining our part toward our client. There must
be an arrangement which I would accept myself. I
like him, I repeat."

The excitement which began to startle Dorsenne
was only augmented during dinner, so much the more
so as, on discussing the conditions of that arrangement
he hoped to bring about, the recollection of his terrible
youth filled the thoughts and the discourse of the former duellist. Was it, indeed, the same personage who
recited the verses of a hymn in the catacombs a few
hours before? It only required the feudal in him to
be reawakened to transform him. The fire in his
eyes and the color in his face betrayed that the duel
in which he had thought best to engage, out of charity,
intoxicated him on his own statement. It was the
old amateur, the epicure of the sword, very ungovern-
able, which stirred within that man of faith, in whom
passion had burned and who had loved all excitement,
including that of danger, as to-day he loved his ideas,
as he loved his flag—immoderately. He no longer

thought of the three women to be spared suspicion, nor of the good deed to be accomplished. He saw all his old friends and their talent for fighting, the thrusts of this one, the way another had of striking, the composure of a third, and then this refrain interrupted constantly his warlike anecdotes: "But why the deuce has Gorka chosen that Hafner for his second? . . . It is incomprehensible." . . . On entering the carriage which was to bear them to their interview, he heard Dorsenne say to the coachman: "Palais Savorelli."

"That is the final blow," said he, raising his arm and clenching his fist. "The adventurer occupies the Pretender's house, the house of the Stuarts." . . . He repeated: "The house of the Stuarts!" and then lapsed into a silence which the writer felt to be laden with more storminess than his last denunciation. He did not emerge from his meditations until ushered into the salon of the *ci-devant* jeweller, now a *grand seigneur* —into *one* of the salons, rather, for there were five. There Montfanon began to examine everything around him, with an air of such contempt and pride that, notwithstanding his anxiety, Dorsenne could not resist laughing and teasing him by saying:

"You will not pretend to say that there are no pretty things here? These two paintings by Moroni, for example?"

"Nothing that is appropriate," replied Montfanon. "Yes, they are two magnificent portraits of ancestors, and this man has no ancestors! . . . There are some weapons in that cupboard, and he has never touched

a sword! And there is a piece of tapestry representing
the miracles of the loaves, which is a piece of audacity!
You may not believe me, Dorsenne, but it is making
me ill to be here. . . . I am reminded of the human
toil, of the human soul in all these objects, and to end
here, paid for how? Owned by whom? Close your
eyes and think of Schroeder and of the others whom
you do not know. Look into the hovels where there
is neither furniture, fire, nor bread. Then, open your
eyes and look at this."

"And you, my dear friend," replied the novelist,
"I conjure you to think of our conversation in the
catacombs, to think of the three ladies in whose names
I besought you to aid Florent."

"Thank you," said Montfanon, passing his hand
over his brow, "I promise you to be calm."

He had scarcely uttered those words when the door
opened, disclosing to view another room, lighted also,
and which, to judge by the sound of voices, contained
several persons. No doubt Madame Steno and Alba,
thought Julien; and the Baron entered, accompanied
by Peppino Ardea. While going through the intro-
ductions, the writer was struck by the contrast offered
between his three companions. Hafner and Ardea
in evening dress, with buttonhole bouquets, had the
open and happy faces of two citizens who had clear
consciences. The usually sallow complexion of the
business man was tinged with excitement, his eyes, as
a rule so hard, were gentler. As for the Prince, the
same childish carelessness lighted up his jovial face,
while the hero of Patay, with his coarse boots, his

immense form enveloped in a somewhat shabby redingote, exhibited a face so contracted that one would
have thought him devoured by remorse. A dishonest
intendant, forced to expose his accounts to generous
and confiding masters, could not have had a face
more gloomy or more anxious. He had, moreover,
put his one arm behind his back in a manner so formal
that neither of the two men who entered offered him
their hands. That appearance was without doubt
little in keeping with what the father and the *fiancé* of
Fanny had expected; for there was, when the four
men were seated, a pause which the Baron was the
first to break. He began in his measured tones, in a
voice which handles words as the weight of a usurer
weighs gold pieces to the milligramme:

"Gentlemen, I believe I shall express our common
sentiment in first of all establishing a point which
shall govern our meeting. . . . We are here, it is
understood, to bring about the work of reconciliation
between two men, two gentlemen whom we know,
whom we esteem—I might better say, whom we all
love." . . . He turned, in pronouncing those words,
successively to each of his three listeners, who all
bowed, with the exception of the Marquis. Hafner
examined the nobleman, with his glance accustomed to
read the depths of the mind in order to divine the
intentions. He saw that Chapron's first witness was
a troublesome customer, and he continued: "That
done, I beg to read to you this little paper." He
drew from his pocket a sheet of folded paper and
placed upon the end of his nose his famous gold *lorg-*

*non:* "It is very trifling, one of those *directives*, as Monsieur de Moltke says, which serve to guide operations, a plan of action which we will modify after discussion. In short, it is a landmark that we may not launch into space."

"Pardon, sir," interrupted Montfanon, whose brows contracted still more at the mention of the celebrated field-marshal, and, stopping by a gesture the reader, who, in his surprise, dropped his *lorgnon* upon the table on which his elbow rested. "I regret very much," he continued, "to be obliged to tell you that Monsieur Dorsenne and I"—here he turned to Dorsenne, who made an equivocal gesture of vexation—"can not admit the point of view in which you place yourself. . . . You claim that we are here to arrange a reconciliation. That is possible. . . . I concede that it is desirable. . . . But I know nothing of it and, permit me to say, you do not know any more. I am here—we are here, Monsieur Dorsenne and I, to listen to the complaints which Count Gorka has commissioned you to formulate to Monsieur Florent Chapron's proxies. Formulate those complaints, and we will discuss them. Formulate the reparation you claim in the name of your client and we will discuss it. The papers will follow, if they follow at all, and, once more, neither you nor we know what will be the issue of this conversation, nor should we know it, before establishing the facts."

"There is some misunderstanding, sir," said Ardea, whom Montfanon's words had irritated somewhat. He could not, any more than Hafner, understand the very simple, but very singular, character of the Marquis, and he added: "I have been concerned in several *rencontres*—four times as second, and once as principal—and I have seen employed without discussion the proceeding which Baron Hafner has just proposed to you, and which of itself is, perhaps, only a more expeditious means of arriving at what you very properly call the establishment of facts."

"I was not aware of the number of your affairs, sir," replied Montfanon, still more nervous since Hafner's future son-in-law joined in the conversation; "but since it has pleased you to tell us I will take the liberty of saying to you that I have fought seven times, and that I have been a second fourteen. . . . It is true that it was at an epoch when the head of your house was your father, if I remember right, the deceased Prince Urban, whom I had the honor of knowing when I served in the zouaves. He was a fine Roman nobleman, and did honor to his name. What I have told you is proof that I have some competence in the matter of a duel. . . . Well, we have always held that seconds were constituted to arrange affairs that could be arranged, but also to settle affairs, as well as they can, that seem incapable of being arranged. Let us now inquire into the matter; we are here for that, and for nothing else."

"Are these gentlemen of that opinion?" asked Hafner in a conciliatory voice, turning first to Dorsenne, then to Ardea: "I do not adhere to my method," he continued, again folding his paper. He slipped it into his vest-pocket and continued: "Let us establish the facts, as you say. Count Gorka, our friend, considers himself seriously, very seriously, offended by Monsieur Florent Chapron in the course of the discussion in a public street. Monsieur Chapron was carried away, as you know, sirs, almost to—what shall I say?—hastiness, which, however, was not followed by consequences, thanks to the presence of mind of Monsieur Gorka. . . . But, accomplished or not, the act remains. Monsieur Gorka was insulted, and he requires satisfaction. . . . I do not believe there is any doubt upon that point which is the cause of the affair, or, rather, the whole affair."

"I again ask your pardon, sir," said Montfanon, dryly, who no longer took pains to conceal his anger, "Monsieur Dorsenne and I can not accept your manner of putting the question. . . . You say that Monsieur Chapron's hastiness was not followed by consequences by reason of Monsieur Gorka's presence of mind. We claim that there was only on the part of Monsieur Chapron a scarcely indicated gesture, which he himself restrained. In consequence you attribute to Monsieur Gorka the quality of the insulted party; you are over-hasty. He is merely the plaintiff, up to this time. It is very different."

"But by rights he is the insulted party," interrupted Ardea. "Restrained or not, it constitutes a threat of assault. I did not wish to claim to be a duellist by telling you of my engagements. But this is the A B C of the *codice cavalleresco*, if the insult be followed by an assault, he who receives the blow is the offended party, and the threat of an assault is equivalent to an actual assault. The offended party has the choice of a duel, weapons and conditions. Consult your authors and ours: Chateauvillars, Du Verger, Angelini and Gelli, all agree.''

"I am sorry for their sakes," said Montfanon, and he looked at the Prince with a contraction of the brows almost menacing, "but it is an opinion which does not hold good generally, nor in this particular case. The proof is that a duellist, as you have just said," his voice trembled as he emphasized the insolence offered by the other, "a *bravo*, to use the expression of your country, would only have to commit a justifiable murder by first insulting him at whom he aims with rude words. The insulted person replies by a voluntary gesture, on the signification of which one may be mistaken, and you will admit that the *bravo* is the offended party, and that he has the choice of weapons.''

"But, Marquis," resumed Hafner, with evident disgust, so greatly did the cavilling and the ill-will of the nobleman irritate him, "where are you wandering to? What do you mean by bringing up chicanery of this sort?"

"Chicanery!" exclaimed Montfanon, half rising.

"Montfanon!" besought Dorsenne, rising in his turn and forcing the terrible man to be seated.

"I retract the word," said the Baron, "if it has insulted you. Nothing was farther from my thoughts. . . . I repeat that I apologize, Marquis. . . . But, come, tell us what you want for your client, that is very simple. . . . And then we will do all we can to make your demands agree with those of our client. . . . It is a trifling matter to be adjusted."

"No, sir," said Montfanon, with insolent severity, "it is justice to be rendered, which is very different. What we, Monsieur Dorsenne and I, desire," he continued in a severe voice, "is this: Count Gorka has gravely insulted Monsieur Chapron. Let me finish," he added upon a simultaneous gesture on the part of Ardea and of Hafner. "Yes, sirs, Monsieur Chapron, known to us all for his perfect courtesy, must have been very gravely insulted, even to make the improper gesture of which you just spoke. But it was agreed upon between these two gentlemen, for reasons of delicacy which we had to accept—it was agreed, I say, that the nature of the insult offered by Monsieur Gorka to Monsieur Chapron should not be divulged. . . . We have the right, however, and I may add the duty devolves upon us, to measure the gravity of that insult by the excess of anger aroused in Monsieur Chapron. . . . I conclude from it that, to be just, the plan of reconciliation, if we draw it up, should contain reciprocal concessions. Count Gorka will retract his words and Monsieur Chapron apologize for his hastiness."

"It is impossible," exclaimed the Prince; "Gorka will never accept that."

"You, then, wish to have them fight the duel?" groaned Hafner.

"And why not?" said Montfanon, exasperated. "It would be better than for the one to nurse his insults and the other his blow."

"Well, sirs," replied the Baron, rising after the silence which followed that imprudent whim of a man beside himself, "we will confer again with our client. If you wish, we will resume this conversation to-morrow at ten o'clock, say here or in any place convenient to you. . . . You will excuse me, Marquis. Dorsenne has no doubt told you under what circumstances—"

"Yes, he has told me," interrupted Montfanon, who again glanced at the Prince, and in a manner so mournful that the latter felt himself blush beneath the strange glance, at which, however, it was impossible to feel angry. Dorsenne had only time to cut short all other explanations by replying to Justus Hafner himself.

"Would you like the meeting at my house? We shall have more chance to escape remarks."

"You have done well to change the place," said Montfanon, five minutes later, on entering the carriage with his young friend.

They had descended the staircase without speaking, for the brave and unreasonable Marquis regretted his strangely provoking attitude of the moment before.

"What would you have?" he added. "The profaned palace, the insolent luxury of that thief, the Prince who has sold his family, the Baron whose part is so sinister. I could no longer contain myself! That Baron, above all, with his *directives !* Words to repeat when one is German, to a French soldier who fought in 1870, like those words of Monsieur de Moltke! His terms, too, applied to honor and that abominable politeness in which there is servility and insolence!

. . . Still, I am not satisfied with myself. I am not at all satisfied."

There was in his voice so much good-nature, such evident remorse at not having controlled himself in so grave a situation, that Dorsenne pressed his hand instead of reproaching him, as he said:

"It will do to-morrow. . . . We will arrange all; it has only been postponed."

"You say that to console me," said the Marquis, "but I know it was very badly managed. And it is my fault! Perhaps we shall have no other service to render our brave Chapron than to arrange a duel for him under the most dangerous conditions. Ah, but I became inopportunely angry! . . . But why the deuce did Gorka select such a second? It is incomprehensible! . . . Did you see what the cabalistic word *gentleman* means to those rascals: Steal, cheat, assassinate, but have carriages perfectly appointed, a magnificent mansion, well-served dinners, and fine clothes! . . . No, I have suffered too much! Ah, it is not right; and on what a day, too? God! That the old man might die!" . . . he added, in a voice so low that his companion did not hear his words.

# CHAPTER VII

### A LITTLE RELATIVE OF IAGO

THE remorse which Montfanon expressed so naïvely, once acknowledged to himself, increased rapidly in the honest man's heart. He had reason to say from the beginning that the affair looked bad. A quarrel, together with assault, or an attempt at assault, would not be easily set right. It required a diplomatic miracle. The slightest lack of self-possession on the part of the seconds is equivalent to a catastrophe. As happens in such circumstances, events are hurried, and the pessimistic anticipations of the irritable Marquis were verified almost as soon as he uttered them. Dorsenne and he had barely left the Palais Savorelli when Gorka arrived. The energy with which he repulsed the proposition of an arrangement which would admit of excuses on his part, served prudent Hafner, and the not less prudent Ardea, as a signal for withdrawal. It was too evident to the two men that no reconciliation would result from a collision of such a madman with a personage so difficult as the most authorized of Florent's proxies had shown himself to be.

They then asked Gorka to relieve them from their duty. They had too plausible an excuse in Fanny's betrothal for Boleslas to refuse to release them. That retirement was a second catastrophe. In his impatience to find other seconds who would be firm, Gorka hastened to the *Cercle de la Chasse*. Chance willed that he should meet with two of his comrades—a Marquis Cibo, Roman, and a Prince Pietrapertoso, Neapolitan, who were assuredly the best he could have chosen to hasten the simplest affair to its worst consequences.

Those two young men of the best Italian families, both very intelligent, very loyal and very good, belonged to that particular class which is to be met with in Vienna, Madrid, St. Petersburg, as in Milan and in Rome, of foreign *clubmen* hypnotized by Paris. And what a Paris! That of showy and noisy *fêtes*, that which passes the morning in practising the sports in fashion, the afternoons in racing, in frequenting fencing-schools, the evening at the theatre and the night at the gaming-table! That Paris which emigrates by turns, according to the season, to Monte Carlo for the *Tir aux Pigeons*, to Deauville for the race week, to Aix-les-Bains for the baccarat season; that Paris which has its own customs, its own language, its own history, even its own cosmopolitanism, for it exercises over certain minds, throughout Europe, so despotic a rule that Cibo, for example, and his friend Pietrapertoso never opened a French journal that was not Parisian.

They sought the short paragraphs in which were related, in detail, the doings of the demi-monde, the last supper given by some well-known *viveur*, the details of some large party in such and such a fashionable club, the result of a shooting match, or of a fencing match be-

[ 229 ]

tween celebrated fencers! There were between them subjects of conversation of which they never wearied; to know if spirituelle Gladys Harvey was more elegant than Leona d'Astri, if Machault made "counters" as rapid as those of General Garnier, if little Lautrec would adhere or would not adhere to the game he was playing. Imprisoned in Rome by the scantiness of their means, and also by the wishes, the one of his uncle, the other of his grandfather, whose heirs they were, their entire year was summed up in the months which they spent at Nice in the winter, and in the trip they took to Paris at the time of the *Grand Prix* for six weeks. Jealous one of the other, with the most comical rivalry, of the least occurrence at the *Cercle des Champs-Elysées* or of the *Rue Royale* in the Eternal City, they affected, in the presence of their colleagues of *la chasse*, the impassive manner of augurs when the telegraph brought them the news of some Parisian scandal. That inoffensive mania which had made of stout, ruddy Cibo, and of thin, pale Pietrapertoso two delightful studies for Dorsenne during his Roman winter, made of them terrible proxies in the service of Gorka's vengeance.

With what joy and what gravity they accepted that mission all those who have studied swordsmen will understand after this simple sketch, and with what promptness they presented themselves to confer at nine o'clock in the morning with their client's adversary! In short, at half-past twelve the duel was arranged in its slightest detail. The energy employed by Montfanon had only ended in somewhat tempering the conditions—four balls to be exchanged at twenty-five paces at the word of command. The duel was fixed for the following morning, in the inclosure which Cibo owned, with an inn adjoining, not very far distant from the classical tomb of Cæcilia Metella. To obtain that distance and the use of new weapons it required the prestige with which the Marquis suddenly clothed himself in the eyes of Gorka's seconds by pronouncing the name, still legendary in the provinces and to the foreigner, of Gramont-Caderousse—*Sic transit gloria mundi!* On leaving that rendezvous the excellent man really had tears in his eyes.

"It is my fault," he moaned, "it is my fault." With that Hafner we should have obtained such a fine official plan by mixing in a little of ours. He offered it to us himself. . . . Brave Chapron! It is I who have brought him into this dilemma! . . . I owe it to him not to abandon him, but to follow him to the end. . . . Here I shall be assisting at a duel, at my age! . . . Did you see how those young snobs lowered their voices when I mentioned my encounter with poor Caderousse? . . . Fifty-two years and a month, and not to know yet how to conduct one's self! Let us go to the Rue Leopardi. I wish to ask pardon of our client, and to give him some advice. We will take him to one of my old friends who has a garden near the Villa Pamphili, very secluded. We will spend the rest of the afternoon practising. . . . Ah! Accursed choler! Yes, it would have been so simple to accept the other's plan yesterday. By the exchange of two or three words, I am sure it could have been arranged."

"Console yourself, Marquis," replied Florent, when

the unhappy nobleman had described to him the deplorable result of his negotiations. "I like that better.
Monsieur Gorka needs correction. I have only one regret, that of not having given it to him more thoroughly. . . . Since I shall have to fight a duel, I would
at least have had my money's worth!"

"And you have never used a pistol?" asked Montfanon.

"Bah! I have hunted a great deal and I believe I
can shoot."

"That is like night and day," interrupted the Marquis. "Hold yourself in readiness. At three o'clock
come for me and I will give you a lesson. And remember there is a merciful God for the brave!"

Although Florent deserved praise for the cheerfulness
of which his reply was proof, the first moments which he
spent alone after the departure of his two witnesses were
very painful.

That which Chapron experienced during those few
moments was simply very natural anxiety, the enerva-
tion caused by looking at the clock, and saying:

"In twenty-four hours the hand will be on this
point of the dial. And shall I still be living?" . . . He
was, however, manly, and knew how to control himself. He struggled against the feeling of weakness,
and, while awaiting the time to rejoin his friends, he
resolved to write his last wishes. For years his intention had been to leave his entire fortune to his brother-
in-law. He, therefore, made a rough draft of his will
in that sense, with a pen at first rather unsteady, then
quite firm. His will completed, he had courage enough

to write two letters, addressed the one to that brother-
in-law, the other to his sister. When he had finished
his work the hands of the clock pointed to ten minutes
of three.

"Still seventeen hours and a half to wait," said he,
"but I think I have conquered my nerves. A short
walk, too, will benefit me."

So he decided to go on foot to the rendezvous named
by Montfanon. He carefully locked the three envelopes in the drawer of his desk. He saw, on passing,
that Lincoln was not in his studio. He asked the footman if Madame Maitland was at home. The reply
received was that she was dressing, and that she had
ordered her carriage for three o'clock.

"Good," said he, "neither of them will have the
slightest suspicion; I am saved."

How astonished he would have been could he, while
walking leisurely toward his destination, have returned
in thought to the smoking-room he had just left! He
would have seen a woman glide noiselessly through the
open door, with the precaution of a malefactor! He
would have seen her examine, without disarranging, all
the papers on the table. She frowned on seeing Dorsenne's and the Marquis's cards. She took from the
blotting-case some loose leaves and held them in front of
the glass, trying to read there the imprint left upon them.
*He would have seen finally* the woman draw from her
pocket a bunch of keys. She inserted one of them in
the lock of the drawer which Florent had so carefully
turned, and took from that drawer the three unsealed
envelopes he had placed within it. And the woman

who thus read, with a face contracted by anguish, the papers discovered in such a manner, thanks to a ruse the abominable indelicacy of which gave proof of shameful habits of espionage, was his own sister, the Lydia whom he believed so gentle and so simple, to whom he had penned an adieu so tender in case he should be killed—the Lydia who would have terrified him had he seen her thus, with passion distorting the face which was considered insignificant! She herself, the audacious spy, trembled as if she would fall, her eyes dilated, her bosom heaved, her teeth chattered, so greatly was she unnerved by what she had discovered, by the terrible consequences which she had brought about.

Had she not written the anonymous letters to Gorka, denouncing to him the intrigue between Maitland and Madame Steno? Was it not she who had chosen, the better to poison those terrible letters, phrases the most likely to strike the betrayed lover in the most sensitive part of his *amour propre?* Was it not she who had hastened the return of the jealous man with the certain hope of drawing thus a tragical vengeance upon the hated heads of her husband and the Venetian? That vengeance, indeed, had broken. But upon whom? Upon the only person Lydia loved in the world, upon the brother whom she saw endangered through her fault; and that thought was to her so overwhelming that she sank into the armchair in which Florent had been seated fifteen minutes before, repeating, with an accent of despair: "He is going to fight a duel. He is going to fight instead of the other!"

# COSMOPOLIS

All the moral history of that obscure and violent soul was summed up in the cry in which passionate anxiety for her brother was coupled with a fierce hatred of her husband. That hatred was the result of a youth and a childhood without the story of which a duplicity so criminal in a being so young would be unintelligible. That youth and that childhood had presaged what Lydia would one day be. But who was there to train the nature in which the heredity of an oppressed race manifested itself, as has been already remarked, by the two most detestable characteristics—hypocrisy and perfidy? Who, moreover, observes in children the truth, as much neglected in practise as it is common in theory, that the defects of the tenth year become vices in the thirtieth? When quite a child Lydia invented falsehoods as naturally as her brother spoke the truth. . . . Whosoever observed her would have perceived that those lies were all told to paint herself in a favorable light. The germ, too, of another defect was springing up within her—a jealousy instinctive, irrational, almost wicked. She could not see a new plaything in Florent's hands without sulking immediately. She could not bear to see her brother embrace her father without casting herself between them, nor could she see him amuse himself with other comrades.

Had Napoleon Chapron been interested in the study of character as deeply as he was in his cotton and his sugar-cane, he would have perceived, with affright, the early traces of a sinful nature. But, on that point, like his son, he was one of those trustful men who did not judge when they loved. Moreover, Lydia and Florent, to his wounded sensibility of a demi-pariah, formed the only pleasant corner in his life—were the fresh and youthful comforters of his widowerhood and of his misanthropy. He cherished them with the idolatry which all great workers entertain for their children, which is one of the most dangerous forms of paternal tenderness; Lydia's incipient vices were to the planter delightful fancies! Did she lie? The excellent man exclaimed: What an imagination she has! Was she jealous? He would sigh, pressing to his broad breast the tiny form: How sensitive she is! . . . The result of that selfish blindness—for to love children thus is to love them for one's self and not for them—was that the girl, at the time of her entrance at Roehampton, was spoiled in the essential traits of her character. But she was so pretty, she owed to the singular mixture of three races an originality of grace so seductive that only the keen glance of a governess of genius could have discerned, beneath that exquisite exterior, the already marked lines of her character. Such governesses are rare, still more so at convents than elsewhere. There was none at Roehampton when Lydia entered that pious haven which was to prove fatal to her, for a reason precisely contrary to that which transformed for Florent the lawns of peaceful Beaumont into a radiant paradise of friendship.

Among the pupils with whom Lydia was to be educated were four young girls from Philadelphia, older than the newcomer by two years, and who, also, had left America for the first time. They brought with them the unconquerable aversion to negro blood and that wonderful keenness in discovering it, even in the most infinitesimal degree, which distinguishes real Yankees. Little Lydia Chapron, having been entered as French, they at first hesitated in the face of a suspicion speedily converted into a certainty and that certainty into an aversion, which they could not conceal. They would not have been children had they not been unfeeling. They, therefore, began to offer poor Lydia petty affronts. Convents and colleges resemble other society. There, too, unjust contempt is like that "ferret of the woods," which runs from hand to hand and which always returns to its point of setting out. All the scornful are themselves scorned by some one—a merited punishment, which does not correct our pride any more than the other punishments which abound in life cure our other faults. Lydia's persecutors were themselves the objects of outrages practised by their comrades born in England, on account of certain peculiarities in their language and for the nasal quality of their voices. The drama was limited, as we can imagine, to a series of insignificant episodes and of which the superintendents only surprised a demi-echo.

Children nurse passions as strong as ours, but so much interrupted by playfulness that it is impossible to measure their exact strength. Lydia's *amour propre* was wounded in an incurable manner by that revelation of her own peculiarity. Certain incidents of her American life recurred to her, which she comprehended more clearly. She recalled the portrait of her grandmother, the complexion, the hands, the hair of her father, and she experienced that shame of her birth and of her family much more common with children than our optimism imagines. Parents of humble origin give their sons a liberal education, expose them to the demoralization which it brings with it in their positions, and what social hatreds date from the moment when the boy of twelve blushes in secret at the condition of his relatives! With Lydia, so instinctively jealous and untruthful, those first wounds induced falsehood and jealousy. The slightest superiority even, noticed in one of her companions, became to her a cause for suffering, and she undertook to compensate by personal triumphs the difference of blood, which, once discovered, wounds a vain nature. In order to assure herself those triumphs she tried to win all the persons who approached her, mistresses and comrades, and she began to practise that continued comedy of attitude and of sentiment to which the fatal desire to please, so quickly leads—that charming and dangerous tendency which borders much less on goodness than falseness. At eighteen, submitted to a sort of continual *cabotinage*, Lydia was, beneath the most attractive exterior, a being profoundly, though unconsciously, wicked, capable of very little affection—she loved no one truly but her brother—open to the invasion of the passions of hatred which are the natural products of proud and false minds. It was one of these passions, the most fatal of all, which marriage was to develop within her—*envy*.

That hideous vice, one of those which govern the world, has been so little studied by moralists, as all too dishonorable for the heart of man, no doubt, that this

statement may appear improbable. Madame Maitland, for years, had been envious of her husband, but
envious as one of the rivals of an artist would be,
envious as one pretty woman is of another, as one
banker is of his opponent, as a politician of his adversary, with the fierce, implacable envy which writhes
with physical pain in the face of success, which is
transported with a sensual joy in the face of disaster.
It is a great mistake to limit the ravages of that guilty
passion to the domain of professional emulation.
When it is deep, it does not alone attack the qualities
of the person, but the person himself, and it was thus
that Lydia envied Lincoln. Perhaps the analysis of
this sentiment, very subtle in its ugliness, will explain
to some a few of the antipathies against which they
have struck in their relatives. For it is not only between husband and wife that these unavowed envies
are met, it is between lover and mistress, friend and
friend, brother and brother, sometimes, alas, father
and son, mother and daughter! Lydia had married
Lincoln Maitland partly out of obedience to her
brother's wishes, partly from vanity, because the
young man was an American, and because it was a
sort of victory over the prejudices of race, of which
she thought constantly, but of which she never spoke.

It required only three months of married life to perceive that Maitland could not forgive himself for that
marriage. Although he affected to scorn his compatriots, and although at heart he did not share any of the
views of the country in which he had not set foot since
his fifth year, he could not hear remarks made in New

York upon that marriage without a pang. He disliked Lydia for the humiliation, and she felt it. The birth of a child would no doubt have modified that feeling, and, if it would not have removed it, would at least have softened the embittered heart of the young wife. But no child was born to them. They had not returned from their wedding tour, upon which Florent accompanied them, before their lives rolled along in that silence which forms the base of all those households in which husband and wife, according to a simple and grand expression of the people, do not live *heart against heart.*

After the journey through Spain, which should have been one continued enchantment, the wife became jealous of the evident preference which Florent showed for Maitland. For the first time she perceived the hold which that impassioned friendship had taken upon her brother's heart. He loved her, too, but with a secondary love. The comparison annoyed her daily, hourly, and it did not fail to become a real wound. Returned to Paris, where they spent almost three years, that wound was increased by the sole fact that the puissant individuality of the painter speedily relegated to the shade the individuality of his wife, simply, almost mechanically, like a large tree which pushes a smaller one into the background. The composite society of artists, amateurs, and writers who visited Lincoln came there only for him. The house they had rented was rented only for him. The journeys they made were for him. In short, Lydia was borne away, like Florent, in the orbit of the most despotic force in the world—that of a celebrated talent. An entire book would be required to paint in their daily truth the continued humiliations which brought the young wife to detest that talent and that celebrity with as much ardor as Florent worshipped them. She remained, however, an honest woman, in the sense in which the word is construed by the world, which sums up woman's entire dishonor in errors of love.

But within Lydia's breast grew a rooted aversion toward Lincoln. She detested him for the pure blood which made of that large, fair, and robust man so admirable a type of Anglo-Saxon beauty, by the side of her, so thin, so insignificant indeed, in spite of the grace of her pretty, dark face. She detested him for his taste, for the original elegance with which he understood how to adorn the places in which he lived, while she maintained within her a barbarous lack of taste for the least arrangement of materials and of colors. When she was forced to acknowledge progress in the painter, bitter hatred entered her heart. When he lamented over his work, and when she saw him a prey to the dolorous anxiety of an artist who doubts himself, she experienced a profound joy, marred only by the evident sadness into which Lincoln's struggles plunged Florent. Never had she met the eyes of Chapron fixed upon Maitland with that look of a faithful dog which rejoices in the joy of its master, or which suffers in his sadness, without enduring, like Alba Steno, the sensation of a "needle in the heart."

The idolatrous worship of her brother for the painter caused her to suffer still more as she comprehended, with the infallible perspicacity of antipathy, the immense dupery. She read the very depths of the souls of the two old comrades of Beaumont. She knew that in that friendship, as is almost always the case, one alone gave all to receive in exchange only the most brutal recognition, that with which a huntsman or a master gratifies a faithful dog! As for enlightening Florent with regard to Lincoln's character, she had vainly tried to do so by those fine and perfidious insinuations in which women excel. She only recognized her impotence, and myriads of hateful impressions were thus accumulated in her heart, to be summed up in one of those frenzies of taciturn rancor which bursts on the first opportunity with terrifying energy. Crime itself has its laws of development. Between the pretty little girl who wept on seeing a new toy in her brother's hand and the Lydia Maitland, forcer of locks, author of anonymous letters, driven by the thirst for vengeance, even to villainy, no dramatic revolution of character had taken place. The logical succession of days had sufficed.

The occasion to gratify that deep and mortal longing to touch Lincoln on some point truly sensitive, how often Lydia had sought it in vain, before Madame Steno obtained an ascendancy over the painter. She had been reduced by it to those meannesses of feminine animosity to manage, as if accidentally, that her husband might read all the disagreeable articles written about his paintings, innocently to praise before him the rivals who had given him offense, to repeat to him with an air of embarrassment the slightest criticisms

pronounced on one of his exhibits—all the unpleasant-
nesses which had the result of irritating Florent, above
all, for Maitland was one of those artists too well satisfied with the results of his own work for the opinion of
others to annoy him very much.   On the other hand,
before the passion for the *dogaresse* had possessed him,
he had never loved.   Many painters are thus, satisfying
with magnificent models an impetuosity of temperament which does not mount from the senses to the
heart.   Accustomed to regard the human form from
a certain point, they find in beauty, which would appear to us simply animal, principles of plastic emotion
which at times suffice for their amorous requirements.
They are only more deeply touched by it, when to that
rather coarse intoxication is joined, in the woman who
inspires them, the refined graces of mind, the delicacy
of elegance and the subtleties of sentiment.

Such was Madame Steno, who at once inspired the
painter with a passion as complete as a first love.   It
was really such.   The Countess, who was possessed
of the penetration of voluptuousness, was not mistaken
there.   Lydia, who was possessed of the penetration of
hatred, was not mistaken either.   She knew from the
first day how matters stood in the beginning, because
she was as observing as she was dissimulating; then,
thanks to means less hypothetic, she had always had
the habit of making those abominable inquiries which
are natural, we venture to avow, to nine women out of
ten!   And how many men are women, too, on this
point, as said the fabulist.   At school Lydia was one
of those who ascended to the dormitory, or who re-

entered the study to rummage in the cupboards and open trunks of her companions. When mature, never had a sealed letter passed through her hands without her having ingeniously managed to read through the envelope, or at least to guess from the postmark, the seal, the handwriting of the address, who was the author of it. The instinct of curiosity was so strong that she could not refrain, at a telegraph office, from glancing over the shoulders of the persons before her, to learn the contents of their despatches. She never had her hair dressed or made her toilette without minutely questioning her maid as to the goings-on in the pantry and the antechamber. It was through a story of that kind that she learned the altercation between Florent and Gorka in the vestibule, which proves, between parentheses, that these espionages by the aid of servants are often efficacious. But they reveal a native baseness, which will not recoil before any piece of villainy.

When Madame Maitland suspected the *liaison* of Madame Steno and her husband, she no more hesitated to open the latter's secretary than she later hesitated to open the desk of her brother. The correspondence which she read in that way was of a nature which exasperated her desire for vengeance almost to frenzy. For not only did she acquire the evidence of a happiness shared by them which humiliated in her the woman barren in all senses of the word, a stranger to voluptuousness as well as to maternity, but she gathered from it numerous proofs that the Countess cherished, with regard to her, a scorn of race as absolute as if Venice had been a city of the United States. . . . That part of the Adriatic abounds in prejudices of blood, as do all countries which serve as confluents for every nation. It is sufficient to convince one's self of it, to have heard a Venetian treat of the Slavs as *Cziavoni,* and the Levantines as *Gregugni.*

Madame Steno, in those letters she had written with all the familiarity and all the liberty of passion, never called Lydia anything but *La Morettina,* and by a very strange illogicalness never was the name of the brother of *La Morettina* mentioned without a formula of friendship. As the mistress treated Florent in that manner, it must be that she apprehended no hostility on the part of her lover's brother-in-law. Lydia understood it only too well, as well as the fresh proof of Florent's sentiments for Lincoln. Once more he gave precedence to the friend over the sister, and on what an occasion! The most secret wounds in her inmost being bled as she read. The success of Alba's portrait, which promised to be a masterpiece, ended by precipitating her into a fierce and abominable action. She resolved to denounce Madame Steno's new love to the betrayed lover, and she wrote the twelve letters, wisely calculated and graduated, which had indeed determined Gorka's return. His return had even been delayed too long to suit the relative of Iago, who had decided to aim at Madame Steno through Alba by a still more criminal denunciation. Lydia was in that state of exasperation in which the vilest weapons seem the best, and she included innocent Alba in her hatred for Maitland, on account of the portrait, a turn of sentiment which will show that it was envy by which that soul was poisoned above all. Ah, what bitter delight the simultaneous success of that double infamy had procured for her! What savage joy, mingled with bitterness and ecstacy, had been hers the day before, on witnessing the nervousness of poor Alba and the suppressed fury of Boleslas!

In her mind she had seen Maitland provoked by the rival whom she knew to be as adroit with the sword as with the pistol. She would not have been the great-grandchild of a slave of Louisiana, if she had not combined with the natural energy of her hatreds a considerable amount of superstition. A fortune-teller had once foretold, from the lines in her palm, that she would cause the violent death of some person. "It will be he," she had thought, glancing at her husband with a horrible tremor of hope. . . . And now she had the proof, the indisputable proof, that her plot for vengeance was to terminate in the danger of another. Of what other?

The letter and will made by Florent disclosed to her the threat of a fatal duel suspended over the head which was the dearest to her. So she had driven to a tragical encounter the only being whom she loved. . . . The disappointment of the heart in which palpitated the wild energies of a bestial atavism was so sudden, so acute, so dolorous, that she uttered an inarticulate cry, leaning upon her brother's desk, and, in the face of those sheets of paper which had revealed so much, she repeated:

"He is going to fight a duel! He! . . . And I am the cause!" . . . Then, returning the letters and the will to the drawer, she closed it and rose, saying aloud: "No. It shall not be. I will prevent it, if I have to cast myself between them. I do not wish it! I do not wish it!"

It was easy to utter such words. But the execution of them was less easy. Lydia knew it, for she had no sooner uttered that vow than she wrung her hands in despair—those weak hands which Madame Steno compared in one of her letters to the paws of a monkey, the fingers were so supple and so long—and she uttered this despairing cry: "But how?" . . . which so many criminals have uttered before the issue, unexpected and fatal to them, of their shrewdest calculations. The poet has sung it in the words which relate the story of all our faults, great and small:

> "The gods are just, and of our pleasant vices
> Make instruments to plague us."

(*Les Dieux sont justes, et des vices où nous nous plaisons, ils font des outils à nous torturer.*) . . . It is necessary that the belief in the equity of an incomprehensible judge be well grounded in us, for the strongest minds are struck by a sinister apprehension when they have to brave the chance of a misfortune absolutely merited. The remembrance of the soothsayer's prediction suddenly occurred to Lydia. She uttered another cry, rubbing her hands like a somnambulist. She saw her brother's blood flowing. . . . No, the duel should not take place! But how to prevent it? How—how? she repeated. Florent was not at home. She could, therefore, not implore him. If he should return, would there still be time? Lincoln was not at home. Where was he? Perhaps at a rendezvous with Madame Steno.

The image of that handsome idol of love clasped in the painter's arms, plunged in the abyss of intoxication which her ardent letters described, was presented to the mind of the jealous wife. What irony to perceive thus those two lovers, whom she had wished to strike, with the ecstacy of bliss in their eyes! Lydia would have liked to tear out their eyes, his as well as hers, and to trample them beneath her heel. A fresh flood of hatred filled her heart. God! how she hated them, and with what a powerless hatred! But her time would come; another need pressed sorely— to prevent the meeting of the following day, to save her brother. To whom should she turn, however? To Dorsenne? To Montfanon? To Baron Hafner? To Peppino Ardea? She thought by turns of the four personages whose almost simultaneous visits had caused her to believe that they were the seconds of the two champions. She rejected them, one after the other, comprehending that none of them possessed enough authority to arrange the affair. Her thoughts finally reverted to Florent's adversary, to Boleslas Gorka, whose wife was her friend and whom she had always found so courteous. What if she should ask him to spare her brother? It was not Florent against whom the discarded lover bore a grudge. Would he not be touched by her tears? Would he not tell her what had led to the quarrel and what she should ask of her brother that the quarrel might be conciliated? Could she not obtain from him the promise to discharge his weapon in the air, if the duel was with pistols, or, if it was with swords, simply to disarm his enemy?

Like nearly all persons unversed in the art, she believed in infallible fencers, in marksmen who never missed their aim, and she had also ideas profoundly, absolutely inexact on the relations of one man with another in the matter of an insult. But how can women admit that inflexible rigor in certain cases, which forms the foundation of manly relations, when they themselves allow of a similar rigor neither in their arguments with men, nor in their discussions among themselves? Accustomed always to appeal from convention to instinct and from reason to sentiment, they are, in the face of certain laws, be they those of justice or of honor, in a state of incomprehension worse than ignorance. A duel, for example, appears to them like an arbitrary drama, which the wish of one of those concerned can change at his fancy. Ninety-nine women out of a hundred would think like Lydia Maitland of hastening to the adversary of the man they love, to demand, to beg for his life. Let us add, however, that the majority would not carry out that thought. They would confine themselves to sewing in the vest of their beloved some blessed medal, in recommending him to the Providence, which, for them, is still the favoritism of heaven. Lydia felt that if ever Florent should learn of her step with regard to Gorka, he would be very indignant. But who would tell him? She was agitated by one of those fevers of fear and of remorse which are too acute not to act, cost what it might. Her carriage was announced, and she entered it, giving the address of the Palazzetto Doria. In what terms should she approach the man to whom she was about to pay that audacious and absurd visit? Ah, what mattered it? The circumstances would inspire her. Her desire to cut short the duel was so strong that she did not doubt of success.

She was greatly disappointed when the footman at the palace told her that the Count had gone out, while at the same moment a voice interrupted him with a gay laugh. It was Countess Maud Gorka, who, returning from her walk with her little boy, recognized Lydia's coupé, and who said to her:

"What a lucky idea I had of returning a little sooner. I see you were afraid of a storm, as you drove out in a closed carriage. Will you come upstairs a moment?" And, perceiving that the young woman, whose hand she had taken, was trembling: "What ails you? I should think you were ill! You do not feel well? My God, what ails her! She is ill, Luc," she added, turning to her son; "run to my room and bring me the large bottle of English salts; Rose knows which one. Go, go quickly."

"It is nothing," replied Lydia, who had indeed closed her eyes as if on the point of swooning. "See, I am better already. I think I will return home; it will be wiser."

"I shall not leave you," said Maud, seating herself, too, in the carriage; and, as they handed her the bottle of salts, she made Madame Maitland inhale it, talking to her the while as to a sick child: "Poor little thing!

How her cheeks burn! And you pay visits in this state. It is very venturesome! Rue Leopardi," she called to the coachman, "quickly."

The carriage rolled away, and Madame Gorka continued to press the tiny hands of Lydia, to whom she gave the tender name, so ironical under the circumstances, of "Poor little one!" Maud was one of those women like whom England produces many, for the honor of that healthy and robust British civilization, who are at once all energy and all goodness. As large and stout as Lydia was slender, she would rather have borne her to her bed in her vigorous arms than to have abandoned her in the troubled state in which she had surprised her. Not less practical and, as her compatriots say, as matter-of-fact as she was charitable, she began to question her friend on the symptoms which had preceded that attack, when with astonishment she saw that altered face contract, tears gushing from the closed eyes, and the fragile form convulsed by sobs. Lydia had a nervous attack caused by anxiety, by the fresh disappointment of Boleslas's absence from home, and no doubt, too, by the gentleness with which Maud addressed her, and tearing her handkerchief with her white teeth, she moaned:

"No, I am not ill. But it is that thought which I can not bear. No, I can not. Ah, it is maddening!" And turning toward her companion, she in her turn pressed her hands, saying: "But you know nothing! You suspect nothing! It is that which maddens me, when I see you tranquil, calm, happy, as if the minutes were not valuable, every one, to-day, to you as well as to me. For if one is my brother, the other is your husband; and you love him. You must love him, to have pardoned him for what you have pardoned him."

She had spoken in a sort of delirium, brought about by her extreme nervous excitement, and she had uttered, she, usually so dissembling, her very deepest thought. She did not think she was giving Madame Gorka any information by that allusion, so direct, to the *liaison* of Boleslas with Madame Steno. She was persuaded, as was entire Rome, that Maud knew of her husband's infidelities, and that she tolerated them by one of those heroic sacrifices which maternity justifies. How many women have immolated thus their wifely pride to maintain the domestic relation which the father shall at least not desert officially! All Rome was mistaken, and Lydia Maitland was to have an unexpected proof. Not a suspicion that such an intrigue could unite her husband with the mother of her best friend had ever entered the thoughts of Boleslas's wife. But to account for that, it is necessary to admit, as well, and to comprehend the depth of innocence of which, notwithstanding her twenty-six years, the beautiful and healthy Englishwoman, with her eyes so clear, so frank, was possessed.

She was one of those persons who command the respect of the boldest of men, and before whom the most dissolute women exercised care. She might have seen the freedom of Madame Steno without being disillusioned. She had only a liking for acquaintances and positive conversation. She was very intellectual, but without any desire to study character.

Dorsenne said of her, with more justness than he thought: "Madame Boleslas Gorka is married to a man who has never been presented to her," meaning by that, that first of all she had no idea of her husband's character, and then of the treason of which she was the victim. However, the novelist was not altogether right. Boleslas's infidelity was of too long standing for the woman passionately, religiously loyal, who was his wife, not to have suffered by it. But there was an abyss between such sufferings and the intuition of a determined fact such as that which Lydia had just mentioned, and such a suspicion was so far from Maud's thoughts that her companion's words only aroused in her astonishment at the mysterious danger of which Lydia's troubles was a proof more eloquent still than her words.

"Your brother? My husband?" she said. "I do not understand you."

"Naturally," replied Lydia, "he has hidden all from you, as Florent hid all from me. Well! They are going to fight a duel, and to-morrow morning. . . . Do not tremble, in your turn," she continued, twining her arms around Maud Gorka. "We shall be two to prevent the terrible affair, and we shall prevent it."

"A duel? To-morrow morning?" repeated Maud, in affright. "Boleslas fights to-morrow with your brother? No, it is impossible. Who told you so? How do you know it?"

"I read the proof of it with my eyes," replied Lydia. "I read Florent's will. I read the letter which he prepared for Maitland and for me in case of accident. . . .

Should I be in the state in which you see me if it were not true?"

"Oh, I believe you!" cried Maud, pressing her hands to her eyelids, as if to shut out a horrible sight. "But where can they be seen? Boleslas has been here scarcely any of the time for two days. What is there between them? What have they said to one another? One does not risk one's life for nothing when he has, like Boleslas, a wife and a son. Answer me, I conjure you. Tell me all. I desire to know all. What is there at the bottom of this duel?"

"What could there be but a woman?" interrupted Lydia, who put into the two last words more savage scorn than if she had publicly spit in Caterina Steno's face. But that fresh access of anger fell before the surprise caused her by Madame Gorka's reply.

"What woman? I understand you still less than I did just now."

"When we are at home I will speak," ... replied Lydia, after having looked at Maud with a surprised glance, which was in itself the most terrible reply. The two women were silent. It was Maud who now required the sympathy of friendship, so greatly had the words uttered by Lydia startled her. The companion whose arm rested upon hers in that carriage, and who had inspired her with such pity fifteen minutes before, now rendered her fearful. She seemed to be seated by the side of another person. In the creature whose thin nostrils were dilated with passion, whose mouth was distorted with bitterness, whose eyes sparkled with anger, she no longer recognized little

Madame Maitland, so taciturn, so reserved that she was looked upon as insignificant. What had that voice, usually so musical, told her; that voice so suddenly become harsh, and which had already revealed to her the great danger suspended over Boleslas? To what woman had that voice alluded, and what meant that sudden reticence?

Lydia was fully aware of the grief into which she would plunge Maud without the slightest premeditation. For a moment she thought it almost a crime to say more to a woman thus deluded. But at the same time she saw in the revelation two certain results. In undeceiving Madame Gorka she made a mortal enemy for Madame Steno, and, on the other hand, never would the woman so deeply in love with her husband allow him to fight for a former mistress. So, when they both entered the small salon of the Moorish mansion, Lydia's resolution was taken. She was determined to conceal nothing of what she knew from unhappy Maud, who asked her, with a beating heart, and in a voice choked by emotion:

"Now, will you explain to me what you want to say?"

"Question me," replied the other; "I will answer you. I have gone too far to draw back."

"You claimed that a woman was the cause of the duel between your brother and my husband?"

"I am sure of it," replied Lydia.

"What is that woman's name?"

"Madame Steno."

"Madame Steno?" repeated Maud. "Catherine Steno is the cause of that duel? How?"

"Because she is my husband's mistress," replied Lydia, brutally; "because she has been your husband's, because Gorka came here, mad with jealousy, to provoke Lincoln, and because he met my brother, who prevented him from entering. . . . They quarrelled, I know not in what manner. But I know the cause of the duel. . . . Am I right, yes or no, in telling you they are to fight about that woman?"

"My husband's mistress?" cried Maud. "You say Madame Steno has been my husband's mistress? It is not true. You lie! You lie! You lie! I do not believe it."

"You do not believe me?" said Lydia, shrugging her shoulders. "As if I had the least interest in deceiving you; as if one would lie when the life of the only being one loves in the world is in the balance! For I have only my brother, and perhaps to-morrow I shall no longer have him. . . . But you shall believe me. I desire that we both hate that woman, that we both be avenged upon her, as we both do not wish the duel to take place—the duel of which, I repeat, she is the cause, the sole cause. . . . You do not believe me? Do you know what caused your husband to return? You did not expect him; confess! It was I—I, do you hear—who wrote him what Steno and Lincoln were doing; day after day I wrote about their love, their meetings, their bliss. Ah, I was sure it would not be in vain, and he returned. Is that a proof?"

"You did not do that?" cried Madame Gorka, recoiling with horror. "It was infamous."

"Yes, I did it," replied Lydia, with savage pride,

[ 256 ]

"and why not? It was my right when she took my husband from me. You have only to return and to look in the place where Gorka keeps his letters. You will certainly find those I wrote, and others, I assure you, from that woman. For she has a mania for letter-writing. . . . Do you believe me now, or will you repeat that I have lied?"

"Never," returned Maud, with sorrowful indignation upon her lovely, loyal face, "no, never will I descend to such baseness."

"Well, I will descend for you," said Lydia. "What you do not dare to do, I will dare, and you will ask me to aid you in being avenged. Come," and, seizing the hand of her stupefied companion, she drew her into Lincoln's studio, at that moment unoccupied. She approached one of those Spanish desks, called *bargenos*, and she touched two small panels, which disclosed, on opening, a secret drawer, in which were a package of letters, which she seized. Maud Gorka watched her with the same terrified horror with which she would have seen some one killed and robbed. That honorable soul revolted at the scene in which her mere presence made of her an accomplice. But at the same time she was a prey, as had been her husband several days before, to that maddening appetite to know the truth, which becomes, in certain forms of doubt, a physical need, as imperious as hunger and thirst, and she listened to Florent's sister, who continued:

"Will it be a proof when you have seen the affair written in her own hand? Yes," she continued, with

17          [ 257 ]

cruel irony, "she loves correspondence, our fortunate rival. Justice must be rendered her that she may make no more avowals. She writes as she feels. It seems that the successor was jealous of his predecessor. . . . See, is this a proof this time?" . . . And, after having glanced at the first letters as a person familiar with them, she handed one of those papers to Maud, who had not the courage to avert her eyes. What she saw written upon that sheet drew from her a cry of anguish. She had, however, only read ten lines, which proved how much mistaken psychological Dorsenne was in thinking that Maitland was ignorant of the former relations between his mistress and Gorka. Countess Steno's grandeur, that which made a courageous woman almost a heroine in her passions, was an absolute sincerity and disgust for the usual pettiness of flirtations. She would have disdained to deny to a new lover the knowledge of her past, and the semi-avowals, so common to women, would have seemed to her a cowardice still worse. She had not essayed to hide from Maitland what connection she had broken off for him, and it was upon one of those phrases, in which she spoke of it openly, that Madame Gorka's eyes fell:

"You will be pleased with me," she wrote, "and I shall no longer see in your dear blue eyes which I kiss, as I love them, that gleam of mistrust which troubles me. I have stopped the correspondence with Gorka. If you require it, I will even break with Maud, notwithstanding the reason you know of and which will render it difficult for me. But how can you be jealous yet? . . . Is not my frankness with regard to that *liaison* the surest guarantee that it is ended? Come, do not be jealous. Listen to what I know so well, that I felt I loved, and that my life began only on the day when you took me in your arms. The woman you have awakened in me, no one has known——"

"She writes well, does she not?" said Lydia, with a gleam of savage triumph in her eyes. "Do you believe me, now? . . . Do you see that we have the same interest to-day, a common affront to avenge? And we will avenge it. . . . Do you understand that you can not allow your husband to fight a duel with my brother? You owe that to me who have given you this weapon by which you hold him. . . . Threaten him with a divorce. Fortune is with you. The law will give you your child. I repeat, you hold him firmly. You will prevent the duel, will you not?"

"Ah! What do you think it matters to me now if they fight or not?" said Maud. "From the moment he deceived me was I not widowed? Do not approach me," she added, looking at Lydia with wild eyes, while a shudder of repulsion shook her entire frame. . . . "Do not speak to me. . . . I have as much horror of you as of him. . . . Let me go, let me leave here. . . . Even to feel myself in the same room with you fills me with horror. . . . Ah, what disgrace!"

She retreated to the door, fixing upon her informant a gaze which the other sustained, notwithstanding the scorn in it, with the gloomy pride of defiance. She went out repeating: "Ah, what disgrace!" without Lydia having addressed her, so greatly had surprise at the unexpected result of all her attempts paralyzed her. But the formidable creature lost no time in regret and repentance. She paused a few moments to think. Then, crushing in her nervous hand the letter she had shown Maud, at the risk of being discovered by her husband later, she said aloud:

"Coward! Lord, what a coward she is! She loves. She will pardon. Will there, then, be no one to aid me? No one to smite them in their insolent happiness." After meditating awhile, her face still more contracted, she placed the letter in the drawer, which she closed again, and half an hour later she summoned a *commissionaire*, to whom she intrusted a letter, with the order to deliver it immediately, and that letter was addressed to the inspector of police of the district. She informed him of the intended duel, giving him the names of the two adversaries and of the four seconds. If she had not been afraid of her brother, she would even that time have signed her name.

"I should have gone to work that way at first," said she to herself, when the door of the small salon closed behind the messenger to whom she had given her order personally. "The police know how to prevent them from fighting, even if I do not succeed with Florent. . . . As for him?" . . . and she looked at a portrait of Maitland upon the desk at which she had just been writing. "Were I to tell him what is taking place. . . . No, I will ask nothing of him. . . . I hate him too much.". . . And she concluded with a fierce smile, which disclosed her teeth at the corners of her mouth:

"It is all the same. It is necessary that Maud Gorka work with me against her. There is some one whom she will not pardon, and that is . . . Madame Steno." And, in spite of her uneasiness, the wicked woman trembled with delight at the thought of her work.

# CHAPTER VIII

## ON THE GROUND

HEN Maud Gorka left the house on the Rue Leopardi she walked on at first rapidly, blindly, without seeing, without hearing anything, like a wounded animal which runs through the thicket to escape danger, to escape its wounds, to escape itself. It was a little more than half-past three o'clock when the unhappy woman hastened from the studio, unable to bear near her the presence of Lydia Maitland, of that sinister worker of vengeance who had so cruelly revealed to her, with such indisputable proofs, the atrocious affair, the long, the infamous, the inexpiable treason.

It was almost six o'clock before Maud Gorka really regained consciousness. A very common occurrence aroused her from the somnambulism of suffering in which she had wandered for two hours. The storm which had threatened since noon at length broke. Maud, who had scarcely heeded the first large drops, was forced to seek shelter when the clouds suddenly burst, and she took refuge at the right extremity of the colonnade of St. Peter's. How had she gone that far? She did not know herself precisely. She remembered vaguely that she had wandered through a labyrinth of small streets, had crossed the Tiber—no doubt by the Garibaldi bridge—had passed through a large garden —doubtless the *Janicule*, since she had walked along a portion of the ramparts. She had left the city by the Porte de Saint-Pancrace, to follow by that of Cavallegieri the sinuous line of the Urban walls.

That corner of Rome, with a view of the pines of the Villa Pamfili on one side, and on the other the back part of the Vatican, serves as a promenade during the winter for the few cardinals who go in search of the afternoon sun, certain there of meeting only a few strangers. In the month of May it is a desert, scorched by the sun, which glows upon the brick, discolored by two centuries of that implacable heat which caresses the scales of the green and gray lizards about to crawl between the bees of Pope Urbain VIII's escutcheon of the Barberini family. Madame Gorka's instinct had at least served her in leading her upon a route on which she met no one. Now the sense of reality returned. She recognized the objects around her, and that framework, so familiar to her piety of fervent Catholicism, the enormous square, the obelisk of Sixte-Quint in the centre, the fountains, the circular portico crowned with bishops and martyrs, the palace of the Vatican at the corner, and yonder the façade of the large papal cathedral, with the Saviour and the apostles erect upon the august pediment.

On any other occasion in life the pious young woman would have seen in the chance which led her thither, almost unconsciously, an influence from above, an invitation to enter the church, there to ask the strength to suffer of the God who said: "Let him who wishes follow me, let him renounce all, let him take up his cross and follow me!" But she was passing through that first bitter paroxysm of grief in which it is impossible to pray, so greatly does the revolt of nature cry out within us. Later, we may recognize the hand of Providence in the trial imposed upon us. We see at first only the terrible injustice of fate, and we tremble in the deepest recesses of our souls with rebellion at the blow from which we bleed. That which rendered the rebellion more invincible and more fierce in Maud, was the suddenness of the mortal blow.

Daily some pure, honest woman, like her, acquires the proof of the treason of a husband whom she has not ceased to love. Ordinarily, the indisputable proof is preceded by a long period of suspicion. The faithless one neglects his hearth. A change takes place in his daily habits. Various hints reveal to the outraged wife the trace of a rival, which woman's jealousy distinguishes with a scent as certain as that of a dog which finds a stranger in the house. And, finally, although there is in the transition from doubt to certainty a laceration of the heart, it is at least the laceration of a heart prepared. That preparation, that adaptation, so to speak, of her soul to the truth, Maud had been deprived of. The care taken by Madame Steno to strengthen the friendship between her and Alba had suppressed the slightest signs. Boleslas had no need to change his domestic life in order to see his

mistress at his convenience and in an intimacy entertained, provoked, by his wife herself. The wife, too,
had been totally, absolutely deceived. She had assisted in her husband's adultery with one of those
illusions so complete that it seemed improbable to the
indifferent and to strangers. The awakening from
such illusions is the most terrible. That man whom
society considered a complaisant husband, that woman
who seemed so indulgent a wife, suddenly find that
they have committed a murder or a suicide, to the great
astonishment of the world which, even then, hesitates
to recognize in that access of folly the proof, the blow,
more formidable, more instantaneous in its ravages,
than those of love—sudden disillusion. When the disaster is not interrupted by acts of violence, it causes an
irreparable destruction of the youthfulness of the soul,
it is the idea instilled in us forever that all can betray,
since we have been betrayed in that manner. It is
for years, for life, sometimes, that powerlessness to be
affected, to hope, to believe, which caused Maud
Gorka to remain, on that afternoon, leaning against
the pedestal of a column, watching the rain fall, instead
of ascending to the Basilica, where the confessional offers pardon for all sins and the remedy for all sorrows.
Alas! It was consolation simply to kneel there, and
the poor woman was only in the first stage of Calvary.

She watched the rain fall, and she found a savage
comfort in the formidable character of the storm, which
seemed like a cataclysm of nature, to such degree did
the flash of the lightning and the roar of the thunder
mingle with the echoes of the vast palace beneath the

lash of the wind. Forms began to take shape in her mind, after the whirlwind of blind suffering in which she felt herself borne away after the first glance cast upon that fatal letter. Each word rose before her eyes, so feverish that she closed them with pain. The last two years of her life, those which had bound her to Countess Steno, returned to her thoughts, illuminated by a brilliance which drew from her constantly these words, uttered with a moan: *How could he?* She saw Venice and their sojourn in the villa to which Boleslas had conducted her after the death of their little girl, in order that there, in the restful atmosphere of the lagoon, she might overcome the keen paroxysm of pain.

How very kind and delicate Madame Steno had been at that time; at least how kind she had seemed, and how delicate likewise, comprehending her grief and sympathizing with it. . . . Their superficial relations had gradually ripened into friendship. Then, no doubt, the treason had begun. The purloiner of love had introduced herself under cover of the pity in which Maud had believed. Seeing the Countess so generous, she had treated as calumny the slander of the world relative to a person capable of such touching kindness of heart. And it was at that moment that the false woman took Boleslas from her! A thousand details recurred to her which at the time she had not understood; the sails of the two lovers in the gondola, which she had not even thought of suspecting; a visit which Boleslas had made to Piove and from which he only returned the following day, giving as a pretext a missed train; words uttered aside on the balcony of the Palais Steno at night, while she talked with Alba. Yes, it was at Venice that their adultery began, before her who had divined nothing, her whose heart was filled with inconsolable regret for her lost darling! *Ah, how could he?* she moaned again, and the visions multiplied.

In her mind were then opened all the windows which Gorka's perfidity and the Countess's as well, had sealed with such care. She saw again the months which followed their return to Rome, and that mode of life so convenient for both. How often had she walked out with Alba, thus freeing the mother and the husband from the only surveillance annoying to them. What did the lovers do during those hours? How many times on returning to the Palazzetto Doria had she found Catherine Steno in the library, seated on the divan beside Boleslas, and she had not mistrusted that the woman had come, during her absence, to embrace that man, to talk to him of love, to give herself to him, without doubt, with the charm of villainy and of danger! She remembered the episode of their meeting at Bayreuth the previous summer, when she went to England alone with her son, and when her husband undertook to conduct Alba and the Countess from Rome to Bavaria. They had all met at Nuremberg. The apartments of the hotel in which the meeting took place became again very vivid in Maud's memory, with Madame Steno's bedroom adjoining that of Boleslas's.

The vision of their caresses, enjoyed in the liberty of the night, while innocent Alba slept near by, and when she rolled away in a carriage with little Luc, drew

[ 267 ]

from her this cry once more: *"Ah, how could he!"*. . .
And immediately that vision awoke in her the remembrance of her husband's recent return. She saw
him traversing Europe on the receipt of an anonymous
letter, to reach that woman's side twenty-four hours
sooner. What a proof of passion was the frenzy
which had not allowed him any longer to bear doubt
and absence! . . . Did he love the mistress who did
not even love him, since she had deceived him with
Maitland? And he was going to fight a duel on her
account! . . . Jealousy, at that moment, wrung the
wife's heart with a pang still stronger than that of indignation. She, the strong Englishwoman, so large, so
robust, almost masculine in form, mentally compared
herself with the supple Italian with her form so round,
with her gestures so graceful, her hands so delicate, her
feet so dainty; compared herself with the creature of
desire, whose every movement implied a secret wave of
passion, and she ceased her cry—*"Ah, how could he?"*
—at once. She had a clear knowledge of the power of
her rival.

It is indeed a supreme agony for an honorable
woman, who loves, to feel herself thus degraded by the
mere thought of the intoxication her husband has
tasted in arms more beautiful, more caressing, more
entwining than hers. It was, too, a signal for the
return of will to the tortured but proud soul. Disgust possessed her, so violent, so complete, for the
atmosphere of falsehood and of sensuality in which
Boleslas had lived two years, that she drew herself up,
becoming again strong and implacable. Braving the

storm, she turned in the direction of her home, with this resolution as firmly rooted in her mind as if she had deliberated for months and months.

"I will not remain with that man another day. To-morrow I will leave for England with my son."

How many, in a similar situation, have uttered such vows, to abjure them when they find themselves face to face with the man who has betrayed them, and whom they love. Maud was not of that order. Certainly she loved dearly the seductive Boleslas, wedded against her parents' will the perfidious one for whom she had sacrificed all, living far from her native land and her family for years, because it pleased him, breathing, living, only for him and for their boy. But there was within her—as her long, square chin, her short nose and the strength of her brow revealed—the force of inflexibility—which is met with in characters of an absolute uprightness. Love, with her, could be stifled by disgust, or, rather, she considered it degrading to continue to love one whom she scorned, and, at that moment, it was supreme scorn which reigned in her heart. She had, in the highest degree, the great virtue which is found wherever there is nobility, and of which the English have made the basis of their moral education—the religion, the fanaticism of loyalty. She had always grieved on discovering the wavering nature of Boleslas. But if she had observed in him, with sorrow, any exaggerations of language, any artificial sentiment, a dangerous suppleness of mind, she had pardoned him those defects with the magnanimity of love, attributing them to a defective training. Gorka at a

very early age had witnessed a stirring family drama—
his mother and his father lived apart, while neither the
one nor the other had the exclusive guidance of the
child. How could she find indulgence for the shameful hypocrisy of two years' standing, for the villainy of
that treachery practised at the domestic hearth, for
the continued, voluntary disloyalty of every day, every
hour? Though Maud experienced, in the midst of her
despair, the sort of calmness which proves a firm and
just resolution, when she reëntered the Palazzetto Doria
—what a drama had been enacted in her heart since
her going out!—and it was in a voice almost as calm as
usual that she asked: "Is the Count at home?"

What did she experience when the servant, after
answering her in the affirmative, added: "Madame
and Mademoiselle Steno, too, are awaiting Madame in
the salon." At the thought that the woman who had
stolen from her her husband was there, the betrayed
wife felt her blood boil, to use a common but expressive
phrase. It was very natural that Alba's mother should
call upon her, as was her custom. It was still more
natural for her to come there that day. For very
probably a report of the duel the following day had
reached her. Her presence, however, and at that moment, aroused in Maud a feeling of indignation so
impassioned that her first impulse was to enter, to
drive out Boleslas's mistress as one would drive out a
servant surprised thieving. Suddenly the thought of
Alba presented itself to her mind, of that sweet and
pure Alba, of that soul as pure as her name, of her
whose dearest friend she was. Since the dread revela-

tion she had thought several times of the young girl. But her deep sorrow having absorbed all the power of her soul, she had not been able to feel such friendship for the delicate and pretty child. At the thought of ejecting her rival, as she had the right to do, that sentiment stirred within her. A strange pity flooded her soul, which caused her to pause in the centre of the large hall, ornamented with statues and columns, which she was in the act of crossing. She called the servant just as he was about to put his hand on the knob of the door. The analogy between her situation and that of Alba struck her very forcibly. She experienced the sensation which Alba had so often experienced in connection with Fanny, sympathy with a sorrow so like her own. She could not give her hand to Madame Steno after what she had discovered, nor could she speak to her otherwise than to order her from her house. And to utter before Alba one single phrase, to make one single gesture which would arouse her suspicions, would be too implacable, too iniquitous a vengeance! She turned toward the door which led to her own room, bidding the servant ask his master to come thither. She had devised a means of satisfying her just indignation without wounding her dear friend, who was not responsible for the fact that the two culprits had taken shelter behind her innocence.

Having entered the small, pretty *boudoir* which led into her bedroom, she seated herself at her desk, on which was a photograph of Madame Steno, in a group consisting of Boleslas, Alba, and herself. The photograph smiled with a smile of superb insolence, which suddenly reawakened in the outraged woman her frenzy of rancor, interrupted or rather suspended for several moments by pity. She took the frame in her hands, she cast it upon the ground, trampling the glass beneath her feet, then she began to write, on the first blank sheet, one of those notes which passion alone dares to pen, which does not draw back at every word:

"I know all. For two years you have been my husband's mistress. Do not deny it. I have read the confession written by your own hand. I do not wish to see nor to speak to you again. Never again set foot in my house. On account of your daughter I have not driven you out to-day. A second time I shall not hesitate."

She was just about to sign *Maud Gorka*, when the sound of the door opening and shutting caused her to turn. Boleslas was before her. Upon his face was an ambiguous expression, which exasperated the unhappy wife still more. Having returned more than an hour before, he had learned that Maud had accompanied to the Rue Leopardi Madame Maitland, who was ill, and he awaited her return with impatience, agitated by the thought that Florent's sister was no doubt ill owing to the duel of the morrow, and in that case, Maud, too, would know all. There are conversations and, above all, adieux which a man who is about to fight a duel always likes to avoid. Although he forced a smile, he no longer doubted. His wife's evident agitation could not be explained by any other cause. Could he divine that she had learned not only of the duel, but, too, of an intrigue that day ended and of which she had known nothing for two years? As she was silent, and as that silence embarrassed him, he tried, in order to keep him in countenance, to take her hand and kiss it, as was his custom. She repelled him with a look which he had never seen upon her face and said to him, handing him the sheet of paper lying before her:

"Do you wish to read this note before I send it to Madame Steno, who is in the salon with her daughter?"

Boleslas took the letter. He read the terrible lines, and he became livid. His agitation was so great that he returned the paper to his wife without replying, without attempting to prevent, as was his duty, the insult offered to his former mistress, whom he still loved to the point of risking his life for her. That man, so brave and so yielding at once, was overwhelmed by one of those surprises which put to flight all the powers of the mind, and he watched Maud slip the note into an envelope, write the address and ring. He heard her say to the servant:

"You will take this note to Countess Steno and you will excuse me to the ladies. . . . I feel too indisposed to receive any one. If they insist, you will reply that I have forbidden you to admit any one. You understand—any one."

The man took the note. He left the room and he had no doubt fulfilled his errand while the husband and wife stood there, face to face, neither of them breaking the formidable silence. They felt that the hour was a solemn one.

Never, since the day on which Cardinal Manning

18       [ 273 ]

had united their destinies in the chapel of Ardrahan
Castle, had they been engaged in a crisis so tragical.
Such moments lay bare the very depths of the character.   Courageous and noble, Maud did not think of
weighing her words.  She did not try to feed her jealousy, nor to accentuate the cruelty of the cause of the
insult which she had the right to launch at the man
toward whom that very morning she had been so confiding, so tender.   The baseness and the cruelty were
to remain forever unknown to the woman who no longer
hesitated as to the bold resolution she had made.   No.
That which she expected of the man whom she had
loved so dearly, of whom she had entertained so exalted an opinion, whom she had just seen fall so low,
was a cry of truth, an avowal in which she would find
the throb of a last remnant of honor.   If he were silent
it was not because he was preparing a denial.   The
tenor of Maud's letter left no doubt as to the nature of
the proofs she had in her hand, which she had there
no doubt.   How?   He did not ask himself that question, governed as he was by a phenomenon in which
was revealed to the full the singular complexity of his
nature.   The Slav's especial characteristic is a prodigious, instantaneous nervousness.   It seems that
those beings with the uncertain hearts have a faculty of
amplifying in themselves, to the point of absorbing the
heart altogether, states of partial, passing, and yet sincere emotion.   The intensity of their momentary excitement thus makes of them sincere comedians, who
speak to you as if they felt certain sentiments of an
exclusive order, to feel contradictory ones the day

after, with the same ardor, with the same untruthful-
ness, unjustly say the victims of those natures, so much
the more deceitful as they are more vibrating.

He suffered, indeed, on discovering that Maud had
been initiated into his criminal intrigue, but he suffered more for her than for himself. It was sufficient
for that suffering to occupy a few moments, a few
hours. It reinvested the personality of the impassioned and weak husband who loved his wife while
betraying her. There was, indeed, a shade of it in his
adventure, but a very slight shade. And yet, he did
not think he was telling an untruth, when he finally
broke the silence to say to her whom he had so long
deceived:

"You have avenged yourself with much severity,
Maud, but you had the right. . . . I do not know who
has informed you of an error which was very culpable,
very wrong, very unfortunate, too. . . . I know that I
have in Rome enemies bent upon my ruin, and I am
sure they have left me no means of defending myself.
. . . I have deceived you, and I have suffered."

He paused after those words, uttered with a tremor
of conviction which was not assumed. He had forgotten that ten minutes before he had entered the room
with the firm determination to hide his duel and its
cause from the woman for whose pardon he would at
that moment have sacrificed his life without hesitation.
He continued, in a voice softened by affection: "Whatever they have told you, whatever you have read, I
swear to you, you do not know all."

"I know enough," interrupted Maud, "since I know

that you have been the lover of that woman, of the mother of my intimate friend, at my side, under my very eyes. . . . If you had suffered by that deception, as you say, you would not have waited to avow all to me until I held in my hands the undeniable proof of your infamy. . . . You have cast aside the mask, or, rather, I have wrested it from you. . . . I desire no more. . . . As for the details of the shameful story, spare me them. It was not to hear them that I re-entered a house every corner of which reminds me that I believed in you implicitly, and that you have betrayed me, not one day, but every day; that you betrayed me the day before yesterday, yesterday, this morning, an hour ago. . . . I repeat, that is sufficient."

"But it is not sufficient for me!" exclaimed Boleslas. "Yes, all you have just said is true, and I deserve to have you tell it to me. But that which you could not read in those letters shown to you, that which I have kept for two years in the depths of my heart, and which must now be told—is that, through all these fatal impulses, I have never ceased to love you. . . . Ah, do not recoil from me, do not look at me thus. . . . I feel it once more in the agony I have suffered since you are speaking to me; there is something within me that has never ceased being yours. That woman has been my aberration. She has had my madness, my senses, my passion, all the evil instincts of my being. . . . You have remained my idol, my affection, my religion. . . . If I lied to you it was because I knew that the day on which you would find out my fault I should see you before me, despairing and implacable as you now are, as I can not bear to have you be. Ah, judge me, condemn me, curse me; but know, but feel, that in spite of all I have loved you, I still love you."

Again he spoke with an enthusiasm which was not feigned. Though he had deceived her, he recognized only too well the value of the loyal creature before him, whom he feared he should lose. If he could not move her at the moment when he was about to fight a duel, when could he move her? So he approached her with the same gesture of suppliant and impassioned adoration which he employed in the early days of their marriage, and before his treason, when he had told her of his love. No doubt that remembrance thrust itself upon Maud and disgusted her, for it was with veritable horror that she again recoiled, replying:

"Be silent! That lie is the worst of all. It pains me. I blush for you, in seeing that you have not even the courage to acknowledge your fault. God is my witness, I should have respected you more, had you said: 'I have ceased loving you. I have taken a mistress. It was convenient for me to lie to you. I have lied. I have sacrificed all to my passion, my honor, my duties, my vows and you.' . . . Ah, speak to me like that, that I may have with you the sentiment of truth. . . . But that you dare to repeat to me words of tenderness after what you have done to me, inspires me with repulsion. It is too bitter."

"Yes," said Boleslas, "you think thus. True and simple as you are, how could you have learned to understand what a weak will is—a will which wishes and which does not, which rises and which falls? . . . And yet, if I had not loved you, what interest would I have in lying to you? Have I anything to conceal now? Ah, if you knew in what a position I am, on the eve of what day, I beseech you to believe that at least the best part of my being has never ceased to be yours!"

It was the strongest effort he could make to bring back the heart of his wife so deeply wounded—the allusion to his duel. For since she had not mentioned it to him, it was no doubt because she was still ignorant of it. He was once more startled by the reply she made, and which proved to him to what a degree indignation had paralyzed even her love. He resumed:

"Do you know it?"

"I know that you fight a duel to-morrow," said she, "and for your mistress, I know, too."

"It is not true," he exclaimed; "it is not for her."

"What?" asked Maud, energetically. "Was it not on her account that you went to the Rue Leopardi to provoke your rival? For she is not even true to you, and it is justice. Was it not on her account that you wished to enter the house, in spite of that rival's brother-in-law, and that a dispute arose between you, followed by this challenge? Was it not on her account, and to revenge yourself, that you returned from Poland, because you had received anonymous letters which told you all? And to know all has not disgusted you forever with that creature? . . . But if she had deigned to lie to you, she would have you still at her feet, and you dare to tell me that you love me when you have not even cared to spare me the affront of learning all

[ 278 ]

that villainy—all that baseness, all that disgrace— through some one else?"

"Who was it?" he asked. "Name that Judas to me, at least?"

"Do not speak thus," interrupted Maud, bitterly; "you have lost the right. . . . And then do not seek too far. . . . I have seen Madame Maitland to-day."

"Madame Maitland?" repeated Boleslas. "Did Madame Maitland denounce me to you? Did Madame Maitland write those anonymous letters?"

"She desired to be avenged," replied Maud, adding: "She has the right, since your mistress robbed her of her husband."

"Well, I, too, will be avenged!" exclaimed the young man. "I will kill that husband for her, after I have killed her brother. I will kill them both, one after the other.". . . His mobile countenance, which had just expressed the most impassioned of supplications, now expressed only hatred and rage, and the same change took place in his immoderate sensibility. "Of what use is it to try to settle matters?" he continued. "I see only too well all is ended between us. Your pride and your rancor are stronger than your love. If it had been otherwise, you would have begged me not to fight, and you would only have reproached me, as you have the right to do, I do not deny. . . . But from the moment that you no longer love me, woe to him whom I find in my path! Woe to Madame Maitland and to those she loves!"

"This time at least you are sincere," replied Maud, with renewed bitterness. "Do you think I have not suffered sufficient humiliation? Would you like me to supplicate you not to fight for that creature? And do you not feel the supreme outrage which that encounter is to me? Moreover," she continued with tragical solemnity, "I did not summon you to have with you a conversation as sad as it is useless, but to tell you my resolution. . . . I hope that you will not oblige me to resort for its execution to the means which the law puts in my power?"

"I don't deserve to be spoken to thus," said Boleslas, haughtily.

"I will remain here to-night," resumed Maud, without heeding that reply, "for the last time. To-morrow evening I shall leave for England."

"You are free," said he, with a bow.

"And I shall take my son with me," she added.

"*Our* son!" he replied, with the composure of a man overcome by an access of tenderness and who controls himself. "That? No. I forbid it."

"You forbid it?" said she. "Very well, we will appeal it. I knew that you would force me," she continued, haughtily, in her turn, "to have recourse to the law. . . . But I shall not recoil before anything. In betraying me as you have done, you have also betrayed our child. I will not leave him to you. You are not worthy of him."

"Listen, Maud," said Boleslas, sadly, after a pause, "remember that it is perhaps the last time we shall meet. . . . To-morrow, if I am killed, you shall do as you like. . . . If I live, I promise to consent to any arrangement that will be just. . . . What I ask of you is—and I have the right, notwithstanding my faults—in the name of our early years of wedded life, in the name of that son himself, to leave me in a different way, to have a feeling, I don't say of pardon, but of pity."

"Did you have it for me," she replied, "when you were following your passion by way of my heart? No!". . . And she walked before him in order to reach the door, fixing upon him eyes so haughty that he involuntarily lowered his. "You have no longer a wife and I have no longer a husband. . . . I am no Madame Maitland; I do not avenge myself by means of anonymous letters nor by denunciation. . . . But to pardon you? . . . Never, do you hear, never!"

With those words she left the room, with those words into which she put all the indomitable energy of her character. . . . Boleslas did not essay to detain her. When, an hour after that horrible conversation, his valet came to inform him that dinner was served, the wretched man was still in the same place, his elbow on the mantelpiece and his forehead in his hand. He knew Maud too well to hope that she would change her determination, and there was in him, in spite of his faults, his folly and his complications, too much of the real gentleman to employ means of violence and to detain her forcibly, when he had erred so gravely. So she went thus. If, just before, he had exaggerated the expression of his feelings in saying, in thinking rather, that he had never ceased loving her, it was true that amid all his errors he had maintained for her an affection composed particularly of gratitude, remorse, esteem and, it must be said, of selfishness.

# PAUL BOURGET

He loved for the devotion of which he was absolutely sure, and then, like many husbands who deceive
an irreproachable wife, he was proud of her, while unfaithful to her. She seemed to him at once the dignity
and the charity of his life. She had remained in his
eyes the one to whom he could always return, the assured friend of moments of trial, the haven after the
tempest, the moral peace when he was weary of the
troubles of passion. What life would he lead when
she was gone? For she would go! Her resolution
was irrevocable. All dropped from his side at once.
The mistress, to whom he had sacrificed the noblest
and most loving heart, he had lost under circumstances
as abject as their two years of passion had been dishonorable. His wife was about to leave him, and
would he succeed in keeping his son? He had returned
to be avenged, and he had not even succeeded in meeting his rival. That being so impressionable had experienced, in the face of so many repeated blows, a disappointment so absolute that he gladly looked forward
to the prospect of exposing himself to death on the
following day, while at the same time a bitter flood
of rancor possessed him at the thought of all the persons concerned in his adventure. He would have
liked to crush Madame Steno and Maitland, Lydia and
Florent—Dorsenne, too—for having given him the
false word of honor, which had strengthened still more
his thirst for vengeance by calming it for a few hours.

His confusion of thoughts was only greater when he
was seated alone with his son at dinner. That morning
he had seen before him his wife's smiling face. The

absence ot ner whom at that moment he valued above all else was so sad to him that he ventured one last attempt, and after the meal he sent little Luc to see if his mother would receive him. The child returned with a reply in the negative. "Mamma is resting. . . . She does not wish to be disturbed." So the matter was irremissible. She would not see her husband until the morrow—if he lived. For vainly did Boleslas convince himself that afternoon that he had lost none of his skill in practising before his admiring seconds; a duel is always a lottery. He might be killed, and if the possibility of an eternal separation had not moved the injured woman, what prayer would move her? He saw her in his thoughts—her who at that moment, with blinds drawn, all lights subdued, endured in the semi-darkness that suffering which curses but does not pardon. Ah, but that sight was painful to him! And, in order that she might at least know how he felt, he took their son in his arms, and, pressing him to his breast, said: "If you see your mother before I do, you will tell her that we spent a very lonesome evening without her, will you not?"

"Why, what ails you?" exclaimed the child. "You have wet my cheeks with tears—you are weeping!"

"You will tell her that, too, promise me," replied the father, "so that she will take good care of herself, seeing how we love her."

"But," said the little boy, "she was not ill when we walked together after breakfast. She was so gay."

"I think, too, it will be nothing serious," replied Gorka. He was obliged to dismiss his son and to go out. He felt so horribly sad that he was physically afraid to remain alone in the house. But whither should he go? Mechanically he repaired to the club, although it was too early to meet many of the members there. He came upon Pietrapertosa and Cibo, who had dined there, and who, seated on one of the divans, were conferring in whispers with the gravity of two ambassadors discussing the Bulgarian or Egyptian question.

"You have a very nervous air," they said to Boleslas, "you who were in such good form this afternoon."

"Yes," said Cibo, "you should have dined with us as we asked you to."

"When one is to fight a duel," continued Pietrapertosa, sententiously, "one should see neither one's wife nor one's mistress. Madame Gorka suspects nothing, I hope?"

"Absolutely nothing," replied Boleslas; "you are right. I should have done better not to have left you. But, here I am. We will exorcise dismal thoughts by playing cards and supping!"

"By playing cards and supping!" exclaimed Pietrapertosa. And your hand? Think of your hand. . . . You will tremble, and you will miss your man."

"A light dinner," said Cibo, "to bed at ten o'clock, up at six-thirty, and two eggs with a glass of old port is the recipe Machault gives."

"And which I shall not follow," said Boleslas, adding: "I give you my word that if I had no other cause for care than this duel, you would not see me in this condition." He uttered that phrase in a tragical voice, the sincerity of which the two Italians felt. They looked at each other without speaking. They were too shrewd and too well aware of the simplest scandals of Rome not to have divined the veritable cause of the encounter between Florent and Boleslas. On the other hand, they knew the latter too well not to mistrust somewhat his attitudes. However, there was such simple emotion in his accent that they spontaneously pitied him, and, without another word, they no longer opposed the caprices of their strange client, whom they did not leave until two o'clock in the morning—and fortune favored them. For they found themselves at the end of a game, recklessly played, each the richer by two or three hundred louis apiece. That meant a few days more in Paris on the next visit. They, too, truly regretted their friend's luck, saying, on separating:

"I very much fear for him," said Cibo. "Such luck at gaming, the night before a duel—bad sign, very bad sign."

"So much the more so that *some one* was there," replied Pietrapertosa, making with his fingers the sign which conjures the *jettutura*. For nothing in the world would he have named the personages against whose evil eye he provided in that manner. But Cibo understood him, and, drawing from his trousers pocket his watch, which he fastened *à l'anglaise* by a safety chain to his belt, he pointed out among the charms a golden horn:

"I have not let it go this evening," said he. "The

worst is, that Gorka will not sleep, and then, his hand!"

Only the first of those two prognostics was to be verified. Returning home at that late hour, Boleslas did not even retire. He employed the remainder of the night in writing a long letter to his wife, one to his son, to be given to him on his eighteenth birthday, all in case of an accident. Then he examined his papers and he came upon the package of letters he had received from Madame Steno. Merely to re-read a few of them, and to glance at the portraits of that faithless mistress again, heightened his anger to such a degree that he enclosed the whole in a large envelope, which he addressed to Lincoln Maitland. He had no sooner sealed it than he shrugged his shoulders, saying: "Of what use?" He raised the piece of material which stopped up the chimney, and, placing the envelope on the fire-dogs, he set it on fire. He shook with the tongs the remains of that which had been the most ardent, the most complete passion of his life, and he relighted the flames under the pieces of paper still intact. The unreasonable employment of a night which might be his last had scarcely paled his face. But his friends, who knew him well, started on seeing him with that impassively sinister countenance when he alighted from his phaeton, at about eight o'clock, at the inn selected for the meeting. He had ordered the carriage the day before to allay his wife's suspicions by the pretense of taking one of his usual morning drives. In his mental confusion he had forgotten to give a counter order, and that accident caused him to escape the two policemen charged by the questorship to watch the Palazzetto Doria, on Lydia Maitland's denunciation. The hired victoria, which those agents took, soon lost track of the swift English horses, driven as a man of his character and of his mental condition could drive.

The precaution of Chapron's sister was, therefore, baffled in that direction, and she succeeded no better with regard to her brother, who, to avoid all explanation with Lincoln, had gone, under the pretext of a visit to the country, to dine and sleep at the hotel. It was there that Montfanon and Dorsenne met him to conduct him to the rendezvous in the classical landau. Hardly had they reached the eminence of the circus of Maxence, on the Appian Way, when they were passed by Boleslas's phaeton.

"You can rest very easy," said Montfanon to Florent. "How can one aim correctly when one tires one's arm in that way?"

That had been the only allusion to the duel made between the three men during the journey, which had taken about an hour. Florent talked as he usually did, asking all sorts of questions which attested his care for minute information—the most of which might be utilized by his brother-in-law—and the Marquis had replied by evoking, with his habitual erudition, several of the souvenirs which peopled that vast country, strewn with tombs, aqueducts, ruined villas, with the line of the Monts Albains enclosing them beyond.

Dorsenne was silent. It was the first affair at which he had assisted, and his nervous anxiety was extreme.

Tragical presentiments oppressed him, and at the same time he apprehended momentarily that, Montfanon's religious scruples reawakening, he would not only have to seek another second, but would have to defer a solution so near. However, the struggle which was taking place in the heart of the "old leaguer" between the gentleman and the Christian, was displayed during the drive only by an almost imperceptible gesture. As the carriage passed the entrance to the catacomb of St. Calixtus, the former soldier of the Pope turned away his head. Then he resumed the conversation with redoubled energy, to pause in his turn, however, when the landau took, a little beyond the Tomb of Cæcilia, a transverse road in the direction of the Ardeatine Way. It was there that *l'Osteria del tempo perso* was built, upon the ground belonging to Cibo, on which the duel was to take place.

Before *l'Osteria*, whose signboard was surmounted by the arms of Pope Innocent VIII, three carriages were already waiting—Gorka's phaeton, a landau which had brought Cibo, Pietrapertosa and the doctor, and a simple *botte*, in which a porter had come. That unusual number of vehicles seemed likely to attract the attention of riflemen out for a stroll, but Cibo answered for the discretion of the innkeeper, who indeed cherished for his master the devotion of vassal to lord, still common in Italy. The three newcomers had no need to make the slightest explanation. Hardly had they alighted from the carriage, when the maid conducted them through the hall, where at that moment two huntsmen were breakfasting, their guns between their knees, and who, like true Romans, scarcely deigned to glance at the strangers, who passed from the common hall into a small court, from that court, through a shed, into a large field enclosed by boards, with here and there a few pine-trees.

That rather odd duelling-ground had formerly served Cibo as a paddock. He had essayed to increase his slender income by buying at a bargain some jaded horses, which he intended fattening by means of rest and good fodder, and then selling to cabmen, averaging a small profit. The speculation having miscarried, the place was neglected and unused, save under circumstances similar to those of this particular morning.

"We have arrived last," said Montfanon, looking at his watch; "we are, however, five minutes ahead of time. Remember," he added in a low voice, turning to Florent, "to keep the body well in the background," these words being followed by other directions.

"Thanks," replied Florent, who looked at the Marquis and Dorsenne with a glance which he ordinarily had only for Lincoln, "and you know that, whatever may come, I thank you for all from the depths of my heart."

The young man put so much grace in that adieu, his courage was so simple, his sacrifice for his brother-in-law so magnanimous and natural—in fact, for two days both seconds had so fully appreciated the charm of that disposition, absolutely free from thoughts of self—that they pressed his hand with the emotion of true friends. They were themselves, moreover, interested, and at once began the series of preparations without which the *rôle* of assistant would be physically insupportable to persons endowed with a little sensibility. In experienced hands like those of Montfanon, Cibo and Pietrapertosa, such preliminaries are speedily arranged. The code is as exact as the step of a ballet. Twenty minutes after the entrance of the last arrivals, the two adversaries were face to face. The signal was given. The two shots were fired simultaneously, and Florent sank upon the grass which covered the enclosure. He had a bullet in his thigh.

Dorsenne has often related since, as a singular trait of literary mania, that at the moment the wounded man fell he, himself, notwithstanding the anxiety which possessed him, had watched Montfanon, to study him. He adds that never had he seen a face express such sorrowful piety as that of the man who, scorning all human respect, made the sign of the cross. It was the devotee of the catacombs, who had left the altar of the martyrs to accomplish a work of charity, then carried away by anger so far as to place himself under the necessity of participating in a duel, who was, no doubt, asking pardon of God. What remorse was stirring within the heart of the fervent, almost mystical Christian, so strangely mixed up in an adventure of that kind? He had at least this comfort, that after the first examination, and when they had borne Florent into a room prepared hastily by the care of Cibo, the doctor declared himself satisfied. The ball could even be removed at once, and as neither the bone nor the muscles had been injured it was a matter of a few weeks at the most.

"All that now remains for us," concluded Cibo, who had brought back the news, "is to draw up our official report."

At that instant, and as the witnesses were preparing to reënter the house for the last formality, an incident occurred, very unexpected, which was to transform the encounter, up to that time so simple, into one of those memorable duels which are talked over at clubs and in armories. If Pietrapertosa and Cibo had ceased since morning to believe in the *jettatura* of the "some one" whom neither had named, it must be acknowledged that they were very unjust, for the good fortune of having gained something wherewith to swell their Parisian purses was surely naught by the side of this —to have to discuss with the Cavals, the Machaults and other professionals the case, almost unprecedented, in which they were participants.

Boleslas Gorka, who, when once his adversary had fallen, paced to and fro without seeming to care as to the gravity of the wound, suddenly approached the group formed by the four men, and in a tone of voice which did not predict the terrible aggression in which he was about to indulge, he said:

"One moment, gentlemen. I desire to say a few words in your presence to Monsieur Dorsenne."

"I am at your service, Gorka," replied Julien, who did not suspect the hostile intention of his old friend. He did not divine the form which that hostility was about to take, but he had always upon his mind his word of honor falsely given, and he was prepared to answer for it.

[ 291 ]

"It will not take much time, sir," continued Bo-leslas, still with the same insolently formal politeness, "you know we have an account to settle. . . . But as I have some cause not to believe in the validity of your honor, I should like to remove all cause of evasion." And before any one could interfere in the unheard-of proceedings he had raised his glove and struck Dor-senne in the face. As Gorka spoke, the writer turned pale. He had not the time to reply to the audacious insult offered him by a similar one, for the three witnesses of the scene cast themselves between him and his aggressor. He, however, pushed them aside with a resolute air.

"Remember, sirs," said he, "that by preventing me from inflicting on Monsieur Gorka the punishment he deserves, you force me to obtain another reparation. And I demand it immediately. . . . I will not leave this place," he continued, "without having obtained it."

"Nor I, without having given it to you," replied Boleslas. "It is all I ask."

"No, Dorsenne," cried Montfanon, who had been the first to seize the raised arm of the writer, "you shall not fight thus. First, you have no right. It requires at least twenty-four hours between the provocation and the encounter. . . . And you, sirs, must not agree to serve as seconds for Monsieur Gorka, after he has failed in·a manner so grave in all the rules of the ground. . . . If you lend yourselves to it, it is barbarous, it is madness, whatsoever you like. It is no longer a duel."

"I repeat, Montfanon," replied Dorsenne, "that I will not leave here and that I will not allow Monsieur Gorka to leave until I have obtained the reparation to which I feel I have the right."

"And I repeat that I am at Monsieur Dorsenne's service," replied Boleslas.

"Very well, sirs," said Montfanon. "There only remains for us to leave you to arrange it one with the other as you wish, and for us to withdraw. . . . Is not that your opinion?" he continued, addressing Cibo and Pietrapertosa, who did not reply immediately.

"Certainly," finally said one; "the case is difficult."

"There are, however, precedents," insinuated the other.

"Yes," resumed Cibo, "if it were only the two successive duels of Henry de Pène."

"Which furnish authority," concluded Pietrapertosa.

"Authority has nothing to do with it," again exclaimed Montfanon. "I know, for my part, that I am not here to assist at a butchery, and that I will not assist at it. . . . I am going, sirs, and I expect you will do the same, for I do not suppose you would select coachmen to play the part of seconds. . . . Adieu, Dorsenne. . . . You do not doubt my friendship for you. . . . I think I am giving you a veritable proof of it by not permitting you to fight under such conditions."

When the old nobleman reëntered the inn, he waited ten minutes, persuaded that his departure would determine that of Cibo and of Pietrapertosa, and that the new affair, following so strangely upon the other, would be deferred until the next day. He had not told an untruth. It was his strong friendship for Julien which had made him apprehend a duel organized in that way, under the influence of a righteous indignation. Gorka's unjustifiable violence would certainly not permit a second encounter to be avoided. But as the insult had been outrageous, it was the more essential that the conditions should be fixed calmly and after grave consideration. To divert his impatience, Montfanon bade the innkeeper point out to him whither they had carried Florent, and he ascended to the tiny room, where the doctor was dressing the wounded man's leg.

"You see," said the latter, with a smile, "I shall have to limp a little for a month. . . . And Dorsenne?"

"He is all right, I hope," replied Montfanon, adding, with ill-humor: "Dorsenne is a fool; that is what Dorsenne is. And Gorka is a wild beast; that is what Gorka is." And he related the episode which had just taken place to the two men, who were so surprised that the doctor, bandage in hand, paused in his work. "And they wish to fight there at once, like redskins. Why not scalp one another? . . . And that Cibo and that Pietrapertosa would have consented to the duel if I had not opposed it! Fortunately they lack two seconds, and it is not easy to find in this district two men who can sign an official report, for it is the mode nowadays to have those paltry scraps of paper. One of my friends and myself had two such witnesses at twenty francs apiece. But that was in

Paris in 'sixty-two." And he entered upon the recital of the old-time duel, to calm his anxiety, which burst forth again in these words: "It seems they do not decide to separate so quickly. It is not, however, possible that they will fight. . . . Can we see them from here?" He approached the window, which indeed looked upon the enclosure. The sight which met his eyes caused the excellent man to stammer. . . . "The miserable men! . . . It is monstrous. . . . They are mad. . . . They have found seconds. . . . Whom have they taken? . . . Those two huntsmen! . . . Ah, my God! My God!". . . He could say no more. The doctor had hastened to the window to see what was passing, regardless of the fact that Florent dragged himself thither as well. Did they remain there a few seconds, fifteen minutes or longer? They could never tell, so greatly were they terrified.

As Montfanon had anticipated, the conditions of the duel were terrible. For Pietrapertosa, who seemed to direct the combat, after having measured a space sufficiently long, of about fifty feet, was in the act of tracing in the centre two lines scarcely ten or twelve metres apart.

"They have chosen the duel *à marche interrompue*," groaned the veteran duellist, whose knowledge of the ground did not deceive him. Dorsenne and Gorka, once placed, face to face, commenced indeed to advance, now raising, now lowering their weapons with the terrible slowness of two adversaries resolved not to miss their mark.

A shot was fired. It was by Boleslas. Dorsenne

was unharmed. Several steps had still to be taken in order to reach the limit. He took them, and he paused to aim at his opponent with so evident an intention of killing him that they could distinctly hear Cibo cry:

"Fire! For God's sake, fire!"

Julien pressed the trigger, as if in obedience to that order, incorrect, but too natural to be even noticed. The weapon was discharged, and the three spectators at the window of the bedroom uttered three simultaneous exclamations on seeing Gorka's arm fall and his hand drop the pistol.

"It is nothing," cried the doctor, "but a broken arm."

"The good Lord has been better to us than we deserve," said the Marquis.

"Now, at least, the madman will be quieted. . . . Brave Dorsenne!" cried Florent, who thought of his brother-in-law and who added gayly, leaning on Montfanon and the doctor in order to reach the couch: "Finish quickly, doctor, they will need you below immediately."

# CHAPTER IX

HE doctor had diagnosed the case correctly. Dorsenne's ball had struck Gorka below the wrist. Two centimetres more to the right or to the left, and undoubtedly Boleslas would have been killed. He escaped with a fracture of the forearm, which would confine him for a few days to his room, and which would force him to submit for several weeks to the annoyance of a sling. When he was taken home and his personal physician, hastily summoned, made him a bandage and prescribed for the first few days bed and rest, he experienced a new access of rage, which exceeded the paroxysms of the day before and of that morning. All parts of his soul, the noblest as well as the meanest, bled at once and caused him to suffer with another agony than that occasioned by his wounded arm. Was he satisfied in the desire, almost morbid, to figure in the eyes of those who knew him as an extraordinary personage? He had hastened from Poland through Europe as an avenger of his betrayed love, and he had begun by missing his rival. Instead of provoking him immediately in the salon of Villa Steno, he had waited, and another had had time to substitute himself for the one he had wished to chastise. The other, whose death would at least have given a tragical issue to the adventure, Boleslas had scarcely touched. He had hoped in striking Dorsenne to execute at least one traitor whom he considered as having trifled with the most sacred of confidences. He had simply succeeded in giving that false friend occasion to humiliate him bitterly, leaving out of the question that he had rendered it impossible to fight again for many days. None of the persons who had wronged him would be punished for some time, neither his coarse and cowardly rival, nor his perfidious mistress, nor monstrous Lydia Maitland, whose infamy he had just discovered. They were all happy and triumphant, on that lovely, radiant May day, while he tossed on a bed of pain, and it was proven too clearly to him that very afternoon by his two seconds, the only visitors whom he had not denied admission, and who came to see him about five o'clock. They came from the races of Tor di Quinto, which had taken place that day.

"All is well," began Cibo, "I will guarantee that no one has talked. . . . I have told you before, I am sure of my innkeeper, and we have paid the witnesses and the coachman.

"Were Madame Steno and her daughter at the races?" interrupted Boleslas.

"Yes," replied the Roman, whom the abruptness of the question surprised too much for him to evade it with his habitual diplomacy.

"With whom?" asked the wounded man.

"Alone, that time," replied Cibo, with an eagerness in which Boleslas distinguished an intention to deceive him.

"And Madame Maitland?"

"She was there, too, with her husband," said Pietra-pertosa, heedless of Cibo's warning glances, "and all Rome besides," adding: "Do you know the engagement of Ardea and little Hafner is public? They were all three there, the betrothed and the father, and so happy! I vow, it was fine. Cardinal Guerillot baptized pretty Fanny."

"And Dorsenne?" again questioned the invalid.

"He was there," said Cibo. "You will be vexed when I tell you of the reply he dared to make us. We asked him how he had managed—nervous as he is— to aim at you as he aimed, without trembling. For he did not tremble. And guess what he replied? That he thought of a recipe of Stendhal's—to recite from memory four Latin verses, before firing. 'And might one know what you chose?' I asked of him. Thereupon he repeated: '*Tityre, tu patulæ recubans.*'"

"It is a case which recalls the word of Casal," interrupted Pietrapertosa, "when that snob of a Figon recommended to us at the club his varnish manufactured from a recipe of a valet of the Prince of Wales. If the young man is not settled by us, I shall be sorry for him."

Although the two *confrères* had repeated that mediocre pleasantry a hundred times, they laughed at the top of their sonorous voices and succeeded in entirely unnerving the injured man. He gave as a pretext his need of rest to dismiss the fine fellows, of whose sympathy he was assured, whom he had just found loyal and devoted, but who caused him pain in conjuring up, in answer to his question, the images of all his enemies. When one is suffering from a certain sort of pain, remarks like those naïvely exchanged between the two Roman imitators of Casal are intolerable to the hearer. One desires to be alone to feed upon, at least in peace, the bitter food, the exasperating and inefficacious rancor against people and against fate, with which Gorka at that moment felt his heart to be so full. The presence of his former mistress at the races, and on that afternoon, wounded him more cruelly than the rest. He did not doubt that she knew through Maitland, himself, certainly informed by Chapron, of the two duels and of his injury. It was on her account that he had fought, and that very day she appeared in public, smiling, coquetting, as if two years of passion had not united their lives, as if he were to her merely a social acquaintance, a guest at her dinners and her *soirées*. He knew her habits so well, and how eagerly, when she loved, she drank in the presence of him she loved. No doubt she had an appointment on the race-course with Maitland, as she had formerly had with him, and the painter had gone thither when he should have cared for his courageous, his noble brother-in-law, whom he had allowed to fight for him! What a worthy lover the selfish and brutal American was of that vile creature! The image of the happy couple tortured Boleslas with the bitterest jealousy intermingled with disgust, and, by contrast, he thought of his own wife, the proud and tender Maud whom he had lost.

He pictured to himself other illnesses when he had seen that beautiful nurse by his bedside. He saw again the true glance with which that wife, so shamefully betrayed, looked at him, the movements of her loyal hands, which yielded to no one the care of waiting upon him. To-day she had allowed him to go to a duel without seeing him. He had returned. She had not even inquired as to his wound. The doctor had dressed it without her presence, and all that he knew of her was what he learned from their child. For he sent for Luc. He explained to him his broken arm, as had been agreed upon with his friends, by a fall on the staircase, and little Luc replied:

"When will you join us, then? Mamma says we leave for England this evening or in the morning. All the trunks are almost ready."

That evening or to-morrow? So Maud was going to execute her threat. She was going away forever, and without an explanation. He could not even plead his cause once more to the woman who certainly would not respond to another appeal, since she had found, in her outraged pride, the strength to be severe, when he was in danger of death. In the face of that evidence of the desertion of all connected with him, Boleslas suffered one of those accesses of discouragement, deep, absolute, irremediable, in which one longs to sleep forever. He asked himself: *"Were I to try one more step?"* and he replied: *"She will not!"* when his valet entered with word that the Countess desired to speak with him. His agitation was so extreme that, for a second, he fancied it was with regard to Madame Steno, and he was almost afraid to see his wife enter.

Without any doubt, the emotions undergone during the past few days had been very great. He had, however, experienced none more violent, even beneath the pistol raised by Dorsenne, than that of seeing advance to his bed the embodiment of his remorse. Maud's face, in which ordinarily glowed the beauty of a blood quickened by the English habits of fresh air and daily exercise, showed undeniable traces of tears, of sadness, and of insomnia. The pallor of the cheeks, the dark circles beneath the eyes, the dryness of the lips and their bitter expression, the feverish glitter, above all, in the eyes, related more eloquently than words the terrible agony of which she was the victim. The past twenty-four hours had acted upon her like certain long illnesses, in which it seems that the very essence of the organism is altered. She was another person. The rapid metamorphosis, so tragical and so striking, caused Boleslas to forget his own anguish. He experienced nothing but one great regret when the woman, so visibly bowed down by grief, was seated, and when he saw in her eyes the look of implacable coldness, even through the fever, before which he had recoiled the day before. But she was there, and her unhoped-for presence was to the young man, even under the circumstances, an infinite consolation. He, therefore, said, with an almost childish grace, which he could assume when he desired to please:

"You recognized the fact that it would be too cruel
of you to go away without seeing me again. I should
not have dared to ask it of you, and yet it was the
only pleasure I could have. . . . I thank you for having given it to me."

"Do not thank me," replied Maud, shaking her
head, "it is not on your account that I am here. It
is from duty. . . . Let me speak," she continued,
stopping by a gesture her husband's reply, "you can
answer me afterward. . . . Had it only been a question of you and of me, I repeat, I should not have
seen you again. . . . But, as I told you yesterday,
we have a son."

"Ah!" exclaimed Boleslas, sadly. "It is to make
me still more wretched that you have come. . . .
You should remember, however, that I am in no condition to discuss with you so cruel a question. . . . I
thought I had already said that I would not disregard
your rights on condition that you did not disregard
mine."

"It is not of my rights that I wish to speak, nor of
yours," interrupted Maud, "but of *his*, the only ones
of importance. When I left you yesterday, I was
suffering too severely to feel anything but my pain.
It was then that, in my mental agony, I recalled words
repeated to me by my father: '*When one suffers, he
should look his grief in the face, and it will always
teach him something.*' I was ashamed of my weakness,
and I looked my grief in the face. It taught me,
first, to accept it as a just punishment for having
married against the advice and wishes of my father."

"Ah, do not abjure our past!" cried the young man; "the past which has remained so dear to me through all."

"No, I do not abjure it," replied Maud, "for it was on recurring to it—it was on returning to my early impressions—that I could find not an excuse, but an explanation of your conduct. I remembered what you related to me of the misfortunes of your childhood and of your youth, and how you had grown up between your father and your mother, passing six months with one, six months with the other—not caring for, not being able to judge either of them—forced to hide from one your feelings for the other. I saw for the first time that your parents' separation had the effect of saddening your heart at that epoch. It is that which perverted your character. . . . And I read in advance Luc's history in yours. . . . Listen, Boleslas! I speak to you as I would speak before God! My first feeling when that thought presented itself to my mind was not to resume life with you; such a life would be henceforth too bitter. No, it was to say to myself, *I will have my son to myself. He shall feel my influence alone.* I saw you set out this morning—set out to insult me once more, to sacrifice me once more! If you had been truly repentant would you have offered me that last affront? And when you returned—when they informed me that you had a broken arm—I wished to tell the little one myself that you were ill. . . . I saw how much he loved you, I discovered what a place you already occupied in his heart, and I comprehended that, even if the law gave

COSMOPOLIS

him to me, as I know it would, his childhood would
be like yours, his youth like your youth.

"Then," she went on, with an accent in which emotion struggled through her pride, "I did not feel justified in destroying the respect so deep, the love so true,
he bears you, and I have come to say to you: You
have wronged me greatly. You have killed within
me something that will never come to life again. I
feel that for years I shall carry a weight on my mind
and on my heart at the thought that you could have
betrayed me as you have. But I feel that for our
boy this separation on which I had resolved is too
perilous. I feel that I shall find in the certainty of
avoiding a moral danger for him the strength to continue a common existence, and I will continue it.
But human nature is human nature, and that strength
I can have only on one condition."

"And that is?" asked Boleslas. Maud's speech,
for it was a speech carefully reflected upon, every
phrase of which had been weighed by that scrupulous
conscience, contrasted strongly in its lucid reasoning
with the state of nervous excitement in which he had
lived for several days. He had been more pained by
it than he would have been by passionate reproaches.
At the same time he had been moved by the reference
to his son's love for him, and he felt that if he did
not become reconciled with Maud at that moment his
future domestic life would be ended. There was a
little of each sentiment in the few words he added to
the anxiety of his question. "Although you have
spoken to me very severely, and although you might

have said the same thing in other terms, although, above all, it is very painful to me to have you condemn my entire character on one single error, I love you, I love my son, and I agree in advance to your conditions. I esteem your character too much to doubt that they will be reconcilable with my dignity. As for the duel of this morning," he added, "you know very well that it was too late to withdraw without dishonor."

"I should like your promise, first of all," replied Madame Gorka, who did not answer his last remark, "that during the time in which you are obliged to keep your room no one shall be admitted. . . . I could not bear that creature in my house, nor any one who would speak to me or to you of her."

"I promise," said the young man, who felt a flood of warmth enter his soul at the first proof that the jealousy of the loving woman still existed beneath the indignation of the wife. And he added, with a smile, "That will not be a great sacrifice. And then?"

"Then? . . . That the doctor will permit us to go to England. We will leave orders for the management of things during our absence. We will go this winter wherever you like, but not to this house; never again to this city."

"That is a promise, too," said Boleslas, "and that will be no great sacrifice either; and then?"

"And then," said she in a low voice, as if ashamed of herself. "You must never write to *her*, you must never try to find out what has become of her."

"I give you my word," replied Boleslas, taking her hand, and adding: "And then?"

"There is no *then*," said she, withdrawing her hand, but gently. And she began to realize herself her promise of pardon, for she rearranged the pillows under the wounded man's head, while he resumed:

"Yes, my noble Maud, there is a *then*. It is that I shall prove to you how much truth there was in my words of yesterday, in my assurance that I love you in spite of my faults. It is the mother who returns to me to-day. But I want my wife, my dear wife, and I shall win her back."

She made no reply. She experienced, on hearing him pronounce those last words with a transfigured face, an emotion which did not vanish. She had acquired, beneath the shock of her great sorrow, an intuition too deep of her husband's nature, and that facility, which formerly charmed her by rendering her anxious, now inspired her with horror. That man with the mobile and complaisant conscience had already forgiven himself. It sufficed him to conceive the plan of a reparation of years, and to respect himself for it—as if that was really sufficient—for the difficult task. At least during the eight days which lapsed between that conversation and their departure he strictly observed the promise he had given his wife. In vain did Cibo, Pietrapertosa, Hafner, Ardea try to see him. When the train which bore them away steamed out he asked his wife, with a pride that time justified by deeds:

"Are you satisfied with me?"

"I am satisfied that we have left Rome," said she, evasively, and it was true in two senses of the word:

First of all, because she did not delude herself with regard to the return of the moral energy of which Boleslas was so proud. She knew that his variable will was at the mercy of the first sensation. Then, what she had not confessed to her husband, the sorrow of a broken friendship was joined in her to the sorrows of a betrayed wife. The sudden discovery of the infamy of Alba's mother had not destroyed her strong affection for the young girl, and during the entire week, busy with her preparations for a final departure, she had not ceased to wonder anxiously: "What will she think of my silence? . . . What has her mother told her? . . . What has she divined?"

She had loved the "poor little soul," as she called the Contessina in her pretty English term. She had devoted to her the friendship peculiar to young women for young girls—a sentiment—very strong and yet very delicate, which resembles, in its tenderness, the devotion of an elder sister for a younger. There is in it a little naïve protection and also a little romantic and gracious melancholy. The elder friend is severe and critical. She tries to assuage, while envying them, the excessive enthusiasms of the younger. She receives, she provokes her confidence with the touching gravity of a counsellor. The younger friend is curious and admiring. She shows herself in all the truth of that graceful awakening of thoughts and emotions which precede her own period before marriage. And when there is, as was the case with Alba Steno, a certain discord of soul between that younger friend and her mother, the affection for the sister chosen becomes so deep that it can not be broken without wounds on both sides. It was for that reason that, on leaving Rome, faithful and noble Maud experienced at once a sense of relief and of pain—of relief, because she was no longer exposed to the danger of an explanation with Alba; of pain, because it was so bitter a thought for her that she could never justify her heart to her friend, could never aid her in emerging from the difficulties of her life, could, finally, never love her openly as she had loved her secretly. She said to herself as she saw the city disappear in the night with its curves and its lights:

"If she thinks badly of me, may she divine nothing! Who will now prevent her from yielding herself up to her sentiment for that dangerous and perfidious Dorsenne? Who will console her when she is sad? Who will defend her against her mother? I was perhaps wrong in writing to the woman, as I did, the letter, which might have been delivered to her in her daughter's presence. . . . Ah, poor little soul! . . . May God watch over her!"

She turned, then, toward her son, whose hair she stroked, as if to exorcise, by the evidence of present duty, the nostalgia which possessed her at the thought of an affection sacrificed forever. Hers was a nature too active, too habituated to the British virtue of self-control to submit to the languor of vain emotions.

The two persons of whom her friendship, now impotent, had thought, were, for various reasons, the two fatal instruments of the fate of the "poor little soul," and the vague remorse which Maud herself felt with regard to the terrible note sent to Madame Steno in the presence of the young girl, was only too true. When the servant had given that letter to the Countess, saying that Madame Gorka excused herself on account of indisposition, Alba Steno's first impulse had been to enter her friend's room.

"I will go to embrace her and to see if she has need of anything," she said.

"Madame has forbidden any one to enter her room," replied the footman, with embarrassment, and, at the same moment, Madame Steno, who had just opened the note, said, in a voice which struck the young girl by its change:

"Let us go; I do not feel well, either."

The woman, so haughty, so accustomed to bend all to her will, was indeed trembling in a very pitiful manner beneath the insult of those phrases which drove her, Caterina Steno, away with such ignominy. She paled to the roots of her fair hair, her face was distorted, and for the first and last time Alba saw her form tremble. It was only for a few moments. At the foot of the staircase energy gained the mastery in that courageous character, created for the shock of strong emotions and for instantaneous action. But rapid as had been that passage, it had sufficed to disconcert the young girl. For not a moment did she doubt that the note was the cause of that extraordinary metamorphosis in the Countess's aspect and attitude. The fact that Maud would not receive her, her friend, in her room was not less strange. What was happening? What did the letter contain? What were they hiding from her? If she had, the day before, felt the "needle in the heart" only on divining a scene of violent explanation between her mother and Boleslas Gorka, how would she have been agonized to ascertain the state into which the few lines of Boleslas's wife had cast that mother! The anonymous denunciation recurred to her, and with it all the suspicion she had in vain rejected. The mother was unaware that for months there was taking place in her daughter a moral drama of which that scene formed a decisive episode, she was too shrewd not to understand that her emotion had been very imprudent, and that she must explain it. Moreover, the rupture with Maud was irreparable, and it was necessary that Alba should be included in it.

The mother, at once so guilty and so loving, so blind and so considerate, had no sooner foreseen the necessity than her decision was made, and a false explanation invented:

"Guess what Maud has just written me?" said she, brusquely, to her daughter, when they were seated side by side in their carriage. God, what balm the simple phrase introduced into Alba's heart! Her mother was about to show her the note! Her joy was short-lived! The note remained where the Countess had slipped it, after having nervously folded it, in the opening in her glove. And she continued: "She accuses me of being the cause of a duel between her husband and Florent Chapron, and she quarrels with me by letter, without seeing me, without speaking to me!"

"Boleslas Gorka has fought a duel with Florent Chapron?" repeated the young girl.

"Yes," replied her mother. "I knew that through Hafner. I did not speak of it to you in order not to worry you with regard to Maud, and I have only awaited her so long to cheer her up in case I should have found her uneasy, and this is how she rewards me for my friendship! It seems that Gorka took offence at some remark of Chapron's about Poles, one of those innocent remarks made daily on any nation—the Italians, the French, the English, the Germans, the Jews—and which mean nothing. . . . I repeated the remark in jest to Gorka! . . . I leave you to judge. . . . Is it my fault if, instead of laughing at it, he insulted poor Florent, and if the absurd encounter resulted from it? And Maud, who writes me that she will never pardon me, that I am a false friend, that I did it expressly to exasperate her husband. . . . Ah, let her watch her husband, let her lock him up, if he is mad! And I, who have received them as I have, I, who have made their position for them in Rome, I, who had no other thought than for her just now! . . . You hear," she added, pressing her daughter's hand with a fervor which was at least sincere, if her words were untruthful, "I forbid you seeing her again or writing to her. If she does not offer me an apology for her insulting note, I no longer wish to know her. One is foolish to be so kind!"

For the first time, while listening to that speech, Alba was convinced that her mother was deceiving her. Since suspicion had entered her heart with regard to her mother, the object until then of such admiration and affection, she had passed through many stages of mistrust. To talk with the Countess was always to dissipate them. That was because Madame Steno, apart from her amorous immorality, was of a frank and truthful nature.

It was indeed a customary and known weakness of Florent's to repeat those witticisms which abound in national epigrams, as mediocre as they are iniquitous. Alba could recall at least twenty circumstances when the excellent man had uttered such jests at which a sensitive person might take offence. She would not have thought it utterly impossible that a duel between Gorka and Chapron might have been provoked by an incident of that order. But Chapron was the brother-in-law of Maitland, of the new friend with whom Madame Steno had become infatuated during the absence of the Polish Count, and what a brother-in-law! He of whom Dorsenne said: "He would set Rome on fire to cook an egg for his sister's husband." When Madame Steno announced that duel to her daughter, an invincible and immediate deduction possessed the poor child—Florent was fighting for his brother-in-law. And on account of whom, if not of Madame Steno? The thought would not, however, have possessed her a second in the face of the very plausible explanation made by the Countess, if Alba had not had in her heart a certain proof that her mother was not telling the truth. The young girl loved Maud as much as she was loved by her. She knew the sensibility of her faithful and delicate friend.

[313]

as that friend knew hers. For Maud to write her mother a letter which produced an immediate rupture, there must have been some grave reason.

Another material proof was soon joined to that moral proof. Granted the character and the habits of the Countess, since she had not shown Maud's letter to her daughter there and then, it was because the letter was not fit to be shown. But she heard on the following day only the description of the duel, related by Maitland to Madame Steno, the savage aggression of Gorka against Dorsenne, the composure of the latter and the issue, relatively harmless, of the two duels.

"You see," said her mother to her, "I was right in saying that Gorka is mad! . . . It seems he has had a fit of insanity since the duel, and that they prevent him from seeing any one. . . . Can you now comprehend how Maud could blame me for what is hereditary in the Gorka family?"

Such was indeed the story which the Venetian and her friends, Hafner, Ardea, and others, circulated throughout Rome in order to diminish the scandal. The accusation of madness is very common to women who have goaded to excess man's passion, and who then wish to avoid all blame for the deeds or words of that man. In this case, Boleslas's fury and his two incomprehensible duels, fifteen minutes apart, justified the story. When it became known in the city that the Palazzetto Doria was strictly closed, that Maud Gorka received no one, and finally that she was taking away her husband in the manner which resembled a flight, no doubt remained of the young man's wrecked reason.

# COSMOPOLIS

Two persons profited very handsomely by the gossiping, the origin of which was a mystery. One was the innkeeper of the *Tempo Perso*, whose simple *bettola* became, during those few days, a veritable place of pilgrimage, and who sold a quantity of wine and numbers of fresh eggs. The other was Dorsenne's publisher, of whom the Roman booksellers ordered several hundred volumes.

"If I had had that duel in Paris," said the novelist to Mademoiselle Steno, relating to her the unforeseen result, "I should perhaps have at length known the intoxication of the thirtieth edition."

It was a few days after the departure of the Gorkas that he jested thus, at a large dinner of twenty-four covers, given at Villa Steno in honor of Peppino Ardea and Fanny Hafner. Reëstablished in the Countess's favor since his duel, he had again become a frequenter of her house, so much the more assiduous as the increasing melancholy of Alba interested him greatly. The enigma of the young girl's character redoubled that interest at each visit in such a degree that, notwithstanding the heat, already beginning, of the dangerous Roman summer, he constantly deferred his return to Paris until the morrow. What had she guessed in consequence of the encounter, the details of which she had asked of him with an emotion scarcely hidden in her eyes of a blue as clear, as transparent, as impenetrable at the same time, as the water of certain Alpine lakes at the foot of the glaciers. He thought he was doing right in corroborating the story of Boleslas Gorka's madness, which he knew better than any one else to be false. But was it not the surest means of exempting Madame Steno from connection with the affair? Why had he seen Alba's beautiful eyes veiled with a sadness inexplicable, as if he had just given her another blow? He did not know that since the day on which the word *insanity* had been uttered before her relative to Maud's husband, the Contessina was the victim of a reasoning as simple as irrefutable.

"If Boleslas be mad, as they say," said Alba, "why does Maud, whom I know to be so just and who loves me so dearly, attribute to my mother the responsibility of this duel, to the point of breaking with me thus, and of leaving without a line of explanation? . . . No. . . . There is something else." . . . The nature of the "something else" the young girl comprehended, on recalling her mother's face during the perusal of Maud's letter. During the ten days following that scene, she saw constantly before her that face, and the fear imprinted upon those features ordinarily so calm, so haughty! Ah, poor little soul, indeed, who could not succeed in banishing this fixed idea: "My mother is not a good woman."

Idea! So much the more terrible, as Alba had no longer the ignorance of a young girl, if she had the innocence. Accustomed to the conversations, at times very bold, of the Countess's salon, enlightened by the reading of novels chanced upon, the words *lover* and *mistress* had for her a signification of physical intimacy such that it was an almost intolerable torture for her to associate them with the relations of her mother,

first toward Gorka, then toward Maitland. That torture she had undergone during the entire dinner, at
the conclusion of which Dorsenne essayed to chat
gayly with her. She sat beside the painter, and the
man's very breath, his gestures, the sound of his
voice, his manner of eating and of drinking, the knowledge of his very proximity, had caused her such keen
suffering that it was impossible for her to take anything
but large glasses of iced water. Several times during
that dinner, prolonged amid the sparkle of magnificent
silver and Venetian crystal, amid the perfume of
flowers and the gleam of jewels, she had seen Maitland's eyes fixed upon the Countess with an expression which almost caused her to cry out, so clearly
did her instinct divine its impassioned sensuality,
and once she thought she saw her mother respond
to it.

She felt with appalling clearness that which before she had uncertainly experienced, the immodest
character of that mother's beauty. With the pearls
in her fair hair, with neck and arms bare in a corsage
the delicate green tint of which showed to advantage
the incomparable splendor of her skin, with her dewy
lips, with her voluptuous eyes shaded by their long
lashes, the *dogaresse* looked in the centre of that table
like an empress and like a courtesan. She resembled
the Caterina Cornaro, the gallant queen of the island
of Cypress, painted by Titian, and whose name she
worthily bore. For years Alba had been so proud of
the ray of seduction cast forth by the Countess, so
proud of those statuesque arms, of the superb carriage,

of the face which defied the passage of time, of the bloom of opulent life the glorious creature displayed. During that dinner she was almost ashamed of it.

She had been pained to see Madame Maitland seated a few paces farther on, with brow and lips contracted as if by thoughts of bitterness. She wondered: Does Lydia suspect them, too? But was it possible that her mother, whom she knew to be so generous, so magnanimous, so kind, could have that smile of sovereign tranquillity with such secrets in her heart? Was it possible that she could have betrayed Maud for months and months with the same light of joy in her eyes?

"Come," said Julien, stopping himself suddenly in the midst of a speech, in which he had related two or three literary anecdotes. "Instead of listening to your friend Dorsenne, little Countess, you are following several blue devils flying through the room."

"They would fly, in any case," replied Alba, who, pointing to Fanny Hafner and Prince d'Ardea seated on a couch, continued: "Has what I told you a few weeks since been realized? You do not know all the irony of it. You have not assisted, as I did the day before yesterday, at the poor girl's baptism."

"It is true," replied Julien, "you were godmother. I dreamed of Leo Thirteenth as godfather, with a princess of the house of Bourbon as godmother. Hafner's triumph would have been complete!"

"He had to content himself with his ambassador and your servant," replied Alba with a faint smile, which was speedily converted into an expression of bitterness. "Are you satisfied with your pupil?" she added. "I am progressing. . . . I laugh when I wish to weep. . . . But you yourself would not have laughed had you seen the fervor of charming Fanny. She was the picture of blissful faith. Do not scoff at her."

"And where did the ceremony take place?" asked Dorsenne, obeying the almost suppliant injunction.

"In the chapel of the *Dames du Cénacle.*"

"I know the place," replied the novelist, "one of the most beautiful corners of Rome! It is in the old Palais Piancini, a large mansion almost opposite the *Calcographie Royale,* where they sell those fantastic etchings of the great Piranese, those dungeons and those ruins of so intense a poesy! It is the Gaya of stone. There is a garden on the terrace. And to ascend to the chapel one follows a winding stair-case, an incline without steps, and one meets nuns in violet gowns, with faces so delicate in the white framework of their bonnets. In short, an ideal re-treat for one of my heroines. My old friend Mont-fanon took me there. As we ascended to that tower, six weeks ago, we heard the shrill voices of ten little girls, singing: *Questo cuor tu la vedrai.** . . . It was a procession of catechists, going in the opposite direc-tion, with tapers which flickered dimly in the remnant of daylight. . . . It was exquisite. . . . But, now per-mit me to laugh at the thought of Montfanon's choler when I relate to him this baptism. If I knew where to find the old leaguer! But he has been hiding since our duel. He is in some retreat doing penance. As

* That heart of Jesus, thou shalt see it.

I have already told you, the world for him has not stirred since François de Guise. He only admits the aims of the Protestants and the Jews. When Monseigneur Guerillot tells him of Fanny's religious aspirations, he raves immoderately. Were she to cast herself to the lions, like Saint Blandine, he would still cry out 'sacrilege.'"

"He did not see her the day before yesterday," said Alba, "nor the expression upon her face when she recited the *Credo*. I do not believe in mysticism, you know, and I have moments of doubt. There are times when I can no longer believe in anything, life seems to me so wretched and sad. . . . But I shall never forget that expression. She saw God! . . . Several women were present with very touching faces, and there were many devotees. . . . The Cardinal is very venerable. . . . All were by Fanny's side, like saints around the Madonna in the early paintings which you have taught me to like, and when the baptism had been gone through, guess what she said to me: 'Come, let us pray for my dear father, and for his conversion.' Is not such blindness melancholy."

"The fact is," said Dorsenne again, jocosely, "that in the father's dictionary the word has another meaning: Conversion, feminine substantive, means to him *income*. . . . But let us reason a little, Countess. Why do you think it sad that the daughter should see her father's character in her own light? . . . You should, on the contrary, rejoice at it. . . . And why do you find it melancholy that this adorable saint should be the daughter of a thief? . . . How I wish

COSMOPOLIS

that you were really my pupil, and that it would not
be too absurd to give you here, in this corner of the
hall, a lesson in intellectuality! . . . I would say to
you, when you see one of those anomalies which renders you indignant, think of the causes.  It is so easy.
"Although Protestant, Fanny is of Jewish origin—that
is to say, the descendant of a persecuted race—which
in consequence has developed by the side of the in-
herent defects of a proscribed people the corresponding
virtues, the devotion, the abnegation of the woman
who feels that she is the grace of a threatened hearth,
the sweet flower which perfumes the sombre prison."

"It is all beautiful and true," replied Alba, very
seriously.  She had hung upon Dorsenne's lips while
he spoke, with the instinctive taste for ideas of that
order which proved her veritable origin.  "But you
do not mention the sorrow.  This is what one can
not do—look upon as a tapestry, as a picture, as an object; the creature who has not asked to live and who
suffers.  You, who have feeling, what is your theory
when you weep?

"I can very clearly foresee the day on which Fanny
will feel her misfortune," continued the young girl.  "I
do not know when she will begin to judge her father,
but that she already begins to judge Ardea, alas, I am
only too sure. . . . Watch her at this moment, I pray
you."

Dorsenne indeed looked at the couple.  Fanny was
listening to the Prince, but with a trace of suffering
upon her beautiful face, so pure in outline that the
nobleness in it was ideal.

21          [ 321 ]

He was laughing at some anecdote which he thought excellent, and which clashed with the sense of delicacy of the person to whom he was addressing himself. They were no longer the couple who, in the early days of their betrothal, had given to Julien the sentiment of a complete illusion on the part of the young girl for her future husband.

"You are right, Contessina," said he, "the decrystallization has commenced. It is a little too soon."

"Yes, it is too soon," replied Alba. "And yet it is too late. Would you believe that there are times when I ask myself if it would not be my duty to tell her the truth about her marriage, such as I know it, with the story of the weak man, the forced sale, and of the bargaining of Ardea?"

"You will not do it," said Dorsenne. "Moreover, why? This one or another, the man who marries her will only want her money, rest assured. It is necessary that the millions be paid for here below, it is one of their ransoms. . . . But I shall cause you to be scolded by your mother, for I am monopolizing you, and I have still two calls to pay this evening."

"Well, postpone them," said Alba. "I beseech you, do not go."

"I must," replied Julien. "It is the last Wednesday of old Duchess Pietrapertosa, and after her grandson's recent kindness——"

"She is so ugly," said Alba, "will you sacrifice me to her?"

"Then there is my compatriot, who goes away tomorrow and of whom I must take leave this evening,

Madame de Sauve, with whom you met me at the museum. . . . You will not say she is ugly, will you?"

"No," responded Alba, dreamily, "she is very pretty." . . . She had another prayer upon her lips, which she did not formulate. Then, with a beseeching glance: "Return, at least. Promise me that you will return after your two visits. They will be over in an hour and a half. It will not be midnight. You know some do not ever come before one and sometimes two o'clock. You will return?"

"If possible, yes. But at any rate, we shall meet to-morrow, at the studio, to see the portrait."

"Then, adieu," said the young girl, in a low voice.

# CHAPTER X

THE Contessina's disposition was too different from her mother's for the mother to comprehend that heart, the more contracted in proportion as it was touched, while emotion was synonymous with expansion in the opulent and impulsive Venetian. That evening she had not even observed Alba's dreaminess, Dorsenne once gone, and it required that Hafner should call her attention to it. To the scheming Baron, if the novelist was attentive to the young girl it was certainly with the object of capturing a considerable dowry. Julien's income of twenty-five thousand francs meant independence. The two hundred and fifty thousand francs which Alba would have at her mother's death was a very large fortune. So Hafner thought he would deserve the name of "old friend," by taking Madame Steno aside and saying to her:

"Do you not think Alba has been a little strange for several days!"

"She has always been so," replied the Countess. "Young people are like that nowadays; there is no more youth."

"Do you not think," continued the Baron, "that perhaps there is another cause for that sadness—some interest in some one, for example?"

"Alba?" exclaimed the mother. "For whom?"

"For Dorsenne," returned Hafner, lowering his voice; "he just left five minutes ago, and you see she is no longer interested in anything nor in any one."

"Ah, I should be very much pleased," said Madame Steno, laughing. "He is a handsome fellow; he has talent, fortune. He is the grand-nephew of a hero, which is equivalent to nobility, in my opinion. But Alba has no thought of it, I assure you. She would have told me; she tells me everything. We are two friends, almost two comrades, and she knows I shall leave her perfectly free to choose. . . . No, my old friend, I understand my daughter. Neither Dorsenne nor any one else interests her, unfortunately. I sometimes fear she will go into a decline, like her cousin Andryana Navagero, whom she resembles. . . . But I must cheer her up. It will not take long."

"A Dorsenne for a son-in-law!" said Hafner to himself, as he watched the Countess walk toward Alba through the scattered groups of her guests, and he shook his head, turning his eyes with satisfaction upon his future son-in-law. "That is what comes of not watching one's children closely. One fancies one understands them until some folly opens one's eyes! . . . And, it is too late! . . . Well, I have warned her, and it is no affair of mine!"

In spite of Fanny's observed and increasing vexation Ardea amused himself by relating to her anecdotes,

more or less true, of the goings-on in the Vatican.
He thus attempted to abate a Catholic enthusiasm at
which he was already offended. His sense of the
ridiculous and that of his social interest made him perceive how absurd it would be to go into clerical society
after having taken for a wife a millionaire converted
the day before. To be just, it must be added that the
Countess's dry champagne was not altogether irre-
sponsible for the persistency with which he teased his
betrothed. It was not the first time he had indulged
in the semi-intoxication which had been one of the
sins of his youth, a sin less rare in the southern cli-
mates than the modesty of the North imagines.

"You come opportunely, Contessina," said he,
when Mademoiselle Steno had seated herself upon the
couch beside them. "Your friend is scandalized by
a little story I have just told her. . . . The one of the
noble guard who used the telephone of the Vatican this
winter to appoint rendezvous with Guilia Rezzonico
without awakening the jealousy of Ugolino. . . . But
it is nothing. I have almost quarrelled with Fanny
for having revealed to her that the Holy Father repeated his benediction in Chapel Sixtine, with a singing master, like a prima donna."

"I have already told you that I do not like those
jests," said Fanny, with visible irritation, which her
patience, however, governed. "If you desire to continue them, I will leave you to converse with Alba."

"Since you see that you annoy her," said the latter
to the Prince, "change the subject."

"Ah, Contessina," replied Peppino, shaking his

head, "you support her already. What will it be later? Well, I apologize for my innocent epigrams on His Holiness in his dressing-gown. And," he continued, laughing, "it is a pity, for I have still two or three entertaining stories, notably one about a coffer filled with gold pieces, which a faithful bequeathed to the Pope. And that poor, dear man was about to count them when the coffer slipped from his hand, and there was the entire treasure on the floor, and the Pope and a cardinal on all fours were scrambling for the napoleons, when a servant entered. . . . Tableau! . . . I assure you that good Pius IX would be the first to laugh with us at all the Vatican jokes. He is not so much *alla mano*. But he is a holy man just the same. Do not think I do not render him justice. Only, the holy man is a man, and a good old man. That is what you do not wish to see."

"Where are you going?" said Alba to Fanny, who had risen as she had threatened to do.

"To talk with my father, to whom I have several words to say."

"I warned you to change the subject," said Alba, when she and the Prince were alone. Ardea, somewhat abashed, shrugged his shoulders and laughed:

"You will confess that the situation is quite piquant, little Countess. . . . You will see she will forbid me to go to the Quirinal. . . . Only one thing will be lacking, and it is that Papa Hafner should discover religious scruples which would prevent him from greeting the King. . . . But Fanny must be appeased!"

"My God!" said Alba to herself, seeing the young

man rise in his turn. "I believe he is intoxicated. What a pity!"

As have almost all revolutions of that order, the work of Christianity, accomplished for years, in Fanny had for its principle an example.

The death of a friend, the sublime death of a true believer, ended by determining her faith. She saw the dying woman receive the sacrament, and the ineffable joy of the benediction upon the face of the sufferer of twenty lighted up by ecstasy. She heard her say, with a smile of conviction:

"I go to ask you of Our Lord, Jesus Christ."

How could she have resisted such a cry and such a sight?

The very day after that death she asked of her father permission to be baptized, which request drew from the Baron a reply too significant not to be repeated here:

"Undoubtedly," had replied the surprising man, who instead of a heart, had a Bourse list on which all was tariffed, even God, "undoubtedly I am touched, very deeply touched, and very happy to see that religious matters preoccupy you to such a degree. To the people it is a necessary curb, and to us it accords with a certain rank, a certain society, a certain deportment. I think that a person called like you to live in Austria and in Italy should be a Catholic. However, it is necessary to remember that you might marry some one of another faith. Do not object. I am your father. I can foresee all. I know you will marry only according to the dictates of your heart. Wait

then until it has spoken, to settle the question. . . . If
you love a Catholic, you will then have occasion to
pay a compliment to your betrothed by adopting his
faith, of which he will be very sensible. . . . From
now until then, I shall not prevent you from following
ceremonies which please you. Those of the Roman
liturgy are, assuredly, among the best; I myself at-
tended Saint Peter's at the time of the pontifical government. . . . The taste, the magnificence, the music,
all moved me. . . . But to take a definite, irreparable
step, I repeat, you must wait. Your actual condition
of a Protestant has the grand sentiment of being more
neutral, less defined."

What words to listen to by a heart already touched
by the attraction of grace and by the nostalgia of eternal life! But the heart was that of a young girl very
pure and very tender. To judge her father was
to her impossible, and the Baron's firmness had
convinced her that she must obey his wishes and
pray that he be enlightened. She therefore waited,
hoping, sustained and directed meanwhile by Cardinal
Guerillot, who later on was to baptize her and to obtain for her the favor of approaching the holy table
for the first time at the Pope's mass. That prelate,
one of the noblest figures of which the French bishopric
has had cause to be proud, since Monseigneur Pie, was
one of those grand Christians for whom the hand of
God is as visible in the direction of human beings as
it is invisible to doubtful souls. When Fanny, already
devoted to her charities, confided in him the serious
troubles of her mind and the discord which had arisen

between her and her father on the so essential point
of her baptism, the Cardinal replied:

"Have faith in God. He will give you a sign
when your time has come." And he uttered those
words with an accent whose conviction had filled
the young girl with a certainty which had never
left her.

In spite of his seventy years, and of the experiences
of the confession, in spite of the disenchanting struggle
with the freemasonry of his French diocese, which
had caused his exile to Rome, the venerable man
looked at Fanny's marriage from a supernatural stand-
point. Many priests are thus capable of a naïveté
which, on careful analysis, is often in the right. But
at the moment the antithesis between the authentic
reality and that which they believe, constitutes an
irony almost absurd. When he had baptized Fanny,
the old Bishop of Clermont was possessed by a joy so
deep that he said to her, to express to her the more
delicately the tender respect of his friendship:

"I can now say as did Saint Monica after the baptism of Saint Augustine: *Cur hic sim, nescio; jam
consumptâ spe hujus saeculi.* I do not know why I
remain here below. All my hope of the age is consummated. And like her I can add—the only thing
which made me desire to remain awhile was to see
you a Catholic before dying. The traveller, who has
tarried, has now nothing to do but to go. He has
gathered the last and the prettiest flower." . . .

Noble and faithful apostle, who was indeed to go
so shortly after, meriting what they said of him, that

which the African bishop said of his mother: "That
religious soul was at length absolved from her body."
. . . He did not anticipate that he would pay dearly
for that realization of his last wish! He did not foresee that she whom he ingenuously termed his most
beautiful flower was to become to him the principal
cause of bitter sorrow. Poor, grand Cardinal! It
was the final trial of his life, the supremely bitter drop
in his chalice, to assist at the disenchantment which
followed so closely upon the blissful intoxication of
his gentle neophyte's first initiation. To whom, if not
to him, should she have gone to ask counsel, in all the
tormenting doubts which she at once began to have in
her feelings with regard to her *fiancé?*

It was, therefore, that on the day following the
evening on which imprudent Ardea had jested so per-
sistently upon a subject sacred to her that she rang at
the door of the apartment which Monseigneur Guerillot occupied in the large mansion on Rue des Quatre-
Fontaines. There was no question of incriminating
the spirit of those pleasantries, nor of relating her
humiliating observations on the Prince's intoxication.
No. She wished to ease her mind, on which rested
a shade of sorrow. At the time of her betrothal, she
had fancied she loved Ardea, for the emotion of her
religious life at length freed had inspired her with
gratitude for him who was, however, only the pretext
of that exemption. She trembled to-day, not only at
not loving him any more, but at hating him, and above
all she felt herself a prey to that repugnance for the
useless cares of the world, to that lassitude of tran-

sitory hopes, to that nostalgia of repose in God, undeniable signs of true vocations.

At the thought that she might, if she survived her
father and she remained free, retire to the *Dames du
Cénacle*, she felt at her approaching marriage an inward
repugnance, which augmented still more the proof of
her future husband's deplorable character. Had she
the right to form such bonds with such feelings?
Would it be honorable to break, without further de-
velopments, the betrothal which had been between
her and her father the condition of her baptism? She
was already there, after so few days! And her wound
was deeper after the night on which the Prince had
uttered his careless jests.

"It is permitted you to withdraw," replied Monsieur
Guerillot, "but you are not permitted to lack charity
in your judgment."

There was within Fanny too much sincerity, her
faith was too simple and too deep for her not to follow
out that advice to the letter, and she conformed to it
in deeds as well as in intentions. For, before taking
a walk in the afternoon with Alba, she took the greatest care to remove all traces which the little scene of
the day before could have left in her friend's mind.
Her efforts went very far. She would ask pardon of
her *fiancé*. . . . Pardon! For what? For having
been wounded by him, wounded to the depths of her
sensibility? She felt that the charity of judgment
recommended by the pious Cardinal was a difficult
virtue. It exercises a discipline of the entire heart,
sometimes irreconcilable with the clearness of the in-

telligence. Alba looked at her friend with a glance full of an astonishment, almost sorrowful, and she embraced her, saying:

"Peppino is not worthy even to kiss the ground on which you tread, that is my opinion, and if he does not spend his entire life in trying to be worthy of you, it will be a crime."

As for the Prince himself, the impulses which dictated to his *fiancée* words of apology when he was in the wrong, were not unintelligible to him, as they would have been to Hafner. He thought that the latter had lectured his daughter, and he congratulated himself on having cut short at once that little comedy of exaggerated religious feeling.

"Never mind that," said he, with condescension, "it is I who have failed in form. For at heart you have always found me respectful of that which my fathers respected. But times have changed, and certain fanaticisms are no longer admissible. That is what I have wished to say to you in such a manner that you could take no offence."

And he gallantly kissed Fanny's tiny hand, not divining that he had redoubled the melancholy of that too-generous child. The discord continued to be excessive between the world of ideas in which she moved and that in which the ruined Prince existed. As the mystics say with so much depth, they were not of the same heaven.

Of all the chimeras which had lasted hours, God alone remained. It sufficed the noble creature to say: "My father is so happy, I will not mar his joy.

I will do my duty toward my husband. I will be so
good a wife that I will transform him. He has religion. He has heart. It will be my *rôle* to make of
him a true Christian. And then I shall have my
children and the poor." Such were the thoughts
which filled the mind of the envied betrothed. For
her the journals began to describe the dresses already
prepared, for her a staff of tailors, dressmakers, needle-
women and jewellers were working; she would have
on her contract the same signature as a princess of
the blood, who would be a princess herself and related
to one of the most glorious aristocracies in the world.
Such were the thoughts she would no doubt have
through life, as she walked in the garden of the Palais
Castagna, that historical garden in which is still to be
seen a row of pear-trees, in the place where Sixte-
Quint, near death, gathered some fruit. He tasted it,
and he said to Cardinal Castagna—playing on their
two names, his being Peretti—"The pears are spoiled.
The Romans have had enough. They will soon eat
chestnuts." That family anecdote enchanted Justus
Hafner. It seemed to him full of the most delightful
humor. He repeated it to his colleagues at the club,
to his tradesmen, to it mattered not whom. He did
not even mistrust Dorsenne's irony.

"I met Hafner this morning on the Corso," said
the latter to Alba at one of the *soirées* at the end of
the month, "and I had my third edition of the pleasantry on the pears and chestnuts. And then, as we
took a few steps in the same direction, he pointed out
to me the Palais Bonaparte, saying, 'We are also related

to them.' . . . Which means that a grand-nephew of the Emperor married a cousin of Peppino. . . . I swear he thinks he is related to Napoleon! . . . He is not even proud of it. The Bonapartes are nowhere when it is a question of nobility! . . . I await the time when he will blush."

"And I the time when he will be punished as he deserves," interrupted Alba Steno, in a mournful voice. "He is insolently triumphant. But no. . . . He will succeed. . . . If it be true that his fortune is one immense theft, think of those he has ruined. In what can they believe in the face of his infamous happiness?"

"If they are philosophers," replied Dorsenne, laughing still more gayly, "this spectacle will cause them to meditate on the words uttered by one of my friends: 'One can not doubt the hand of God, for it created the world.' Do you remember a certain prayer-book of Montluc's?"

"The one which your friend Montfanon bought to vex the poor little thing?"

"Precisely. The old leaguer has returned it to Ribalta; the latter told me so yesterday; no doubt in a spirit of mortification. I say *no doubt* for I have not seen the poor, dear man since the duel, which his impatience toward Ardea and Hafner rendered inevitable. He retired, I know not for how many days, to the convent of Mount Olivet, near Sienna, where he has a friend, one Abbé de Negro, of whom he always speaks as of a saint. I learned, through Rebalta, that he has returned, but is invisible. I tried to force an entrance. In short, the volume is again in the shop of the curiosity-seeker in the Rue Borgognona, if Mademoiselle Hafner still wants it!"

"What good fortune!" exclaimed Fanny, with a sparkle of delight in her eyes. "I did not know what present to offer my dear Cardinal. . . . Shall we make the purchase at once?"

"Montluc's prayer-book?" repeated old Ribalta, when the two young ladies had alighted from the carriage before his small book-shop, more dusty, more littered than ever with pamphlets, in which he still was, with his face more wrinkled, more wan and more proud, peering from beneath his broad-brimmed hat, which he did not raise. "How do you know it is here? Who has told you? Are there spies everywhere?"

"It was Monsieur Dorsenne, one of Monsieur de Montfanon's friends," said Fanny, in her gentle voice.

"*Sara sara*,"* replied the merchant with his habitual insolence, and, opening the drawer of the chest in which he kept the most incongruous treasures, he drew from it the precious volume, which he held toward them, without giving it up. Then he began a speech, which reproduced the details given by Montfanon himself. "Ah, it is very authentic. There is an indistinct but undeniable signature. I have compared it with that which is preserved in the archives of Sienna. It is Montluc's writing, and there is his escutcheon with the turtles. . . . Here, too, are the half-moons of the Piccolomini. . . . This book has a history. . . .

*That may be. It is possible.

The Marshal gave it, after the famous siege, to one of the members of that illustrious family. And it was for one of the descendants that I was commissioned to buy it. . . . They will not give it up for less than two thousand francs."

"What a cheat!" said Alba to her companion, in English. "Dorsenne told me that Monsieur de Monfanon bought it for four hundred."

"Are you sure?" asked Fanny, who, on receiving a reply in the affirmative, addressed the bookseller, with the same gentleness, but with reproach in her accent: "Two thousand francs, Monsieur Ribalta? But it is not a just price, since you sold it to Monsieur de Montfanon for one-fifth of that sum."

"Then I am a liar and a thief," roughly replied the old man; "a thief and a liar," he repeated. "Four hundred francs! You wish to have this book for four hundred francs? I wish Monsieur de Montfanon was here to tell you how much I asked him for it."

The old bookseller smiled cruelly as he replaced the prayer-book in the drawer, the key of which he turned, and turning toward the two young girls, whose delicate beauty, heightened by their fine toilettes, contrasted so delightfully with the sordid surroundings, he enveloped them with a glance so malicious that they shuddered and instinctively drew nearer one another. Then the bookseller resumed, in a voice hoarser and deeper than ever: "If you wish to spend four hundred francs I have a volume which is worth it, and which I propose to take to the Palais Savorelli one of these days. . . . Ha, ha! It must be one of the

22                    [ 337 ]

very last, for the Baron has bought them all." In uttering, those enigmatical words, he opened the cupboard which formed the lower part of the chest, and took from one of the shelves a book wrapped in a newspaper. He then unfolded the journal, and, holding the volume in his enormous hand with his dirty nails, he disclosed the title to the two young girls: *Hafner and His Band; Some Reflections on the Scandalous Acquittal. By a Shareholder.* It was a pamphlet, at that date forgotten, but which created much excitement at one time in the financial circles of Paris, of London and of Berlin, having been printed at once in three languages—in French, in German and in English—on the day after the suit of the *Crédit Austro-Dalmate.* The dealer's chestnut-colored eyes twinkled with a truly ferocious joy as he held out the volume and repeated:

"It is worth four hundred francs."

"Do not read that book, Fanny," said Alba quickly, after having read the title of the work, and again speaking in English; "it is one of those books with which one should not even pollute one's thoughts."

"You may keep the book, sir," she continued, "since you have made yourself the accomplice of those who have written it, by speculating on the fear you hoped it would inspire. Mademoiselle Hafner has known of it long, and neither she nor her father will give a centime."

"Very well! So much the better, so much the better," said Ribalta, wrapping up his volume again; "tell your father I will keep it at his service."

[ 338 ]

"Ah, the miserable man!" said Alba, when Fanny and she had left the shop and reëntered the carriage. "To dare to show you that!"

"You saw," replied Fanny, "I was so surprised I could not utter a word. That the man should offer me that infamous work is very impertinent. My father? . . . You do not know his scrupulousness in business. It is the honor of his profession. There is not a sovereign in Europe who has not given him a testimonial."

That impassioned protestation was so touching, the generous child's illusion was so sincere, that Alba pressed her hand with a deeper tenderness. When Alba found herself that evening with her friend Dorsenne, who again dined at Madame Steno's, she took him aside to relate to him the tragical scene, and to ask him: "Have you seen that pamphlet?"

"To-day," said the writer. "Montfanon, whom I have found at length, has just bought one of the two copies which Ribalta received lately. The old leaguer believes everything, you know, when a Hafner is in the question. . . . I am more skeptical in the bad as well as in the good. It was only the account given by the trial which produced any impression on me, for that is truth."

"But he was acquitted."

"Yes," replied Dorsenne, "though it is none the less true that he ruined hundreds and hundreds of persons."

"Then, by the account given you of the case, it is clear to you that he is dishonest," interrupted Alba.

PAUL BOURGET

"As clear as that you are here, Contessina," replied Dorsenne, "if to steal means to plunder one's neighbors and to escape justice. But that would be nothing. The sinister corner in this affair is the suicide of one Schroeder, a brave citizen of Vienna, who knew our Baron intimately, and who invested, on the advice of his excellent friend, his entire fortune, three hundred thousand florins, in the scheme. He lost them, and, in despair, killed himself, his wife, and their three children."

"My God!" cried Alba, clasping her hands. "And Fanny might have read that letter in the book."

"Yes," continued Julien, "and all the rest with proof in support of it. But rest assured, she shall not have the volume. I will go to that anarchist of a Ribalta to-morrow and I will buy the last copy, if Hafner has not already bought it."

Notwithstanding his constant affectation of irony, and, notwithstanding, his assumption of intellectual egotism, Julien was obliging. He never hesitated to render any one a service. He had not told his little friend an untruth when he promised her to buy the dangerous work, and the following morning he turned toward the Rue Borgognona, furnished with the twenty louis demanded by the bookseller. Imagine his feelings when the latter said to him:

"It is too late, Monsieur Dorsenne. The young lady was here last night. She pretended not to prefer one volume to the other. It was to bargain, no doubt. Ha, ha! But she had to pay the price. I would have asked the father more. One owes some consideration to a young girl."

[ 340 ]

COSMOPOLIS

"Wretch!" exclaimed the novelist. "And you can jest after having committed that Judas-like act! To inform a child of her father's misdeeds, when she is ignorant of them! . . . Never, do you hear, never any more will Monsieur de Montfanon and I set foot in your shop, nor Monseigneur Guerillot, nor any of the persons of my acquaintance. I will tell the whole world of your infamy. I will write it, and it shall appear in all the journals of Rome. I will ruin you, I will force you to close this dusty old shop."

During the entire day, Dorsenne vainly tried to shake off the weight of melancholy which that visit to the brigand of the Rue Borgognona had left upon his heart.

On crossing, at nine o'clock, the threshold of the Villa Steno to give an account of his mission to the Contessina, he was singularly moved. There was no one there but the Maitlands, two tourists and two English diplomatists, on their way to posts in the East.

"I was awaiting you," said Alba to her friend, as soon as she could speak with him in a corner of the salon. "I need your advice. Last night a tragical incident took place at the Hafner's."

"Probably," replied Dorsenne. "Fanny has bought Ribalta's book."

"She has bought the book!" said Alba, changing color and trembling. "Ah, the unhappy girl; the other thing was not sufficient!"

"What other thing?" questioned Julien.

"You remember," said the young girl, "that I told you of that Noé Ancona, the agent who served Hafner as a tool in selling up Ardea, and in thus forcing the marriage. Well, it seems this personage did not think himself sufficiently well-paid for his complicity. He demanded of the Baron a large sum, with which to found some large swindling scheme, which the latter refused pointblank. The other threatened to relate their little dealing to Ardea, and he did so."

"And Peppino was angry?" asked Dorsenne, shaking his head. "That is not like him."

"Indignant or not," continued Alba, "last night he went to the Palais Savorelli to make a terrible scene with his future father-in-law."

"And to obtain an increase of dowry," said Julian.

"He was not by any means tactful, then," replied Alba, "for even in the presence of Fanny, who entered in the midst of their conversation, he did not pause. Perhaps he had drunk a little more than he could stand, which has of late become common with him. But, you see, the poor child was initiated into the abominable bargain with regard to her future, to her happiness, and if she has read the book, too! It is too dreadful!"

"What a violent scene!" exclaimed Dorsenne. "So the engagement has been broken off?"

"Not officially. Fanny is ill in bed from the excitement. Ardea came this morning to see my mother, who has also seen Hafner. She has reconciled them by proving to them, which she thinks true, that they have a common interest in avoiding all scandal, and arranging matters. But it rests with the poor little one. Mamma wished me to go, this afternoon, to beseech her to reconsider her resolution. For she has told her father she never wishes to hear the Prince's voice again. I have refused. Mamma insists. Am I not right?"

"Who knows?" replied Julien. "What would be her life alone with her father, now that her illusions with regard to him have been swept away?"

The touching scene had indeed taken place, and less than twenty-four hours after the novelist had thus expressed to himself the regret of not assisting at it. Only he was mistaken as to the tenor of the dialogue, in a manner which proved that the subtlety of intelligence will never divine the simplicity of the heart. The most dolorous of all moral tragedies knit and unknit the most often in silence. It was in the afternoon, toward six o'clock, that a servant came to announce Mademoiselle Hafner's visit to the Contessina, busy at that moment reading for the tenth time the *Eglogue Mondaine*, that delicate story by Dorsenne. When Fanny entered the room, Alba could see what a trial her charming god-daughter of the past week had sustained, by the surprising and rapid alteration in that expressive and noble visage. She took her hand at first without speaking to her, as if she was entirely ignorant of the cause of her friend's real indisposition. She then said:

"How pleased I am to see you! Are you better?"

"I have never been ill," replied Fanny, who did not know how to tell an untruth. "I have had pain, that is all." Looking at Alba, as if to beg her to ask no question, she added:

"I have come to bid you adieu."

[ 343 ]

"You are going away?" asked the Contessina.

"Yes," said Fanny, "I am going to spend the summer at one of our estates in Styria." And, in a low voice: "Has your mother told you that my engagement is broken?"

"Yes," replied Alba, and both were again silent. After several moments Fanny was the first to ask:

"And how shall you spend your summer?"

"We shall go to Piove, as usual," was Alba's answer. "Perhaps Dorsenne will be there, and the Maitlands will surely be."

A third pause ensued. They gazed at one another, and, without uttering another word, they distinctly read one another's hearts. The martyrdom they suffered was so similar, they both knew it to be so like, that they felt the same pity possess them at the same moment. Forced to condemn with the most irrevocable condemnation, the one her father, the other, her mother, each felt attracted toward the friend, like her, unhappy, and, falling into one another's arms, they both sobbed.

# CHAPTER XI

ER friend's tears had relieved sad Alba's heart while she held that friend in her arms, quivering with sorrow and pity; but when she was gone, and Madame Steno's daughter was alone, face to face with her thoughts, a greater distress seized her. The pity which her companion in misery had shown for her—was it not one more proof that she was right in mistrusting her mother?

Alas! The miserable child did not know that while she was plunged in despair, there was in Rome and in her immediate vicinity a creature bent upon realizing a mad vow. And that creature was the same who had not recoiled before the infamy of an anonymous letter, pretty and sinister Lydia Maitland—that delicate, that silent young woman with the large brown eyes, always smiling, always impenetrable in the midst of that dull complexion which no emotion, it seemed, had ever tinged. The failure of her first attempt had exasperated her hatred against her husband and against the Countess to the verge of fury, but a concentrated fury, which was waiting for another occasion to strike, for weeks, patiently, obscurely. She had thought to wreak her vengeance by the return of Gorka, and in what had it ended? In freeing Lincoln from a dangerous rival and in imperilling the life of the only being for whom she cared!

The sojourn at the country-seat of her husband's mistress exasperated Lydia's hidden anger. She suffered so that she cried aloud, like an imprisoned animal beating against the bars, when she pictured to herself the happiness which the two lovers would enjoy in the intimacy of the villa, with the beauties of the Venetian scenery surrounding them. No doubt the wife could provoke a scandal and obtain a divorce, thanks to proofs as indisputable as those with which she had overwhelmed Maud. It would be sufficient to carry to a lawyer the correspondence in the Spanish *escritoire*. But of what use? She would not be avenged on her husband, to whom a divorce would be a matter of indifference now that he earned as much money as he required, and she would lose her brother. In vain Lydia told herself that, warned as Alba had been by her letter, her doubt of Madame Steno's misconduct would no longer be impossible. She was convinced by innumerable trifling signs that the Contessina still doubted, and then she concluded:

"It is there that the blow must be struck. But how?"

Yes. How? There was at the service of hatred in that delicate woman, in appearance oblivious of worldliness, that masculine energy in decision which is to be found in all families of truly military origin. The blood of Colonel Chapron stirred within her and gave her the desire to act. By dint of pondering upon those reasonings, Lydia ended by elaborating one of those plans of a simplicity really infernal, in which she revealed what must be called the genius of evil, for there was so much clearness in the conception and of villainy in the execution. She assured herself that it was unnecessary to seek any other stage than the studio for the scene she meditated. She knew too well the fury of passion by which Madame Steno was possessed to doubt that, as soon as she was alone with Lincoln, she did not refuse him those kisses of which their correspondence spoke. The snare to be laid was very simple. It required that Alba and Lydia should be in some post of observation while the lovers believed themselves alone, were it only for a moment. The position of the places furnished the formidable woman with the means of obtaining the place of espionage in all security. Situated on the second floor, the studio occupied most of the depth of the house. The wall, which separated it from the side of the apartments, ended in a partition formed of colored glass, through which it was impossible to see. That glass lighted a dark corridor adjoining the linen-room. Lydia employed several hours of several nights in cutting with a diamond a hole, the size of a fifty centime-piece, in one of those unpolished squares.

Her preparations had been completed several days when, notwithstanding her absence of scruple in the satiating of her hatred, she still hesitated to employ that mode of vengeance, so much atrocious cruelty was there in causing a daughter to spy upon her mother. It was Alba herself who kindled the last spark of humanity with which that dark conscience was lighted up, and that by the most innocent of conversations. It was the very evening of the afternoon on which she had exchanged that sad adieu with Fanny Hafner. She was more unnerved than usual, and she was conversing with Dorsenne in that corner of the long hall. They did not heed the fact that Lydia drew near them, by a simple change of seat which permitted her, while herself conversing with some guest, to lend an ear to the words uttered by the Contessina.

It was Florent who was the subject of their conversation, and she said to Dorsenne, who was praising him:

"What would you have? It is true I almost feel repulsion toward him. He is to me like a being of another species. His friendship for his brother-in-law? Yes. It is very beautiful, very touching; but it does not touch me. It is a devotion which is not human. It is too instinctive and too blind. Indeed, I know that I am wrong. There is that prejudice of race which I can never entirely overcome."

Dorsenne touched her fingers at that moment, under the pretext of taking from her her fan, in reality to warn her, and he said, in a very low voice that time:

"Let us go a little farther on. Lydia Maitland is too near."

He fancied he surprised a start on the part of Florent's sister, at whom he accidentally glanced, while his too-sensible interlocutor no longer watched her! But as the pretty, clear laugh of Lydia rang out at the same moment, imprudent Alba replied:

"Fortunately, she has heard nothing. And see how

one can speak of trouble without mistrusting it. . . . I have just been wicked," she continued, "for it is not their fault, neither Florent's nor hers, if there is a little negro blood in their veins, so much the more so as it is connected by the blood of a hero, and they are both perfectly educated, and what is better, perfectly good, and then I know very well that if there is a grand thought in this age it is to have proclaimed that truly all men are brothers."

She had spoken in a lower voice, but too late. Moreover, even if Florent's sister could have heard those words, they would not have sufficed to heal the wound which the first ones had made in the most sensitive part of her *amour proprc!*

"And I hesitated," said she to herself, "I thought of sparing her!"

The following morning, toward noon, she found herself at the atelier, seated beside Madame Steno, while Lincoln gave to the portrait the last touches, and while Alba posed in the large armchair, absent and pale as usual. Florent Chapron, after having assisted at part of the sitting, left the room, leaning upon the crutch, which he still used. His withdrawal seemed so propitious to Lydia that she resolved immediately not to allow such an opportunity to escape, and as if fatality interfered to render her work of infamy more easy, Madame Steno aided her by suddenly interrupting the work of the painter who, after hard working without speaking for half an hour, paused to wipe his forehead, on which were large drops of perspiration, so great was his excitement.

"Come, my little Linco," said she, with the affectionate solicitude of an old mistress, "you must rest. For two hours you have not ceased painting, and such minute details. . . . It tires me merely to watch you."

"I am not at all tired," replied Maitland, who, however, laid down his palette and brush, and rolling a cigarette, lighted it, continuing, with a proud smile: "We have only that one superiority, we Americans, but we have it—it is a power to apply ourselves which the Old World no longer knows. . . . It is for that reason that there are professions in which we have no rivals."

"But see!" replied Lydia, "you have taken Alba for a Bostonian or a New Yorker, and you have made her pose so long that she is pale. She must have a change. Come with me, dear, I will show you the costume they have sent me from Paris, and which I shall wear this afternoon to the garden party at the English embassy."

She forced Alba Steno to rise from the armchair as she uttered those words, then she entwined her arms about her waist to draw her away and kissed her. Ah, if ever a caress merited being compared to the hideous flattery of Iscariot, it was that, and the young girl might have replied with the sublime words: *"Friend, why hast thou betrayed me by a kiss?"* Alas! She believed in it, in the sincerity of that proof of affection, and she returned her false friend's kiss with a gratitude which did not soften that heart saturated with hatred, for five minutes had not passed ere Lydia had put into execution her hideous project. Under the pretext of reaching the linen-room more quickly, she took a servant's staircase, which led to that lobby with the glass partition, in which was the opening through which to look into the atelier.

"This is very strange," said she, pausing suddenly. And, pointing out to her innocent companion the round spot, she said: "Probably some servant who has wished to eavesdrop.—But what for? You, who are tall, look and see how it has been done and what it looks on. If it is a hole cut purposely, I shall discover the culprit and he shall go."

Alba obeyed the perfidious request absently, and applied her eye to the aperture. The author of the anonymous letters had chosen her moment only too well. As soon as the door of the studio was closed, the Countess rose to approach Lincoln. She entwined around the young man's neck her arms, which gleamed through the transparent sleeves of her summer gown, and she kissed with greedy lips his eyes and mouth. Lydia, who had retained one of the girl's hands in hers, felt that hand tremble convulsively. A hunter who hears rustle the foliage of the thicket through which should pass the game he is awaiting, does not experience a joy more complete. Her snare was successful. She said to her unhappy victim:

"What ails you? How you tremble!"

And she essayed to push her away in order to put herself in her place. Alba, whom the sight of her mother embracing Lincoln with those passionate kisses inspired at that moment with an inexplicable horror, had, however, enough presence of mind in the midst of her suffering to understand the danger of that mother whom she had surprised thus, clasping in the arms of a guilty mistress—whom?—the husband of the very woman speaking to her, who asked her why she trembled with fear, who would look through that same hole to see that same tableau! . . . In order to prevent what she believed would be to Lydia a terrible revelation, the courageous child had one of those desperate thoughts such as immediate peril inspires. With her free hand she struck the glass so violently that it was shivered into atoms, cutting her fingers and her wrist.

Lydïa exclaimed, angrily:

"Miserable girl, you did that purposely!"

The fierce creature as she uttered these words, rushed toward the large hole now made in the panel —too late!

She only saw Lincoln erect in the centre of the studio, looking toward the broken window, while the Countess, standing a few paces from him, exclaimed:

"My daughter! What has happened to my daughter? I recognized her voice."

"Do not alarm yourself," replied Lydia, with atrocious sarcasm. "Alba broke the pane to give you a warning."

"But, is she hurt?" asked the mother.

"Very slightly," replied the implacable woman with the same accent of irony, and she turned again toward the Contessina with a glance of such rancor that, even in the state of confusion in which the latter was plunged by that which she had surprised, that glance paralyzed her with fear. She felt the same shudder which had possessed her dear friend Maud, in that same studio, in the face of the sinister depths of that dark soul, sud-denly exposed. She had not time to precisely define her feelings, for already her mother was beside her, pressing her in her arms—in those very arms which Alba had just seen twined around the neck of a lover —while that same mouth showered kisses upon him. The moral shock was so great that the young girl fainted. She regained consciousness and almost at once. She saw her mother as mad with anxiety as she had just seen her trembling with joy and love. She again saw Lydia Maitland's eyes fixed upon them both with an expression too significant now. And, as she had had the presence of mind to save that guilty mother, she found in her tenderness the strength to smile at her, to lie to her, to blind her forever as to the truth of that hideous scene which had just been enacted in that lobby.

"I was frightened at the sight of my own blood," said she, "and I believe it is only a small cut. .... See! I can move my hand without pain."

When the doctor, hastily summoned, had confirmed that no particles of glass had remained in the cuts, the Countess felt so reassured that her gayety returned. Never had she been in a mood more charming than in the carriage which took them to the Villa Steno.

To a person obliged by proof to condemn another without ceasing to love her, there is no greater sorrow than to perceive the absolute unconsciousness of that other person and her serenity in her fault. Poor Alba felt overwhelmed by a sadness greater, more depress-ing still, and which became materially insupportable,

when, toward half-past two, her mother bade her farewell, although the *fête* at the English embassy did not
begin until five o'clock.

"I promised poor Hafner to go to see him to-day.
I know he is bowed down with grief. I would like to
try to arrange all. . . . I will send back the carriage
if you wish to go out awhile. I have telephoned Lydia
to expect me at four o'clock. . . . She will take me."

She had, on detailing the employment so natural of
her afternoon, eyes too brilliant, a smile too happy.
She looked too youthful in her light toilette. Her feet
trembled with too nervous an impatience. How could
Alba not have felt that she was telling her an untruth?
The undeceived child had the intuition that the visit
to Fanny's father was only a pretext. It was not the
first time that the Countess employed it to free herself
from inconvenient surveillance, the act of sending back
the carriage, which, in Rome as in Paris, is always the
probable sign of clandestine meetings with women of
their rank. It was not the first time that Alba was possessed by suspicion on certain mysterious disappear-
ances of her mother. That mother did not mistrust that
poor Alba—her Alba, the child so tenderly loved in spite
of all—was suffering at that very moment and on her account the most terrible of temptations. . . . When the
carriage had disappeared the fixed gaze of the young
girl was turned upon the pavement, and then she felt
arise in her a sudden, instinctive, almost irresistible
idea to end the moral suffering by which she was devoured. It was so simple! . . . It was sufficient to
end life. One movement which she could make, one

single movement—she could lean over the balustrade, against which her arm rested, in a certain manner—so, a little more forward, a little more—and that suffering would be terminated. Yes, it would be so very simple. She saw herself lying upon the pavement, her limbs broken, her head crushed, dead—dead—freed! She leaned forward and was about to leap, when her eyes fell upon a person who was walking below, the sight of whom suddenly aroused her from the folly, the strange charm of which had just laid hold so powerfully upon her. She drew back. She rubbed her eyes with her hands, and she, who was accustomed to mystical enthusiasm, said aloud:

"My God! You send him to me! I am saved." And she summoned the footman to tell him that if M. Dorsenne asked for her, he should be shown into Madame Steno's small salon. "I am not at home to any one else," she added.

It was indeed Julien, whom she had seen approach the house at the very instant when she was only separated from the abyss by that last tremor of animal repugnance, which is found even in suicide of the most ardent kind. Do not madmen themselves choose to die in one manner rather than in another? She paused several moments in order to collect herself.

"Yes," said she at length, to herself, "it is the only solution. I will find out if he loves me truly. And if he does not?"

She again looked toward the window, in order to assure herself that, in case that conversation did not end as she desired, the tragical and simple means remained at her service by which to free herself from that infamous life which she surely could not bear.

Julien began the conversation in his tone of sentimental raillery, so speedily to be transformed into one of drama! He knew very well, on arriving at Villa Steno, that he was to have his last *tête-à-tête* with his pretty and interesting little friend. For he had at length decided to go away, and, to be more sure of not failing, he had engaged his sleeping-berth for that night. He had jested so much with love that he entered upon that conversation with a jest; when, having tried to take Alba's hand to press a kiss upon it, he saw that it was bandaged.

"What has happened to you, little Countess? Have my laurels or those of Florent Chapron prevented you from sleeping, that you are here with the classical wrist of a duellist? . . . Seriously, how have you hurt yourself?"

"I leaned against a window, which broke and the pieces of glass cut my fingers somewhat," replied the young girl with a faint smile, adding: "It is nothing."

"What an imprudent child you are!" said Dorsenne in his tone of friendly scolding. "Do you know that you might have severed an artery and have caused a very serious, perhaps a fatal, hemorrhage?"

"That would not have been such a great misfortune," replied Alba, shaking her pretty head with an expression so bitter about her mouth that the young man, too, ceased smiling.

"Do not speak in that tone," said he, "or I shall think you did it purposely."

"Purposely?" repeated the young girl. "Purposely? Why should I have done it purposely?"

And she blushed and laughed in the same nervous way she had laughed fifteen minutes before, when she looked down into the street. Dorsenne felt that she was suffering, and his heart contracted. The trouble against which he had struggled for several days with all the energy of an independent artist, and which for some time systematized his celibacy, again oppressed him. He thought it time to put between "folly" and him the irreparability of his categorical resolution. So he replied to his little friend with his habitual gentleness, but in a tone of firmness, which already announced his determination:

"I have again vexed you, Contessina, and you are looking at me with the glance of our hours of dispute. You will later regret having been unkind to-day."

As he pronounced those enigmatical words, she saw that he had in his eyes and in his smile something different and indefinable. It must have been that she loved him still more than she herself believed, as for a second she forgot both her own pain and her resolution, and she asked him, quickly:

"You have some trouble? You are suffering? What is it?"

"Nothing," replied Dorsenne. "But time is flying, the minutes are going by, and not only the minutes. There is an old and charming French ode, which you do not know and which begins:

"*Le temps s'en va, le temps s'en va, Madame.*"
"*Las, le temps? Non. Mais nous nous en allons.*"

[ 357 ]

"Which means, little Countess, in simple prose, that this is no doubt the last conversation we shall have together this season, and that it would be cruel to mar for me this last visit."

"Do I understand you aright?" said Alba. She, too, knew too well Julien's way of speaking not to know that that mannerism, half-mocking, half-sentimental, always served him to prepare phrases more grave, and against the emotion of which her fear of appearing a dupe rose in advance. She crossed her arms upon her breast, and after a pause she continued, in a grave voice: "You are going away?"

"Yes," he replied, and from his coat-pocket he partly drew his ticket. "You see I have acted like the poltroons who cast themselves into the water. My ticket is bought, and I shall no longer hold that little discourse which I have held for months, that, *Sir executioner, one moment. . . . Du Barry.*"

"You are going away?" repeated the young girl, who did not seem to have heeded the jest by which Julien had concealed his own confusion at the effect of his so abruptly announced departure. "I shall not see you any more! . . . And if I ask you not to go yet? You have spoken to me of our friendship. . . . If I pray you, if I beseech you, in the name of that friendship, not to deprive me of it at this instant, when I have no one, when I am so alone, so horribly alone, will you answer *no?* You have often told me that you were my friend, my true friend? If it be true, you will not go. I repeat, I am alone, and I am afraid."

"Come, little Countess," replied Dorsenne, who be-

COSMOPOLIS

gan to be terrified by the young girl's sudden excitement, "it is not reasonable to agitate yourself thus,
because yesterday you had a very sad conversation
with Fanny Hafner! First, it is altogether impossible for me to defer my departure. You force me to
give you coarse, almost commercial reasons. But my
book is about to appear, and I must be there for the
launching of the sale, of which I have already told you.
And then you are going away, too. You will have all
the diversions of the country, of your Venetian friends
and charming Lydia Maitland!"

"Do not mention that name," interrupted Alba,
whose face became discomposed at the allusion to the
sojourn at Piove. "You do not know how you pain
me, nor what that woman is, what a monster of cruelty
and of perfidy! Ask me no more. I shall tell you
nothing. But," the Contessina that time clasping her
hands, her poor, thin hands, which trembled with the
anguish of the words she dared to utter, "do you not
comprehend that if I speak to you as I do, it is because I
have need of you in order to live?" Then in a low voice,
choked by emotion: "It is because I love you!" All
the modesty natural to a child of twenty mounted to her
pale face in a flood of purple, when she had uttered that
avowal. "Yes, I love you!" she repeated, in an accent
as deep, but more firm. "It is not, however, so common
a thing to find real devotion, a being who only asks to serve
you, to be useful to you, to live in your shadow. And
you will understand that to have the right of giving
you my life, to bear your name, to be your wife, to
follow you, I felt very vividly in your presence at the

[ 359 ]

moment I was about to lose you. You will pardon my lack of modesty for the first, for the last time. I have suffered too much."

She ceased. Never had the absolute purity of the charming creature, born and bred in an atmosphere of corruption, and remaining in the same so intact, so noble, so frank, flashed out as at that moment. All that virgin and unhappy soul was in her eyes which implored Julien, on her lips which trembled at having spoken thus, on her brow around which floated, like an aureole, the fair hair stirred by the breeze which entered the open window. She had found the means of daring that prodigious step, the boldest a woman can permit herself, still more so a young girl, with so chaste a simplicity that at that moment Dorsenne would not have dared to touch even the hand of that child who confided herself to him so madly, so loyally.

Dorsenne was undoubtedly greatly interested in her, with a curiosity, without enthusiasm, and against which a reaction had already set in. That touching speech, in which trembled a distress so tender and each word of which later on made him weep with regret, produced upon him at that moment an impression of fear rather than love or pity. When at length he broke the cruel silence, the sound of his voice revealed to the unhappy girl the uselessness of that supreme appeal addressed by her to life.

She had only kept, to exorcise the demon of suicide, her hope in the heart of that man, and that heart, toward which she turned in so immoderate a transport, drew back instead of responding.

# COSMOPOLIS

"Calm yourself, I beseech you," said he to her. "You can understand that I am very much moved, very much surprised, at what I have heard! I did not suspect it. My God! How troubled you are. And yet," he continued with more firmness, "I should despise myself were I to lie to you. You have been so loyal toward me. . . . To marry you? Ah, it would be the most delightful dream of happiness if that dream were not prevented by honesty. Poor child," and his voice sounded almost bitter, "you do not know me. You do not know what a writer of my order is, and that to unite your destiny to mine would be for you martyrdom more severe than your moral solitude of to-day. You see, I came to your home with so much joy, because I was free, because each time I could say to myself that I need not return again. Such a confession is not romantic. But it is thus. If that relation became a bond, an obligation, a fixed framework in which to move, a circle of habits in which to imprison me, I should only have one thought—flight. An engagement for my entire life? No, no, I could not bear it. There are souls of passage as well as birds of passage, and I am one. You will understand it to-morrow, now, and you will remember that I have spoken to you as a man of honor, who would be miserable if he thought he had augmented, involuntarily, the sorrows of your life when his only desire was to assuage them. My God! What is to be done?" he cried, on seeing, as he spoke, tears gush from the young girl's eyes, which she did not wipe away.

"Go away," she replied, "leave me. I do not want you. I am grateful to you for not having deceived me.

But your presence is too cruel. I am ashamed of having spoken to you, now that I know you do not love me. I have been mad, do not punish me by remaining longer. After the conversation we have just had, my honor will not permit us to talk longer."

"You are right," said Julien, after another pause. He took his hat, which he had placed upon a table at the beginning of that visit, so rapidly and abruptly terminated by a confession of sentiments so strange. He said:

"Then, farewell." She inclined her fair head without replying.

The door was closed. Alba Steno was again alone. Half an hour later, when the footman entered to ask for orders relative to the carriage sent back by the Countess, he found her standing motionless at the window from which she had watched Dorsenne depart. There she had once more been seized by the temptation of suicide. She had again felt with an irresistible force the magnetic attraction of death. Life appeared to her once more as something too vile, too useless, too insupportable to be borne. The carriage was at her disposal. By way of the Portese gate and along the Tiber, with the Countess's horses, it would take an hour and a half to reach the Lake di Porto. She had, too, this pretext, to avoid the curiosity of the servants: one of the Roman noblewomen of her acquaintance, Princess Torlonia, owned an isolated villa on the border of that lake. . . . She ascended hastily to don her hat. And without writing a word of farewell to any one, without even casting a glance at the objects among which she had lived and suffered, she descended the staircase and gave the coachman the name of the villa, adding: "Drive quickly; I am late now."

The Lake di Porto is only, as its name indicates, the port of the ancient Tiber. The road which leads from Transtevere runs along the river, which rolls through a plain strewn with ruins and indented with barren hills, its brackish water discolored from the sand and mud of the Apennines.

Here groups of eucalyptus, there groups of pine parasols above some ruined walls, were all the vegetation which met Alba Steno's eye. But the scene accorded so well with the moral devastation she bore within her that the barrenness around her in her last walk was pleasant to her.

The feeling that she was nearing eternal peace, final sleep in which she should suffer no more, augmented when she alighted from the carriage, and, having passed the garden of Villa Torlonia, she found herself facing the small lake, so grandiose in its smallness by the wildness of its surroundings, and motionless, surprised in even that supreme moment by the magic of that hidden sight, she paused amid the reeds with their red tufts to look at that pond which was to become her tomb, and she murmured:

"How beautiful it is! "

There was in the humid atmosphere which gradually penetrated her a charm of mortal rest, to which she abandoned herself dreamily, almost with physical voluptuousness, drinking into her being the feverish fumes of that place—one of the most fatal at that season and at that hour of all that dangerous coast—until she shuddered in her light summer gown. Her shoulders contracted, her teeth chattered, and that feeling of discomfort was to her as a signal for action. She took another *allée* of rose-bushes in flower to reach a point on the bank barren of vegetation, where was outlined the form of a boat. She soon detached it, and, managing the heavy oars with her delicate hands, she advanced toward the middle of the lake.

When she was in the spot which she thought the deepest and the most suitable for her design, she ceased rowing. Then, by a delicate care, which made her smile herself, so much did it betray instinctive and childish order at such a solemn moment, she put her hat, her umbrella and her gloves on one of the transversal boards of the boat. She had made a great effort to move the heavy oars, so that she was perspiring. A second shudder seized her as she was arranging the trifling objects, so keen, so chilly, so intense that time that she paused. She lay there motionless, her eyes fixed upon the water, whose undulations lapped the boat. At the last moment she felt reënter her heart, not love of life, but love for her mother. All the details of the events which would follow her suicide were presented to her mind.

She saw herself plunging into the deep water which would close over her head. Her suffering would be ended, but Madame Steno? She saw the coachman growing uneasy over her absence, ringing at the door of Villa Torlonia, the servants in search. The loosened boat would relate enough. Would the Countess know that she had killed hersélf? Would she know the cause of that desperate end? The terrible face of Lydia Maitland appeared to the young girl. She comprehended that the woman hated her enemy too much not to enlighten her with regard to the circumstances which had preceded that suicide. The cry so simple and of a significance so terrible: "You did it purposely!" returned to Alba's memory. She saw her mother learning that her daughter had seen all. She had loved her so much, that mother, she loved her so dearly still!

Then, as a third violent chill shook her from head to foot, Alba began to think of another mode, and one as sure, of death without any one in the world being able to suspect that it was voluntary. She recalled the fact that she was in one of the most dreaded corners of the Roman Campagna; that she had known persons carried off in a few days by the pernicious fevers contracted in similar places, at that hour and in that season, notably one of her friends, one of the Bonapartes living in Rome, who came thither to hunt when overheated. If she were to try to catch that same disease? . . . And she took up the oars. When she felt her brow moist with the second effort, she opened her bodice and her chemise, she exposed her neck, her breast, her throat, and she lay down in the boat, allowing the damp air to envelop, to caress, to chill her, inviting the entrance into her blood of the fatal germs. How long did she remain thus, half-unconscious, in the atmosphere more and more laden with miasma in proportion as the sun sank? A cry made her rise and again take up the oars. It was the coachman, who,

[ 365 ]

not seeing her return, had descended from the box and was hailing the boat at all hazards. When she stepped upon the bank and when he saw her so pale, the man, who had been in the Countess's service for years, could not help saying to her, with the familiarity of an Italian servant:

"You have taken cold, Mademoiselle, and this place is so dangerous."

"Indeed," she replied, "I have had a chill. It will be nothing. Let us return quickly. Above all, do not say that I was in the boat. You will cause me to be scolded."

# CHAPTER XII

. . . . . . .

AND it was directly after that conversation that the poor child left for the lake, where she caught the pernicious fever?" asked Montfanon.

"Directly," replied Dorsenne, "and what troubles me the most is that I can not doubt but that she went there purposely. I was so troubled by our conversation that I had not the strength to leave Rome the same evening, as I told her I should. After much hesitation—you understand why, now that I have told you all—I returned to the Villa Steno at six o'clock. To speak to her, but of what? Did I know? It was madness. For her avowal only allowed of two replies, either that which I made her or an offer of marriage. Ah, I did not reason so much. I was afraid. . . . Of what? . . . I do not know. I reached the villa, where I found the Countess, gay and radiant, as was her custom, and *tête-à-tête* with her American. 'Only think, there is my child,' said she to me, 'who has refused to go to the English embassy, where she would enjoy herself, and who has gone out for a drive alone. . . . Will you await her?' "

[ 367 ]

"At length she began to grow uneasy, and I, seeing that no one returned, took my leave, my heart oppressed by presentiments. . . . Alba's carriage stopped at the door just as I was going out. She was pale, of a greenish pallor, which caused me to say on approaching her: 'Whence have you come?' as if I had the right. Her lips, already discolored, trembled as they replied. When I learned where she had spent that hour of sunset, and near what lake, the most deadly in the neighborhood, I said to her: 'What imprudence!' I shall all my life see the glance she gave me at the moment, as she replied: 'Say, rather, how wise, and pray that I may have taken the fever and that I die cf it.' You know the rest, and how her wish has been realized. She indeed contracted the fever, and so severely that she died in less than six days. I have no doubt, since her last words, that it was a suicide."

"And the mother," asked Montfanon, "did she not comprehend finally?"

"Absolutely nothing," replied Dorsenne. "It is inconceivable, but it is thus. Ah! she is truly the worthy friend of that knave Hafner, whom his daughter's broken engagement has not grieved, in spite of his discomfiture. I forgot to tell you that he had just sold Palais Castagna to a joint-stock company to convert it into a hotel. I laugh," he continued with singular acrimony, "in order not to weep, for I am arriving at the most heartrending part. Do you know where I saw poor Alba Steno's face for the last time? It was three days ago, the day after her death, at this hour. I called to inquire for the Countess! She was receiving! 'Do you wish to bid her adieu?' she asked me. 'Good Lincoln is just molding her face for me.' And I entered the chamber of death. Her eyes were closed, her cheeks were sunken, her pretty nose was pinched, and upon her brow and in the corners of her mouth was a mixture of bitterness and of repose which I can not describe to you. I thought: 'If you had liked, she would be alive, she would smile, she would love you!' The American was beside the bed, while Florent Chapron, always faithful, was preparing the oil to put upon the face of the corpse, and sinister Lydia Maitland was watching the scene with eyes which made me shudder, reminding me of what I had divined at the time of my last conversation with Alba. If she does not undertake to play the part of a Nemesis and to tell all to the Countess, I am mistaken in faces! For the moment she was silent, and guess the only words the mother uttered when her lover, he on whose account her daughter had suffered so much, approached their common victim: '*Above all, do not injure her lovely lashes!*' What horrible irony, was it not? Horrible!"

The young man sank upon a bench as he uttered that cry of distress and of remorse, which Montfanon mechanically repeated, as if startled by the tragical confidence he had just received.

Montfanon shook his gray head several times as if deliberating; then forced Dorsenne to rise, chiding him thus:

"Come, Julien, we can not remain here all the afternoon dreaming and sighing like young women! The child is dead. We can not restore her to life, you in despairing, I in deploring. We should do better to look in the face our responsibility in that sinister adventure, to repent of it and to expiate it."

"Our responsibility?" interrogated Julien. "I see mine, although I can truly not see yours."

"Yours and mine," replied Montfanon. "I am no sophist, and I am not in the habit of shifting my conscience. Yes or no," he insisted, with a return of his usual excitement, "did I leave the catacombs to arrange that unfortunate duel? Yes or no, did I yield to the paroxysm of choler which possessed me on hearing of the engagement of Ardea and on finding that I was in the presence of that equivocal Hafner? Yes or no, did that duel help to enlighten Madame Gorka as to her husband's doings, and, in consequence, Mademoiselle Steno as to her mother's? Did you not relate to me the progress of her anguish since that scandal, there just now? . . . And if I have been startled, as I have been, by the news of that suicide, know it has been for this reason especially, because a voice has said to me: 'A few of the tears of that dead girl are laid to your account.'"

"But, my poor friend," interrupted Dorsenne, "whence such reasoning? According to that, we could not live any more. There enters into our lives, by indirect means, a collection of actions which in no way concerns us, and in admitting that we have a debt of responsibility to pay, that debt commences and ends in that which we have wished directly, sincerely, clearly."

"It would be very convenient," replied the Marquis,

with still more vivacity, "but the proof that it is not true is that you yourself are filled with remorse at not having saved the soul so weak of that defenseless child. Ah, I do not mince the truth to myself, and I shall not do so to you. You remember the morning when you were so gay, and when you gave me the theory of your cosmopolitanism? It amused you, as a perfect dilettante, so you said, to assist in one of those dramas of race which bring into play the personages from all points of the earth and of history, and you then traced to me a programme very true, my faith, and which events have almost brought about. Madame Steno has indeed conducted herself toward her two lovers as a Venetian of the time of Aretin; Chapron, with all the blind devotion of a descendant of an oppressed race; his sister with the villainous ferocity of a rebel who at length shakes off the yoke, since you think she wrote those anonymous letters. Hafner and Ardea have laid bare two detestable souls, the one of an infamous usurer, half German, half Dutch; the other of a degraded nobleman, in whom is revived some ancient *condottiere*. Gorka has been brave and mad, like entire Poland; his wife implacable and loyal, like all of England. Maitland continues to be positive, insensible, and wilful in the midst of it all, as all America. And poor Alba ended as did her father. I do not speak to you of Baron Hafner's daughter," and he raised his hat. Then, in an altered voice:

"She is a saint, in whom I was deceived. But she has Jewish blood in her veins, blood which was that of the people of God. I should have remembered it and the beautiful saying of the Middle Ages: 'The Jewish women shall be saved because they have wept for our Lord in secret.' . . . You outlined for me in advance the scene of the drama in which we have been mixed up. . . . And do you remember what I said: 'Is there not among them a soul which you might aid in doing better?' You laughed in my face at that moment. You would have treated me, had you been less polite, as a Philistine and a *cabotin*. You wished to be only a spectator, the gentleman in the balcony who wipes the glasses of his lorgnette in order to lose none of the comedy. Well, you could not do so. That *rôle* is not permitted a man. He must act, and he acts always, even when he thinks he is looking on, even when he washes his hands as Pontius Pilate, that dilettante, too, who uttered the words of your masters and of yourself. What is truth? Truth is that there is always and everywhere a duty to fulfil. Mine was to prevent that criminal encounter. Yours was not to pay attention to that young girl if you did not love her, and if you loved her, to marry her and to take her from her abominable surroundings. We have both failed, and at what a price!"

"You are very severe," said the young man; "but if you were right would not Alba be dead? Of what use is it for me to know what I should have done when it is too late?"

"First, never to do so again," said the Marquis; "then to judge yourself and your life."

"There is truth in what you say," replied Dorsenne, "but you are mistaken if you think that the most intellectual men of our age have not suffered, too, from that abuse of thought. What is to be done? Ah, it is the disease of a century too cultivated, and there is no cure."

"There is one," interrupted Montfanon, "which you do not wish to see. . . . You will not deny that Balzac was the boldest of our modern writers. Is it necessary for me, an ignorant man, to recite to you the phrase which governs his work: 'Thought, principle of evil and of good can only be prepared, subdued, directed by religion.' See?" he continued, suddenly taking his companion by the arm and forcing him to look into a transversal *allée* through the copse, "there he is, the doctor who holds the remedy for that malady of the soul as for all the others. Do not show yourself. They will have forgotten our presence. But, look, look! . . . Ah, what a meeting!"

The personage who appeared suddenly in that melancholy, deserted garden, and in a manner almost supernatural, so much did his presence form a living commentary to the discourse of the impassioned nobleman, was no other than the Holy Father himself, on the point of entering his carriage for his usual drive. Dorsenne, who only knew Leon XIII from his portraits, saw an old man, bent, bowed, whose white cassock gleamed beneath the red mantle, and who leaned on one side upon a prelate of his court, on the other upon one of his officers. In drawing back, as Montfanon had advised, in order not to bring a reprimand upon the keepers, he could study at his leisure the delicate face of the Sovereign Pontiff, who paused at a

[ 373 ]

bed of roses to converse familiarly with a kneeling gardener. He saw the infinitely indulgent smile of that *spirituelle* mouth. He saw the light of those eyes which seemed to justify by their brightness the *lumen in cœlo* applied to the successor of Pie IX by a celebrated prophecy. He saw the venerable hand, that white, transparent hand, which was raised to give the solemn benediction with so much majesty, turn toward a fine yellow rose, and the fingers bend the flower without plucking it, as if not to harm the frail creation of God. The old Pope for a second inhaled its perfume and then resumed his walk toward the carriage, vaguely to be seen between the trunks of the green oaks. The black horses set off at a trot, and Dorsenne, turning again toward Montfanon, perceived large tears upon the lashes of the former zouave, who, forgetting the rest of their conversation, said, with a sigh: "And that is the only pleasure allowed him, who is, however, the successor of the first apostle, to inhale his flowers and drive in a carriage as rapidly as his horses can go!" They have procured four paltry kilometers of road at the foot of the terrace where we were half an hour since. And he goes on, he goes on, thus deluding himself with regard to the vast space which is forbidden him. I have seen many tragical sights in my life. I have been to the war, and I have spent one entire night wounded on a battlefield covered with snow, among the dead, grazed by the wheels of the artillery of the conquerors, who defiled singing. Nothing has moved me like that drive of the old man, who has never uttered a complaint and who has for himself only that

COSMOPOLIS

acre of land in which to move freely. But these are
grand words which the holy man wrote one day at the
foot of his portrait for a missionary. The words explain his life: *Debitricem martyrii fidem*—Faith is
bound to martyrdom."

"*Debitricem martyrii fidem*," repeated Dorsenne,
"that is beautiful, indeed. And," he added, in a low
voice, "you just now abused very rudely the dilettantes
and the sceptic. But do you think there would be
one of them who would refuse martyrdom if he could
have at the same time faith?"

Never had Montfanon heard the young man utter a
similar phrase and in such an accent. The image returned to him, by way of contrast, of Dorsenne, alert
and foppish, the dandy of literature, so gayly a scoffer
and a sophist, to whom antique and venerable Rome
was only a city of pleasure, a cosmopolis more paradoxical than Florence, Nice, Biarritz, St. Moritz, than
such and such other cities of international winter and
summer. He felt that for the first time that soul was
strained to its depths, the tragical death of poor Alba
had become in the mind of the writer the point of remorse around which revolved the moral life of the
superior and incomplete being, exiled from simple
humanity by the most invincible pride of mind. Montfanon comprehended that every additional word would
pain the wounded heart. He was afraid of having
already lectured Dorsenne too severely. Hhe took
within his arm the arm of the young man, and he
pressed it silently, putting into that manly caress all the
warm and discreet pity of an elder brother.

[ 375 ]

www.ingramcontent.com/pod-product-compliance
Lightning Source LLC
Chambersburg PA
CBHW030354030726
47497CB00002B/335